TENDER TRUST

"What are you thinking, Lady Anne?"

"Oh!"

Sir James's softly spoken question broke into Anne's thoughts and she twisted around to stare up at him.

"You startled me," she said. Her gaze was caught by the kindness, the interest . . . the . . . She didn't know what it was, but it warmed her. He smiled and she remembered he'd spoken to her. "What did you ask?"

James repeated his query and Anne bit her lip. "Nothing in particular." She shifted slightly, her gaze dropping to her fingers.

"Lady P. would tell you that to lie is a sin," teased James and then stepped forward when Anne's skin paled to a sickly white. "Lady Anne, don't! I did not mean . . ."

"Whatever you meant, what you said is true. Lying *is* sinful. And my thoughts *were* of something in particular, so when I said they were not, I *did* lie." Anne felt odd prickles under the skin of her face. "It was wrong of me to do so."

"But all you were truly saying was that your thoughts were none of my business, was it not? And perhaps also, that I should take myself away because you'd prefer to be private. It wasn't really a lie, Lady Anne, but only a common form of conventional politeness."

Anne glanced at him, saw that he still smiled, but that there was also . . . a tenderness? . . . revealed that was both frightening and seductive. Could she trust him? Did she dare to do so?

Books by Jeanne Savery

THE WIDOW AND THE RAKE
A REFORMED RAKE
A CHRISTMAS TREASURE
A LADY'S DECEPTION
CUPID'S CHALLENGE

Published by Zebra Books

Cupid's Challenge
JEANNE SAVERY

ZEBRA BOOKS
KENSINGTON PUBLISHING CORP.

Many times the idea for a book comes from a single bit or the combination of a few bits of information which must then be fleshed out with research. Occasionally, finding a source for that research is difficult.

The existence of the use of electricity in medicine during the Regency era was not in doubt: Finding enough detail to make use of the notion was.

Therefore . . .

This book is dedicated to
Abraham Liboff, Professor
Oakland University

. . . who told me about . . .

The Bakken Library and Museum
and
Elizabeth Ihrig, Librarian

. . . who made this book possible.

Thank you.

One

Sir James glared down his noble nose at the barely opened door. "Jaycee will see *me*."

"Lady Montmorency is *not* at home," lied the butler and shivered as a chill blast swept in the crack between door and frame.

"Tibbet, come down out of the boughs and get out of my way. I will see my sister. At once."

"Sir James, her ladyship is not at home," insisted the harassed butler, but his eyes wandered in every direction but where they might meet those of her ladyship's brother.

"Nonsense. Jaycee may be cowering in her room hoping to avoid me, but it's far more likely she's sleeping like the innocent babe she is *not*. However that may be, *she'll see me*."

Sir James waited one more moment in the January cold outside his brother-in-law's country residence before he pushed against the heavily carved oak of the Montmorency Park door. He widened the opening enough to allow entry and set the shorter but decidedly plumper, Tibbet to one side. While he removed his five-caped driving coat and handed it and his fur-lined driving gloves to the butler, he gently admonished the man for attempting to keep him out. Finishing the mild scold, he turned toward the stairs, intending to berate his sister far more roundly for her latest idiocy.

"Stop!" a no-nonsense voice commanded.

Startled, Sir James did just that. He raised his gaze to the top of the broad flight of steps and, scrabbling for his quizzing glass, raised it to his eye. The horribly magnified orb did *not* have its usual effect. The woman toward whom he directed the social weapon merely raised her nose another notch and stared back. Glared back? Sir James frowned and took a step—only to halt at the peremptorily raised hand.

"The *devil*," he said.

"Is that an announcement of identity or a prayer to the nether regions?" asked the unknown woman in an icy tone.

Deciding he was amused rather than angry, Sir James bit back a chuckle. He actually *looked* through his glass, instead of using it as a social weapon, and realized the regal figure with haughty stance and unconscious self-confidence was a mere waif wrapped in an ancient brown robe, her hair bundled up under the most monstrous old-fashioned nightcap he'd ever been privileged to see. What was more, that "regal" figure was, perhaps, all of five foot and an inch tall—but only when out in the rain wearing pattens!

"I've come to see Jaycee, child. Now be a good little girl and tell me where to find her. Her boudoir, do you think?"

The strange girl's pert little nose rose a further fraction of an inch. "You were informed that *Lady Montmorency* is not at home."

How, wondered James, could such a little wisp of a chit manage to give off the air of a dowager duchess? "*Jaycee* is always at home to me, my dear," he said calmly, but added with just a shade of irritation, "Who in creation are you, anyway?"

"I, my lord, am a lady. Since *you* are no gentleman, you are excused from recognizing that fact." The short straight nose tipped still higher although it hardly seemed possible. "Tibbet," she said, as she turned on her heel. "Show this intruder out."

It should have been a good exit. In fact, James was silently admiring the child's style when her heel caught in the over-long robe and horror replaced all thought. James rushed forward, but there was no way he could save her. Her arms cartwheeled, reaching for a railing just beyond grasp. For an instant, huge frightened blue-green eyes stared into James's equally wide brown ones and then, with no more than a stifled gasp, one quickly muffled groan of pain, the thin figure continued its disastrous descent, tumbling and rolling and bouncing, settling into an ungainly heap at the foot of the steps where James stood helplessly.

"Tibbet," ordered James, "I want Bobson—my groom, you know—and this wee brown wren's maid. *At once,* Tibbet!"

Gently, James felt along the girl's arms. Birdlike, they were terribly thin but strongly muscled, as was the whole, *nearly* childish, body. Forcing his attention away from that last intriguing fact, James moved his probing fingers from her ribs downward to check her legs.

"Move, man!" he demanded when the shiny black shoes near his side *did not.* "*Tibbet* why do you stand like a block?"

"She has no maid, my lord."

"My *groom,* Tibbet, and then a woman, *any* woman so I may take Miss . . . whoever . . . to her room."

James spoke more harshly than usual although his hands continued a gentle foray as he searched for broken bones. Finding none, he cautiously straightened the body—reluctantly covering the well-formed ankles as propriety demanded. For the moment he didn't move her further, merely staring at the fragile-seeming girl in perplexity.

Who is she? he wondered. *Where did she come from?*

Minutes later he glanced up at his groom, who also stared down at the girl, an old hat held tightly in the man's grip, a hat which didn't match his livery but which the man, superstitiously, refused to replace.

"Ah. Bobson. At last. Take the team back to London and return with Dr. Mac as quickly as you can. Don't accept any excuse. Tell him I need him. You'll most likely find him at St. Bartholomew's Hospital. And hurry, lad," he added as the groom turned. "Tibbet, stop gobbling. Where is a woman?"

"I don't know this Dr. Mac, Sir James," said the butler, a stubborn note matching a stubborn stance. "We always call in Dr. . . ."

James raised a silencing hand, which was instantly obeyed. "I'll have no country doctor who, if you tied his hands behind him, couldn't find his . . . Ah—" He stopped in mid-harangue. "—Mrs. Tibbet! At last." James picked up the unconscious figure carefully. "Lead the way, now. We'll get her to bed and you'll tell me from what nest this young bird fell."

Mrs. Tibbet took in the situation in half a glance. "This way, Sir James." She started up the stairs.

He was not surprised when forced to climb the second flight to the floor devoted to family and guest bedrooms—only thankful the slim form he carried was no heavier. But, when Mrs. Tibbet climbed to the rarely used third floor and then led the way down the hall to where she opened a door on another, much narrower, staircase, he balked.

"Mrs. Tibbet? I believe she said she's a lady?"

"Yes, Sir James."

Mrs. Tibbet gestured to the stairs, her face a study of servile blankness, an expression which, as Sir James well knew, was totally out of character.

James held his ground. "If she's a lady, her room should be on the floor below."

"A room was prepared in the family wing, my lord, but she prefers those above."

The blank look of the well-trained servant was replaced by a concerned glance at his burden. Sir James gritted his teeth and followed. When he found himself under the low ceilings of the attics his brows rose under the hair resting on his forehead, hair, which, that morning, had been arranged in a fashionable Brutus style, but which, thanks to the wind and quite by accident, had become a perfect example of the popular and difficult to achieve "wind-blown" style.

"Through here, Sir James."

James glanced around the miniature, but comfortable-looking sitting room which had been made up in a recently painted attic room. Shelves full of books lined one wall; two smallish armchairs and a small but comfortable looking sofa took up much of the cozy space. The grouping was centered on a small hearth flanked by a pair of color-washed, India ink drawings. James moved on behind Mrs. Tibbet who passed a small desk to enter a narrow doorway.

James was forced to duck his head as he followed the housekeeper into an ill-lit region that was either a wide hall or a narrow room and seemed to function as the most utilitarian dressing room he'd ever seen. A tiny mirror above a small table holding a bowl and jug painted with a wreath of spring flowers, was the only hint of vanity.

If that, he thought, peering to where a handful of plain unflounced dresses and a cloak the color of aged tobacco hung on pegs against the wall, *is the chit's entire wardrobe, then Jaycee, with her inexhaustible supply of pin money, has been treating her guest dratted shabbily.*

Beyond the dressing room was an equally Spartan bedroom. He waited beside the narrow cot only long enough for Mrs. Tibbet to straighten the mussed bedding before laying down his burden which, despite her pocket size, had begun to weigh on him. He removed his right arm from beneath her legs and reached to lift her shoulders slightly so he could remove his left from under her back. The rough material of his sleeve caught on the absurd nightcap, pulling it away and revealing a flood of deep auburn tresses which tumbled over the pillow and dripped over the side of the bed.

"My God in heaven," he said on a soft breath of sound.

It wasn't blasphemy, as Mrs. Tibbet might have been excused for thinking, but in praise of the glory revealed.

"Mrs. Tibbet," he whispered, awed, "who is she?" He reached out but didn't quite touch the unbelievably beautiful hair.

"You really don't know? I assumed you were joking me, Sir James," Mrs. Tibbet frowned. "She's Lady Anne, of course."

"Lady Anne," mused James. "Anne?" he repeated, straightening and coming within a fraction of an inch of bumping his head on the ceiling. "Martin's half-sister? Jaycee's *sister-in-law?* The one she said was coming, at long last, to live with them?"

"She *is* living here. Right here," said the housekeeper, her gesture encompassing the small apartment.

"She's just arrived, then? I seem to recall she was due six—perhaps as much as eight weeks ago. I gave up expecting that she'd come at all."

"She arrived exactly as scheduled," contradicted the housekeeper. When James stared, a defensive note entered her voice as she added, "Lady Anne has been here nigh on two months."

"Nonsense. I've seen neither hide nor hair of her." *Especially the hair,* thought James, finally touching an errant wave with one finger. "I'd have met her if she'd been a guest in this house."

"No, sir." Again James's frowning, insistent stare forced Mrs. Tibbet to elaborate. "Lady Anne has refused to go into company, Sir James. If things weren't at sixes and sevens I'm sure she'd not have spoken to you below stairs. She's shy as a bird, poor dear."

"Lady Anne is shy?" James reviewed his memory of the militant woman ordering Tibbet to show him the door.

"Shy?" She'd acted the hunting hawk then, rather than a wee wary quail. "I don't believe it. More, I don't understand it. Any of it."

And what Sir James didn't understand, he got to the bottom of with no hesitation.

"Mrs. Tibbet, there's no more we can do for Lady Anne except await the doctor. So, while we wait, you come over to this nice window seat—" He took the gray-haired woman by the shoulders, turned her, and gently pushed her away from the bed. "—and you sit yourself down. Yes, just like that. And now you explain why that child is hidden away up here in the attics." A sudden thought sent his eyes scurrying toward the bed. *Surely not!* "I've never heard of a strain of insanity in the Montmorency family," he said hesitantly, not quite a question but something more than a statement.

"Lord love you, *no,* of course not! Although—" Mrs. Tibbet sighed. "—I don't suppose you can be blamed for thinking so. Now, where to begin."

James opened his mouth to make the obvious suggestion and she reverted to a manner she'd last used when James was still in short pants and had been brought to play with Martin.

"Now be still, do," she scolded. "Just you let me think." Mrs. Tibbet mused a moment. "Her mother died when Anne was not quite twelve."

Sir James, to whom mental calculations were something of a game, interrupted. "The late Lady Montmorency died at least a dozen years ago. That child cannot possibly be twenty-four years old."

"Oh but she *can.* She *is.*" James shook his head. "She is not a child, Sir James." Mrs. Tibbet glared at him and relaxed only when his expression shifted to acceptance.

James, remembering his accidental discovery of the girl's slight breasts when he'd checked her ribs, reassessed the tiny figure with knowledge of her age. Even now, better informed, he arrived at the same conclusion he'd reached earlier. Lady Anne seemed no more than a delightful child. He glanced at the hair. A feisty child, and one he'd very much like to know better, but still . . .

"If she is actually twenty-four years old," he objected, "she might, by the highest of sticklers, be considered well laid upon the shelf! Even those not so high in the instep would suggest she's fast approaching an age where she'll sink into spinsterhood. So, why, if she's such a great age, was she never presented?"

"Now Sir James, will you ask questions or should I just tell you Lady Anne's history?"

Sir James suppressed a grin at the scold, something he'd not heard for many a long year. "I'll be good," he replied in the cowed tone he'd used as a boy when he and Martin were caught in mischief.

Mrs. Tibbet knew her man and glared over the rims of her spectacles but a resigned sigh escaped her when he merely reached out and pushed them up her nose. She batted away his hand and continued her tale. "Lady Anne was sent away upon the death of her mother which followed, in short order, as you'll recall, that of her father." Mrs. Tibbet cast a speculative glance his way. "Do you remember Lady Preminger?" she asked.

"Sister to the old lord's first wife? *That* old witch? Lady Anne was sent to her?"

Mrs. Tibbet nodded.

Sir James's eyes widened painfully as he stared at the solemn-faced housekeeper. "Lady Preminger was half mad, and an obsessive chapel-goer, was she not? That beldame was no proper guardian for a sensitive young girl. And for a bereaved child? Even less suitable!"

"Beldame and witch. I'd say worse, myself," admitted Mrs. Tibbet softly. "Lady Anne was such a bright cheerful child. It's my belief her ladyship beat all the spirit out of our little girl; that's what she must have done."

"Beat her!" James looked horrified, his eyes shifting to the still figure in the bed. *"Beat* her?"

"Well," Mrs. Tibbet contradicted herself, "I'll not say she actually laid hands on the child, although I'll not say she didn't either. But, since you remember Lady Preminger, you'll recall what a vicious tongue was in her ladyship's head. She could flay a man at twenty paces with that tongue of hers, lecturing him on his sinful ways, so what—" The housekeeper glared over the tops of her glasses. "—do you think she might do to a child whose every need depended on her?"

James and Mrs. Tibbet stared at each other, that thought sending shivers up two very different spines. Finally James said, "I believe Lady P. died some years ago?" Another swift calculation and the brows disappeared again. *"Seven* years ago, if I mistake not?"

"Yes, sir."

"So?"

"So Lady Anne went into mourning for a year." Mrs. Tibbet shrugged as if he should have known that.

"But when *that* was over? She had, by then, reached the age of seventeen, if I've not erred in my calculations?" James's tone was as nearly neutral as he could make it, but he was very angry for reasons not entirely clear to him.

Mrs. Tibbet glanced at the bed where the young lady rolled her head from side to side.

"Excuse me, sir." The housekeeper went to Anne's side. "Lady Anne, dear. Can you open your eyes, love?"

There was no response but the restlessness subsided and, after a moment, Mrs. Tibbet resumed her story. "Lady Anne's half-brother had her sent to the Exbridge estate for the duration of her mourning where she had Miss Mary and Miss Jane Merryweather to act as chaperons."

"Martin did something so stupid as that?" James didn't believe his friend and brother-in-law could possibly have been so completely insensitive but, making still another calculation, realized he erred. "Forgive me. That would have been Martin's brother Vincent, would it not? Yes, Vincent was selfish enough and thoughtless enough to have wanted a young nuisance of an unwanted half-sister out of his hair and as far out of mind as possible." An arrested look widened Sir James's usually heavily lidded eyes. "Oh no."

"Oh yes." Mrs. Tibbet nodded several times. "His lordship was thrown at that five bar gate only days before Lady Anne would have come out of mourning for Lady Preminger."

"Still another year of mourning . . . But there are five years for which you've not yet accounted, Mrs. Tibbet," said Sir James, a certain grimness around the eyes also evident in his words.

"Yes sir. But you see Miss Mary had the bad taste to succumb to a cold in the chest part way through Lady Anne's mourning for her brother and that added some months to it and then Miss Jane, celebrating her release from mourning for her sister—Miss Jane always did have a penchant for overly bright colors, Sir James—she insisted they go instantly into Exbridge to order new clothes. It was the worst possible weather and, as any sensible person might have predicted, the carriage overturned. Miss Jane was drowned in the ditch and it is no more than a miracle that dear Lady Anne didn't succumb to pneumonia."

"Which added more time to Lady Anne's mourning. Poor chit. She's been unlucky in her associates, has she not? But there are *still* several years for which you've not accounted and you haven't explained why she's never been presented."

Mrs. Tibbet sighed. "Sir James, I don't understand it myself. But by the time mourning for Miss Jane was done, Lady Anne refused to come to London. She insisted she was quite happily settled and only under protest accepted a new chaperone—another indigent cousin, I believe."

"It seems the family has a plethora of them instantly available," said James absently as he rose to his feet. "I wonder why Martin allowed it, but, then, come to that, he was rather preoccupied just then. No longer on *active* duty, of course, but he was, if I remember rightly, still running errands for the war office . . . ?" James crossed the room to stand beside Lady Anne's bed. He stared down at their patient before reaching toward her. Lifting a bright curl, he wound it around his finger. "Beautiful," he murmured.

"Sir James," scolded the housekeeper, "You get your hands out of Lady Anne's hair! 'Tisn't the least proper to play with it that way."

"In a moment. I may never again have an opportunity to touch it, Mrs. Tibbet and I've never seen anything so magnificent. No one will know if you don't tell."

The housekeeper's mouth snapped into a disapproving line which Sir James ignored—assuming he noticed it.

"Lady Anne," he said, "can you hear me?" He rested his palm against her forehead. "Did you see, Mrs. Tibbet? Her eyes flickered which is good, but she should have come out of her swoon by now. I don't like it that she has not." Nor did he like it when Anne *continued* unconscious.

It seemed hours, although less than two, before help arrived in the big burly form of his friend, Ewen Macalister, the son of a minor Scottish laird. Relief filled him when he finally heard a commotion on the stairs and then, in the sitting room, a deep voice with a strong Scottish accent swearing roundly.

"If I've been turned out on a wild-goose chase, I'll see that Jimmy-lad suffers for it. I dinna know what may-game he thinks to make of me this time, but I swear I'll have his guts for garters! No *lady* would be living up under the roof this way!"

"Through here, Mac," called James. "And she is a lady. She's also been unconscious far too long," he finished more quietly as the doctor ducked his head of wild carroty-colored hair and entered the small bedroom, exuding a restless energy which seemed to fill it.

The doctor elbowed Sir James away and, ignoring Mrs.

Tibbet's gasp of outrage, rudely uncovered his patient. He listened to James's description of the fall as he made an even more thorough examination than James had made. "There's a bump the size of a bully-boy's fist on the back of her head, laddie. Ice, madam," he ordered and Mrs. Tibbet, after only a moment's hesitation, and muttering about the ice house, scurried off to relay his order. "Lovely hair," mused the doctor. "Hope we don't have to cut it."

"Don't you dare cut it."

"Nae then, Jimmy. None of that. If it must go, go it must . . . but," he added when he saw his friend about to explode, "I see no immediate need for it." The doctor chuckled. "I can understand, m'lad, why you'd nae wish it gone, but I'll not let your randy nature dictate what's best for my patient." He cast a disparaging glance around the attic room. "Lady, indeed."

"She is Lady Anne Montmorency, Mac," said James a touch dangerously. "She's a daughter of the house, and you'll dub your mummer right tight. No more of that sort of talk!"

"Oh, aye." The doctor glanced even more skeptically at the low ceilinged chamber, thought of the four flights of stairs he'd been forced to climb and nodded. "Certainly now. It's the newest thing, of course. These fine days the unmarried daughters of peers are hidden away in the attics. . . ." Mr. Macalister's quick mind echoed James's earlier thought and his glance sharpened as his finger made a circle beside his head. "Or is she . . . ?"

"No, she is *not*," said James in an offended tone before he grinned and admitted, "I wondered that same thing, but it seems she is merely of a retiring nature. Mrs. Tibbet says she refuses to go into company, which is certainly a loss to society. You should have heard the set-down the chit gave me just before she fell. You'd have approved her spirit, Mac."

"I'm glad to hear she's got spirit," said the doctor.

A funny note in his voice drew James's eyes.

"The puir bonny lass'll likely have a need of it," added Mac softly as he gently recovered Lady Anne.

"What have you discovered? What's the matter with her? I couldn't find a thing wrong with her—beyond that bump you mentioned."

"I fear she may have lost the use of her legs, Jimmy-lad. Perhaps her arms, as well," he added when he'd finished testing her reactions by firmly pinching her extremities. "Temporarily we must hope."

"Surely not!" James stared down at the childish figure and suddenly realized just how much he looked forward to a continuation of the short battle which had raged between them before her tumble. "She must be able to move. So lovely a girl—no. It's impossible."

"Ye well know accidents happen to anyone. I fear she'll need special care, Jimmy."

James drew in a deep breath. "Why do you think she'll be unable to move when she wakes?"

"Reflexes, mon. They've gone. See you?" Once again Mac pinched Lady Anne's finger. There was no reaction. "She should ha' twitched, you see. Even unconscious as she is." He accepted the pan of chipped ice a young maid handed him. "Nae lass, none of that," he added, glancing at the blubbering servant. "Tears won't help your mistress," he scolded gruffly.

"Bain't no one like Lady Anne." The ungainly maid sniffed inelegantly. "Doctor, she bain't goin' ta *die* is she? Tell me she be all right? I want—we all want to know."

Mac glowered. "She won't die . . . as for all right, well, we'll have to wait and see, will we not?"

Throwing her apron over her head, the maid bawled noisily as she rushed from the room. Sir James filed away the information that the servant loved Lady Anne. It said much for her ladyship's character and made him more curious than ever about what went on behind the narrow face with its pointy chin and the high slanted brows which gave her a perpetual air of surprise. The memory of the horror he'd glimpsed in the clear blue green eyes which had met his as she fell twisted his insides and he discovered he was more intrigued by this unusual girl-woman than he'd been by anything for a long time. He watched as the doctor made up an ice pack and applied it gently to the back of the young woman's head.

"What else can we do, Mac?" he asked, staring down at the bird-boned girl about whose condition he felt excessively guilty. If only he'd not arrived just when he did . . . if only he'd taken himself off, rather than argue . . . Mac's voice penetrated his thoughts. "What did you say?"

"Ye can do nothing," repeated the doctor, "beyond getting the swelling down. 'Tis all one can do for the moment, Jimmy-lad. Get it down as quick as may be, before it does any permanent damage to the brain in there under that pretty skull. Then we must see she's kept quiet. If she canna move she'll be frightened. She mustna panic. Explain to her it is only temporary and that soon, maybe several weeks however, she'll have the use of her body back again."

"Will she?"

"Often times, aye," said the doctor on a grim note, his native burr stronger when he added, "Then again, the answer is nae. We wait in each case to see and we deal with whatever happens." Dr. Macalister glared down at the still unconscious girl. "If only we knew more, mon. So much we canna tell, so much to learn."

James ignored a complaint he'd heard often. "I'm to replace the ice as it melts until the bump goes down?"

"You do that. I must get back to London and the hospital where I've got patients without such fancy pocketbooks, but, nae-the-less, in need of a doctor. Luckily, just beyond Chelsea as you are, you aren't *too* far from town. I'll ride out late this evening." Macalister's brows rose. "Will you tell that bloody-minded butler to let me in?"

"I'll be here." James eyes were on the narrow face with its neat features. She must *not* be permanently paralyzed. He wouldn't have it.

"And the butler, mon?" Macalister repeated, grinning. "I don't think he approved of me, Jimmy-lad."

James didn't spare the doctor a glance. "Tibbet will let you in and Mrs. Tibbet will have a room prepared for you so you needn't return in the dark," he said absently. He didn't bother to turn as his old friend nodded and left with his usual tightly restrained energy.

Sir James began his vigil, totally forgetting he'd come that morning to rake his wayward sister over the coals for her outrageous behavior of the night before. Once he *did* remember and asked Mrs. Tibbet for the truth about Jaycee, he discovered she'd arrived in the middle of the night and was keeping to her room. Lady Montmorency, said Mrs. Tibbet, insisted she was no good in a sick room—which James knew to be the true—and was, besides, not very well herself.

That last, James suspected, might also be true—at least to the extent she was sick with fear that she might finally be forced to pay the piper for her latest descent into idiocy.

James wished his friend Martin would return from diplomatic doings at the Congress of Vienna and would once again take over the management of his wife. Jaycee had always been unpredictable, but, with her husband absent, his sister was more rackety than ever, and James had had enough.

James blamed Martin, who'd blithely gone to play-act the diplomat with no care for James, who was left to worry about Jaycee in his absence. James had grown very tired of keeping track of his sister as she grew into womanhood and had been more than happy to marry her off to his friend, who, obligingly, tumbled head over heels into love with the chit. The marriage had, temporarily, relieved James of the need to watch over Jaycee and, with a sigh of relief, he'd assumed his part was played.

But then Martin had had the audacity to take himself off to Vienna without his wife! Sir James decided, as he'd done more than once since Martin crossed the Channel, that he'd have a few words to say to his friend. Not that he didn't understand. Jaycee loose in Vienna at a time like this? The mind boggled.

As for her latest stupidity, Jaycee had arrived, according to Mrs. Tibbet, at four in the morning. James himself left London as soon as he was informed by a sneering acquaintance that his sister had attended a cyprian's ball. A masquerade given by and for London's whores, it was an entertainment she'd no business attending in the first place but, while indulging in such an escapade, *less* business allowing herself to be recognized!

In any case, according to Mrs. Tibbet, upon arriving at the Park, Jaycee had turned her household out of bed and upside down. The servants had been required to unload her coach which she'd had piled with seemingly random possessions from the Montmorency town house. It had pulled on around the house not fifteen minutes before James's arrival at about six. All of which explained why Lady Anne was downstairs at such a ridiculous hour and dressed in her night clothes, but *not* why she'd stayed to bandy words with a total stranger. Assuming she were half so shy as Mrs. Tibbet insisted, of course.

In any case, Jaycee had secluded herself in her suite. So, for just this moment, James felt he could safely forget about his sister. If she were here at Montmorency Park, then she was out of the way and, perhaps, out of trouble. For the moment, at least.

"Careful now, Lady Anne. No, don't be afraid. I'm a pussy cat and no danger to you. Shhh."

Anne blinked her eyes rapidly, hazily assessing her situation. Her room was deeply shadowed, the lamp well-shielded from shedding light directly over her bed. Her head ached abominably. And that voice. She vaguely recalled hearing that voice somewhere, but it hadn't sounded so mellow, so soothing. She turned her head, trying to find the owner, wanting to put a name to it.

"Very good. Now, can you hold this cup if I raise you up?"

There was a sigh, one of relief, she thought, as she automatically reached for the much desired drink. She drank thirstily, handing the cup back, her eyes following it as it disappeared to the side.

At the look which hinted she wished more the voice said, "You may have another sip after awhile. Mac said you shouldn't have too much too soon for fear your stomach should be unsettled. Be patient."

"You . . . doctor?" she whispered with difficulty.

"No. I wished very much to become one, but it wasn't to be."

James bit his tongue. Beyond Mac, who had known him from school days and guessed that particular secret, he'd never discussed it with a soul. Not from the moment his father sat him down and gently explained why it could not be. It was a secret so well hidden even his sister, Jaycee, who was supernaturally sensitive in some ways, had never guessed. And if *she* hadn't, why had he revealed it to this tiny creature no bigger than his thumb?

"What hap—?"

"You don't recall?" James explained. "You fell down the stairs very early this morning. You've been unconscious far too long, my dear." He grasped her hand and squeezed it gently. "Welcome back to us, Lady Anne." At least, thought James, her arms work! Now if he could just think of a way to test her lower limbs. . . .

Anne accepted the information without flinching. She

couldn't remember falling, but knew such falls resulted, usually temporarily, in mental confusion and assumed that that had happened to her. She sighed. Her fingers picked at the coverlet, touched her forehead, moved on to her hair. Her whole being stilled instantly. Then her fingers trembled, her eyes widened.

"My cap!" she breathed, her eyes raised anxiously to meet his.

"It got in the way of the ice packs," lied James.

Mrs. Tibbet had wished to put a new nightcap on their patient but he'd not allowed it, not wishing to hide the girl's crowning glory.

"Must . . ."

"Must?"

"Cover it." She yanked at a handful of hair, a grimace distorting her face. "Must . . ."

James frowned. Lady Anne was obviously distressed and her upset appeared to be centered on her hair but that surely didn't make sense. "You wish to hide your hair," he clarified, speaking rather hesitantly.

"Yes." Lady Anne relaxed at this stranger's understanding, nodding her head and then wincing when the movement worsened the headache. "At once, please."

James hesitated. "Lady Anne, truly, I think it better to leave it this way. At least until we've completely reduced the swelling at the back of your head. Truly." Truly? Ha! Why didn't he simply tell her he couldn't bear to cover her hair?

Her voice slurred, but there was a hint of desperation in it as well. "Must hide the ugly mop."

James blinked. Had he heard correctly? "Ugly, Lady Anne?"

"This awful hair. Must hide it. Please."

"Awful?"

"Yes. Terrible. *Must* hide it."

She thought that beautiful hair awful? "Lady Anne, I

don't know who told you your hair was ugly but whoever it was did so out of spite or jealousy or both. Your hair is beautiful. Magnificent. Absolutely wonderful." He frowned when she shook her head. "You should *never* hide it."

A wistful smile narrowed her surprisingly full mouth. "How kind of you. But you should not perjure yourself that way. A cap? Please?"

She was, despite the polite phrasing, obviously agitated. Mac had said she must not become upset if it could be avoided. James hadn't been able to resist testing to see if she could use her arms, but there was no sly way to test her lower limbs. At least her upper body was all right and she had not yet complained about anything else.

But she was agitated! And agitation was bad for her. Mac insisted it be avoided.

James stifled a sigh and crossed the room to where he'd tossed the nightcap Mrs. Tibbet had brought him. Very gently he fit it over Lady Anne's head and slowly, enjoying every moment even as he regretted the necessity, he pushed her hair, lock by lock, under the unruffled, undecorated hem and, when he had no more excuse to touch her, gently pulled the draw string firm, tying it in a bow beside one ear. He patted it and reluctantly withdrew his hand.

"There. All covered."

He watched as Anne relaxed and, almost before he straightened away from her, she was asleep.

About nine, Mrs. Tibbet walked into the room hiding a yawn. "I'll take over now, Sir James. The blue room at the back of the house is ready when you wish it since I don't suppose you'll return to London until we know how she progresses."

"You know me well, Mrs. Tibbet, but not well enough. I'll catch a wink out in Lady Anne's sitting room so that I'll be near at hand if you need me."

"Sir James, you sat with Lady Anne all of the day and

you need your sleep. You'll be no good for anything tomorrow if you get none tonight."

"Don't worry about me. On any number of occasions I've been several nights in a row with little sleep. I'm responsible and I've never been one to shirk an obligation. Lady Anne would not have stopped at the top of those stairs when she did if I'd not been below and, if she'd not stopped, she'd not have fallen. Now no argument," he said when the housekeeper opened her mouth to object. He turned away, turned back. "She woke briefly and insisted I put that ridiculous cap over her hair. She said it was ugly and must be hidden."

"She's said that before. Joking like. But it's true enough she never, *never* appears anywhere with a strand of hair showing."

"I wonder why."

"I haven't a notion. In fact, I'd forgotten just how lovely it is. I've not seen it myself, you see, since before her mother died."

"We'll have to convince her she's wrong to hide it, Mrs. Tibbet. I don't think I can go through life knowing it exists but never allowed a glimpse of it!"

"Oh, Sir James, you are the one! Now off with you and get what sleep you can." Mrs. Tibbet yawned again, hiding it as well as she could. "You really should go down to a decent bed. We'll be fine. She's wakened once and that's good. But she'll most likely sleep the rest of the night now."

"But she might not. You heard Dr. Mac. If she wakes and is worried or upset you may be glad of my help. I'll be in the other room."

Mrs. Tibbet knew when to stop arguing. And from the look on the baronet's face this was certainly one of those times. She pressed her lips tight against further words and turned to sit in the comfortable chair Sir James had brought from Lady Anne's sitting room. It would be, thought the housekeeper, a long, long night. Laying her head against the back of the chair Mrs. Tibbet focused on the soft glow of the shielded lamp. Almost immediately it seemed to grow and grow and then to fade and fade—and before many moments had passed, without ever meaning to, the tired woman drifted into a deep, deep sleep.

Half an hour later, Sir James remembered he'd not told Mrs. Tibbet Lady Anne could move her arms. Returning to the bedroom to do so, he smiled, a trifle sardonically perhaps, but kindly, with it. It was, after all, little more than he'd expected. Mrs. Tibbet had been roused in the middle of *last* night by the unexpected arrival of her mistress and, thanks to Lady Anne's fall, hadn't had much, if any, sleep since.

James lifted the extra blanket from the chest at the end of the bed and gently tucked it around the exhausted housekeeper. Then he returned to the sitting room and brought the second chair through. He placed it near the bed and hoped, wryly, no one else wished to enter the tiny bedroom. There wasn't room left for a cat to wander through! He looked at the sleeping girl and sighed. It would be, he thought, unknowingly echoing Mrs. Tibbet, a long, long night.

"Well noo, m'lassie, how are ye this morning?"

Dr. Mac had arrived late the evening before after an overly long day with patients. He'd talked quietly with James and decided he'd not wake Lady Anne who was sleeping normally. Instead, he'd taken the bed prepared for him and slept very well indeed. Now he smiled down at an alert woman who stared back, the flaring brows emphasizing a look of caution.

"I don't know how I do," said Lady Anne absently, in belated response to his question. Her wary eyes examined the overly large Scotsman and was somewhat soothed by the kindness she saw in him.

"Don't know?" Mac's brows wiggled up and down. "And who's to know if ye do not!"

She smiled at his grin and relaxed slightly. "I can't seem to move my legs." She blushed, her cheeks glowing with the flush of blood rising under pale skin. "My lower limbs, I mean."

"Don't go all missish on me, noo. I know a leg when I see it and a fine pair you have, m'lassie. We'll just have to get them working again. Noo, do you feel that?" asked Macalister, pinching a tempting pink toe. He wasn't surprised when she shook her head in the negative. "So. Two legs malfunctioning, but arms working fine. That's good. That's verra good. When I first saw you they had no sensation either, you see. Not a twitch when I pinched your wee finger like this. Yes, that's a very good twitch, m'lassie," he said, approvingly, when she jerked her arm away and scowled at him. "Now, a look at that bump, m'lady."

Mac reached for the hideous nightcap only to have her hands come up protectively to hold it in place.

"Nae, there," he said soothingly. "What's to do, noo?"

"You mustn't uncover my hair."

"Such a solemn wee chick you are. Why must I no take off that ridiculous bonnet so I may take a look at the wee bump, then?"

"I must never never show my hair."

"And who told you such a canard as that, lass? Why, I saw it myself only yesterday. Lovely hair it is, too. There must be something of the Scots in you, m'lady, that you have hair that magnificent color," he teased, but his brows pulled together when he got no response and his eyes searched her averted face for a clue. "Well, now," he said, finally, "I suppose I might just edge my fingers under the hem here if I loosen the strings a wee bit."

The swelling was nearly gone. The lump had been reduced to a tender spot which was only slightly puffy. Macalister gently resettled the edge of the ugly cap, pushing a straying lock back into hiding and made an awkward bow. He patted the girl's shoulder with his great paw which could be amazingly gentle when necessary. He told her not to worry, that when the swelling was all gone, then her *legs* would likely move again. If not, then at some point in the next few weeks they'd begin working. It would just take time and patience and worry was the worst thing she could do.

"I'll try to be good, Mr. Macalister. Patience is not a virtue with which I'm overly familiar, but I'll find some way to keep myself occupied."

"You send someone out to the nearest circulating library and have them bring home a pile of novels. *Pride and Prejudice* is very good noo."

A tiny smile which tucked her mouth into a perfect heart shape, also limned faint laugh lines to the corners of Anne's eyes. "You recommend some lady's novel over your own Scott's work?"

"Now then," scolded Macalister, pretending earnestness, "dinna I say you must no get excited? We canna have you reading a work so stirring as Scott's *Marmion* or his *Lady of the Lake* until you feel more the thing, lassie."

Anne sighed. "I was only jesting, sir. I don't read novels, of course. Or narrative poems. They are not the thing," she scolded, "as you must know."

Mac was startled into stating his opinion in no uncertain terms. "I dinna know that at all and where you came by such an odd notion I canna tell." He eyed her for a moment and, with the barest hint of a chiding note, asked, "If ye've never read one, then ye canna be a judge, can ye, m'lassie? I recommend you do so before again expressing such a nincompoopish opinion." He turned on his heel and, remembering just in time to duck, disappeared through the door.

Anne blinked at his stern words. What a strange man. But then, doctors were not truly gentlemen, she assured herself. At least not usually, although this one seemed . . . but, no. Surely he merely aped manners he'd observed? And therefore, he could know nothing of what was proper and what was not.

Anne reran that thought through her mind and blushed, plucking nervously at the coverlet. *How smug. How priggish. Could he possibly be correct?* It was certainly true she'd never opened the covers of a novel. Why, Aunt Prem would roll over in her grave if she *dared* do anything so sinful! It was silly to even contemplate the notion she might read one.

Instead she'd think about Sir James and how kind and . . . But no. That wasn't a very good notion either, was it? Not when it led to feelings which . . . no! She'd think about . . .

Well, she didn't know, but something. Anything which would take her mind from formerly unknown but easily recognizable impulses which could lead to nothing but her downfall. Aunt Prem had explained very carefully how the devil made one feel sinful desire, exactly what it led to, and how, as Anne got older, she must carefully guard against all such urges.

Anne's hands covered the burning in her cheeks at the memory of Aunt Prem's vivid descriptions of the act between men and women necessary for the procreation of children. She must root out all curiosity about such things, since, as Aunt Prem had assured her, she was not the sort a man would wish to wed—not with her horrid hair and independent nature—and it went without saying she couldn't be the *other* sort of woman lustful-minded men required in their lives!

All of which meant she must *not* think about the tall man with the kind brown eyes who looked at her in that singular way that led her to wonder . . . but there it was again! That exceedingly odd, wonderfully tingly warmth . . . The devil must surely be laughing up his sleeve that she could be so easily suborned from the path of righteousness!

Two

"Well, Mrs. Tibbet, when she puts her mind to it, Jaycee does things very well, does she not?" Sir James smiled at his sister who blushed at the praise.

To hide her confusion, Jaycee asked, "But will Lady Anne like it?"

His hands on hips, Sir James turned slowly, looked around the dainty, essentially feminine room and wondered if aught else *could* be done to make it more welcoming, more comfortable. His sister had ordered hothouse flowers, all sorts and sizes and colors. Those nodded cheerful greeting from nearly every surface which would hold a vase. The table beside the bed held the natural impedimenta necessary to an invalid, such as a crystal handled solid silver hand-bell and a carafe of clear fresh water; it also held a stack of books which James hoped might interest Lady Anne, some of which had had to be wrested forcibly from Jaycee.

Was there anything else . . . ?

"I think it will do," Jaycee said, interrupting his thoughts, *"assuming,* of course, that Anne can be convinced to move down from those rooms at the top of the house which she insists are all she wants and more than she needs. You've no notion, James, how stubborn she has been about having her own, very private apartment. I gave up arguing weeks ago."

A muscle twitched in James's cheek. "I'll convince her,

Jaycee, even if it is necessary to become a trifle manipulative. She must not be allowed to hide herself away in the attics. If she's shy, as Mrs. Tibbet suggests—" He bowed slightly toward the silent housekeeper. "—such standoffish behavior on her part will only make the condition worse. If it is something else—" James was quite certain it *was*. "—then we must get to the bottom of it and convince her she is wrong to act the hermit."

"I hope you can, James, but you are up against more than you know. Anne is the oddest creature."

"Jaycee, it is that sort of attitude which has kept her locked in her current way of living!"

"Well!" Jaycee turned on her heel and stalked out the door, her usual answer at any hint of contradiction or opposition.

Mrs. Tibbet stared after her mistress. She sighed, before saying, "I must return to my duties, Sir James, but I'll be free directly after lunch if you wish to move Lady Anne then?"

Only half hearing her, James nodded absently. In his mind, he was debating whether he should share his suspicions that Lady P., jealous of Lady Anne's mother, had imbued her rival's daughter with the odd notions which had led to the child's isolation and her very lonely existence.

Child, he thought, a sense of confusion filling him. *Lady Anne is no child. . . . On the other hand,* the rueful notion intruded a moment later, when he had another, fully understood, reaction to the memory of her slight form, *perhaps it is safer to think her one?*

James pushed aside his awareness of an inappropriate physical reaction to Lady Anne and returned to the problem of her odd behavior. What could be done? At this point? Nothing, James concluded. He must wait until he accumulated more evidence before revealing his suspicion.

Once again he looked around the prepared bedroom. He noticed the housekeeper had gone off somewhere and, forgetting Mrs. Tibbet's half-heard comment concerning when they could move Lady Anne, he muttered, "I'll just bring her down now. A maid can move her belongings later once she's here and able to direct the girl from her bed."

James climbed the stairs slowly, marshaling his thoughts for the argument he faced. He'd begun to know Lady Anne and, if he was not mistaken, there was *one* argument she could not refute and, given her nature would not dispute. He'd save that for last, since it would hurt her if he must point it out to her.

If she didn't think of it herself, of course, and perhaps she would. . . . More cheerfully Sir James climbed the rest of the way to the attics.

Nothing worked. James stared down at the stubborn face turned slightly away from him. The time had come to be underhanded and a trifle cruel even, since kindness and patience proved insufficient. James looked at Anne and shook his head that he must tweak her conscience and thereby pain her in order to do her a kindness. He moved to the window where he stared out at the bit of blue sky which was all that was visible. He realized he didn't want to face Anne when she realized she *must* submit, but, turning back, he did.

"You are very selfish," he began. "I didn't think that of you."

That a twist of pain spiraled through Anne was obvious from the grimace which crossed her face. She clenched her jaw and said, "I do not see why it is selfish to wish to remain in my own rooms. I am comfortable here. I have made my home in this apartment. Do you know how difficult it is to make a place for oneself in another person's house?"

Anne blinked and blushed and dipped her head. She twisted a bit of the coverlet between nervous fingers. Obviously, thought James, the girl hated controversy. Yet it was also obvious she believed she had a right to her own life, even though she must live it in her brother's home.

"I wish I was considered old enough for my own home," she added with only the faintest trace of bitterness.

"Why would a lovely intelligent young woman such as yourself want such a thing? Where?"

She glared. "It is my dream to have a cottage in some under-populated district where I can be *alone*."

"Thank goodness you *are* too young to be allowed to do anything so foolish," said James quickly, putting away the information to think about when he wasn't in the midst of an important argument. He eyed her and, with a sigh, returned to his reasoning. "Since I do not believe you are truly selfish, you *will* move down to the room prepared for you."

"You simply don't understand," she said rather dolefully.

"I wonder if I don't understand more than you think, my dear." Again James turned to the low window, fearing his face would reveal his distaste at tricking her into agreeing to the move—not that his argument was invalid, of course. It was the very truth of it which would win the day.

"No one understands. . . ."

He decided it was doing nobody any good to put it off, drew in a deep breath, and said, "I am forced, then, to consider your reluctance selfish."

"And I must be exceedingly stupid—" Her voice was both plaintive and yet held a determined note. "—because I don't understand."

James forced his features into a stern mold and turned. "When you chose these rooms, Lady Anne, you had two good limbs which carried you wherever you wished to go." He ached himself when he saw understanding dawning. "You've guessed what I'll say next, but I'll say it anyway." He forced a frown. "Is it fair, Lady Anne, to require of the servants the extra work of carrying your every need up and down two unnecessary flights of stairs?" He caught and held her gaze.

Anne bit her lip, a stricken look in the eyes which met his. Finally she turned away to stare at the slanted ceiling. James felt compassion for her, but could not yield on this. Lady Anne must move to a room on a lower floor, not merely for the well being of the servants, but for *her own future well being as well*.

"I didn't think, did I?" she asked in a small voice. Her lips quivered but she quickly controlled the revealing movement.

"You are willing to remove to the room Jaycee and Mrs. Tibbet have prepared for you?"

There was the briefest of hesitations before Lady Anne nodded.

James carefully hid his satisfaction. Moving her to the floor she should occupy was only his first step toward introducing the imp to the society in which she should and, if he had anything to say about it, *would* shine. Assuming his theory was correct, the child had imbibed some very strange notions from Lady Preminger and they must be removed from beneath that shining head of deeply burnished hair as quickly as possible.

Oh yes, he thought, his mind's eye on the hidden beauty of her hair, *certainly as soon as might be!*

James approached the bed, shaking out the old robe Lady Anne had worn when he'd first seen her. "We must get you into this, I suppose, so as to not outrage propriety."

"You mean because you are here with no vestige of a chaperone in sight?" Anne chuckled softly. "How very silly of you!" she said, wide eyes more innocent looking than ever under the flaring brows. "No one would believe you to be the least interested *that way* about an ugly squab of a goose like me."

Sir James froze, his hands clenching, white knuckled, around the rough brown material of the robe. Lady Anne spoke with such utter belief, such acceptance, such complete and bewildering certainty, he couldn't move.

"What's the matter?" Those big fairy-green eyes met his, questioningly. "Are you in pain, Sir James?" She struggled to raise herself onto her elbows, the covers slipping to her waist. "Sir James?"

"Great Caesar's ghost," he whispered, his eyes flicking to the plain white gown she wore, and back to her eyes. *"You believe that nonsense."*

"I don't understand."

"No you don't, you little fool. And unfortunately I'm too much the gentleman to show you just how wrong you are. Lady Anne, once we have you well again and back on your feet and in fighting trim, I promise you I'll convince you of the stupidity of what you've just said. But for now we must get you into this ridiculous garment, not only for propriety's sake—" His gaze again flicked to where small breasts pushed against thin cotton. "—but to aid my rapidly disintegrating self-control. Then I'll carry you down to your new room."

Since she was still leaning up on her elbows it was the work of a moment to pull her farther forward and drape the robe around her. Forcing himself to look anywhere but at her slim form, he threw back the covers and shifted her, lifting her to allow the robe to fall around her legs and set her on the side of the bed. He steadied her with one hand long enough to pull it around her with the other and, once her arms were in the sleeves, Lady Anne tied the ties, her eyes lowered in embarrassment.

"There," he said, lifting her into his arms in one further smooth motion. "That should do the trick."

Now that she was enveloped in the ugly robe, he allowed himself to smile down into her bemused features and then, unable to help himself, shifted just enough to allow the stupid nightcap to pull down and away. Once again he revealed that cascade of red-gold hair and he did one further thing he knew he'd likely regret. He bent his head and kissed her, an ephemeral touching of lips that satisfied him not at all.

"You told me once I was no gentleman, Annie, m'girl. I think I've just proved it." He grinned at her, the grin widening as she blushed. "Do you remember telling me that, my sweet little wren?"

"If you refer to our silly argument just before I fell, of course I do." She lifted her eyes in a shy look, and glanced away. "I apologize."

"Apologize?" James frowned very slightly. "One needn't apologize for speaking the truth, Anne."

"But you *are* a gentleman, Sir James." The faintest hint of humor could be heard when she added, "You yourself said so not more than a moment ago."

"I said I was *enough* of one," he contradicted her, "that I'll not prove you a gudgeon for believing you are unattractive and safe from men's desires."

"I've years of experience which prove me correct, Sir James," she said with that surprising dignity which had, from the first, intrigued him.

The rueful thought crossed James's mind that, if she looked at men in just that particular way, there would be few brave enough to attempt her defenses. Luckily, he thought smugly, he'd never thought himself a coward!

Anne glanced up at him then quickly away. "If I must be moved to another room, do you think we might get on with it?"

"Why? Are you uncomfortable in my arms?"

"Yes."

James choked back a laugh. He should have expected agreement, but had automatically looked for a social lie along the lines of *not at all*. "In that case I'd best carry you off. But, little one, you really shouldn't be so honest. It only tempts a man to make you, hmm, more uncomfortable."

"You are such a tease, Sir James."

He looked down at her for a moment, questioning whether she flirted with him. She wasn't. "Lady Anne, you have a great deal to learn. Or perhaps it is a question of *unlearning,* but now, unfortunately, is *not* the time to teach you." Before he could be tempted further, he told her to hush. "Not another word, sparrow. Or I might change my mind."

Mrs. Tibbet appeared as he reached the family bedroom wing, fluttering her hands. She frowned deeply and followed as James carried his slight burden into Lady Anne's bedroom. "Sir James, you really must not do such things."

"And just who is to know?" he asked.

Anne looked from the housekeeper to the overly pugnacious chin all too close to her own. "Know what?" she asked.

"He had no business going up to get you without me there to help," scolded the housekeeper. "Why, a lovely young lady like you? And a handsome man like Sir James? It was bad enough I let him sit with you yesterday without a maid in the room, but you were unconscious and he insisted and I was too tired and worried to think. But now my mind's working and I've had a good long *think.* I've had a long talk with Lady Montmorency, too," she finished half in triumph and half defensively, "and told her you must be properly chaperoned.

"Jaycee?" James gritted his teeth. The last thing he wanted was the presence of his sister hovering in the background whenever he had a moment with Anne. "Why?"

"Because, Sir James," said the housekeeper, "I know you. You aren't about to go away and leave Lady Anne to Lady Montmorency and me. So, if *you* are here, then Lady Anne must be chaperoned and no one will believe me suitable even if I'm far more a dragon than our dear Lady Montmorency could ever be."

"Jaycee won't thank you for that bit of officiousness, Mrs. Tibbet," said James. "For that matter, neither will I.

Besides," he added, the notion of propriety reminding him, "my sister is a complication all in herself, is she not? Given her latest doings? While under a cloud of scandal herself, she's no chaperone at all!" Mrs. Tibbet didn't relax her expression one jot and James sighed. "Perhaps there is some other we might ask—if you are certain it is necessary."

"It is Lady Montmorency's home and her right and her duty," insisted the housekeeper stubbornly. "I didn't approve of how her ladyship arrived in such a scrambling way, but so hysterical the poor dear was there was no arguing with her! However that may be, she's needed and so it's good she's here. Besides, this is a way of taking her ladyship out of herself, thinking of another as she must do, and you'll not change my mind, Sir James, however much you glower!"

Mrs. Tibbet collected herself and blushed at her presumption. Lecturing her betters that way was outside of enough! It was an impertinence, even if she had known Lady Montmorency from a toddler and Sir James for still longer, first as the newest Lord Montmorency's boyhood friend and then as his brother-in-law.

"Now, you put Lady Anne down and I'll get her straight," scolded the housekeeper, compounding her original error to hide her embarrassment at the first offense! "Then, Sir James, you get yourself some sleep. You were up all night, as you should not have been, though it was your own fault, letting me sleep when it was my duty to sit with Lady Anne."

"Sir James sat with me?" Anne had a vague memory of a kind-voiced man leaning over her in the night. She'd thought it one of her rare dreams of the affectionate but often absent father she barely recalled.

"He insisted." Mrs. Tibbet pointed at James. "Just you see him yawn! You lay Lady Anne down, and take yourself off, Sir James."

James, suddenly very tired, obeyed. He drew his arms

from under his burden, letting his fingers trail along the
hair with which he'd fallen in love, and, with one last touch,
the end of his finger to the tip of her turned-up nose, he
exited.

Mrs. Tibbet watched the girl's bemused eyes follow Sir
James from the room. What would come of this she didn't
know, although she feared it. She'd had the cheek to pray
that something would wake up Lady Anne and bring her
out of the shell into which she'd withdrawn. But, oh dear!
Perhaps it was true that one should beware what one prayed
for? It certainly wasn't a fall down the front stairs she'd
had in mind when she'd prayed that Lady Anne be shaken
up!

But perhaps Sir James was the true means to that wished-
for end? Even if he were to put a few cracks into the young
heart of her with that handsome face and kind nature,
wouldn't that be better than the way things were? Mrs. Tibbet, ambivalent about that possibility, swore to watch and
wait and interfere only if she felt things—she didn't wish
to define exactly what she meant by *things*—appeared to
be getting out of hand.

For the moment Sir James had her approval. He'd brought
Lady Anne down out of those rooms at the top of the house,
out of the attics and into a proper bedroom and for that, if
nothing else, Mrs. Tibbet was deeply grateful. Now if Lady
Anne would only regain the use of her legs—but not so
soon as to undo what good had been done so far, of course,
and perhaps not before *more* good were done . . . ?

Alone at last, Anne stared with sad eyes around the room
to which she'd been forced to move by her consideration
for the servants. She wrinkled her nose at the lavish bou-
quets. Flowers should not, she believed, be picked. Their
lives were far too short and they died still more quickly
when cut.

Besides, forming a handful of flowers into an acceptable bouquet was time-consuming nonsense. Time better spent elsewhere on practical matters. That simple truth had been one of her first lessons at the hands of Lady Prem when, one day soon after she was taken to live with her ladyship, she'd shyly brought her new guardian a bouquet, something she'd been taught by her father that her mother liked. Aunt Prem soon taught her it was merely frivolous.

Anne's glance roamed on, and settled, finally, on the pile of books which had been left within easy reach. Curious, she lifted them, one by one, onto the bed beside her.

The first was poetry, *The Curse of Kehama,* by Robert Southey, and by its very title, the current laureate's work must be deemed unsuitable. The next, another slim volume, horrified her, the first stanza revealing it was another romantic effusion in poetic form and it too was pushed away. She'd been taught all such books were the work of the devil and, despite being strongly tempted by *Sense and Sensibility* about which even she had heard, she sternly set aside those three slim leather-bound volumes as well. So what remained?

She picked up the last two. One was, she discovered, a rather light-hearted and tongue-in-cheek diary of an anonymous lord's travels in India and although she didn't approve the levity, it would teach one something about the poor heathen's way of life and the land in which he lived, and perhaps, despite the man's jesting style, was educational and could be permitted.

Finally, she picked up a volume by someone named Lamb entitled *Specimens of the English Dramatic Poets who Lived about the Time of Shakespeare.* Even Aunt Prem allowed Shakespeare's plays to be read on a long cold winter's evening, although not, of course, attendance at a theater where one might see them produced. So perhaps Lamb's work about Shakespeare's contemporaries would be all right.

Even there, however, she mustn't indulge herself. Reading *was* an indulgence, after all, unless it taught one something.

Anne realized that *not* indulging herself would be a problem, given the fact she hadn't the freedom to move nor the privacy in which to get on with her work.

She sighed, her mouth drooping slightly. How was she to finish her manuscript if she was unable to rise and lock her door, assuring her privacy, and was unable to move to her desk where she did that work? She'd promised to get the manuscript to her publisher before the spring Season began, too. Oh dear. She sighed. But, in a day or two, if she were lucky, her limbs would again function and she could return to her rooms and to her usual schedule of work.

One thing she *could* finish while lying in bed was the pencil sketch of poor awkward Kitty which the maid wished to present to her parents, both of whom had natal days in the month of February, her mother's on St. Valentine's name day. It was a shame, thought Anne, that she'd be unable to get the portrait framed as she'd meant to do, but it wasn't as if she'd *told* Kitty of that intention, so, at least, there'd be no disappointment.

Anne sighed again. Softly. It would be necessary that Kitty retrieve the sketch book and pencils from upstairs. She hated asking anyone to wait upon her, but, in her current condition, it was unavoidable. Then, once she had her equipment, the girl must sit here, beside the bed rather than *exactly so* in the dormer window where the light came in around her in *just* the right way. All that was bad enough, but worst of all, in this room, she was no longer assured of privacy while she worked and she so disliked anyone knowing of it. Even when it was nothing more serious than a maid's portrait.

Very likely it had been a mistake to believe she'd finally achieved a way of life which might make her comfortable and . . . not *happy* precisely, but . . . content? The fall and the resulting paralysis changed that and for the worse, of course.

Aunt Prem, she knew, would remind her the world was a harsh place and even simple contentment should not be taken for granted, but, for a long moment, Anne felt extremely sorry for herself. Then she remembered another of Aunt Prem's strictures, this one on self-pity and forced herself to count her blessings as she'd been taught to do.

The trick for turning her mind to better things had been unnecessary for weeks now. Once she'd organized her life in her half-brother's home and convinced his rather flighty wife of her wishes, life had seemed full and interesting and—well, much more bearable. Perhaps it had become too comfortable? The accident, therefore, had occurred to remind her of the seriousness of life?

From long practice Anne accepted her situation. Thanks to Aunt Prem, she'd incorporated into her very being the rules whereby one must live. Lady Preminger had seen to that during the five years her young and impressionable charge lived under her tutelage. Now Anne must think how best to handle this newest hurdle. And she would.

First she'd finish Kitty's portrait. She couldn't bring herself to work on the text of her book when that would mean others knowing what she did, but a sudden notion occurred to her, a way to improve what she'd thought were finished drawings. She would add small insets, showing how the herbs looked at various seasons of the year so they could be found and watched until the proper time for harvesting arrived.

A distinct improvement, she decided, a sense of contentment returning to calm her and soothe away the last of her anxiety. Because, once again, she'd been given proof that every bad had some good in it if one only searched for it. Not that Aunt Prem would have agreed. She'd insist the paralysis was punishment for the forwardness of attempting to stop Sir James's entry when Tibbet had failed to keep him out. Anne, according to Aunt Prem, should not have presumed to think she, such an insignificant figure as she was, might succeed in shutting out the visitor when someone else had failed.

Why *had* she tried? Anne never, voluntarily, spoke to a stranger—and certainly not a stranger of the male persuasion! Aunt Prem had impressed on her all the reasons for avoiding men. So, on this occasion when she had *not* refrained from speech with a man, see what came of it? See how she now suffered for it!

Shoving that self-pitying thought away with the rest of those in which it was wrong to indulge, Anne set to planning the new design for the plates for the new book. What was that pompous title Mr. Gregory insisted they use? Humor put a small smile on her face. *A Small Volume of Plates and Simple Explanations for the Finding of Common Herbs and Preparation of Same for Use in the Care of a Family's Health.*

And the subtitle? *A Necessary Addition to Every Household. Now that,* thought Anne, *was a truly presumptuous claim.* She'd pointed out that fact to Mr. Gregory, but that gentleman had nevertheless insisted, so, since he seemed to know his business, she'd not felt she'd a right to argue.

But worse still the subtitle was to be followed by the statement that: "This book will be exceedingly useful for those women of sense and sensibility who wish to train the poor and uneducated females who come into their purview to better care for their families." And that was a statement, now she thought of it, which must be changed, for it was difficult to understand to whom the word "their," in its second usage, referred: the instructor's family or those of the women she taught. Mr. Gregory would be chagrined he'd not noticed!

Anne chuckled.

"How nice to hear that sound. Unexpected, of course, but verra nice."

"Doctor?"

"You call me Dr. Mac, m'lass. Or Mac will do. I'm easily pleased."

"I have wondered why you were called in to see me instead of Lady Jaycee's usual doctor."

"Jimmy-lad gave me no choice, lassie, but I'm verra glad he did not. Now, let us see how you do. . . ."

He approached the bed and felt more than saw the fine-boned young woman flinch.

"You know I'll nae hurt you, Lady Anne," he said with a frown, glancing briefly to where Mrs. Tibbet stood beside the door, her hands folded at her waist. "Surely you dinna fear me." When Anne bit her lip instead of responding, his tone revealed bemusement. "Do you, now, lass?"

"No, of course not," said Anne. She bit her lip at her foolish reaction. Her memory of earlier visits was a trifle hazy, but she recalled she'd liked, even trusted him. So why did she now feel this irritation of the nerves?

Ah, she thought, enlightened. It was because she'd been thinking about Aunt Prem's strictures! He was a male even if a doctor, and males, according to Aunt Prem were not to be trusted—not the *best* of them and there were, again according to Aunt Prem, few enough of *those*.

A vision of Sir James floated into Anne's head, a comforting vision, but she pushed it out again. Now was no time to think of the irritating man—or to wonder why she had. It certainly could not be that she considered him one of those one might label *best!*

"I'll just have a look now," Mac said, still watching her cautiously. He lifted the blankets over her legs and folded them away so he revealed her lower limbs below the knee. He noted Lady Anne's shock that her extremities were bare and, seeing the edge of her nightgown, pulled it down for her, noting the fact she was grateful to him for doing so. "Have you any pain, Lady Anne?" he asked, holding her gaze and, while her eyes were captured by his own, pinching the same toe which had received similar treatment on each occasion he'd seen her.

Again there was no reaction and, mentally, where the patient could not see it, Dr. Macalister sighed. The longer she went with no response, the less likely she'd recover. He didn't like this at all. She was too placid about it, too accepting. Why didn't she cry and rant and rave at the unfairness, even at the *fact* of paralysis? It was unnatural, this passive acceptance.

Anne had seen his action out of the corner of her eye. For an instant her mouth tightened. "Still no change, is there?"

Mac blinked. So Jimmie's wounded bird was not to be tricked. "Nae change yet, but we must be patient. These things take time, ye ken." Her next words surprised him still more.

"Time," she said thoughtfully. "I recall a case near my home in Shropshire where the patient recovered months later. By then her poor limbs were reduced to toothpicks and it took more months to strengthen them until she could walk again. She was never the same, of course."

The faintest of frowns creased her brow, but no more than might be the case if she were thinking of some odd fact. Mac frowned far more deeply himself. How could the child disassociate herself so completely from the fact it was *herself* who was unable to move? A deep dark anger filled him that she did not respond as she should do.

"Ye seem unaccountably familiar with the problem, m'dear," he said with the slightest of acid bite to his tone.

Anne glanced at him, away. "I've made something of a hobby of discovering what I can about health problems— and what can be done about them, of course."

Anne said it calmly, making her life's work sound like the casual, if rather odd, interest of a lady with nothing of any particular importance to do. She'd had practice making such statements, quickly learning to dissemble after seeing her first auditors' reactions to learning the depth of her interest in medicine. Their reactions had ranged from patronizing amusement to the titillation of horrified curiosity. As a result, she made light of her work which was by far the best way—especially since it was such an unladylike interest.

Beyond a woman's necessary work in the still room, of course, which had piqued her curiosity in the first place. It was one thing Aunt Prem had not simply *allowed* but had *demanded*. That the old woman hated the work perhaps explained why she assumed everyone did. It had been the one terrible secret Anne had kept from her guardian, her great interest in it and the satisfaction she gained from learning all she could.

As she got older, Anne's interest in herbal lore had led to her becoming known as a healer. She'd made her first drawings as a teaching device, to aid the village women in identifying those herbs they were paid to gather. The vicar saw one such drawing, collected more, and sent them to Mr. Gregory, who had asked for a complete set. Lady Anne's first publication was nothing more than a collection of the illustrations. A request soon followed for a more complete book on the subject.

Her new book would not only include improved plates, but would explain the uses of various herbs and how to make them into salves and powders or distill beneficial home remedies from them. It was the result of much research into books she bought or borrowed and correspondence with herbalists to whom Mr. Gregory got her introductions. She'd found that much of what was in print included extraneous ingredients to say nothing of some really dangerous concoctions, mixtures which should be guarded against. Almost as bad were the cosmetic preparations since she disapproved pandering to vanity. Her book would contain only those compounds which helped in illness and accident. Lady Anne would put nothing into her book which had not been sworn efficacious by someone she trusted or thoroughly tested by herself.

Mac cleared his throat, his eyes twinkling. "Ho, there, Lady Anne. Have ye gone to sleep, then?"

"What? Oh. Mr. Macalister." Anne's cheeks turned the bright rosy red of embarrassment and tiny white teeth slipped over her bottom lip. "I was wool-gathering, was I not? Did you ask a question?"

"I asked," he said, a twinkle in his eye, "if ye had yet found a moment in which you might dip into this verra fine novel, and if, thereby, ye had changed your opinion of such writings?" He held up the first volume of *Sense and Sensibility* by A Lady.

"Do not tempt me, Mr. Macalister, to do something I know I should not. I am far too easily drawn from the path I must tread as it is. Otherwise I would not be lying here in this condition."

"Nonsense."

"That because of my presumption I've been punished? It is the truth."

Mac blinked. "You *believe* that foolishness!"

"It is not foolishness and of course I do. You should, too."

Mac's mouth firmed into a hard line, his cold clear eyes raking her face. "Now, then," he asked, "who has been filling your pretty little head with such idiocy?"

"It is not that, I assure you."

"Lady Anne, I do not like to contradict an intelligent woman, but for the sake of your health, I must."

Anne, who had been girding herself to resist temptation, found herself disarmed. "For my *health's* sake?"

"You lay there accepting your fate as if it were deserved and there was naught ye could do." His anger at her attitude rose again and, in a scolding tone, he added, "By such a silly attitude, ye may well *make* permanent what likely should be merely temporary. Lady Anne, you must not only push aside witless idiocy, but you must *believe* ye'll be well again."

Anne's stubborn little chin lifted. "I'll be well again if and only if it is God's will that I recover," she said, her magnificent eyes sparking fire.

"Aye, it is true the good Lord will play His part," Mac agreed but added, "For all a that, your recovery will not come aboot if it is not willed by *yerself,* there, lassie, *as well.*"

It was Anne's turn to blink. "By *myself?*"

"Oh, aye, now. I've seen it again and again. The ill who recover are those who *wish* to recover. It must come from within ye, lassie. I know from what Jimmy-lad told me ye have the spirit for it. What we must do is rid your mind of the idiotish notions which will, if you do not set them aside, leave you lying here pacifically accepting your fate for the rest of your life." Mac almost growled. *"Nonsense,* I say. Rank and evil nonsense!"

Anne thought back over patients she'd nursed during her years in Shropshire. Several times there had been women she'd believed could get well but the poor wretches had had no heart for the trials of their lives and had slipped away despite all her efforts to save them.

Then there was Mrs. Cooper. Mrs. Cooper had been badly broken up when dragged into a gear of the mill wheel. The local apothecary had shaken his head and given up practically before he'd begun cleaning those awful wounds. Anne had done all she could, but she too had felt despair. She'd never seen a human body so wracked in so many ways.

Mrs. Cooper had gritted her teeth, insisted she'd had more pain birthing her firstborn, that she was needed by husband and babes and that she didn't have time just now to die. Didn't *dare* go off and leave her man with the youngsters to raise! And she hadn't. Today she worked beside her man just as she'd always done, although there was a weakness in one arm the woman cussed in terms which made Anne blush and run away. Mrs. Cooper *should* have died. Miss Jenkins, the retired governess who had lived in the third cottage from the end of the village street, had come down with a minor chill and should *not*—but she'd lain in her narrow bed and simply drifted out of life.

"Yes," said Anne, slowly, "I see what it is to which you refer, but . . ."

Mac rolled his eyes. "But it is against what you've been taught to believe for yourself and ye must think about it, reet, Lady Annie?" asked the doctor kindly.

"Exactly. Do you always send your patients into a brain-fever by making them reexamine their beliefs?"

"Missy," he said sternly, "ye may believe I'll do anything I must to see my patients well again. And if that means fighting the devil himself I'll do it."

Anne closed her eyes tightly and shuddered. "Don't. Don't joke about such things." She stared up at him. "You do jest, of course?"

Mac straightened. He stared down his nose. "Lady Anne, I dinna joke about my work." He glared, noted her wide eyes and faint blush, and nodded firmly before turning to leave her.

Anne forgot to say goodbye. At that moment she was not only paralyzed from her fall, but from his words and could not speak until it was too late. The notion one could *fight* the devil in any but passive ways was too radical to be absorbed instantly.

Fight the devil? *How did one go about it?*

"Lady Anne?" asked the housekeeper, interrupting her thoughts.

"Yes, Mrs. Tibbet?"

"Can I get you anything?"

Forcing herself to return to everyday things and reminding herself of the portrait she must finish, Anne asked,

"When she has finished her day's tasks, could you send me Kitty?"

"Today is Kitty's half day, Lady Anne," said Mrs. Tibbet. "I'll tell her you've asked for her and that she should come to you before she leaves."

"I'd forgotten it is her day, Mrs. Tibbet. Please forget my request. Kitty will wish to visit her parents as usual and their cottage is a far walk for her. I'll not take time from what she'll need if she is to have any sort of visit at all before she must turn around and come back." Anne tried hard to hide a sigh at this delay in finding something to do with herself. "Tomorrow will do."

"Very well, my lady."

Mrs. Tibbet excused herself and moved to the door where she paused to look back at Lady Anne. What was this about Kitty walking far to visit her family? Was *that* why the maid was always so tired the day after her half day? The housekeeper felt herself blushing at the reasons she'd attributed to the girl for her lethargic behavior. She'd even, when she'd had to scold the maid for laxness, thought of sending the girl packing and hiring someone who could keep her eyes open after a half-day holiday!

But how had Lady Anne known what Kitty did, when she, Mrs. Tibbet, whose duty it was to know such things, did *not*? Well, she soon *would* and she would see what, if anything, could be done to relieve the situation. Depending on *where* the parents lived, of course.

A ride part of one way, perhaps? The weekly delivery wagon which took fresh vegetables, meat, and game birds for the table and flowers and fruit from the succession houses to the London house went up on this day. Mrs. Tibbet had a notion Kitty came from nearer the city but on the Kentish side of the Thames. Perhaps she could profit from a ride?

Mrs. Tibbet felt shamed indeed, that Lady Anne knew more about the servants than she did. She'd become lax, herself, in not ascertaining the facts and keeping that information in mind instead of jumping to conclusions as she had about Kitty.

"Oh dear. Oh dearie me," muttered Mrs. Tibbet.

"Is she worse?"

Mrs. Tibbet jumped, straightened her shoulders and turned. "Sir James, you half frightened me to death."

"Has Lady Anne's condition worsened?"

"Now why would you think such a thing? No, of course not, although from what I overheard your Mr. Macalister say, she's no better either and not like to be as long as she won't fight to get better."

"Mac has seen her and gone without seeing me? I'll have a word or two to say to *him*. You may bet on it, Mrs. Tibbet."

"I do not wager my meager income on anything, Sir James. Such doings are not for the likes of me," she said bitingly, taking a bit of her irritation at herself out on the baronet.

"But, it's a sure thing, Tibby." Sir James grinned, *her* unexpected crossness lightening *his* mood.

"And if it is, then who would take my mite, knowing it certain I'll win from them? Enough of your nonsense, Sir James," she scolded. "I suspect Lady Anne is bored with her own company and thinking too much and too deeply for her own good. You be a good lad and go in and distract her. But leave the door open," she added, her eyes narrowing, her gaze studying his face. "I'll send up a maid to sit with you. We don't need to compromise the poor dear child more than you already have done."

Sir James, itching to be with Lady Anne, suddenly remembered why he'd first stopped to talk to the housekeeper. "Another moment, Mrs. Tibbet. You've not explained the heaving of mournful sighs which I overheard as I came along the hall."

" 'Tis nothing, Sir James, about which you need worry your head. Merely that Lady Anne in her gentle way and not meaning to at all has brought to mind a duty I've been lax in performing. I'll see to changing my ways, sir. And a good thing it'll be, too. I might have done something terrible without her words to set me right."

Shaking her head Mrs. Tibbet made for the servant's stair at the back of the hall and a much-needed conversation with Kitty. Sir James stared after the woman until she disappeared.

Three

"Mrs. Tibbet thinks you're bored, Anne, my wee brown wren. So I've come to do something about it. Do you play chess?"

"Chess?" Anne's eyes widened. "I know the game," she admitted. "I once nursed the vicar when he was recovering from a broken leg. He had to keep off his feet for weeks. I was forced to learn to play in order to keep him quiet. It was not, you understand," she added, earnestly, "a frivolous doing on my part."

"Frivolous, Lady Anne?" James's voice remained casual and no one would have realized he was suddenly alert to every nuance in her voice.

"A *game,* Sir James. Not something with which one should fritter away one's time under normal conditions."

"Well," he said, perhaps a trifle too quickly, "no one could consider the present circumstances normal, now could they?"

Anne glowered. "I must take great care in what I say to you, Sir James, must I not? It is obvious you would trifle with my very soul, were I to allow it."

"Nonsense. You well know you must keep occupied and quiet until you've recovered the use of your limbs. As you must have discovered when nursing your vicar, nothing is more conducive to stillness than chess. Will you play me?" He held up a hand. "I warn you, I'm considered a dab hand at the game and will not give you quarter simply because you are a novice. You must win or lose on your own."

"I will play you, my lord. I was surprised to discover that chess is a game with merit. Some. It makes the player think, does it not? One must plan ahead if one is to win and that is good training for life itself."

"So, the fact chess is a game is not, in itself, enough to condemn it?"

Anne hesitated a moment before nodding. "True enough."

James eyed her and decided to take the chance. "Lady Anne, do you suppose that, if you were to read this novel which you have scorned, that you might discover there can also be merit in that form of writing?" He touched the cover of *Sense and Sensibility*.

Anne's gaze swung to meet James's, and swung away. He noted the faintest hint of worry, revealed by a tiny crease between her brows and the faint darkening of her expression. Lady Anne glanced down to her tightly clasped hands, then looked into the distance as her thoughts whirled. Novels were evil. They were, *by definition,* evil. Aunt Prem had been very clear on the point and scathing about the squire's daughters who were allowed to read them—after their Mama finished with the volumes, of course! She lifted her gaze to meet Sir James's, a solemn look in her eyes beyond any need he could understand.

"Please," she said, "do not attempt to undermine my beliefs. Do not tempt me from my path. It is unkind of you to wish me ill." Having had her say, she again dropped her gaze to her hands.

James bit his lip, his eyes on the bent head, the nape of her slender neck. Fine reddish hairs lay just there, swirled against pale skin, silky looking, tempting him to lay his fingers on their shiny surface. He restrained himself with effort, sensing that she was on the verge of ordering him from her room, ordering him to never come near her again.

He reminded himself, no matter impatient he was, he *could* not push her too quickly.

"Chess, Lady Anne," he said softly. "We'll play a quiet game of chess and I'll not tell you I think you a silly little pigeon who has imbibed ridiculous notions from a woman everyone considered half mad."

Anne choked back what James was almost certain was a chuckle. After a moment she looked up at him. "The board and chessmen?" Her eyes were wide open and innocent of anything other than the question. "Do you have them with you, or must you ride into town to your own residence to obtain them?"

"I left Martin's set on the hall table until I ascertained whether you'd knowledge of the game. Just a moment."

And so began their battles with the chessmen. Mrs. Tibbet, uncertain about allowing Sir James so much time in Lady Anne's bedroom, consulted with Lady Montmorency. When Jaycee could see nothing wrong with the games, the housekeeper grew resigned, especially when she saw how deeply involved the two became. She even ceased to demand a maid sit with them for the simple reason the maids were threatening to resign from the boredom of it all! And truly, she decided, there was no need. Surely? But whatever she told herself, her sensibilities could not *quite* be convinced such behavior was proper.

"What do you think you're doing?" asked Anne a day or so later after they'd finished a game. She eyed the old brown robe Sir James was shaking out and turning just so.

"I'm preparing to hold this for you, my lady, so you, my lady, may put your arms in it and we may then arrange it and tie it and . . ."

"Stupid!"

Anne's eyes widened in shocked surprise at her own outburst. She shivered, bowed her head, and waited for him to blast her for the insult. Instead he burst into chuckles. Carefully she turned her head to look at him. His expression invited her to join his laughter. Anne didn't understand it.

"Why are you not angry?" she asked. "Why are you laughing? I shouldn't have said that!"

"Anne," he responded quickly, softly, "to me you may say anything which comes into your head. I'm laughing," he continued before she could respond, "because I was teasing you, knew I was teasing you, and deserved to be called a great gawk."

"Teasing?"

He nodded.

The shy expression James had come to look for returned to her face. "I cannot remember anyone teasing me. Ever. Unless my mother did. But I'm never truly certain I remember her." The shy look was lost in sadness. "Aunt Prem thought it best I forget my early years."

"And, I'll wager, made it as difficult as possible for you to remember," said James, unable to control a grim note. Having said too much already, if Anne's shocked expression were to be believed, he gave a mental shrug and went still further. "I wish I could get my hands on that vicious old woman!" He tipped his head, forced himself to relax and, although it could not be said to be his best effort, managed a grin before adding, "On the other hand, I'll wager the devil is having great sport with her soul, so I'll assume you are well avenged and cease to—What's the matter, Anne?"

"You *mustn't*. No. It is terrible to say such things." Anne's voice rose, tension revealed in a shrill note. "Aunt Prem was *good*. She was the most strict of all the members of her chapel in obeying the laws which guarantee one's salvation."

Anne's eyes were wide, painfully open, a pulse pounding in her forehead. At James's look of shock mixed with curiosity, she bowed her head, her hands tightly clasped. She breathed deeply and, after a moment, looked up.

Her voice once again normal, Anne continued more quietly, "You don't understand, Sir James. One must be very careful if one is to save one's soul and *no one* was more careful than Aunt Prem."

James's grim look returned. His chin rose and he drew her gaze, and held it. "Your step-aunt," he said, "was a joyless rigid task-mistress who had more bees in her bonnet than brains. She was determined the rest of the world be as unhappy as she was herself and did her best, which was unfortunately talented, to see no one around her enjoyed themselves." He recalled what the Tibbets had accidentally revealed the preceding evening. "What, for instance, did her ladyship do about your music?"

The switch in his attack from her aunt's religious training to music left Anne blinking, uncertain what to respond to first. While she was bemused, James got her into the ugly old brown robe which, at some time in its long and useful existence, had belonged to a much larger woman. James reminded himself to have Jaycee order more attractive night wear for his young obsession. He'd do it, but a gift of such apparel from himself was impossible, of course. However careless Sir James might *seem* concerning social shibboleths, he was very careful he not actually ruin any young lady's reputation.

But obsession? Yes, he thought as he swung Lady Anne up into his arms, *that is exactly what she's become. An obsession. I'll straighten out that head of hers or else.*

"Now what do you think you're doing?" Anne held herself rigid, not daring to relax against his shoulder as she wished to do. Nor did she have the nerve to swing her arm around his neck although she felt such an action would make her position seem far less precarious.

"Music, Anne. Have you lost all interest in playing? It has been weeks since you arrived and not once did you go near the piano. According to Tibbet, a specialist was sent for just as soon as it was known you were coming. The pianoforte was tuned especially for your pleasure." James shifted her slightly in his arms, attempting to ease the dead weight. "I remember hearing you play when still a child. You were already very good."

"The piano . . . ! But that was nonsense. Just catering to the childish pride in me."

"If that is what Lady P. told you, you've given me another reason to wish she'd been boiled in oil prior to her death. Your music teacher felt you had a God-given talent, one which it would be a sin to discourage, but your aunt didn't allow it to grow, did she? Despite your mother's wishes."

"My mother wished me to play?" asked Anne on a thread of sound.

"Oh yes. Mrs. Tibbet remembers how definite your mother was on that point, how Lady P. swore to your mother she'd encourage you to continue your lessons and remind you to practice—not that that was necessary. You loved the piano." James finally noticed how unsettled his precious burden had become. He went on in a more kindly tone. "Mrs. Tibbet was in the room when that conversation occurred, Anne, helping to care for your mother during her last illness. Last night Mrs. Tibbet described the scene to me after Tibbet mentioned they'd had the piano tuned for you, saying it was a waste of time since you didn't seem to care." He paused, wondering if he dared criticize Lady P. again, adding still another straw to those he'd already piled up. Hoping he'd soon reach that final straw, he decided to do so, but kept his voice casual as he asked, "Your aunt was forsworn, was she not?"

"Aunt Prem made a *promise* to my mother. . . ."

Sir James's hold tightened around his white-faced burden. Had he gone too far? "Don't think about that terrible old woman's perfidy, Lady Anne. But would you not like to see a piano again? Shouldn't you like to play—as your mother wished? I've fixed a chair for you, one you won't fall out of, so that you can practice as much as you wish. Mac said it would be all right. . . ."

Anne bit her lip to control the trembling besetting it but the trembling merely transferred itself to her whole body. Aunt Prem had sworn something and had not . . . her aunt had been *forsworn?* Such a thought about Lady Preminger was very nearly blasphemous! No. She couldn't bear to think of it just now. She must change the subject. Something . . . anything. . . .

"Sir James," she asked, a faint hint of her hope in her tone, "did *you* know my mother? Do *you* remember her?"

For a moment James considered simply taking her to the piano, but something in Anne's gaze made him desist. "Yes, of course I remember her. She was a lovely, loving, gentle woman with more love in her than any other I've ever known, including my own mother who was also an exceptional person. Why do you ask?"

"She was loving? *Gentle?*" Anne's eyes again widened. *"Not* a useless butterfly flitting on her merry way to perdit—"

Anne clenched her jaw and, given her expression, James decided, again, not to push her.

After a moment she asked wistfully, "Did she have long hair? Sort of dark but when she allowed the sun to shine on it, were there reddish glints in it? And eyes not quite the color of mine but more blue?"

James's brows flew together. "Anne, haven't you a likeness of your parents?"

"Oh *no.*" Her eyes widened. "Of course not. That would be a graven image, would it not?"

"No." James chuckled at Anne's shocked surprise. "Anne, it *would* be if you were to *worship* it, but I don't think you the sort to indulge in ancestor worship."

"Ancestor worship? What is that?"

"Something about which I've read. For some heathen peoples in the East it is a sort of religion, a special way of remembering and honoring their dead." He shifted direction from the music room toward the library. His burden was beginning to weigh on him, but he had no desire to put it down. "Since you are less than enthusiastic about the piano, shall we take a look at your mama? She was truly lovely, Anne. Not the most beautiful woman I've ever seen, but one I'll never forget as I *will* most of the beauties I've met. Your mama had character and courage and talent and . . . Oh dear, I wonder . . . ?"

He eyed his burden, wondering if he dared. . . .

"Sir James?"

Of course he did. He'd dare anything . . . !

"Anne, you don't suppose it possible that Lady Preminger was *jealous* of your mother, do you? Something Mrs. Tibbet said reminded me I once heard my mother say Lady P. set her cap for your father when her sister died. He, of course, had far too much sense to have anything to do with such a wicked witch and quite sensibly fell in love with your mama instead. . . . But, given that is so, might Lady P. not have disliked your mama a great deal?"

Anne ignored his calling Lady Prem a witch, for the far more shocking revelation. *"Aunt Prem set her cap for my father?"*

Anne's world was upside down. Her aunt, who had hated all men, distrusted each and every one of them, had once wished to wed one? And she'd actually sworn an oath and broken it?

James nodded to the footman standing near the library. The doors were flung open and James bore Lady Anne toward the fireplace.

"Look up, my lady. Unlike Vincent, my friend Martin loved your mother very much. When he came into the title he brought her portrait from the room where Vincent hid it. Your elder half brother never accepted the fact his father remarried and, after your mother died, he tried to forget it by pushing you out of sight and the portrait where he'd never see it. Actually, come to that, I sometimes had the impression Vincent didn't particularly like much of anyone." James shifted Anne and, automatically, she put her arm around his neck. That made the weight in his arms much more tolerable. *Besides,* thought James, *it is a burden I like. Somehow she fits there. . . .*

"Sir James," breathed Anne softly after staring for a time at the portrait, "I thought it was an angel coming to me in my dreams to ease the burden when life seemed most unbearable. I didn't know it was my memory of my mother. Oh dear, I hope I haven't been sinning all these years, depending on that memory as I have."

James very nearly allowed tongue-room to all the swear words he knew. But, if he swore as he wished to do, Anne would, he believed, find it necessary to deny him her presence for fear she be contaminated by blasphemous language. She was very near to doing so for one reason or another all too often as it was!

When he had control of his tongue, James said, "I think, Lady Anne, that perhaps you should return to your room and we'll try the music room another day. You seem rather pale and I fear I've upset you and that's a great mistake on my part: I've recalled that Mac said you were *not* to be agitated."

"Yes, please take me back. I've much to think on." There was a pause while James removed them from the library and then she added, "When I'm settled, I'd like to see Mrs. Tibbet, please. If you'd be so kind as to tell her to come to me? When she has a free moment, of course."

For just an instant James felt panic, worried he'd hurt her, that that was why Anne asked for the housekeeper, but then he remembered. Aha, he thought, the promise made to her mother. Anne wishes to hear the story from Mrs. Tibbet herself. Good. Anything that shook Lady Anne's belief Lady P. was an ideal to be emulated was, surely, a step in the right direction. "Very well, Lady Anne." James started down the hall toward the staircase in the front entry but stopped when a row broke out, catching their attention.

"What is that noise?" Lady Anne asked. "Oh dear! What is happening?"

James's brows snapped together. "I haven't a notion," he said and, before he'd thought, he added, "Shall we find out?"

It was too late when he remembered Mrs. Tibbet's strictures on compromising Lady Anne, because Lady Anne had already nodded, so James, who also wished to discover what was going forward, once again headed for the entrance hall. They paused at the entrance to it and James grinned.

Tibbet, his eyes bobbling in his white face, was attempting to shut the door, but a brawny footman in strange livery casually held it open with one arm, his other hand extended to a very short, very chunky woman bundled into furs and veils and carrying a monstrously huge reticule.

"Well, Tibbet?" said a harsh, almost masculine, voice from the woman half hidden behind the footman.

"But Lady Fuster-Smythe . . . !"

Tibbet stared at the traveling coach from which the elderly lady had descended and from which her possessions were being removed. The clatter of boxes and trunks and the noise of voices rising steadily toward a roar as grooms and footmen argued about how best to do the job forced Tibbet to raise *his* voice above what he believed proper.

"Were we, er," he asked, while patting his damp forehead with his handkerchief, "hmm, expecting you, my lady? I mean . . ."

"Of course not, dolt. If you were you'd not stand there like a bobbing-block, but would allow me entrance as you should have done instantly when you saw it was *me*. No," she added as a chair was detached from the rear of the coach and carried toward her by two wrangling servants, "do not hold it that way. You will hit something with the legs. Turn it around now."

The men obediently set the chair down and picked it up again, then looked toward their mistress for approval. She scowled and they put it down and tried another hold. She tipped her head, gave the door a measuring look and then, her lips compressed as if she knew a better way but would not lower herself to explaining it, she nodded. Tibbet backed away out of necessity as the chair was borne toward him just as if he were not standing there, futilely attempting to shut the door.

"I'll have my usual room, Tibbet," said Lady Fuster-Smythe, following the chair into the hall.

"But . . ."

"Tibbet, you booberkin, don't dither. You have much to order done if I'm to be accommodated properly before night falls."

"The fact the sun is nearly straight overhead does not," whispered James to Anne, "make that an untrue statement!"

"Ah—" Lady Fuster-Smythe smiled with satisfaction as Mrs. Tibbet arrived on the scene. "—*now* we'll see the way things should be done. Mrs. Tibbet, how can you bear being married to yon block? He has yet to order my men to the room I require." As Lady Fuster-Smythe spoke she bore down on the harassed housekeeper, her hands on the supporting arms of a pair of footmen who trailed along willy-nilly.

"Lady Fuster-Smythe." Mrs. Tibbet curtsied. "I believe Tibbet hesitates because Lady Anne is presently in your usual room. He is also hesitant because we are not properly prepared for company, the situation being what it is. I've sent up word to Lady Montmorency of your arrival. She'll be down shortly to greet you, I'm sure."

"You needn't stand on ceremony with *me*," said Lady Fuster-Smythe.

"Now there's a bit of hypocrisy if I ever heard one," whispered James to Anne. "Everyone knows her ladyship will complain loud and long if anyone dispenses with one jot of proper form!"

"I do not blame *you* for her ladyship's tardy appearance,"

continued Lady Fuster-Smythe. "Nor can I fairly blame Lady Montmorency, when," she added with reluctant justice, "she did not know I was coming. Nor—" She sighed at the burden of it all. "—can I blame you that my usual room is unavailable. I'll have the blue room overlooking the rose garden instead."

Mrs. Tibbet shook her head, her face reddening. "I'm sorry, Lady Fuster-Smythe, but . . ."

"What she would say to you, Lady Fussy-puss, is that *I* have that room," James interrupted from where he stood in the shadow of an arch. "What brings you here, my lady?" he asked, strolling forward. He shifted Lady Anne slightly to ease overburdened muscles. "When I last saw you, you insisted you were going home and never leaving it again. Certainly you would never, you said, come within fifty miles of London. You said, 'The city is nasty and filthy and, with the little season ended, an utterly boring place' and you added, you would *never* set foot in it again if the ton would only have the good taste to meet elsewhere come next spring.' Your exact words, Lady Fussy-puss."

"And *that*," muttered her ladyship, casting surreptitious looks toward Lady Anne, "is exactly what they may do this year. Meet elsewhere, I mean. Are not you, too, planning to travel to Paris, Sir James, along with all the world and its neighbor?" Lady Fuster-Smythe waved her hand dismissively and the long plumes decorating the wide brim of her hat swayed gently. She pretended to note the girl in James's arms for the first time and her deep bosom swelled. "Never mind that." She pointed one arthritic finger. "Tell me, James, why you stand there holding that badly dressed wench? And, why, in any case, are you living in your brother-in-law's house when he is absent?"

"It is also my sister's home," said James, answering her last question first. "And I'm here for very good reason. My sister's guest fell and hurt herself. Someone must care for her and you know my sister is no good with the ailing.

Moreover this is *not* a wench, Lady Fussy-puss." James deliberately used his childhood pet name for the harridan whom half the ton feared and therefore avoided and the other half didn't dare avoid simply *because* they feared her. "This is Lady Anne Montmorency. Lady Anne, do be pleased to meet my godmother, Lady Fuster-Smythe. Her bark is far worse than her bite—not that she can't, if the occasion demands it, draw blood, of course, but you'll discover she can, when she wishes, be as kind a lady as you are ever likely to meet." James said the last with just the hint of a warning and hoped his godmother caught it.

Lady Fuster-Smythe, who had puffed up like a threatened hen when she'd commented on Anne's position in James's arms, became her normal size in much the way a balloon deflates.

Yes, thought James critically, *just* like a balloon he'd once seen. Rapidly changing weather had canceled the ascension. The balloon, as the gas drained, had softened and become less awesome much as Lady Fuster-Smythe was doing. James managed to uncramp a few of the muscles which had tightened the instant he'd realized who had arrived.

Her ladyship's voice was less harsh when she said, "I *knew* there was a reason I felt a sudden urge to come here." Her eyes narrowed and she tipped her head sideways, looking at James from their corners. "But, now I think on it, I recall I'd the notion it was your *sister* who required my aid." A suspicious note returned to her voice which even the most obtuse could not fail to hear.

James groaned silently. He'd just remembered a half rueful, half angry comment he'd once heard about his godmother. Disaster of some sort had visited the family and her ladyship arrived soon after. There had been three additional tales contributed in which her ladyship had simply shown up just when she was least wanted—and had proceeded, in her well-meaning way, to complicate matters beyond all expectation.

"If it is my sister you wish to see, Lady Fuster-Smythe. . . ."

Jaycee interrupted from the head of the stairs. "I can think of no reason at all why you should wish to see *me,* my lady, but if you truly do, here I am." Jaycee tripped down the stairs. She tossed a harassed look toward her brother and turned a sweet smile toward her unexpected guest. "I don't know why you have come, Lady Fuster-Smythe, but, of course," lied Jaycee while adopting her best social manner, "you are very welcome."

"Of course you are," agreed James blandly, automatically drawing her ladyship's fire which had been about to fall on his sister's head.

Her ladyship stared at him. "Nincompoop." One more glare to make certain she'd silenced her godson and Lady Fuster-Smythe turned to inspect the piles of trunks and boxes which had been brought in and set around the hall. "Oh dear. Did I truly bring all that?" She sighed. "Well, it cannot be helped. Is everything in from the coach?"

"Except for Miss Perfect, the coach has been fully unloaded," emoted a spider-thin man whose sole function in Lady Fuster-Smythe's life was to act as courier whenever her ladyship traveled—even if a particular day's travel involved no more than a few miles to visit a friend for less than an hour.

Lady Fuster-Smythe's froglike eyes turned to glare at the man. "And why has Perfect remained in the coach?"

"She insists she'll only remove herself if and when you determine you will stay. Why, she asks, should she go to the effort of extricating herself from the coach when she would merely have to insert herself back into it?" The words were spoken in the same dramatic fashion as had been the less interesting information.

"Tell Perfect we stay."

Lady Fuster-Smythe glowered first at James who raised his brows but remained silent and then at Tibbet who

stepped one step back and finally at Mrs. Tibbet who nodded and turned to lead the way up the stairs, motioning to
Lady Fuster-Smythe's servants to carry up her ladyship's
possessions.

Oh dear, thought Mrs. Tibbet, *oh deary me. Well, forgetting all the upset, at least one may be sure she'll play the
proper chaperone for dear Lady Anne and that is one worry
off my mind . . . !*

Not so very much later, Lady Anne, who felt no need
for a chaperone, was wishing Perfect had been correct and
that the old trout ensconced with her tatting in the chair
two of her footmen carried from room to room, had *not*
stayed. The chair was, just then, in Anne's room and, now
they had an audience, Anne found it difficult to concentrate
on chess. What had James called her? Lady Fussy-puss?
How *dare* he? Realizing Sir James was waiting for her
move, Anne lifted a bishop's pawn and set it down two
squares forward.

"Is that truly what you wish to do?"

"Yes."

Then she looked at the board and wished she'd said no.
The board was opened up by the move, giving her opponent
so many options he'd have the game won in no time. She
sighed, waited for the inevitable defeat, and realized that
defeat was the consequence of all her confrontations with
this handsome emissary of the devil. He was unsettling her
life in a hundred different ways to say nothing of worrying
her mind into a brain-fever by introducing contradictions
into her thoughts.

But she *must* think upon such things and clear her mind.
She'd had to smother, again, the tiny flame of hope which
Sir James repeatedly lighted. As did Dr. Macalister, come
to that. Anne didn't *dare* to dream her life might be made
different, become more interesting, go on more like that of
others.

She simply must not forget, ever, that she was to have

*the greatest possible care for her soul. After all, her hair
already marked her, as Aunt Prem had repeatedly pointed
out, as, potentially, one of the devil's own.*

"Well, well," boomed Dr. Macalister as he entered Anne's
room late that afternoon. "Damn my eyes, if it isn't dear
old Lady Fussy-pussy herself! How the carrion crows do
gather where disaster occurs. How *do* you know, Lady Fuster-Smythe? What sort of scent or sound brings you time
and again to stick your long nose into other people's business just when they most wish privacy in which to settle
their problems or peace in which to lick their wounds?"

His questions were asked in such an innocent questioning
manner he barely set up the lady's back despite the impertinence of his words. Lady Fuster-Smythe merely sniffed.
"I go where I'm needed, lad. And anyone with a smidgen
of intelligence can see I'm needed here, what with Lady
Montmorency hiding herself away from society for some
havey-cavey reason I've not yet determined and that peep-
o-day boy I'm required to call godson consorting with such
a pretty lady and nary a chaperone in sight. Why, they'd
have found themselves leg-shackled in a trice if it were to
get out he'd compromised Lady Anne as he's done by his
frequent presence in her bedroom."

"I'm not so sure he'd find that all a bad thing," muttered
Mac as he reached to test Anne's reflexes, his words startling that young lady very much. "You're not trying, my
lady," he insisted when he got no response to his daily toe-
nipping procedure. "Now you pay attention here and
twitch," he ordered.

But, despite his second pinch and Anne's attempts at a
twitch, there was no sign of recovery and he and Lady Anne
sighed in concert.

"No matter," she said and stared at nothing in particular.

"Lady Anne," Mac said, his visage stern, "I'll be quite

frank with you. The longer ye go along this way, the less likely there is to be any change." His eyes narrowed and he rubbed his nose. "I canna like it that you don't seem to *care.*"

She faced him squarely, challenging him, if she'd known her own motives, to contradict her. "One cannot fight one's fate, Dr. Mac. I know when I'm being punished for my sins."

"Nonsense! Besides," joked the doctor, his eyes narrowing in that way they had, "you *like* being carried in the arms of my handsome friend, dinna ye? If you could walk, lass, he'd have no choice but to let you trot along on your own two good legs, would he not, then?"

Anne blanched to a sickly shade, a prickling under her skin warning her she was in danger of fainting. She raised stricken eyes to face her tormentor. "It cannot be. Surely? I could not be so blind as to want. . . ." She swallowed. "Could I truly wish . . . ?"

Alerted by her loss of color, Mac asked, "What canna be, lass?"

"Surely," she said bravely, "I'm not reveling in close contact with a male body, deliberately courting such behavior. . . ." But she had wished it so, had she not? Anne felt the heat of a flush rising up her cheeks, felt it fade and that funny prickly feeling return. "No!" she insisted. "Surely I know better than to wish for . . . for . . . I cannot want. . . ."

"And why should you *not?*" interrupted the doctor.

"But the sin of it all . . . ," she whispered, the gray look changing to merely white.

"The normal human behavior of it all, you mean, assuming there's anything to the notion. Lass, I was bamming you," he scolded. At her questioning look, he nodded. "Yes. Merely teasing." He tipped his head. "But since you yourself have raised the point, when did it become a sin to wish to be loved?"

"But . . ."

"Lassie, I *was* teasing you. It canna really have anything to do with your not getting better, now. After all, you could get *much* closer to the man if your limbs worked properly, couldn't you now?" His brows arched, then wiggled up and down.

Anne went from white to painfully red. She lifted her hands to cover her burning cheeks. "Dr. Mac!"

"That's quite enough nasty talk," agreed Lady Fuster-Smythe, her voice harsh, but the physician tossed her a roguish look which had her lips twitching before she forced her features into stern lines by adopting a fierce frown. "Instead of such unacceptable nonsense, tell me this. Is there nothing at all which may be done to help our dear little Anne walk again?"

The doctor looked into the distance. A muscle twitched along side his cheek. Finally his eyes came back into focus and he shrugged, seeming to settle his coat more closely around his husky shoulders. "I canna like the only potential cure that's occurred to me. . . ." His words trailed off.

James, entering just in time to hear his friend's half comment, asked, "What is it you do not like?"

"Something which *might* help. Perhaps. Occasionally it does, but more often it does not. . . ."

When James demanded an explanation Macalister shook his head, but, when his friend strode toward him in a belligerent fashion, he gave in. "Galvanism, James. Electricity *occasionally* has beneficial results."

James glanced from Macalister to Anne and back again. "You don't mean drawing sparks . . . ?"

"That is one method. There are others. But the whole notion . . . I canna like it," repeated the doctor. "If results were more certain, then . . ." He shook his head. "No. We'll wait a wee bit and see if nature does not take a hand and mend matters."

"Electricity?" asked Anne in a small voice which was ignored by the two men who glared at each other.

"But it's an excellent notion," said James. "Great things are done with electricity every day. It is even an aid for those suffering toothache!"

"But our wee lass is *not* suffering toothache," objected Mac and frowned mightily.

"Newfangled balderdash," said Lady Fuster-Smythe from her corner.

"Not balderdash," objected Mac, but rather hesitantly. "But my reading shows the techniques are not consistent in their beneficial aspects. One report contradicts another. So much is written it is very difficult to sift through it and, too, most reports are unclear on the details." He paused, his lips tightly compressed. When he spoke, Mac's voice indicated combined despair and anger. "We do not know enough! Will we *ever* know enough?"

"Bah. The old ways are good enough for anyone," said Lady Fuster-Smythe. When three pairs of eyes turned to stare at that trite comment, two spots of color appeared in her cheeks. "Enough about this young lady. Tell me instead, is Lady Montmorency as sick as she claims to be or is she merely hiding from me so she need not face a scold?"

"Jaycee! Dash it all, I'd forgotten about her latest idiocy." Sir James scowled. "How, by the way, did you hear of it?"

"I doubt if there is a soul who hasn't heard your sister made a fool of herself," said Lady Fuster-Smythe with unwonted airiness—because she *hadn't* known when she arrived, *not for certain,* that there *was* a problem. On the other hand, she'd known Lady Montmorency from a child, so it was not difficult to guess a situation existed. It seemed she'd guessed correctly. Would Sir James describe how the silly chit had tried to put herself beyond the pale? "Has she, do you suppose, succeeded in ostracizing herself?" she asked.

"Please, Sir James, if you don't object to explaining," asked Anne, "just what *did* Lady Montmorency do? I didn't quite like to ask why she arrived so unexpectedly and in such a hurly-burly way—she was quite distraught, I thought—but I admit to being curious."

James almost teased Anne about the minor sin of curiosity, but managed to bite his tongue. Unfortunately the impulse allowed Lady Fuster-Smythe time to jump in with her own demands for a round tale of his sister's latest doings—now that she hadn't had to raise that exact question herself.

James, unable to repress his irritation once his sister's fall from grace was brought to mind, responded with an acid note. "My charming sister, in her usual bird-witted fashion managed to make a by-word of herself in the worst way possible."

"But how?" asked an avid Lady Fuster-Smythe.

"How? She attended an impromptu Cyprian's ball disguised as a ladybird. She was recognized."

"But I don't understand," said Anne. "What is a Cyprian's ball?"

"Don't you dare, Lady Fussy-puss!" ordered James when he saw his godmother was about to answer that question in her undoubtedly imitable fashion.

Sir James's warning gave her ladyship a moment in which to think. Recalling that Anne was unmarried and an innocent, she closed her mouth with a snap and subsided.

Once assured his godmother would not interfere, James turned to Anne. "If you don't understand, Lady Anne, then simply believe that what my sister did was exceedingly bad of her. She disgraced herself and her husband, and me come to that, and it is just as well she's sequestered herself in her rooms where she may think over her impulsiveness. Not that she will." He scowled. "Knowing my sister, it will not be long before she is up to more devilment! Even though she is rusticating because of her *last* prank, she won't refrain from kicking up another lark as soon as she becomes bored. Which will happen soon enough. That she's under an obligation to behave in such a way people will forget and forgive her *last* escapade won't occur to her as she runs merrily on to new disaster."

"Oh, dear," murmured Anne softly. "Just the other day she mentioned something about holding a ball on St. Valentine's Day. . . ."

"You have the right of it, James," said Lady Fuster-Smythe. "Your sister is still a hoyden with no notion of how to go on. Lord Montmorency was a fool to leave her in England as he did." A new thought occurred to the long-tongued old woman. "Or perhaps he left her enceinte?" Her arched brows queried James on that point and he shook his head. "Too bad. Such a condition might have prevented her from making a still bigger fool of both of them by getting herself into that particular difficulty while he's gone."

"You are speaking of my sister, Lady Fuster-Smythe, and I won't have you abusing her in that nasty way."

"Of course you won't," agreed her ladyship sweetly. "You hold that prerogative to yourself, do you not?"

James's temper cleared and he chuckled at his own foibles. "That I do. *I* am allowed to scold her up one side and down the other, but I deny anyone else the right. Except Martin, of course."

"Ah yes. Lord Montmorency. Now why *did* he go running off and leave her here? He knows what she is."

James sighed. "I don't know the whole story, Lady Fussy-puss. There was a falling out of charity with each other at just the wrong moment and no time to make it up. Sometimes I suspect Martin left her behind as punishment and Jaycee is behaving as badly as she can, which is far more badly than one would like to think possible, to punish *him*. This last escapade, though, got out of hand."

James frowned, tipped his head thoughtfully and continued more slowly. "Somehow, I cannot believe she dreamed up that particular lark all on her own. I'd like very much indeed to discover who put the notion into her head and then, once it took root, saw that the greatest possible scandal resulted. Jaycee, once she'd decided to play such a prank, is far too intelligent to have allowed anyone to guess her identity. She *must* have been betrayed."

"Betrayed?" Anne looked thoughtful. "Could it be?" She nodded, answering her own question. "Very likely, I think. I never liked him."

"Who, Lady Anne?" asked Lady Fuster-Smythe, her ears on the prick and her beady eyes glittering avidly.

"Lord Runyon."

James sputtered, his eyes widening. *"That rake has been making free of Jaycee's presence?"*

"I believe one might call it that. Mrs. Tibbet commented several times she wished he'd not visit so often, that it wasn't at all the thing. That resulted in Lady Jaycee deciding to move back to the town house. I met his lordship once before she left. Or rather, I didn't actually *meet* him." Anne blushed rosily. "Later, it occurred to me he must have believed me one of the maids." She met James's wry look and the blush deepened.

"Tried to kiss you, did he?" asked Lady Fuster-Smythe absently and didn't notice how Anne's face flamed still more at her comment. "Well, now we know your villain, James. And a smooth sort of villain he is, too. Does he hate you or is it Lord Montmorency he's out to do a mischief?"

"Both of us, belike," said James morosely. "We spoiled his game once. He was running off with the Moorfield chit. *You'll* remember her, Lady Fussy-puss. A pie-faced heiress with suspiciously low, if excessively wealthy, connections in Yorkshire. Two, maybe three years ago now, she was looking for a husband?"

Lady Fuster-Smythe snorted. "I remember and I'll wager she didn't thank you for rescuing her, either. A feather-brained chit if I ever saw one."

Anne, shocked, moved restlessly. James fastened his gaze on her legs wondering if he'd seen the covers shift. Had he? Or had he not? His hopes and fears centered there, he dropped from the discussion. His gaze turned to Macalister, but the doctor was listening to the women and had, obviously, noted nothing. James looked back. No movement at all. . . . He decided he was likely mistaken and forced his mind to the conversation.

Anne was asking, "If Lord Runyon is known for such a villain, how can his lordship have been welcomed here?"

James nearly growled. "Because Runyon is a smooth-tongued devil, a favorite with women everywhere. The important hostesses will not give him the cut direct, which might put him beyond the pale. Instead, they invite him to parties, even though they know him for what he is. For a certainty," said James, not even trying to hide the acid in his tone, "he's gotten around my bacon-brained sister with just such cozening ways. Besides, it couldn't have been too difficult. After her falling out with Martin, she'd be in the mood to lap up effusive compliments which are that rake's stock in trade."

"Very true." Lady Fuster-Smythe nodded and continued thoughtfully, "Do you think he'll be content with the storm he's raised or do you think he'll try for further villainy?"

James's teeth ground together. "Runyon will not be content until he sees Martin and myself dragging our tails in the dirt, so . . ."

"What a terrible expression, James. Very descriptive, of course, but don't let me hear you using such cant language ever again." Lady Fuster-Smythe dropped her scolding tone for a more thoughtful one. "It would be just like your sister to have sent the man a message as to where she could be found, would it not?" Her ladyship blinked rapidly and rose to her feet. "I *knew* it was Lady Montmorency who needed me and not Lady Anne."

Her ladyship waited for James to offer his arm but James was wool-gathering. She cleared her throat. Again. But it wasn't until Anne poked him that James realized he was remiss in his social duty. He walked her ladyship to the door and would have bowed her out but she retained a hold on his wrist with one clawlike hand.

"Oh no you don't, James! Come along now. And you, too, Dr. Macalister. Before *my* arrival Lady Anne and my godson very likely made all too free with the conventions, but there'll be no more of it. And you, doctor, need not think I'll allow *you* to remain alone with my charge either."

James winked at Anne before he closed the door behind them all. Before they'd gotten beyond earshot, she heard him teasing Lady Fuster-Smythe for being her usual fussy-puss self, an impertinence that made her smile.

But now that Anne was alone she had work to do. She rang for Kitty. When the maid came she directed the girl to get the sketchbook from its drawer and place a chair for another sitting. With luck she'd finish the portrait while Lady Fuster-Smythe kept James occupied elsewhere.

The light changed with the waning day and Anne held the sketchpad away. She tipped her head slightly and glanced from it to the maid. Yes, it was very nearly done and one of her better efforts at that. Young as she was, the maid had character which showed in Kitty's face. Anne felt she'd managed to capture some of that in the portrait.

If she ever managed to get that small home of her very own for which she'd yearned and hoped and wished and had done everything but pray—after all, it wasn't at all proper to pray for indulgences for oneself—why, then if she *did* someday manage it, she'd ask Kitty to be her house-keeper. The notion pleased her very much indeed and, later when she went to sleep, thinking about a home of her own, her lips curved into a gentle smile of contentment.

For the first night since her accident, Lady Anne did not have nightmares about her place in the hell which Lady Preminger had repeatedly described in vivid detail as Anne's certain fate for all eternity . . . assuming Anne failed to obey her ladyship's every stricture.

Four

Early the next morning Macalister lay in the comfortable bed he'd been given for his own use until Lady Anne's condition was determined. After staring at the ceiling for some time, Macalister rose and stared out his window into the clear cold light of the dawning day. He stood there for a long time thinking about his all too patient patient. Then, after dressing and breaking his fast, he went to Lady Anne's room before leaving for his day's work in London.

"You aren't trying, my lady," he scolded when his pinch elicited nothing at all.

"I do not know how to counter fate, Dr. Macalister. I've lived too long accepting what comes and working around the blows I receive from her to think it possible I might actually win a battle with her."

"Hmm. Let me have a go at that cap of yours."

He loosened the tie and slipped his fingers up under to where the swelling had completely disappeared.

"I no longer have the headache," she said and he nodded.

"That is verra good, but we must find a way to teach you to fight if you are not to lay on your couch for the rest of you life. It will not do," he scolded. "Dinna ye wish to walk again?"

"I wish it very much," she said, "and, when alone, I do try, but my silly limbs will not move."

"Ah. Then perhaps it is that you've been trying *too hard*," he said and grinned at her obvious confusion. "I'm a doctor, lass," he said and a faint hint of apology could be heard in his voice. "I dinna have to be consistent." When that elicited a smile he continued. "I think it a bonny notion Jimmy-lad has had. He asked if you might not only play your piano, but if you might not spend your days downstairs. I see no harm and perhaps some good in the idea, so Mrs. Tibbet is to make ready a salon for you and, whenever you wish it, you may go down to it."

What Mac did not explain was why James made the suggestion. Conscious of the dangers Jaycee ran from Lord Runyon's plots, he'd discussed them with Mac when they'd left Anne's room with Lady Fuster-Smythe. James wished to be in the areas of the house open to company in case the rake had the gall to call on his sister, but he also wished to entertain Lady Anne.

Mrs. Tibbet gave the actual orders concerning changes in Jaycee's favorite salon, but James checked more than once that everything was done for Lady Anne's comfort. Finally Mrs. Tibbet approved her girl's work. James asked her to remain for a moment once she'd sent the maids to their next task.

"Mrs. Tibbet . . . did Anne ever ask you about her music?"

"Yes, she did. It was pitiful, Sir James. I felt so sorry for the poor dear. And since we had that talk I've become rather concerned about her. She only picks at her breakfast trays and, although the luncheon tray I sent up yesterday came back empty, I'd almost be willing to wager my quarterly wages Kitty ate the lot at Lady Anne's encouragement, and, as you know, I'm *not* a betting woman!" Mrs. Tibbet let out a mournful sigh. "She's the merest wisp of a girl as it is. If she loses more weight, well, I don't know but what she'll dry up and blow away."

Sir James, who had carried the "wisp's" dead weight around the house on any number of occasions, thought that unlikely. There wasn't, it was true, much of her, but what there was was solid muscle. "Why don't I take a small tray up now," he suggested, "asking her to join me in a dish of tea. It is getting on for luncheon, is it not?"

"Which you never eat," said the housekeeper.

James grinned. "Very true, so I'll fancy very little now." When the housekeeper moved to prepare a tray, he added, "Just slice a bit of bread, Mrs. Tibbet, for toasting and put on a chunk of cheese—a nursery tea, you see. She is, I think, more likely to nibble if we're informal than if asked to eat a proper meal."

How Sir James knew that about his Sweet Obsession, he hadn't a clue, but he soon discovered how correct he was. When he entered her room, he found Lady Anne concentrating on a tome which looked far too heavy for her to hold and which, Sir James discovered when he peered more closely, was so old and well used its binding showed signs of imminent disintegration.

"I could take that into London and have it rebound for you," he said, "when you've no use for it for a day or two."

Anne very nearly dropped the book in her reaction to the sudden intrusion of his voice. "Goodness me, how long have you been spying on me?" she asked as her eyes searched the room to see if anything was visible which she didn't wish seen. Then she remembered Kitty had put her manuscript and portfolio neatly into a dresser drawer.

It was abominable that a woman could not take a serious interest in scholarly things without finding herself labeled odd and unfeminine. On the other hand, she wondered why she cared what Sir James thought of her. She *shouldn't* concern herself about the opinion of a mere man—or so Lady Prem would have insisted. But Lady Prem had insisted on many things which seemed rather odd to Anne now that she lived with friendly, non-censorious, relatives.

Thinking about that, Anne absently accepted the tea cup James filled for her and, equally absently, the slab of toasted bread with cheese melted over it which he gave her a minute or two later.

As the aroma of warm cheese and toasted bread reached her nostrils, her mouth watered. It surprised her to discover she was actually hungry and, pushing bitter thoughts away, she nibbled around the edges as she watched Sir James deftly toast his own piece of bread and melt cheese on it.

"You do that very well," she said, as she finished up her slice and blew on her tea.

James grinned. "Learned it in the nursery, but haven't done it in years and now I wonder why. Do you remember how good it tasted when nanny let you do your very own? Somehow, it was always just that little bit better—even if you scorched the cheese and burned the toast." His chuckle faded at the expression which crossed her face. "What's the matter, my lady?"

"I don't believe I had that experience, or if I did, it is simply another thing I've forgotten. But this *is* very good," she said, licking the last crumb off her fingers while eying the toast James was about to bite into. He handed the piece he'd just prepared to her and set to toasting still another slice.

"So much you've missed in life, little Annie." He said it softly, almost as if he said it to himself, then looked up at her and grinned. "You can't have this one, if that's why you're watching it so closely. I brought the tray up because I didn't get breakfast this morning. You see, I rode into London at an early hour. After I saw my solicitor in the city I ran all over town on errands for Lady Fussy-puss. As a result I'm starving. Kitty," he called as the maid passed the open door, "come in here and make your mistress another piece of cheese toast while I eat this one."

"No, no. Kitty, don't you dare! I won't eat dinner at this rate and Mrs. Tibbet will scold. I don't know why everyone thinks I don't eat enough," she sighed. "Did you accomplish all Lady Fuster-Smythe asked of you?"

"Only a small portion. You didn't see the list, my dear Anne, or you'd not even ask. I'll have a word or two to say to her about the one or two little things she claimed to require!"

"How brave of you."

"You refuse to believe me when I tell you she barks a lot, but doesn't bite," he retorted with a put-upon accusation in his tone. Then he grinned and added the caveat, "At least, she never bites me."

"I guess I'm not overly fond of the barking," responded Anne thoughtfully. "I heard far too much of it when Aunt Prem was alive. Unfortunately, *her* bark was often followed by a bite. The bite of a willow switch. She said it hurt her more than it hurt me, but I could never quite believe that," added the slip of a woman with no more emotion than if it were a comment about which flowers should be planted in a new border or the colors for a new cushion cover.

James discovered he'd lost his appetite and laid down the last of his bread and cheese. He excused himself brusquely and stalked out, leaving behind a bemused young woman— but he had to leave, dared not trust himself. He'd wanted so desperately to take Anne into his arms, cuddle her close, tell her no one would hurt her ever again. Unfortunately, he knew that, if he gave into such urges, not only would Anne be justifiably angry with him, but so would her protectors. They might toss him out the door and refuse him further access to her, no longer trusting him to hold the line.

James slammed his bedroom door and strode the half-dozen steps from one end of his room to the other. He wished he were in his own house on a street just off Grosvenor Square where the library furniture was arranged to leave proper space for pacing. If he hadn't already ridden into London once today, he'd take himself off to Gentleman Jackson's for a round or two of sparring.

Or something. He badly needed to participate in something excessively violent, something requiring a great deal of energy, something which would satisfy the unsatisfiable need to take Lady Preminger by the throat and shake her as a terrier shakes a rat. Unfortunately, by her death, she'd escaped any punishment he might deal out.

But still, there was this need. . . . James stared at the vases atop his mantel. They were, he decided, excessively ugly. Just as Lady Prem had had her ugly side. James reached for the first. It made a most satisfying crash which was immediately followed by another. James swiped the palms of his hands back and forth after hurling the second vase into his grate, which was now piled with porcelain shards.

His door swung open after a brief tap and two servants gawked at him. "Sir James?" the braver asked. "We heard something breaking . . . ?"

"Don't just stand there," said James cheerfully. "As you see, there's been an, hmm—" His brows arched. "—accident? Clean it up, please." He grinned, feeling much better. "Ah, yes, clean it up, and then bring up water for a bath, if you'd be so kind."

James turned away and strolled to his window to look down into the walled garden fitted in where a wing of the house made a sheltered spot. He'd relaxed once his temper found release. He gave a quick look over his shoulder to where one of the maids knelt removing pottery pieces from the grate and felt a faint heat in his ears.

Taking a small booklet from the pocket in the tails of his coat, he made a note to replace his sister's gewgaws. With something better, something less ugly . . . and then, finally realizing what his temper had led him to do, he prayed Jaycee hadn't been particularly attached to those vases!

Anne, for the first time since her accident, had been brought to the dinner table. She was *not* enjoying herself. She shivered at the argument raging over her bent head and moved a spoonful of peas from one side of the plate to the other. Then she moved them back again.

She hated controversy and Lady Fuster-Smythe and Sir James had engaged in an on-going argument every since her ladyship fired the opening salvo with the clear soup, insisting he was a villain for forgetting her peppermints. James promptly retorted she'd sent him off with more errands to do than the Duke of Wellington's whole army might accomplish in a day and he'd found it necessary to pick and choose.

From there the argument had escalated to open warfare. Sometime late in the fish course James realized Anne was upset and he interrupted Lady Fuster-Smythe's diatribe about the uselessness of the modern young man. "Lady Fussy-puss, I am not one of your hirelings with no responsibility but to obey your orders. I warned you I had things to do while in town and would have time for only one or two errands and you insisted that was all you asked. So why do you complain now that I have proved to you the truth of what I said?"

James grinned at the glower he received, but when she opened her mouth to blast him, he hurried on. "Yes, be just as angry as you like, but you are well aware that what I say is true. I did manage," he added in a coaxing tone, "to retrieve your forwarded mail from Martin's town house, did I not, which you insisted was the most important item on your list?"

"Hmm. You did do that." Her eyes widened and she nodded comprehension when James gestured toward Anne who had a hang-dog air as if it were she herself who had been scolded. Her ladyship's tone was far more friendly when she added, "You might be interested in the news from Vienna."

Jaycee looked up her nose almost quivering. "Vienna?" she asked softly.

"I, too, had several letters from the continent. Some were

from friends in Paris, but some are from those attending the festivities surrounding the congress," said James. "It is thought that the Duke of Wellington will soon arrive there."

"News?" asked Jaycee still more softly.

"Speaking of Vienna," asked a nervous Lady Anne who was the only one to notice Jaycee's sudden interest, "was there, perhaps, a letter from Lord Montmorency?"

"From your brother?" Sir James tipped his head. "Why do you refer to Martin by his title, Lady Anne, as if he were a stranger?" Before Anne could find words to explain tactfully, Sir James continued, "Of course! Because Martin *is* a stranger. How stupid of me not to realize that instantly. There was a letter from him. Vienna is the madhouse he expected and even less appears to get accomplished than was our most pessimistic guess, although, he says, everyone is constantly maneuvering in involved patterns which have been likened to the complexities of a contra-dance. And speaking of dancing, I'm told an inordinate amount of time and money is spent on lavish balls and other frivolities as each sovereign attempts to outdo the others in display."

Anne studied his tight features, then glanced at Jaycee who was pretending great interest in a rather sad-looking chicken wing. She sighed softly. "Jaycee, you haven't written to him, have you?"

Jaycee grimaced.

"Obviously not," said James on a dry note. "But then, my stubborn friend as much as admitted that he hasn't written *Jaycee* either."

Jaycee's lips tightened.

Sir James stared in irritation mixed with pity at his sister. He felt soft and comforting fingers on the back of his wrist and looked down. Carefully he unclenched his white-knuckled fist. "Jaycee, why will you not see sense?" When she didn't respond, he added, "I never could make you do so when we were children and nothing seems to have changed in our relationship although the both of us have, supposedly, become adults."

Jaycee rose to her feet and left the table.

He watched her leave the room, his lips compressed. He sighed, shook away his irritation and said, "It is obvious I needn't expect a better result this time although I always hope she'll behave with sense and sensibility . . . as the novel has it." He sent a teasing glance at Anne, but turned to Lady Fuster-Smythe when that lady spoke.

"You refer to the Montmorencys' little spat, do you not?" asked her ladyship. "You never explained what, exactly, it was, about which they fought."

Anne had forgotten her ladyship's presence and blushed scarlet. It was improper to speak of such things before someone not in the family. She felt the fool, but when her eyes met Sir James's and she saw the rueful look there, she realized she was not alone in her foolishness and smiled slightly. It was nice, she decided, having someone who understood one's moods so well and entered into them as Sir James so often did.

However that might be, James couldn't explain to her ladyship what he didn't understand himself and was too intelligent to try. "I don't have a notion what, exactly, happened before Martin left for Vienna, Lady Fussy-puss, but, knowing the two of them, I'd guess the quarrel was my sister's fault."

Lady Fuster-Smythe snorted. "Despite her skitter-witted ways, I doubt it. Men never have the sense they were born with when dealing with their women—as you've proved once again." She nodded toward Jaycee's empty chair. "Not that Lady Jaycee is a sweet innocent. The two of them, though! Just like babes in the woods, aren't they?" She turned a glare Anne's way. "Don't, I beg you, make a love match. So full of Sturm and Drang—as that German fellow wrote. Goethe, I think his name was. Romance is a lot of twaddle, and, all too often, becomes very uncomfortable, as you'll agree when you think on this situation between James's sister and your brother."

"I don't understand."

"It's simple, my dear. Just like April and May, the two of them, for weeks, perhaps months. Then each discovers the other isn't quite perfect! They feel cheated in each other and the arguments begin. It's always that way. Don't do it, Lady Anne. Find a steady man of rank and fortune who won't gamble away his substance and grab him with both hands. When you've provided the necessary heir, why, *then* you may look about yourself for the romance everyone thinks so wonderful." Lady Fuster-Smythe snorted softly. "Wonderful 'til we experience it, of course. Then we know better. But each must learn that for herself it seems." Lady Fuster-Smythe shook her head slowly in a disbelieving way. "I do *not* understand why the young will not listen to older and wiser heads."

"Did *you?*" asked James, twirling his wineglass between long fingers. When Lady Fuster-Smythe looked at him blankly he elaborated in a lazy voice, "Did you listen to your elders, Lady Fussy-puss?"

The old lady's cheeks turned fuchsia under her rouge. "You are impertinent."

He nodded judiciously, his eyes brimming with suppressed laughter. "I rather thought you the sort who wouldn't."

Lady Fuster-Smythe stood and glared at James who lounged slightly in his chair. "Someday, Cupid will give you your comeuppance, James Collingwood, and I hope I'm there to see it!" She looked at Lady Anne. "Come, my dear," she said, forgetting the girl couldn't. "Let us leave this scapegrace to his port."

"Don't go," coaxed Sir James. "I hate drinking port in state all by myself." Then he saw the pair of footmen exchange a glance. "On second thought," he said, when the servants then looked at the sideboard which needed clearing, "we'll have the decanter and my glass taken into the sitting room and we'll *all* go. The servants may finish their work early."

Anne, seeing this further evidence Sir James was not a thoughtless hey-go-mad peep-o-day boy, but a caring mature adult, felt her heart give another lurch of the sort she'd experienced several times recently. Once or twice she'd wondered if she should describe the odd sensation to Dr. Macalister, that perhaps her fall had done damage they'd not previously noticed, but now, after listening to Lady Fuster-Smythe's lecture, she realized the truth and hid her despair by looking at the hands clenched in her lap.

Lady Fuster-Smythe's views about love matches had opened Anne's eyes to what was happening in her own heart. She was falling in love! Anne compressed her lips tightly, angry at herself for allowing such a situation to arise when it was so impossible that anything come of it.

Marriage was not for such as she. Aunt Prem had been very certain on that subject! First, she couldn't seem to live from day to day without doing something sinful. To lay such a burden as that on another was out of the question. Such an exceedingly selfish thing to do, to ask another to put up with her misbehavior! But secondly and perhaps more important in the way of things between a man and woman, no man in his right mind would care to ally himself to an ugly woman with hair she dared not show the world.

"What's the matter, Lady Anne?" asked Sir James, standing beside her chair and waiting to pick her up. "Was studying that heavy book and then coming down to dinner too much for one day? Should I take you to your room for an early night?"

Escape, she thought. "Yes, please." She raised emotionally empty eyes to meet his, lowered them at the questioning worried look she read in his expression. "I am not in pain, if that concerns you. You take very good care of me, Sir James." Which, she thought, was surprisingly true. She trusted him to see to her comfort, to make the hours of her convalescence as easy as possible. Which was strange, was it not? He was a *man*.

Aunt Prem, she thought, *must be rolling over in her grave!*

Then Anne recalled, again, that Aunt Prem had not been the paragon she'd taught Anne to believe her to be. She'd forsworn herself concerning music training for Anne.

But surely Sir James's suggestion the woman had been jealous of Anne's mother was impossible. Jealousy was a sin. *Surely* Aunt Prem would not be ruled by it. She would have rooted it out, would have forced herself to eschew such emotion. . . .

Would she not?

Five

Sir James, returning once again from a day in London, deftly eased his team into the last difficult turns in the drive up to the Park. A mild curse escaped him that his friend Martin had yet to straighten the approach to the sprawling house with its multitude of wings springing from the ancient entrance centered in the front.

The oldest portions of the Park had been constructed in far different times. In those wicked days a winding drive with well placed groves and dense shrubbery allowed defenders opportunities for ambush. A much younger Martin, over-turning a curricle and injuring a favorite mare, had sworn that, if he were ever unlucky enough to succeed to his brother's title, his first duty would be to straighten the drive. James wished he'd done so! He steadied his team after the final turn and glanced toward the entrance which had been furnished with a stately portico by Martin's grandfather. This time when he swore, it was far more vehemently and for an entirely different reason.

"Perhaps," he said to Bobson, an acid note creeping into his voice, "modern times are not so peaceful as I believed. How does that lowlife have the temerity to break through our defenses and visit my sister?"

"Lord Runyon, ye be meaning?" asked his groom. He pulled his ancient hat lower around his ears and added, "Don't much like that man of his." Bobson sucked thoughtfully on his teeth.

Sir James slowed his team. "Why?" he asked.

"Has a reputation, that one, in the lower taverns of a type you'd be knowing nothing about." When more seemed required, he added, "For being a bit nasty to womenfolk, ye ken? A wise host hides his females when that one comes in. 'Course," added Bobson, judiciously, "one or two are always more willing to bite a golden boy than to have a care to a mere maid. There be dozens to take a maiden's place if she's . . . damaged."

James couldn't remember hearing such distaste in his long-time groom's voice. But, since he felt the same disgust himself, he easily understood it. "That sort, is he?"

"Aye." The groom settled into stolidity, facing straight forward and appearing not to notice the departing sporting carriage passing them too near the curve and at a rather dangerous clip. "You know the saying," he added thoughtfully.

"Like master, like man," growled James, proving he did.

He also knew Lady Fuster-Smythe. And knowing Lady Fuster-Smythe's ability to make mountains from little or nothing, he hoped her ladyship had been fully occupied elsewhere during Runyon's visit. James didn't need Lady Fussy-Puss scolding Jaycee for her sins. That was a duty he kept for himself. And one which needed no help from anyone else! James pulled up under the portico and stared down into the pouting face of his sister who, seeing his carriage approach, had pulled her shawl around her shoulders and awaited his arrival.

"He's a really nasty man," said James without even a pretense of a formal greeting. "Why do you allow him anywhere near you?" He noted the way her eyes flickered away from his and then returned, defiant as they always were when he'd attempt to make her understand the error of her ways. "Ah," he said, enlightened. "I see. You've chosen this means of punishing Martin. Well, it won't fadge, Jaycee. *He'll* not suffer; *you'll* be punished when you become scandal-bait and

Martin divorces you and you are banished forever from polite society."

Lady Jaycee Montmorency's eyes widened and she gasped. "He wouldn't!"

"Runyon wouldn't ruin you? He would. Or is it that you believe you can go your length again and again and Martin will, forever, forgive the scandal you brew?"

"He shouldn't have flir—" Jaycee bit her lip, glanced quickly at her brother and away. She stamped her foot. "Why did you come back? Why don't you go home? We don't need you. I didn't invite you."

"No. You invite the dregs of society, but don't raise a finger to protect a young woman under your care. If I were the sort to whom you so warmly said goodbye just now, Lady Anne would long ago have found herself an outcast as a result of my attentions. But you don't care, do you? You know, Jaycee, if Martin does *not* divorce you, I believe I *will.*"

She blinked, blinked again, obviously pondering his words. "That's nonsense, James. You *can't* divorce me. I'm your *sister.*"

"Hmm. I cannot count how often you've made my life so difficult I've wished that that were not true. Perhaps I cannot divorce you, but I *can* wash my hands of you, if I so decide."

"You love me." The words were said in a confident manner, but the look his sister sent his way was a trifle hesitant and had a questioning element in it.

He nodded, a judicious movement of his head. "For my sins, Jaycee, I do." He paused a moment during which he noted complacency return to her mien, and added, in a polite tone, "Must you continually test the love others have for you? Can you explain why you find it necessary to see just how much we, who wish you only the best, will swallow before we finally are *forced* to turn from you?"

For half an instant Jaycee's eyes lost focus. "Test . . . ?"

she muttered. She glared at her brother and, turning on her heel, entered the house.

"Where are you going?"

"Do you care?"

"I'm a guest, Jaycee, as well as your brother."

"I don't *want* you as a guest in my house."

James's brows arched. "But it is not your house, Jaycee," said her brother, his tone silky. "It is Martin's house."

"It *is too* my home."

"Home yes, house no. Can you not see the distinction?"

She pouted again, flouncing around to present her back to him, her arms folded across her chest. "You are not kind."

"You think that anyone who contradicts you or will not let you have your way is unkind. You've never understood that if we did *not* care for you, it is *then* we'd let you go your length and shrug at the pit you dig for yourself." He tipped his head and gave her a sad look.

Jaycee seemed to shrink. "Why did he flirt with Lady Commerce?"

"Why," asked James in exactly the same tone, "did you flirt with Lord Northfield? And His Grace, Duke of Grimstoke? And . . ."

"But . . ."

"It is *exactly* the same, Jaycee," said James, a tired note in his voice. "Exactly."

"How did you know what I was going to say?"

"How long have I known you?"

The unexpected question startled her and Jaycee giggled. "Since I was born, silly."

"Well?"

She pokered up again. "He had no right—"

James held her gaze until it fell, but, as was Jaycee's way, her eyes, when they raised to meet his, were filled with defiance and, he thought, contained a certain amount of resentment.

She veered to a slightly different topic. "Perhaps you are right about that, then, but my dear husband certainly hasn't a right to make a byword of himself in Vienna!"

"What makes you think he's doing any such thing?"

"Willy—" She glanced at her brother and bit her lip. "—Lord Runyon, I mean . . . he's had word from a friend. . . ."

James interrupted, scorn dripping from his tongue, "You *believed* him!"

"Why should I not? He showed me the letter. It did come from Vienna—which is one more letter than *I've* had."

"Have you written Martin?"

"It was *his* fault."

"Was it? Believing that nonsense, to say nothing of being something of child," said James in a judicious tone, "you'll refuse to write first and will, thereby, cut off your nose to spite him, will you not? Did it not occur to you that Lord Runyon had *asked* someone to write that letter?"

Jaycee's eyes filled with tears and, this time when she turned and moved into the house, he did not call her back. Instead he turned to the Montmorency butler and glared until the man's skin reddened. "Tibbet," said James when his victim was nicely rosy, "you did *not* hear me help Lady Jaycee make a fool of herself just now."

"No, Sir James."

"You have forgotten all that was said between my sister and myself?" he demanded.

"Every word."

"Good."

James handed over his coat, hat, and gloves and strolled down the hall to the room which was now Anne's daytime abode. He paused in the door when he discovered his sister there, pacing from one end of the salon to the other in something far from her usual dainty steps.

"He is impossible!" she said, her back to the door. "How can you bear to have anything to do with him?"

Anne glanced at James who quirked one brow. Anne had to smile at his expression. "I've not found him difficult, Jaycee, dear. I apologize if my accident has kept him here far longer than you find comfortable, but I don't know what I can do about that."

"I cannot see where *you* need apologize. I doubt you have a choice in the matter since my dear brother began organizing your life as he does mine."

"Attempts to do yours," said James, a dry note not hidden. "You were never a child who could be led and still will not be broken to the most gentle of bridling." He strolled on into the room.

Jaycee swung around, her delicate features distorted by a ferocious frown. "I don't believe you ever tried *leading* me. You only *drove* me on the route you wished me to take."

"Attempted . . ."

"Attempted! James, you are *always* telling me what to do and what not to do and it is a dead bore."

"I'm certain your brother only did what he . . ." said Anne pacifically.

"Now, don't you start!" said Jaycee whirling around to glare at Anne. "I won't have two of you against me."

"I don't believe either of us is against you, Jaycee," said James. "It is what you never see: we are not against you merely because we do not agree with you."

"You are correct. I do *not* see how that can be. Do you, Anne?"

"It is very true, Jaycee. One need not agree with a loved one on every detail. Indeed, I find it impossible to believe one *could* agree with another to that extent. And, besides," added Anne slowly, "I feel that too might be a dead bore if it *were* possible!"

Jaycee laughed. "You are a one, Anne!" Her temper evaporating in laughter as quickly as it had been roused by opposition, she moved to seat herself before her tambour frame. After a moment she asked, "Will you do me a great favor, Anne, and come tell me what I'm doing wrong with this embroidery? Usually I know exactly what it is I wish to paint with my threads, but this time, something is not quite right and I cannot put my finger on it."

"Jaycee!" James turned a shocked look at Anne who again smiled, this time shaking her head at him.

"Jaycee," she said, in turn, "I cannot come to you. You'll have to bring your work here if you truly wish my advice."

"Cannot come to me?" Jaycee turned shocked eyes on her sister-in-law. "It is not possible that you are *still* unable to move!"

"My lower limbs will not obey my commands, Jaycee," said Anne with the simple acceptance Macalister did not like.

"I knew you couldn't move before, when you first fell, but still? Oh dear, why did no one tell me?" Jaycee's complexion paled. "James, truly, I didn't know. I thought . . ."

"I do not see how you can help but have known," said James, moving to Anne's side and picking up her hand, wishing to comfort her. "Surely Mrs. Tibbet has given you daily reports?"

"I told her not to bother. I was too concerned about . . . about something else." After a moment she added in a small high voice, "I'm sorry."

"You are always sorry when it is made clear to you that you've done the thoughtless thing."

"I *am* sorry. Truly. I thought Anne would recover quickly. . . ."

"Of course you did," said Anne firmly. Quietly she added, "And now I wish we might change the subject."

But Jaycee was embarrassed. Also, she feared James would return to scolding about Lord Runyon and, if Anne's condition was not a topic for discussion, Lord Runyon was one *she* wished to avoid. She cast her mind around for an excuse to go to her room, noticed her hem was coming down, and immediately, completely involved in this new disaster, she fled the salon, insisting no one must ever see her looking such a ragtag!

"She is a dear child," said Anne softly, smiling after her retreating sister-in-law.

"I'm aware. Now if she would only grow up and be a dear *adult*," said James, an equally soft note in his voice.

"I wonder if she would be half so delightful. . . ."

"I cannot believe she'd be anything but *more* of a delight. Martin showed signs of disillusionment when he left. He'd thought she loved him, but her behavior . . . ! Anne, it could *not* be described as that of an adoring wife."

"I think she loves him."

"Then why did she behave so badly from the instant they returned from their wedding journey?"

"Did she? Perhaps it is because she was determined to—" Anne frowned. "—I believe the phrase she used was *cut a dash?*"

James grinned. "That's not proper language for a lady. I think you might say she wished to make a splash, or," he asked, with a roguish look, "is that, too, unacceptable?"

Anne gave him a reproving look. She'd, finally, learned to distinguish between James's serious and joking manners, but had not yet become comfortable with the latter. "Whatever you would call it, perhaps she knew no way other to achieve her goal than to behave as she did?"

A muscle jerked at the side of James's jaw. "You have been with my sister for a mere two months. How, in that brief time, have you managed to understand her so well?"

"I've often had little to interest me in life," said Anne diffidently, "and much time to watch others and think about why they behave as they do. It has become almost a game with me, which is something I do not like in myself. On the other hand, I believe I *have* learned something of why people act in the ways they do."

"Has she said . . . anything . . . ?"

"About her argument with her husband?"

"Yes." The muscle twitched again.

"Now and again," said Anne. She heard steps and raised a warning finger. Looking around the salon, she asked, "This is a very pleasant room, is it not, Sir James? Nothing like I think it was in my childhood when I believe the panels were merely painted pale green with dark woodwork. Do you suppose Jaycee planned and executed the design? It is almost like a garden, is it not?"

James looked at the flower-topped cushions, the various greens in the carpet, the drapery, and the covers on the furniture. Each wall panel framed a hand-painted trellis with vines and flowers; each was different and each delightful. The woodwork was painted white. Behind green drapes were sheer white curtains which billowed slightly in a draft from the French doors which led to the winter-drab garden beyond. But the draft was not so insistent it chilled one. It was, all in all, a very pleasant room indeed.

Lady Fuster-Smythe swept in, followed by a maid with a tray of refreshments. "That excuse for a butler said I'd find you here and here I find you. How nice." She too looked around. "What a pleasant room," she said, her surprise-filled words echoing James's thoughts of moments earlier. "Very pleasant indeed. Oh. I passed Lady Montmorency on the stairs and she said she'd have cook send up a bite to eat and something to drink, but I had already ordered it. I don't know why it is, but invariably I need just a little something about this time of day."

"We were just speaking of this room and wondered if Jaycee had had a hand in its decorating," said Anne.

"You truly think this is her work?" asked James, and then wished he'd kept his mouth shut when Jaycee entered in time to hear him.

Understandably, her response was cool. "I did not do the actual *work*, James. Merely supervised the changes. Last summer, it was, when we were here briefly." She looked

around and found only approving looks where she'd expected teasing at best and disbelief at worse. "I thought it
went well," she added a trifle shyly. She smoothed down
her skirts, hoping to hide the warmth brightening her
cheeks.

James gave her a quick look, realized their opinions were
important to her and said, "It turned out very well indeed.
I did not know you had such talent, Jaycee."

The blush deepened. "Th—th—ank . . . thank . . . you."

Jaycee was stuttering? But, she hadn't done that since
she was a child! She'd started it after their mother died but
the fit had passed.

Anne immediately asked just how Jaycee had come to
think of such a lovely notion as bringing a garden indoors,
which roused the young matron to animation and she
laughed at a compliment Anne gave her on the wonderful
petit point embroidery on the cushions.

"They are a lot of work," agreed Jaycee, "but it is something I enjoy very much. Choosing just the right colors,
watching a pattern I've planned grow to completion. It is
usually very satisfying." She grimaced. "Unlike the one I
asked you to look at earlier which isn't working out so very
well at all."

"You did the cushion tops?" asked Lady Fuster-Smythe,
peering suspiciously around the room. She wandered from
panel to panel, studying each painted rendition. "This is a
very odd notion, I think."

"But very nice," said Anne quickly, noting Jaycee fade
under what was perceived as criticism.

"Oh, yes, quite pleasant. I suspect it is particularly nice
at this time of year when the gardens are so particularly
ugly," said her ladyship in an off-hand manner.

James could almost see the old witch storing up ideas
which she'd have copied in her own home! He must remember to tell Jaycee that suspicion. It would please her.
Then he wondered just when his volatile sister found time

to do quite so much embroidery. Especially since her marriage. His eyes narrowed. "How long ago did you have this idea?" he asked, holding his voice to neutral.

"It occurred to me several years ago during the winter we were mewed up for so long at Ashton Place. No one could travel safely and we were told they even hoped there'd be a frost fair on the Thames's ice as they had last year. We were alone for *weeks*. I began the cushions then and have kept one by me ever since. It is amazing how much one can do in the odd moment. . . ." She looked from one to the other. "What is it? Why do you look at me *just so?*"

"I don't believe any of us have ever thought of you as *working* at anything, Jaycee. You are such a butterfly one has difficulty thinking of you as an industrious ant, but you have eight cushions if I have not miscounted and each is different. . . ."

"But I *like* doing it. It is *not* work."

"Whatever you call it, Jaycee," said Lady Fuster-Smythe, "you have done well."

Her ladyship eyed the tiny cakes and small toast rounds heaped with some indecipherable mixture. Jaycee noted her interest and offered the food around, but only Lady Fuster-Smythe accepted, since everyone but James, who rarely ate at noon, had had a nuncheon a mere hour or so earlier. Everyone, however, accepted a cup of tea.

James watched his sister as she sat behind the tea table and served what was wanted. He noted her expressions, first of irritation, then of worry and finally satisfaction, and could, knowing her so well, almost read her mind as it moved from the subject of the room to that of Anne's condition and on to her own particular friendship with Lord Runyon.

He wondered just how far Runyon had managed to get with her, to say nothing of how often the rake was in the habit of visiting. That last question he'd soon answer. Tibbet would tell him. . . .

Setting aside his questions about his sister, James turned to look at Anne. His eyes narrowed when he perceived how exceedingly tired she looked. Was she in pain? Deeply concerned, he rose to his feet.

"Anne," he said, bending over her chaise, "you would tell us if there were something wrong, would you not?"

Lady Anne glanced up, smiled, but also wore a faint frown. "Something wrong?" she asked and looked at her legs.

"Something more than is *already* wrong," he modified his question. "Moving you downstairs during the day hasn't harmed you, has it?"

"I believe I am merely tired."

James straightened, frowning. "Jaycee, I'm taking Lady Anne up to her room. She's tired. She should return to her bed."

Anne raised her hand, shaking her head. "No, no. Do not disturb yourself. I am perfectly all right."

"But tired," said James. He picked Anne up. "We can't have that."

Lady Anne blushed. Noticing Jaycee's speculative look, she blushed still more—although perhaps for slightly different reasons—but the rosy result confirmed Jaycee's suspicions concerning the relationship between her brother and her sister-in-law. She made a mental note to write Martin that James had finally succumbed to Cupid's arrow and . . .

And then remembered she wasn't speaking to Martin—writing him, that was. She recalled she was very angry with Martin. She sighed, turned back, and discovered Lady Fuster-Smythe staring at her.

It was Jaycee's turn to blush rosily although she couldn't for the life of her think why she did so.

James returned to the Green Salon with a vague hope of finding his sister only to discover she was alone and awaited

him. She'd obviously been hoping he'd return. She stood
with arms crossed and her toe tapping and a frown creasing
her delightful brow. "That woman must go," said Jaycee,
before James could fire his own opening salvos.

Her words, however, gave him an opening and he returned fire instantly. *"That woman,* assuming you mean
Lady Fuster-Smythe, may protect your reputation from the
wolves and will, if I have anything to say about it, go nowhere farther than the rose garden or perhaps the long sheltered walk between the yews for a bit of exercise!"

"I will not have her here, scolding and nagging and lecturing and making life miserable."

"Behave yourself and she'll not scold, nag, or lecture and
your life will not be miserable."

"You are an unfeeling brute." But as she said the words,
Jaycee was reminded that perhaps her brother was feeling
more than might be proper for her sister-in-law. "And
speaking of what one would laughingly call your feelings,
just what are you feeling for Anne?"

James's brows arched, one rising slightly higher than the
other. "That was very well done of you, Jaycee. You have
learned that attack is an excellent form of defense, have
you not?"

"I haven't a notion what you mean," she said, tossing
her head in what would have been a delightful manner if
her audience had been someone other than her brother. He
didn't explain and she sighed. "Whatever you mean, I *will*
have an answer. James, what are your intentions toward
Anne? I'll not have her hurt," she said in a warning tone.

"Coming from you who most recently hurt her, I don't
know if I need answer that. But I will," he added before
she could spit and claw like the kitten she often successfully
emulated. "I've not completely delved into the question,
and haven't had time to come to a firm conclusion, but—"
A smile hovered around James's lips. "—I suspect I wish
to wed her."

"Wed her!" Jaycee's volatile emotions shifted yet again. She clapped her hands. "Oh! Very good! I guessed it might be so, but I remembered what a curmudgeon you are and decided you could not possibly have fallen in love." She tipped her head, compressing her lips and suppressing giggles, but couldn't rid herself of twinkling eyes. "There is a problem, of course."

"There are several problems. What, in particular, do you have in mind?"

"She'll not wish to marry a curmudgeon! It will be quite a challenge for Cupid, I think, to make *any* woman fall in love with you." said Jaycee smiling, the roguish look appearing which was her most delightful expression. She sobered, placing one finger under her chin and the backs of the fingers of her other hand to her forehead in an attitude which had been labeled Lady At Thought. "I have played with the notion of holding a ball, but now I will do it. Perhaps in February. St. Valentine's Day, I think."

"Ball?" Something warned James he'd better delve into just what was in his sister's mind. "A ball is always acceptable, Jaycee, but why now, particularly?"

"For the announcement, of course. St. Valentine's Day is when birds choose their mates, is it not, and you are always teasing Anne about being a little bird, so that date will do very well, will it not?"

James frowned. "Jaycee, Lady Anne is in no condition to think of anything but getting well and you'll not tease her with this. Although I have admitted to you a partiality for Anne, I hope you'll not burden her with the information?" When Jaycee didn't respond, he added, "It would not be kind while she still suffers from her fall."

Jaycee was silent for still another moment, a puzzled frown creasing her brow. "You are saying you've not told her?"

"Of course I have not. She is *paralyzed,* Jaycee. Can you not understand how unsettling that is, how terrible it must be for her that she cannot walk? I will not burden her with my feelings and hopes until, one way or another, we sort out the immediate problem."

"You mean," said Jaycee complacently, "when she can walk again."

"Either that, or if the time comes we must accept she never will and she, accepting it, can go on to plan what she'll do with her life."

Horror settled onto Jaycee's expressive face. Her whole body twisted slightly in rejection of the notion. "But . . . *surely* she'll walk again!"

"Perhaps not, Jaycee."

For the first time it seemed to register on Jaycee just how badly Anne had been injured. "But that is terrible!"

"We'll deal with it if it happens."

"Deal with it? How does one deal with something so awful? I would die if it were me!"

"Then, Jaycee, we must be very glad it is not you, must we not?"

James, irritated by his sister's attitude which only emphasized fears he could not quite suppress, turned on his heel and left her standing in the middle of the Green Salon.

Jaycee, frowning, watched him go. She tipped her head, a motion indicative of her puzzlement, and then, shrugging, returned to her seat and the tambour frame holding her latest and not entirely successful needlework. Unable to understand her brother, it was a relief to deal with something she *did* understand. She studied the design carefully, and realizing the leaf she was stitching was far too large, set herself to the tedious but necessary task of carefully unpicking the fine silk threads.

Six

A few days later Lady Anne lay back against the pillows on the chaise longue in Jaycee's garden room and watched tiny white clouds float in the deep blue of the sky above the ancient dark, nearly black, green of the yews. The yews, striding in stately manner from left to right, protected and made a dark background for the lawn which glittered with frost the sun had not yet burnt off. Anne's fingers itched to hold pencil and sketchpad. Or, better, brush and water colors. The scene cried out for color. Would it be wrong to indulge that desire? Was it a sin that she yearned to reproduce that lovely peaceful scene?

Anne closed her eyes and recalled how pleased Kitty was that she'd been able to deliver her portrait to her parents on her last half day. Then Anne recalled Lady Prem's objections to Anne's viewing her own mother's portrait, calling it an icon. Why had she, Anne wondered, felt no guilt while drawing Kitty's face? Wasn't it too an icon? Wasn't that a contradiction? A huge hole in the logic of her existence? Why?

"Of what are you thinking, Lady Anne?"

"Oh!"

Sir James's softly spoken question broke into Anne's thoughts and she twisted around to stare up at him.

"You startled me," she said. Her gaze was caught by the kindness, the interest . . . the. . . . She didn't know what it was, but it warmed her. He smiled and she remembered he'd spoken to her. "What did you ask?"

James repeated his query.

Anne bit her lip. "Nothing in particular." She shifted slightly, her gaze dropping to where her fingers showed white.

"Lady P. would tell you that to lie is a sin," teased James and then stepped forward when Anne's skin paled to a sickly white. "Lady Anne, don't! I did not mean. . . ."

"Whatever you meant, what you said is true. Lying is sinful. And my thoughts *were* of something in particular, so when I said they were not, I *did* lie." Anne felt odd prickles under the skin of her face. "It was wrong of me to do so."

"But all you were truly saying was that your thoughts were none of my business, was it not? And perhaps also, that I should take myself away because you'd prefer to be private. It wasn't really a lie, Lady Anne, but only a common form of conventional politeness."

She glanced at him, saw that he still smiled, but that there was also . . . a tenderness? . . . revealed that was both frightening and seductive. Could she trust him? Dare she do so?

"Should I go?" he asked, obviously prepared to do so if that should be her decision.

So. She must give the word and he'd go. She drew in a deep breath to do just that and was shocked to discover, instead, that the words issuing from her mouth explained her dilemma concerning the portraits. James listened attentively. He nodded when she pointed out the contradiction. And then he asked, "Did you never have a portrait of your parents? I mean, did you not take one with you when you went to live with Lady P.?"

Anne frowned, again staring at her clasped hands, this time as if hoping they might open up and reveal an answer. From somewhere in her mind came a faint memory of a small picture in an oval frame. Not much larger than the two hands which held it, touched it, brought it to lips which kissed it. . . .

Anne glanced up. "A miniature . . ."

"Of your mother?"

"I believe it must have been," she said slowly.

"Think again, Anne. What happened to it?"

Stress brought tension and caused Anne to fidget. She plucked at the light cover over her lower limbs, bit her lip, turned her head from side to side. "I do not know. . . ."

"Do you not? Are you certain?"

An expression of bewilderment took up residence on her features. "Aunt Prem *never* lost her temper!" She stared at James, an intensity of expression that both questioned and pleaded, although she could not have said what it was for which she begged. "Never!"

"What is it you recall, Anne?" he asked even more softly than when he'd first spoken to draw her attention.

"Aunt Prem." Anne stared blindly out the window at the peaceful scene. "I can see her. She . . . she screams at me. She takes the miniature from me and she . . . she throws it in the fire." Anne closed her eyes, pressing her head back into the cushions. "It cannot be a true memory. Such behavior is . . . well, it's insane!"

James's brows arched. "But, of course. Have I not said that Lady P.'s reputation was that of a madwoman?"

"Then why was she given command of me?" Again Anne felt her eyes straining in her head in a painful way as she stared at James, hoping for, *needing,* an answer. "She cannot have been a bad woman. Surely no one would give a child into the care of one who was not in their right mind."

A thoughtful frown took up residence on James's forehead. "I think *Vincent* might easily have done so." He moved a chair near and seated himself so they faced each other. "Vincent was more than a trifle odd himself, Lady Anne, and he hated your mother very nearly as much as Lady P. hated her."

"Hate." For a moment Anne stared out the window. "But hate is an evil thing. I don't understand. . . ."

James sighed. "If only Martin had been older. He'd not have allowed you to suffer so. Not if he'd known what was happening, but his father had bought him his colors only a few years earlier. A young soldier, who must learn all he needs to know in order to survive war, has little time or opportunity to help a child with whom he has no contact and when, added to that, he was dealing with the problems of growing up himself . . . well! One can, if I remember that age correctly, be rather unthinking of others."

Anne smiled a swift little smile with just a touch of sadness. "You need not excuse Martin to me, Sir James. He has been all that is kind since he came into the title. He came to see me, you know, very soon after he returned from the Peninsula, and even then he was willing to have me to live with him."

"But you refused."

"Yes." Her mind was elsewhere and she answered absently. "But the miniature. Why do I feel a rendition of my mother wrong, but other portraits do not trouble me?"

"You were totally dependent on Lady P. I would guess she impressed on you certain notions which were not true."

"I have told you that that cannot be. Lady Prem was a most righteous woman. She would not have lied." There was a stubborn tension in Anne's jaw. She felt it, forced herself to relax, but wondered at it. . . .

"Lady Anne, you have learned her ladyship was not perfect."

Stubbornly, Anne shook her head.

"You know," he insisted, "that she made a promise she had no intention keeping. Is that not a lie of sorts?"

"I'm so confused," said Anne, deep hurt revealed by the drowned look of her greenish eyes when she looked up at James. "I have believed . . . have *had* to believe . . . what Lady Prem taught me." She paused, the tension returning to her body doubled. "One can so easily be damned, find oneself suffering all the pain and horror of an eternity in hell. . . ."

James hesitated. "Anne, Lady P. did you a vicious disservice if she encouraged you to believe you are likely to be damned. I don't know *why* you believe it, but when you think about it, will you please remember that Lady P. may have done her best to destroy *you* as a means of gaining revenge against your mother who stole the man her ladyship wanted for herself?"

Again Anne felt prickles under her skin. "Please . . ."

"I'll go. But somehow, my dear, we must convince you Lady P. was *wrong*," said James, his voice again revealing that much to be desired tenderness.

Anne craved to hear that softness, but she'd believed such softness was not for her. Wanting so much to believe him, not *daring* to believe. . . . She forced herself to look away from him and stared at the lovely winter scene beyond the window. It had changed. The frost was gone and clouds had gathered to cover much of the sky.

"Anne?

Anne didn't respond. She would not ask that her paints be brought to her. It would be an indulgence to waste time putting color on paper however enjoyable it might be. Or *because* it was enjoyable? Anne pushed that thought away since, either way, she would not indulge herself. Instead, she'd ask that Kitty bring her her most useful herbal, *Medicina Britannica,* which had been written in the last century and dealt with all sorts of plants found in fields and gardens and an account of their nature.

"Anne . . ."

"Hmm?" She glanced up, away. "Oh. As you leave, will you pull the bell cord? I'd like Kitty to come to me, please."

James's lips stretched into a thin line, but Anne didn't notice. He moved to the fireplace and yanked the bell pull, then looked back to where Anne stared out the window.

James stiffened into immobility, all irritation fleeing. When he'd entered the room, hadn't Anne's ankles been crossed right over left? Weren't they now crossed the other way? Had she moved? *Could* Anne move? But, if so, why had she not told them?

On the other hand, her limbs were hidden under the shawl spread across them. Could he be certain they'd been crossed the other way . . . ? Surely he was wrong in his recollection of her original position. . . .

Kitty entered, curtsied, and gave him a questioning look. He motioned toward her mistress and, after half a moment's hesitation, left the room. Somewhere there was an argument which would prove to Anne she was wrong to suffer as Lady P. wished her to suffer! Somehow he must find that argument and convince Anne she could live a normal life. He *would* discover it, *convince* her. . . . At least, he'd do his best to do so.

He had to, because, in the long hours of the night when he'd tossed and turned and wondered and questioned and analyzed his emotions and thought and dreamed and thought some more, he'd been forced to conclude he'd not been teasing his sister when he'd said he wished to wed Lady Anne.

His wee wren had become something of more than momentary importance in his life. Her intelligence. Her thoughtfulness for others and gentleness. . . . And, of course, he would not, *could* not, forget that magnificent head of hair!

He'd been forced to conclude that Lady Anne was just the woman for whom he hadn't known he was looking, but for whom it seemed he'd searched forever. Now he'd found her, he'd straighten out her head and then convince her he was the man for whom *she'd* searched—even if she was unaware she'd ever pursued such a course! Or perhaps she truly hadn't. Searched, that is. Once again Sir James quietly cursed Lady P. and her evil care of poor defenseless Anne.

* * *

"So," said Sir James, "the only person who might recall the weeks just before Lady Anne's mother died, other than yourself and Mrs. Tibbet, of course, is Betty Wright who is now Betty Simpson who was a nurse here during the period Lady Anne's mother was ill, is that correct? Then I wish to speak to this Betty Simpson. She may remember more of that time than you do, might recall something which will help me."

Tibbet straightened to his full height of five foot, two inches and somehow gave the impression of looking down his nose. "To do that, Sir James, it would be necessary for you to go to the inn."

"Yes," said James judiciously. A chord of humor vibrated at the butler's tone. "I believe that *would* be necessary, unless one could convince Mrs. Simpson to come here, of course. Why should I *not* go to the inn?"

Spots of color marred the old man's pale cheeks and he looked away. "I cannot say, Sir James."

"Can you not! Then I will. Lord Runyon is putting up at the inn, perhaps?"

Tibbet sighed, his eyes looking everywhere but at Sir James. "I believe he is, Sir James."

"And it is your belief we should not meet?"

"It would be best if you did not," agreed the butler, nodding, his eyes still wandering.

"Best for whom, Tibbet?"

The spots of color returned, larger and more obvious. "Sir James . . ."

"How often, when my sister lived here before moving back to town, did Lord Runyon visit this house, Tibbet?"

"I could not say, Sir James."

"*Will* not, is perhaps more accurate." James eyed the man. "So." Still no response beyond a tightening of the butler's lips. "In my opinion, Tibbet, your refusal to speak is, itself, an answer. No, do not look guilty. I had already determined that I must discover an answer to that question. I'll not put you to the blush by asking you what the two of them do when he comes visiting, villain that he is."

"Oh, no, Sir James." Pomposity punctured by the fear Sir James would hold wrong-headed notions, the old man seemed to shrink. His eyes widened, and swung to meet James's brown orbs. "Nothing like *that*," the butler hastened to add, and thereby answered another question, one James had had too much delicacy to ask in just so many words!

"I am glad to hear his visits have not gone beyond the line."

"Her ladyship ordered that the doors to the hall remain open when he visits and that a footman be stationed nearby. In case she wishes to order refreshments, you know," said Tibbet, his voice earnest.

"Of course." James managed to remain sober for only a moment, but then he grinned broadly. "I'll admit, Tibbet, I hadn't a notion my sister had such good sense. I'm exceedingly pleased to discover she's not the complete skitterwit she seems to wish the world to believe her! And, given that news, I've a letter to write before I ride into the village. I wish it may catch the mail as it goes through today."

"Very good, Sir James," said the butler in a voice of doom.

"Tibbet, you old humbugger, you don't think it good at all!"

Sir James clapped the old man on the shoulder and moved off to the library where he'd find paper, ink, and, if he were lucky, a reasonably decent pen. There too would be found the wafers necessary to seal up his scrawled efforts.

Not more than an hour later James's gelding clattered onto the cobbles paving the bit of road before the inn and two small shops which, along with a small church and a handful of cottages, *were* the village. He dismounted and threw his reins to a boy playing with homemade marbles and strode into the first shop which boasted a shelf of boiled sweets and other candies.

Sir James bought a small bag of the most expensive sort and turned to go, but, just about to exit, he caught sight of Lord Runyon turning out of the inn's stable yard. He paused. Today he had other things on his mind, and therefore no desire for a confrontation with the man. The situation must be faced eventually, but there was no reason to push it forward—especially since he'd learned Jaycee was behaving in a far more circumspect fashion than he'd believed possible.

When Runyon turned the corner and disappeared, James left the shop and strolled across the street, motioning the boy to follow with his horse. "Tell the hostler to give him a drink, but not to untack him, that I'll be back shortly, will you, lad?" The boy deftly caught the coin James flipped his way. "By the way, can you, perhaps, tell me where Mistress Simpson is to be found at this time of day?"

"Inna kitchen," mumbled the boy, more interested in ridding himself of the gelding than answering questions. He very obviously wished to return to the shop James had exited where he would likely choose himself a large enough quantity of sweets, they'd make him thoroughly sick.

"Ah. Around the rear, then," said James.

He picked a careful way through the mud, to say nothing of worse muck, which made the yard a danger for highly polished boots. Behind the ill-kept inn, James found an equally neglected yard including a badly weeded winter garden and *there* he saw the woman for whom he searched. Mrs. Simpson stared at her vegetables as if watching would produce something beyond Brussels sprouts which she might pick to serve her paying guest with his mutton that day for dinner.

"Mrs. Simpson," said James and the slatternly woman turned to stare at him. "May I have a word or two with you?"

"What about?" she asked.

A certain sullenness in her heavy face made James wonder if perhaps he'd not wasted his blunt on the sweets he'd bought to give her. A more blatant bribe might have done better, he thought.

"You were," he said, "nurse to Lady Montmorency, Lady Anne's mother?"

"Urr," she said.

When she spoke no more, but waited for whatever it was he'd say next, James decided the sound must mean yes. "Do you recall the days of Lady Montmorency's last illness?" He held out the bag of sweets.

The woman reached eagerly, feeling every piece before pulling one out and popping it into her mouth. "That were easy done," she said around the large hard candy. "I were there most every day, o'course," she said. She mopped away a sickly pink drool from the side of her mouth and sucked noisily.

"Then," said Sir James patiently, "could you tell me about Lady Montmorency and Lady Preminger?"

"Urr," she said, her eyes glued to the bag as she moved the candy she sucked from one side of her mouth to the other.

"Would it be too much trouble," he asked, suppressing as much of a sarcastic note as he was able, "to tell me what went on between them?"

"Urr . . . ?"

Perhaps the sound didn't mean yes? James sighed. "I suppose you'll tell me when you have thought about it a bit?"

" 'Course I will." The small, too closely set eyes, widened in a frightful parody of innocence. "Why not, then?"

"Ah. And when will you have thought?"

The woman blinked, a sly look crossing her face and she glanced again at the bag. James finally understood and handed it over, something he'd intended to do eventually in any case.

The bag disappeared down the dirty front of the woman's dress. She patted it to see that it was well settled and moved the hard lump in her mouth to a more comfortable location. Again a bit of drool escaped and again she mopped it up. Finally, it seemed she could delay no longer. "Ol' witch jollied poor sick lady. Told her all sorts of lies to make her die happy."

"What sort of lies?" James asked when it seemed the woman had once again shot her bolt.

"That pee-anaforty." She continued when James's brows arched. "Said the girlee could play all she wanted."

"The pianoforte. I see. How do you know that was a lie?"

"Ol' witch had a maid, dinna she, then?"

James accepted that as the obvious source of the slattern's information. "What else did Lady Preminger lie about?"

"Churching," said the woman promptly. "Said she wouldn't make the girlee go to that chapel her la'yship favored but tol' her maid she most certainly *would.*"

"And?"

More long moments of thought while sucking loudly on the sweet. "Tol' my sick lady she'd see the girlee' had a proper come-out just like other girlees, that she'd see the queen all right and proper and have the nice clothes and all. But she died an' I heard there was no pretties and dancing and like that, were there?"

James could hear jealousy in the woman's voice and began to understand why she'd never bothered to tell anyone Lady Preminger was a woman with no conscience and the totally wrong person to raise Anne. The acid note which had become all too common recently in James's tone could readily be heard. "You are a really nasty person, are you not?"

The woman glowered, but said nothing.

"I'll pay you to come to Lady Anne and tell her what you've told me."

"Arr . . ." The sly speculative look returned. "How much, then?"

James named a figure. The woman doubled it. Since James had expected as much, he said nothing, merely nodded and the woman looked as if she might cry. James suspected she'd have asked far more if she'd thought him that easy a touch and for the first time since he'd ridden out toward the village, he felt an urge to chuckle.

"I'll send a gig for you," he said. "You'll come when it arrives, or you'll not see a cent of that exorbitant fee."

James, forgetting the letter in his pocket, rode quickly back toward the Park. But the thought of a mere child exposed to such infamy caused a combination of anger and pain to rise in him and all thought of laughter fled. The anger grew and, leaving the road for high ground, James set his mount to a fast pace, hoping to ride off some of the emotion before he reached home and all the problems awaiting him there.

Like Lord Runyon!

He put that problem to one side, thanking heaven he needn't, at the moment, worry about his sister and the shady character pursuing her! Lady Fuster-Smythe was there, now knew the situation, and would see that Jaycee was chaperoned. With any luck, the old harridan would set up Runyon's back and he'd go away in high dudgeon and forget his plot to ruin Jaycee. Not likely, of course, but one could hope.

James eventually reached the stables and immediately sent Bobson off in the gig for the woman who might, with a little luck, convince Lady Anne her life could be led in as normal a fashion as that of anyone else.

Tibbet scowled as he lay the table in the small dining room for their ladyships and the guest who had arrived an hour earlier. Tibbet had once wondered at the man's habit of arriving just at meal time. Then he'd learned Lord Runyon was putting up at the Golden Shield. That almost made the butler feel sorry for his lordship—and would have done, if it were anyone else.

But it seemed to Tibbet that eating Betty Simpson's cooking was an entirely suitable punishment for the man who was sitting in her ladyship's pocket and was, Tibbet believed, determined to cause trouble. Because of the impossibility that he himself do something about Lord Runyon, Tibbet was pleased Sir James had come. He even went so far as to wonder if, *perhaps,* it was a good thing that that old besom, Lady Fuster-Smythe, had arrived all on her own and unexpected, like.

Even now, Lady Fuster-Smythe sat with Lady Jaycee, thwarting the villain from sweet-talking Lady Montmorency into rash behavior! Not that Tibbet thought his lordship would succeed. Not through honest seduction, that is, using only his considerable charm of manner.

No, if Lord Runyon managed to ruin her ladyship, then some underhanded move would be required. Tibbet clattered another setting of silver onto the table and moved it into place as he turned possibilities over in his mind. Abduction, for instance. Lord Runyon and that nasty groom of his might carry her ladyship off somewhere and ravish her. . . . For a moment Tibbet scolded himself for an overactive imagination, but it didn't stop him from enjoying the sort of titilation one feels when dreaming up disaster to others.

Still, the butler liked both Lord and Lady Montmorency and he *didn't* like the notion that either of them might be hurt. Besides, it never did the servants in a family a bit of good, either, when scandal was afoot. Yes, on the whole, even the presence of old Lady Fuster-Smythe, along with her useless army of servants eating their heads off in the servant's hall, was better than *that.*

Seven

Jaycee, Lord Runyon, and Lady Fuster-Smythe ate in near silence, the old woman glaring at the gentleman in such a way as to put him off his food. Jaycee felt extreme embarrassment at the situation but could think of no way of improving it. However much the young matron wished to think herself up to every rig and row in town, she was too inexperienced a hostess to pull together such diverse guests as Lord Runyon and Lady Fuster-Smythe.

Then, when she thought things could not possibly be worse, her unwanted chaperone instigated an intensive catechism into Lord Runyon's past behavior—which, quite unbelievably, changed Jaycee's mood for the better. She found it very difficult not to laugh outright at Runyon's growing discomfort.

". . . Well," Lady Fuster-Smythe said, after his lordship, with increasing difficulty, laughed off yet another question concerning past exploits, "you needn't bite my nose off. Just wondered what led to your failing interest in Lady Westindyke, that's all," said Lady Fuster-Smythe, pouting. "No need to get in a snit," she added when he didn't respond.

Jaycee wondered if Lord Runyon's neck would be stained permanently red, given how often Lady Fuster-Smythe put him to the blush. During the soup course she'd felt sorry for him, but now, near the end of the fish course, she was much strained to hold back giggles.

"I am not," insisted his lordship, "in a snit because you enjoy yourself at my expense, my lady. It is merely I do not believe you should mention such things before the servants." He glanced toward the impassive Tibbet who was, at that moment, offering a platter of meat delicately sauced in a tarragon cream, to Lady Montmorency. "That I have enjoyed the company of a number of lovely women in the past," he continued, "does not make my feelings for dear Jaycee any the less." He smiled at Jaycee.

" 'Course it don't mean that, since you don't *have* any feelings," said the unwanted chaperone, agreeably.

Lady Fuster-Smythe ignored Runyon's indignant sputtering, turning to serve herself potatoes from the bowl held by a poker-faced, stiff-backed, obviously disapproving Tibbet. Tibbet, too, had strong views concerning what should and should not be said before servants. He had, the moment he saw the way the wind blew, sent away the footmen. He now met her ladyship's hooded gaze and nodded very slightly.

"I don't know why you doubt my sincere feelings of friendship toward Jaycee," said Lord Runyon.

Jaycee heard something very close to a whine in his tone and he must have heard it too, because he cleared his throat.

"In the first place, it is Lady Montmorency to you, my lord, and *not* Jaycee, whatever pet name her *friends* may choose to call her," chided her ladyship. "And in the second, it is obvious why you've chosen just this moment to espouse warm regard for Jaycee—what with her husband in Vienna."

"Lord Montmorency doubtlessly cares little how his wife entertains herself," said Runyon carelessly. He believed in taking every opportunity handed him to pour more oil on the jealous fires he nurtured in Jaycee's heart. "He is enjoying himself very much—or so I hear."

"Yes," said her ladyship, eying a sauce boat she'd not previously noticed. "I heard about that letter." Lady Fuster-

Smythe remembered she did not particularly like that style of sauce and raised her eyes to meet Lord Runyon's. "Did you," she asked with specious interest, "write out a clean copy for your friend to put into his own hand, or did you merely give him a general notion of the sort of letter you wished him to write?"

"I never did! Nonsense!" It was bluster and Runyon moderated his voice. "Why would one have any need to do such a terrible thing?"

With mild interest Jaycee again watched the red rise in Runyon's neck and saw how he pulled at his cravat with a finger tucked into the tight, heavily starched fold laying against his throat. She could almost read his thoughts as he wondered how Lady Fuster-Smythe could possibly have guessed that something of that sort had been his stratagem. Jaycee shook her head at Tibbet's offer of a neatly carved and arranged roast chicken.

"Because," said her ladyship, another who leapt on any opportunity baring its throat to her teeth, "you would like nothing better than to embarrass Lord Montmorency, to say nothing of Sir James." Lady Fuster-Smythe accepted a nice portion of boiled chicken in aspic. Her ladyship glanced up. "You said something?" she asked Lord Runyon as he folded his napkin and rose to his feet. It would, she thought, be far more amusing if Runyon weren't such a pitiful enemy—which was not to imply he was not dangerous, of course.

"Merely," he said now, "that I have enjoyed a very good meal—" They avoided glancing at his plate with its untouched food. "—but I must depart. Immediately. I'd forgot I've an appointment for which I must not be late. Will you ride with me tomorrow, Jaycee?" He cast a defiant glance toward the chaperone as he used the informal name her ladyship had forbidden him.

Jaycee didn't miss the defiant sidelong look, but Lady Fuster-Smythe, who was carefully choosing between fairy cakes, small tartlets, and a very nice-looking ginger biscuit didn't see it.

"I must see how the weather looks, of course," said Jaycee, "but it sounds delightful. Perhaps my brother will wish . . ." She frowned slightly when Runyon could not quite repress a faint shake of his head. "You do not care for my brother's company, Lord Runyon?" she asked sweetly.

"It is only that I cannot help but wish to have you to myself alone."

"With my groom riding behind, of course," added Jaycee, demurely.

"That goes without saying. But a groom! That is not the same as having another of our own sort accompany us who will distract our attention."

"I will think about it," said Jaycee, flirting a little with her lovely eyes before lowering them demurely and then raising them again. "And the weather, of course. I'd have found today far too chilly, I think."

"Oh, of course. We must have a perfect day for our ride, my lady," he said, bowing over her hand and looking deep into her widened eyes in that hot way he'd long ago discovered made a woman's heart beat faster.

Very often that alone was enough to have his prey fall ripe and willing into his hands. Lady Montmorency had not done so. Yet. But neither had she pushed him away. But eventually she'd come to his arms, his bed, and soon thereafter, fulfill his plan to take her to Paris where "arrangements" such as he had in mind were well understood. And then he'd act out the denouement of his carefully devised scheme, which was, stated simply, that, once every Englishman in Paris knew Jaycee's status as his mistress, he'd drop her cold.

He'd show Lord Montmorency and Sir James they could not interfere in his plans with impunity! Opportunity for revenge had been long in coming, but would, for that very reason, be the sweeter. As he left the house, he savored the

image of his beaten enemies, wasting not a thought on Jay
cee's suffering. The feelings of a mere woman were, of
course, totally irrelevant.

Back in the dining room, Lady Fuster-Smythe carefully
peeled her pear which had been grown in his lordship's
succession house. "There goes a dangerous man," she said
calmly when Runyon was beyond hearing. "He'll ruin you
if he can."

"But he cannot if I do not allow it." Jaycee eyed the fruit
tart offered to her inspection. She shook her head. She
waved away the whole tray which Tibbet began to turn to
offer another choice.

"That might have been true once. He was willing to play
a waiting game and take things slowly," responded her la
dyship thoughtfully, feeling no guilt that she'd spent the
luncheon complicating an already complicated situation.
"But now? I fear he'll change his plans." She pointed the
fruit knife at Jaycee for emphasis. "I think it exceedingly
unlikely he'll wait for your permission, child. Not now I've
arrived. And James, too, of course."

Jaycee's eyes widened. "But what else *can* he do?"

"Abduct you?"

Jaycee frowned. "But he wouldn't . . . surely not . .
that would be . . ."

"Ungentlemanly? Irregular? Unfair?" suggested Lady
Fuster-Smythe. "Whatever gave you the notion that particu
lar man played fair?"

Jaycee's frown deepened, then it cleared. "I see." She
gave one quick determined nod. "Thank you for your ad
vice, my lady. I'll take care he has no opportunity for such
underhanded ploys." She chose to accept a pear and bit of
cheese dug from a ripe Stilton before she looked up. "You
mustn't worry, my lady," she said in a kindly tone.

"What makes you think I'd worry? Wouldn't waste my
energy. No bed of *my* making if you wish to make a foo

of yourself." Lady Fuster-Smythe popped a last bite of pear into her mouth and, turning abruptly, she called, "You!"

Tibbet, who had been as silently as possible rearranging the trays on the server, jumped slightly and turned to face her. "Yes, my lady?"

"Coffee. Good strong hot coffee."

"Yes, my lady." Tibbet chose a large cup and saucer and set it by Lady Fuster-Smythe's elbow. Then he returned to get a French-made porcelain pot which stood over a small flame. He poured. "Coffee, my lady," he said.

"You may leave the pot here," she said to Tibbet and pointed to where she could conveniently reach it. "Oh," she added, as Tibbet reached for the last few plates on the table, "you might leave a few of those biscuits as well."

Cook's secret recipe for ginger snaps was truly delightful. Lady Fuster-Smythe wondered if it would be possible to bribe Cook? Or steal the recipe, perhaps? Might Perfect find and copy . . . no. Very unlikely. Her silly maid hadn't the slightest understanding of subterfuge.

Once the coffee and biscuits were arranged to her liking, Lady Fuster-Smythe settled comfortably in her special chair and ignored Jaycee to the point her young hostess decided that, whatever the dictates of politeness might demand, she would not sit forever waiting for her guest to finish. She would, she decided, take herself to the Green Salon as she'd have done on any other day and do another of the cluster of dog violets which were a major part of her newest design for her latest pillow top.

Jaycee didn't even apologize or ask if her ladyship had plans for the afternoon. Lady Fuster-Smythe's plans appeared to include finishing the large pot of coffee and demolishing the whole plate of ginger biscuits, a plan which she would, undoubtedly, follow up with a much-needed nap! *How could she help but do so?* wondered Jaycee.

Lady Fuster-Smythe did no such thing. Well, actually, she did finish the coffee, thought of calling for another biscuit or two to go with the last cup, but touching her ample girth, decided to refrain. When completely satisfied, she too went into the Green Salon where again she ignored her hostess. She spent an intense twenty minutes thinking about what she should do to meet this latest crisis which she'd been called in to fix.

Finally, having decided her course of action, she rang for a footman and asked for her writing desk. When it arrived in Perfect's jealous hands, she wrote briskly for some minutes and then closed and sealed her missive.

While Tibbet muttered and fussed and completed his after-luncheon work in the dining room, the gig arrived and James, called by a footman, led Mrs. Simpson to Anne's room where the innkeeper's wife greedily watched Anne spoon up a spoonful of broth. James retired to the corner ready to interfere if the slattern did or said something she should not. The warning glare he turned her way had the woman scowling for a moment before she looked back at Anne.

"She did it, dinna she?" asked Betty, a gloating tone drawing Anne's gaze.

Anne looked up. "She? Did what?" asked Anne, slowly lowering her spoon back into the bowl.

"Lady Preminger."

"You knew her ladyship?"

"Was nurse here, wasn't I? For your mama, when her sick."

"You?"

Even Betty Simpson could hear the insult in that. "Good nurse!" she said. When Anne merely compressed her lips, the slattern relaxed and began again in her sly voice. "Said she'd see you never did to another what your mama did to *her.*"

"She?"

"Lady Preminger," said the woman, scowling.

"She told you that?"

Betty nodded, ignoring that she'd actually gotten her information from her ladyship's overly repressed, and therefore, overly talkative maid. "Said she'd ruin you for any man's wanting, make you suffer as *she* should ha' done."

"She?"

"Your mama."

"Why should my mother have suffered? She loved my father."

"Bah. All nonsense, love," said the dirty woman in a voice steeped in scorn. "Lord Montmorency what was should have done his duty and married Lady Preminger and not her sister the way her ladyship's father arranged. Instead, she was forced to wed that old man who treated her badly but, bless the lord, din't last so very long, after all."

"I haven't a notion of what you speak," said Anne, fearing she did. "You mean she, instead of her sister, was supposed to wed my father?"

"Tha's right. And then," said Betty, gloating, but speaking carefully, as if to someone who was not quite all there, "her la'yship were widowed and suppose to wed your father *after* her sister died, but the old lord ran off and wed your mama who stole him away."

"I don't believe you."

"Lady Preminger said . . ."

"I do not think my father thought there was any such arrangement or he'd not have married my mother. He had married Lady Prem's sister as his father wished; why should he wed another from that family? In fact," she asked, thoughtfully, "was such an arrangement even possible?"

"Their fathers . . ."

"Oh, no," said Anne interrupting, the trembling disappearing in her determination she not allow insult to her father. "Fathers make arrangements between one young man and one young woman. That first marriage made Lady

Preminger my father's sister so he'd not have been allowed
to wed Lady Prem even if he'd wished to do so. It is not
done. It would not be legal."

"Lady Preminger . . ."

"I am forced to conclude," said Anne stiffly, "assuming,
that is, that what you say is correct, that Lady Preminger
believed, or pretended to believe, exactly what she wished
to believe! If she envied her sister her husband, that was
not the fault of my mother who was a good woman and
not the sort who would steal another's promised husband!"

At least Anne hoped that was true. Memories of her years
before her mother's death were returning. She'd had several
visions of herself: Playing the piano, sitting at her mother's
side in a cloud of light floral scent and doing simple embroidery, running in the garden after a roly-poly puppy with
the lovely sound of tinkly laughter coming from where her
mother sat with her father, the both of them watching her
play, and many more small things which added up to a very
happy life, one which had, for years, been eradicated from
her mind by the woman who took her in after her parent's
deaths.

Anne was forced to the conclusion Lady Prem had *not*
been the paragon she'd have had Anne believe her to be! It
was a shocking notion, one which was not easily accepted,
but the evidence kept pointing that way and now here was
Mrs. Simpson giving more proof of Lady Prem's perfidy!

"However *that* may be, Lady Preminger must have done
what she said she'd do," the innkeeper's wife insisted. "She
said she'd make you so fearful for your soul, you'd never
dare impose yourself on a gentleman as your mother did.
She said she make it impossible for you to believe a man
could love you. And she did, dinna she, or you'd not be
such a great age and unwed! An ape leader, you be," gloated
Mrs. Simpson.

Anne stared at her visitor. "You didn't like my mother,
did you? Why?"

Mrs. Simpson pouted. "Said I was dirty, she did, and she didn't want me around her. Tried to be rid of me," said the nurse, a sullen note entering her tone. "But Lord Vincent saw what she was about and he didn't let it happen. Lord Vincent was—" The woman's eyes took on a glow Anne would have thought impossible in such a cold, hard woman. "—wonderful. He . . ." Suddenly her gaze sharpened, focused on Anne. "Never you mind about *that*. You wouldn't understand."

"That Vincent took you to his bed and had you in keeping until he tired of you?" asked Anne in a bland, unaccented voice. "And, when he wished to be rid of you he paid the innkeeper to marry you, your reward for the, er, service you'd done him?"

Ugly rosy circles of color blotched the woman's face. "You," she said sternly, "shouldn't know about such things!"

"I've run my own home for some time, Mrs. Simpson. I deal with respectable village women and tenants' wives and with the less respectable when necessary. One doesn't long remain ignorant of the world's ways. What I do not understand is why you wish *me* to suffer for something you blame on another. Can you explain that to me?"

"Can't get revenge on your mother, can 'e? So, then, the sins of the parent descend to the children, don' they?" She pointed a grimy finger at Anne. "That means you, don' it?"

"Just how did my mother sin? Merely her wish to relieve you of your duties here?"

Betty scowled. "Shouldn't have done it."

"You shouldn't have done what?"

"Me!" An indignant look crossed the thin face. "Not *me*. She shouldn't have tried to be rid of me."

"And for that, that you didn't wish to bathe," said Anne pensively, "you, hmm, forgot to tell anyone what you knew and condemned me to live with Lady Preminger? It seems a bit extreme to me."

"Weren't my business what they did with a mere brat, were it? Vin—I mean Lord Montmorency . . . he said you deserved to suffer. He said it was good you suffered." She shrugged.

Lady Anne sighed. "Well, if it makes you happy, you may know that I *have* suffered. You may go."

"Pay me first." The sly look was back, this time directed between Lady Anne and Sir James.

James sighed, wondering if the slut had done it on purpose hoping to undo any good that might have come of her visit. He looked at Anne who looked back at him, her gaze steady. Then the corner of her mouth twitched and her eyes twinkled.

"Pay the woman, Sir James. She has earned her fee, has she not?" asked Anne innocently. But one eyelid drooped in a hint of a wink.

James tried to suppress a grin. Then Anne and he laughed merrily.

"Here now! What's toward?"

"I'll pay you and thank you very much, Mrs. Simpson." He bowed to her in as royal a fashion as he knew how. "You did exactly what I hoped you'd do and I'm very pleased with you."

The woman looked sullenly from Anne to James and back again. "Urr . . ." was all she said, but in such an utterly dejected tone it again set James and Anne to chuckling.

Anne's eyes turned toward the closed door after they'd gone, a pensive look about her. Then, her tummy grumbling, she put thoughts of Lady Prem from her mind and looked at her broth. It was cold. There was a pear to one side and she cut it, peeling the sections. It, the chunk of cheese, and Cook's truly wonderful ginger biscuits, would be sufficient. . . . But what had passed would not stay repressed. What a very unpleasant woman that was to try to undo the good she'd done. Why did people wish to make others un-happy? Was it merely because they were unhappy them-selves and couldn't bear that others feel differently?

A movement caught Anne's eye and she looked to where the tip of her left foot seemed to tap the air as it had been known to do whenever she thought deeply on an unsettling subject. She stared, a bite of pear suspended midway to her open mouth, but the foot moved no more. Nor, when she made the attempt, could she make it do so.

Had she really seen it? Or had she dreamed it?

Anne felt a chill up her spine and, once she'd finished eating, rang for Kitty and asked that her writing desk be brought her. Dr. Macalister, who no longer came daily to the Park, might be able to explain to her whether it was possible that her foot moved when she was paying it no heed, but would *not* move when she strove to make it do so! Surely she'd merely seen what she'd thought to see rather than anything real. Surely it was not possible. . . .

Anne grasped her pen firmly, wrote steadily, and prayed Dr. Macalister would answer promptly.

James watched the gig disappear around the first curve. He turned to look back up the stairs, wondering if he should return to Anne and discuss Mrs. Simpson's visit which must have been exceedingly upsetting. On the other hand, wasn't just such emotional turmoil needed to change Anne's mind? Wasn't it necessary to unsettle her deeply in order to bring her to admit she was a perfectly normal young woman who had been imposed upon by an evil old lady? How could he possibly avoid giving Anne some pain in the process of undoing Lady P.'s vicious doings?

James sighed. He longed to go to Anne and sooth her, tell her it didn't matter, that he loved his sweet wren just as she was . . . except for that silly cap, of course and she'd never remove that cap while in her current way of thinking!

So. If he could *not* go to Anne just now, what could he do? He paced the hall until Tibbet came in from the servants area and discovered him there. James had no desire to explain to Tibbet why he couldn't decide what to do with himself, so took himself off to the stables where it was assumed he wished a horse. His gelding was saddled in a trice and, having nothing else to do, James took himself off for a long ride, west along the Thames.

It was late in the afternoon when James arrived back at the Park and, for a moment, he wondered if he were too late to bathe before dressing for dinner, but then he remembered the Montmorency habit of keeping city hours even in the country, so he went in search of Lady Anne.

With a wry, self-deriding smile, he approached the pleasant Green Salon in which Anne chose to spend her days. If she were there and if she did not send him away because he smelled of the stables, he'd very likely spend, with her, every second between now and the last instant before he must change!

But she was *not* there. James could not bear the sudden sharp disappointment that he could not immediately . . . what? Ask her how she felt? Or if there were anything he could do? Offer, perhaps, a game of chess?

Whatever he'd had in mind, assuming he'd had anything at all other than a straightforward and simple need to see that she was *there,* he'd been thwarted in the easiest possible way: she was *not!* His step was far heavier when he returned the way he'd come and plodded up the stairs to his room.

Tibbet was rather astonished at the amount of post to be sent off that day. Not that it was unusual in a country home for there to be a great deal, since the writing of letters was, as he knew from discussing such things with his equals, a common pastime among the upper orders, but that had *not* been particularly true in this house. Four letters!

Tibbet glanced around the hall and quickly flipped down through the stack before dropping them into the pouch a groom would take into the village. Her ladyship, the Fuster-Smythe woman, had written some bigwig in the Foreign Office. It was not a long letter but Tibbet was very curious as to its contents.

Next was in a clear spidery hand he attributed to Lady Anne, although he'd never before seen her writing. *It* was addressed to Dr. Macalister in care of St. Bartholomew's Hospital. Tibbet still thought it strange a mere Bartholomew Hospital doctor was called in to Lord Montmorency's sister rather than a more prestigious doctor—even if this one were a friend of the family.

There was a second letter to Macalister, this one addressed in James's quick unruly fist to the doctor's private address, rooms in the Albany. The Albany? Tibbet corrected his view of Dr. Macalister! After all, not just *anyone* could arrange for rooms in the Albany! There was a second in James's hand, this one to Lord Montmorency directed to Vienna via the Foreign Office. Very likely, Tibbet decided, that one would be sent off to the continent in one of the government's dispatch bags and would find its way there in double quick time. Even if the courier ran into bad winter weather it wouldn't be more than three weeks, surely.

Tibbet heaved a great sigh of pure relief. It was about time someone contacted his lordship about what was going on in his home. Not that anything *was,* of course, but it *might,* and then where would they be? It was with a far lighter heart that Tibbet sent a footman to the stables with orders the mailbag go off at once! Sir James would see that Lord Runyon did nothing untoward and Lord Montmorency would return home and all would be well. By mid-February it would all be over. By St. Valentine's Day perhaps!

Tibbet felt so much better he actually cracked a mild joke while overseeing the footmen setting the table, startling the two men to no end.

Eight

Once he'd dismounted, Ewen Macalister pushed back his hat and looked along the frontage of the Montmorencys' country home. The word "impressive" crossed his mind but it held no extraneous baggage of emotions such as envy. It was not the house nor the entertainment to be found in the country which brought the doctor hotfoot from London.

It was, instead, an exceedingly interesting essay in a book recently arrived from the continent, from Switzerland to be exact, in which was described an experiment on a young man who could not walk. The treatment had involved the interesting but frustrating science of Galvanism about which Macalister had such conflicting thoughts. This particular essay, however, was exceedingly detailed concerning the exact method which brought about total recovery in the patient.

Nor should one discount the letters which had reached him at two very different addresses: Mac's always high energy had been raised still more by the information Lady Anne might have movement she could not control. The essay and letters together had him up half the night arranging that the necessary equipment and its owner accompany him immediately to Montmorency Park.

It never occurred to Macalister it might be easier to transfer the *patient* to the *equipment*. He and it were in London. The patient was in the country. Ergo. Retire with said equipment into the country. Therefore, at a far slower pace than Macalister moved, a wagon trundled along the roads accompanied by an anxious young scientist who watched over its contents as if they were his children. In the wagon was an odd machine about which Macalister still had his doubts.

On the other hand, the essay was very well written, very specific as to the equipment required and the procedure and there had resulted a cure! Even though he could not entirely suppress his skepticism, Macalister's excitement was such he could barely contain it. That machine might, if they were lucky, literally jerk Lady Anne from her paralysis and set her walking again. Particularly, it might be expected to do so if she were already moving, even if she couldn't *make* her legs do as she wished them to do.

Macalister spun on his heel, a frown on his face. How long, he wondered, would it take the benighted equipment to arrive? Its owner suggested it might well be tomorrow. Surely not. The frown deepened. He didn't *wish* to wait so long to discover how his patient reacted! This was far too exciting, far too interesting, far too possible. . . .

But, despite all Mac could say, the young scientist had been sternly pessimistic. The equipment was delicate, it was fragile, it must be packed very carefully, it was . . . bah!

But true.

Macalister heaved a huge sigh of pure impatience. He shoved his hands into the coat pockets he'd had sewn into the seams and glared at nothing in particular. It wasn't that he truly *expected* the world to run to his demands—because he knew very well it did *not*. It was just such a bore *when* it did not!

A groom strolled around the corner of the Park nearest the stables. He noticed the horse calmly cropping dry grass near the edge of the drive and the visitor whose features were distorted by an odd grimace. The groom hesitated, giving Macalister and his gelding a further startled glance, and then hurried forward. "Sir!"

"Hmm? Oh." Mac waved a languid hand at the roan. "Aye, you may have him," he said. He patted the horse,

which had been trained to stand patiently with its reins dragging whenever Mac got off. The doctor gave the animal
one last pat and strolled toward the Park's heavily carved
front door.

"Sir?" asked the groom who had not previously met the
doctor. He wished to question this stranger's right to wander
unattended, but, given Mac's assurance, didn't quite dare to
do so.

"Yes, yes, that's quite all right," said Macalister, "you
will nae forget to take great care of the wagon when it
comes, of course."

That particular order had the groom lifting his hat and
scratching his head. He looked down the entrance road toward the first curve leading to the unseen gate and back at
the roan.

The groom spat. "Jist like the quality, ain't it!" he said,
to no one in particular. "Think a man can read their minds!"

Mac's horse nodded as if in full agreement and, with
seeming tolerance of the many foibles of human race,
merely snatched one more mouthful of grass before allowing himself to be led away.

Macalister, unaware he'd left confusion behind, stepped
into the dusky interior of the Park's great hall and waited
for his eyes to adjust. When they did, he discovered no one
on duty. For a moment he actually waited, but, when no
one appeared, Mac wandered on.

What room was it, he wondered, which they used as a
family gathering place? His last visit was getting on for a
week earlier, and, never a very important piece of information in Mac's busy mind, he could not remember. More
surprising, given how busy a country house usually appeared to be, with comings and goings at all hours, he met
no one in his ramble. Not until he wandered nearly to the
back of the house did he even hear voices. Luckily these
came from a room with an open door.

"Ah ha!" he said, poking his head in. "There you are,

lass. I did wonder," he said and beamed at Anne who, startled, glanced up from her day lounge where she'd been discussing with Kitty the best disposition of her writing desk and papers.

"Doctor Macalister!" She blushed scarlet and glanced around herself.

Anne had decided that if she were to finish her manuscript by the date she'd promised her publisher, then she would have to stop being secretive about her work, whatever consequences ensued.

If no one else, she was forced to take Kitty into her confidence. The maid had arranged Anne's reference books and the notebook in which Anne recorded her own work, on a table set to one side. A large lap desk rested over Anne's limbs and to the other side Kitty was moving another small table a few inches at a time, while Anne decided where the easel set upon it would best show whichever of her ink drawings she wished to describe and discuss.

"You didn't expect to see me?" asked the doctor, pretending chagrin, but looking curiously at the arrangement of tables and lap desk.

"Of course I did not. I merely hoped you could explain to me whether . . ." Anne's face turned a fiery red. "But it is surely impossible."

"That legs move all on their ain, but willna when you wish it?" He struck a thoughtful pose. "I deem it possible," he said after a moment, finger laid firmly along side his nose.

"But that is quite ridiculous, is it not? That they *will* move but I cannot *make* them move?"

Macalister chuckled. "You, lass, have the look of one deeply insulted."

A muscle jumped along Anne's jaw. "Do you not think it insulting?"

"Insulting? Hmm." No longer pretending, Macalister merely rubbed his nose. "Nae, I canna say it's an *insult*."

Anne didn't quite glower but came close and Macalister carefully restrained a laugh he decided would not be appreciated. "But, since I'm here, perhaps ye'll allow me to check those wee reflexes?"

Anne tucked the rug more closely around her thighs. "I have had Kitty do so. There is no reaction."

"Hmm. I would see for myself." He gained no encouragement from his patient and decided he'd need to go slowly with Lady Anne. Perhaps it was not altogether a bad thing the equipment was delayed since, obviously, he must prepare her before she was likely to cooperate. Macalister moved all the way into the room. "What is this?" he asked when he'd approached the couch. He tipped up several of the heavy tomes laying on the table and read the titles. "Ye be looking for your ain cure, perhaps?" he asked, only half teasing.

"Studying old herbals is a . . . a hobby," said Anne, faintly defensively, and looking away from the doctor.

"And drawing bonny pictures," as well?" he asked softly, as he flipped down through the stack of carefully inked pages laid near the easel.

"I've had an interest in such things for a very long time," she said, the defensive note growing.

"Oh, aye, a *verra* long time, such an ancient crone as ye be!" He smiled, taking the sting from his teasing. "These are verra good."

"You know herbs?"

"I firmly believe that what heals should be used to heal." He thought of his reason for coming to the Park, but shoved it back until he'd once again wormed his way into Anne's confidence. "Where I grew up, in Scotland ye mind, there was an herb woman who taught me a great deal." He looked through the pages again. "These should be published," he said and glanced up in time to see the deepening red in Anne's cheeks, her hands flying to cover it. "Nae then. What is this?"

"Yes," said James from the doorway. "How have you upset my Anne?"

"Not your Anne," she denied, turning chagrin into anger.

James sighed. "No, not mine. I only wish it so." Again there was no response from the young woman—except, perhaps, a deepening of the flush staining her cheeks. "Mac," asked James, when he realized he was embarrassing Anne, "just when did you arrive?"

"Hmm? Oh, some time ago. Have you seen these, Jimmy-lad?" He handed a few of the drawings. "Verra good indeed!"

Then, his eye caught by a movement to the side, Macalister glanced at his patient. *Her lower limbs moved.* There was no doubt. He himself had seen them slide restlessly against each other.

"Oh aye, published indeed," he muttered, wondering if he could induce another twitch, but Anne had calmed herself and now raised her eyes to his. "Lady Anne?" he asked. "Nae then, is it so difficult an admission?" he asked, guessing what she would say.

"They *are* to be published," she managed, "along with text concerning the collection and curing of herbs and simple recipes for their use." The blush grew less hectic. "I fear it is presumptuous of me to do anything of the sort, but the publisher insists my work will be of some little benefit."

"Of great benefit, I should think, then," said Macalister, impressed. "Have you *used* all these different herbs, lass?"

"I will include nothing in my book I've not tested myself or that is not strongly recommended by one of the respected correspondents who have been kind enough to share their work with me."

"Hmm." Macalister repressed a chuckle at the young author's slightly pompous tone. It wasn't that he didn't take her seriously but only her tone, after all, and he didn't wish to discourage her. Instead, he looked at another drawing. "Rue. It is not often used these days."

Anne blushed again and stared at the far corner of the room. "I've found," she mumbled, "that it is efficacious for women who, well, when they feel, hmm, when there is some discomfort when, er, when . . ."

"When," said Macalister firmly, "the bonny dears are being their most womanly." He winked at the maid when Kitty smothered a giggle, both hands over her mouth. "Aye." Mac pulled a chair near and settled his large frame, again studying one and another of the drawings. "This noo. I dinna recognize this," he said and held it out toward his patient.

Soon the two were deep into a technical discussion concerning the proper care and combining of herbs for various illnesses and problems ranging from fever, scraped knees, sore throats, ear aches, broken heads, burns, and the tummy aches acquired from eating green apples or too much rich food.

James's throat tightened, making the taking of a breath difficult and the notion of speaking impossible. This was Anne. This wide-awake, much alive, animated young woman was . . . incredible. It had never once occurred to him she could be so *happy*. As he accepted that her delight had nothing to do with *him*, panic engulfed him. He couldn't even join the widely ranging discussion and encourage it because, as much as he'd always longed for a medical career, his furtive studies hadn't included the humble herb!

Mac enjoyed every word the two exchanged, but he didn't lose sight of his goal, that they make Anne walk again. He gradually rearranged everything around the chaise longue so that he could sit close to it facing his patient. Eventually, with a little luck, perhaps when Anne read to him from her writing as she did now and again, he could reach under the cover over her lower limbs to check those blasted reflexes she said were not there!

Finally Anne turned to one side, searching among her books for a certain volume which expounded a theory contrary to one she believed. While she was occupied, Mac reached under the shawl, but Anne was neatly shod and those tempting toes well out of his reach. He managed to right himself, returning his hands to his coat pockets, before she turned back, but his eyes met James and the two men shared a wry look of understanding.

James gained control over his rampaging emotions as he remembered Macalister was never roused to this degree by interest in a mere *woman*. He reminded himself that the *subject* of the conversation might enthrall his old friend, but it was as *patient* and as an *expert* in her field he'd find Anne worth his time, his conversation and, of course, a good argument.

Pushing aside his jealousy, James was left with a great deal of warm satisfaction that Mac had dropped everything to come help when he'd only been asked for advice! James was disabused of that notion almost immediately he and Mac removed themselves from Anne's presence some little time later and met the butler in the hall.

"Tibbet, has the wagon arrived?" asked Mac, as they followed the butler down the hall.

"Wagon, Dr. Macalister?"

"It has not, then. Take every care when it comes, mon," he ordered and continued up the stairs. "The man with it will tell you what to do."

"What man?" asked James, curious, as they started up the second set of stairs.

The enthusiasm of the scientist on the trail of information lit up Macalister's whole being as he described to James the experiment about which he'd read.

". . . But the machine is aye delicate," he finished, thinking sadly of how many hours must pass before he could actually *try* it on Anne. It occurred to him the scientist would insist on testing it thoroughly, too, which would delay them yet more. He sighed.

"It will hurt her! Mac, I forbid it!"

"Bah. I'll use it on you first and you'll see it is not so," threatened the doctor.

Macalister entered his room already stripping off his coat and shirt. He tossed one after the other toward a chair, each slipping off the far side to land on the floor. Mac poured water into the basin, dipped it up and sluiced it over his face, neck, and down his torso while James picked up the clothes he made all neat, but, knowing from past experience Mac's form of ablutions, he prudently moved both himself and the apparel far away from the splashing.

Macalister groped for the towel and James handed it over, retaining hold of one end. When Mac, having used his part to wipe his face, looked up, James caught his gaze. "Mac, if this is at all dangerous, you must not attempt it. Better that she never walk again then that she be badly burned or even dead!"

Mac stared arrogantly, angered that James would question anything he wished to do, but almost immediately he subsided. James allowed the towel to slip through his fingers and the doctor slowly wiped away the drips running a zig-zag path through the ruddy hairs swirling across his barrel chest and on down toward his trousers.

"I am," he said slowly, "occasionally carried away and a wee bit thoughtless. I sometimes rush ahead into things without full preparation. I admit it. But this . . ." His eyes glowed. "Jimmy-lad, I canna tell you how interesting it is." He thumped the cover of a book lying on the bed table. "You would have to know more than you do, which, for someone who is not a doctor, is a great deal, for me to explain it. I can only tell you it has been done safely with no danger to the patient."

"And was it successful?"

"In one case, yes. Generally? I dinna know. It's not been tried often. Ye ken?"

James's rising hope instantly subsided. "You would say it has not proven consistent. Why do you think, then, in Lady Anne's case, it may be helpful?"

"Because," said Mac instantly, swinging around on his heel, "in *this case* our fine lady *could* walk if only she *believed* she could! She has *moved,* Jimmy-my-lad! Ye dinna ken that would make a difference when you wrote me of it, did ye?"

Mac's triumph was pricked when James shrugged. "You think that the deciding factor? That she believe? And how will you make her believe this will make her walk?"

"She'll believe it a cure because I'll tell her it is and it will then *be* a cure," said Mac arrogantly. He moved to the armoire in which the changes of clothes he'd brought stuffed into saddlebags had been hung.

"I'm not so sure of that."

Mac gave him a rueful grin. "Ye have that right. Lady Anne is unlikely to take my word alone, is she? But she *can* move and that's important."

"Did you actually see movement?" asked James.

"Oh aye. Just a restlessness, one leg rubbing against the other, but movement nae-the-less."

James bit his lip. He eyed his old friend who, after mumbling about the odd habits of butlers, found where his brushes were hidden from him—in plain sight, of course—on a dressing table. He busied himself with pulling them through his wind-tangled locks.

"Mac . . ."

The doctor turned, a brow quirked. He tossed the brushes back over his shoulder. One actually stayed on the dressing table. The other skittered across and onto the floor but, like the clothing earlier, was ignored.

"Mac, she's very important to me."

"Noo why did I ever think differently!"

Mac gave James a wide-eyed innocent look which would fool no one. He grinned again and turned back to the armoire where he pulled down his best coat, decided it was not *too* wrinkled, and pulled it on, grunting a trifle because it was a tighter than his everyday and slightly old-fashioned coats. He glanced around the room, down at his boots which needed dusting and then, that done, back at James.

"I'm ready," he said.

James was startled from his thoughts. "Ready?"

"Dinner, Jimmy-lad," said his friend and tut-tutted, muttering, just loudly enough for James to hear, at how love turned the best of men into blithering idiots.

James straightened. "Dinner!" He turned toward the door. *"You* are ready, but I am *not.* Come along," he added and removed himself to his own room.

His bath awaited him and, although he had little time, James decided to make quick use of it. A long ride had left him in a condition where he didn't much like himself, so he thought it perhaps rude to impose that self in this condition on anyone else! Especially at mealtime. He settled in the steaming water before calling around the screen to Macalister.

"Mac, I may actually have brought Anne to believe Lady P. did *not* have her best interests at heart!" He related his experience with Mrs. Simpson and that lady's attempt to spoil the whole. "But she didn't manage to do so!"

"Do you think so, then? But the wee lass hasn't removed that ugly cap," objected Mac.

James huffed. "Help me convince her to do so, will you?" Silence followed his request for help. His lips pursed, James scrubbed quickly. He knew his friend well enough to realize he was not being ignored, but that Mac had no immediate answer—an ominous answer all in itself. Somehow, some way, Lady Anne Montmorency must be made to accept that she was a perfectly normal human being, with faults, perhaps, but that she was a good woman with beautiful hair. Especially she must be convinced about the hair!

Blast Lady P., anyway, thought James. On occasion his curiosity had led him into odd paths and he'd read until he could stomach no more in the dissenting ministry's writings. Now he swore long, if softly, at the existence of the bleak and cheerless sect which believed *anything* which detracted one's attention from a vengeful God was a sin.

It was from such as they that Lady Preminger had drawn her code of behavior toward Anne. The strictest sect, the one James most disliked, went so far as to believe a parent's love of his children was distraction, especially when such children must be taught, firmly, even viciously if necessary, the behavior which they believed led to salvation in the hereafter!

Had Lady Preminger *truly* believed such harsh concepts or had she adopted them to justify her treatment of Anne? James pondered the question, but pushed it aside as one for which there could be no proof one way or the other, and therefore, no answer. When the silence had gone on too long James got out, dried off, and dressed to the point modesty would not be offended. He stepped around the screen and looked across to where Macalister, sitting in the comfortable armed chair before the fire, brooded.

"Mac?" he asked. "Have you any thoughts on the subject?"

"There is Goodwin. He was raised in the most joyless of families and yet managed to become a sensible man. One might give her his *An Enquiry Concerning the Principles of Political Justice and its Influence on General Virtue and Happiness,* I suppose."

"You are the only person who doesn't call that simply *An Enquiry,*" said James a trifle testily. "But the *Enquiry!* You wish to push Lady Anne into a brain fever on top of having useless limbs and a baseless fear of eternity?"

"Really, Jimmy-lad, do you truly think a little study

would give that one a brain fever? Nonsense. She's a verra bright woman, our little Annie!"

"She is, is she not?" agreed James and looked down to where his valet held an evening pump with a slight heel. "Not those. The soft leather slippers which are more comfortable will do. Lady Anne," he went on, "is a very fine chess player."

"I'd guessed she could play, since the board was in her room. And I suspected she played well, or you'd not have spent verra much time at it, but from something which was said, ye did? Play together quite often, I mean?"

"Daily. She wins almost as often as I do." James didn't try to hide his pride in Anne.

Macalister chuckled and gave a sly look which bordered on a leer but was inoffensive with it. "Aye then, the perfect mate for you!"

"She is, Mac." James turned from where he'd forced his arms into the evening coat held by his valet and spoke as he buttoned modest silver buttons. "I thought her wonderful from the beginning and everything I discover only confirms me in that belief. Help me, Mac . . ."

The doctor sighed. "Jimmy-lad, I'm a medical man, not a miracle worker. I dinna ken *how* to help."

"Well, think about it. . . ."

"Oh aye, I'll think. . . ."

The men stared at each other. Simultaneously they sighed, noticed the coincidence, and the sigh disappeared in chuckles. The moment's humor lightened their respective moods and they were in far better spirits when they removed themselves to the salon where the household met before dinner.

Once again, minutes after reaching the room, Macalister could not have told you how he'd gotten there and certainly could not have found it again by himself. He'd been far too interested in his conversation with James to pay attention!

* * *

Anne, who had previously thought to remain in her room for dinner, decided at the last moment she would not. She was nearly ready to go down before it occurred to her to wonder why she'd changed her mind. Was it because it would be impolite to avoid the doctor's company? She would not like to insult a man who made the long ride out from London merely to check on her suspicion she'd moved in that odd way.

For an instant Anne allowed herself to believe her reason for going down was that innocent. Then, with a wry twist to her lips, she faced the fact that not only would the doctor be at table, but Sir James would as well.

Sir James. Although all her concentration had seemed to be on her conversation with Macalister as they'd discussed their varying opinions about the efficacy of various herbs, a part of her had been aware of James's quiet presence. She'd not understood his early agitation but had been warmed, later, by his pride in her as he listened.

Pride? How strange. Instead of sneering at her for her interest or teasing her or even berating her for presuming to be a minor authority, he'd been *proud*. But, *why* had he felt that way? Why would a man she barely knew—Anne's cheeks heated and her hands flew to cover them—feel pride in her? Could it be because of that odd affection he seemed to bear for her? Might it grow to be more . . . ?

Anne moaned. He *must* not! It would be unfair to him, to her. . . .

Kitty, who was brushing her hair, paused, glanced down at the young woman she very nearly worshiped. "Are ye in pain?" asked the maid anxiously.

"What? Oh. No pain. I mean, my limbs do not ache," she clarified, since, somewhere inside there was another sort of barely definable hurt, one concerned with the impossibility that she'd ever love and be loved.

"But you can't deny it is *something*," persisted Kitty.

Anne didn't respond.

"So, if not your limbs," the maid asked, "then what?"

Anne sighed. "Kitty, I am not always as accepting as I should be of my situation. Occasionally I feel sorry for myself."

"And why would you not? It's a terrible thing you cannot walk, and unfair and . . ."

"No!" interrupted Anne. "You don't understand," she said sternly.

"I don't? Then explain to me, please," requested Kitty, her hands moving the brush rhythmically through Anne's beautiful hair which, much to her disgust, she'd soon be asked to cover with one of Anne's ugly caps.

Anne relaxed under the steady brushing. If Kitty were to stay with her, were to someday even take over the management of her home as housekeeper, then Kitty should know the truth. "I believe I must take extra care to never do anything which would endanger my soul." Anne explained in detail the condition of the human soul. "You see, I am exceedingly prone to sin."

"Nonsense."

Anne's cheeks turned a deep rose and she jerked her hair from the maid's hands. She twisted around. "Kitty!" she said, "You must *not.*"

"Must not tell you nonsense is nonsense?" asked Kitty as she gently turned Anne back and began braiding Anne's hair.

"But Kitty . . . !"

Angry, Kitty forgot her place and scolded, "I dunno who tole you such silly dangerous lies, but must a bin an ignorant foolish bit who never been loved and didn't want anyone else to be loved either."

"Kitty . . ."

"You put such foolishness out of your head, my lady," said Kitty and, reluctantly, but without being asked, she settled Anne's cap over her hair.

"Kitty . . ." This time Anne's voice held a touch of anguish.

"Shush, now. I don't want to hear you ever say such an evil thing again. Not loved? Not lovable? Poppycock!"

"You don't know . . ."

"*I* love you. Sir James loves you. And I know my family's reverend would say shame to anyone who says God's love would let you do without!"

"Your reverend . . ." Anne turned to stare at her maid.

"Hmm. A very good man. Some have called him a saint. Next time I'm home I'll ask him to write down some texts from the Bible and you can read for yourself. . . ."

"Read for myself . . . ?" interrupted Anne.

"You never read the bible?" asked Kitty, shocked.

"I was told it wasn't for the likes of me. . . ."

"Someone truly hated you, dinnit they?" asked Kitty, wonderingly.

"Hated me . . ."

Anne sat, hands folded, staring blankly at the mirror in which she was reflected, but it was a reflection she did not see. Instead her mind traveled back over the years of her adolescence, counted up times her guardian had been overly stern and had punished her with excessive harshness. All too often Anne had not understood why she should be punished at all.

Could that awful Mrs. Simpson be correct? Had Lady Preminger actually hated her mother so much she wished harm to a child? Was Sir James's guess correct? Had Lady Preminger been jealous? Had the stern woman merely wished to ruin Anne's life rather than save the child's soul? Did she dare hope . . . ?

"Kitty," said Anne impatiently and urgently caught and held her maid's reflected gaze, "I would very much like to read a bible. . . . Have you one?"

"I surely do and you're welcome to it, but not right now this moment, my lady," said the maid, casting an exasperated look toward the hall door, "I hear the footmen coming to carry you down! And, what with all this driveling on we've been doin'," she added in a disgusted tone, "I haven't quite finished dressing you!"

Nine

With guilty pleasure Lady Anne saw that Sir James was watching for her entrance. It was yet more gratifying that he came immediately to her side when the footmen carried her in and led the way to where he'd placed a chair near the fire, a petit point covered stool ready to receive her feet. She smiled shyly when he smiled at her and then, guilt fighting the hope Kitty's words had roused, she colored and looked at her fingers.

Lady Jaycee joined them then, using Anne's arrival as an excuse to avoid any more of Lady Fuster-Smythe's ongoing lecture concerning the dangers of allowing Lord Runyon within miles of her. "Are you feeling more the thing, Lady Anne?" she asked, not quite knowing what to say, but feeling it not quite right to avoid any mention at all of Anne's condition.

"I have, I think, made an adequate adjustment to my situation," said Anne.

Once again there was no emotion in her voice when she spoke of her inability to move. There was not even the resignation one might have expected from such a comment. Sir James looked at Mac who frowned.

"Nae then! Why should you adjust?" asked the doctor before James could make his own objection to her seeming acceptance. "Why do you nae swear and cuss—or if that is not your way, then cry and scream and demand something be done to relieve the situation?"

"Especially when you are able to move. When it is only a question of your not moving?" added James and discovered the doctor's frown was now turned his direction.

"But is it *true? Can* I move?" asked Anne quickly, looking from one to the other. "I have never been certain it is so."

"Ach," said Mac, irritated. He'd not determined the best way to approach her about the Galvanism procedure and was not quite ready for this discussion. He looked at James who stared expectantly and sighed. "You may not be sure, Lady Anne, but you do move."

"I . . . ?" she began. When he nodded her eyes widened painfully. "You truly *know?* You have *seen,* perhaps . . . ?"

"Oh, aye. It happens, I conclude, when you are not trying—when ye have the whole of your wee mind putting itself to the business of thinking of something else, ye ken?"

Relief swept through Anne, leaving a lightness in her head. *She could move.* "My mind is not, I am to understand, large enough to think of two things at once?" An elusive smile tipped the corners of her mouth.

Mac started up. "Nae, then, I dinna say that! How you take one up, my lady," he scolded. When Anne chuckled softly, he heaved an exaggerated sigh of relief and grinned. "Ach, then." He mopped his forehead. "It was a jest, I see. Verra good, my lady. I am glad. My Scottish manner of speaking is all too often taken amiss. I am glad it is nae the case here!"

Sir James decided he'd been left from the discussion quite long enough. "There is nothing at all wrong with your mind, Lady Anne. Mac and I were discussing your ability at the chess board less than an hour ago. We think you a very bright woman."

"For a woman, of course," responded Anne quickly, the little smile returning. She looked from one man to the other and gave a tiny sideways glance to Jaycee to see if she was listening and what she thought of their banter. Jaycee obviously didn't think it a bit odd. Relieved she was not doing something for which she'd be censured, Anne brought her mind back to the conversation. "It is well known women are creatures of small account."

"Nae then!" sputtered Mac.

Sir James, too, immediately denied any such thing. "Are you not an author?" he asked to clinch the matter. "A writer must have a great deal of intelligence."

"But then it is still worse." She glanced from one to the other. "What you mean to say is that I am unwomanly and *blue.*"

"You will instantly stop putting words in my mouth, Lady Anne! I like you just the way you are. Don't, I pray, pretend you are something you are not—something one sees far too often among the buds opening upon the social scene each spring."

Anne tipped her head, a querying look in her expression.

"The young women attempt to make of themselves what they are taught is man's ideal. Fearing to put a foot wrong, they become impossibly insipid. Any one of them might be interchanged for another, and no one know the difference." James reached for Anne's hand, caught her gaze and held it. "Now that I've found a woman who affects no pretense at all, please don't change her!"

Heat flooded Anne's cheeks and she felt a sense of pure relief that, at that moment, Tibbet announced dinner. In the general upheaval resulting from the move to the dining room, she'd not be required to respond to such blatant admiration. But, however deeply embarrassed she was, it didn't destroy the pleasure she felt when Sir James lifted her into his arms.

Lady Fuster-Smythe, aided by her footmen, led the way and Jaycee followed on Mac's arm. Anne fussed with the drape of her skirt and, when that was found to be properly demure, worried her cap might have slipped. Checking that

it had not took the time needed for James to reach her seat
at the table and, by then, it was no longer necessary to find
reasons for not responding to Sir James's alarming comment, nor to the warmth in his expression!

The moment had passed and Anne, unsure of her whole,
suddenly alarming, world, had to be glad. She could not
deal with Sir James's courtship, assuming that was what it
was, when she was concerned with her inability to walk.
Even more important, Lady Anne could not think of something so wonderful as the possibility she might actually be
loved when she wondered if such a glorious thing would
or *should* be permitted. Kitty insisted her fears were nonsense and *everyone* told her Lady Prem had had vicious
and selfish reasons for forcing Anne's beliefs. . . . But
enough of that.

Nor would she think of Sir James's exceedingly interesting comment. She couldn't. Daren't. Life was much too
confusing already to add Sir James's possible feelings—to
say nothing of her own—to the bubbling pot!

Instead, she'd ask if something might be done for her
problem now it was proved she could move. She did and
looked from Sir James to the doctor and back again when
it seemed to her sensitive soul that Macalister somehow
withdrew just when she most wished him to be open with
her.

"Is there not some means of making me walk again?"
she repeated when James looked toward the doctor and neither man spoke immediately.

Mac sighed. "I had thought, lass, we might discuss the
procedure which has come to my attention tomorrow when
you were rested. But I see it cannot be put off." He nodded
impatiently to a footman who was offering to ladle an aro-
matic broth into his bowl, but then he ignored the steaming
soup, putting his elbows to either side of it and leaning his
chin on his clasped hands as he stared with intensity at his
patient. "You see, lass, it's like this. The patient is laid upon

a very odd sort of table with glass legs. Then a silly looking machine is hooked up. The operator holds a wand which he touches to the exact spot which is not functioning properly. Energy moves from the machine to the body and makes it move. Ye see?"

"The machine makes energy? How can that be?"

"Now dinna worry your head about *that* wee problem," said Mac.

"What should I worry my head about?"

Mac looked at James who scowled back. Mac sighed. "Not a thing. The machine will make you walk again."

"And when they take the machine away, will I still be able to walk?"

"Of course ye will, lass. The young man in Switzerland did!"

But there was the faintest hint of bluster in his tone. Mac was not the best in the world when it came to telling taradiddles and it showed. Anne sighed and spooned up a taste of her broth. One taste and she laid her spoon back down. It seemed that just perhaps it might be possible that maybe, if she were lucky, Mr. Macalister's remedy would result in a cure! But then again, if she read him rightly, perhaps it would not.

"Tell her more about the Swiss," suggested James as he too laid down his spoon, his broth half finished.

Macalister gave an enthusiastic lecture on the cure which had so excited him when he'd first read about it. He ended by saying, "You see, lass, the cases are similar. Verra similar. We will do exactly as was done before, and you, too, will soon be back on your feet!"

The doctor nodded impatiently when the footman, hesitantly, reached to take away his untouched soup. Anne's soup, too, looked untouched. James's bowl was partly empty, but far more remained than the Montmorency cook would approve. Since Jaycee rarely ate more than a very small portion of anything, only Lady Fuster-Smythe appeared to have enjoyed it!

"It may take days—a few weeks, even," added Mac with a movement of his hand. "One does not undo major damage in only an instant."

"But you *will* walk," agreed James earnestly, holding Anne's gaze with all the power of his mind, body, and soul. She would walk. She *must*.

"By good Saint Valentine's Day at the very latest," interrupted Jaycee, nodding to the footman who waited patiently at her elbow with a serving tray. "I'm holding a ball on Saint Valentine's Day," she added with a sly look toward her brother. "You truly must be walking by then, Anne. It's important."

"I do not dance, Jaycee," said Anne. "My walking isn't important."

"Oh, but it is," said Jaycee with more earnestness than was usual. "You see, Anne, I intend . . ."

"You intend to introduce Anne to all your friends, is that not it?" inserted James before Jaycee could say something he'd regret. Something about announcing a betrothal which did not exist! Yet. Jaycee simply would, or perhaps *could,* not understand the delicacy of Anne's position. Not only was she paralyzed, but there was still all those wrongheaded notions Lady P. had beaten into her. Literally beaten into her, he now knew, since Anne's calm mention of a willow switch.

That memory caused James's appetite to disappear. The fish he'd been about to place in his mouth was returned untasted to his plate. He laid aside his knife and fork and turned his attention to his pouting sister. "Do not worry, Jaycee. I'm quite certain Anne will walk by Saint Valentine's Day. Perhaps we can even teach her one or two dances," he added, casting a merry look toward Anne. He didn't feel at all like laughing, but it was, he guessed, important for the cure that Anne be in the best of moods.

"And this all important cure," inserted Lady Fuster-Smythe, after she'd finished her steamed trout with finely cut root vegetables, "will you attempt it here at Montmorency Park or will we remove to London for the experiment?"

"Oh, here, of course," said Mac. He too laid aside his utensils and made a funny tale of his argument with the owner of the necessary equipment. "It should arrive tomorrow at the latest. Mr. Ryder will wish a day or two to test it and see there has been no damage, of course. We shall begin, I think, day after next." He reached for his knife and fork, but, at a thought, again laid them down. "That is, o'course, if you approve, lass?"

"Did you," Lady Anne asked slowly, "bring the essay which led to your wishing to try this?"

"Aye." There was a pause and Mac added, "You wish to read it."

It wasn't a question, but Anne said that, indeed, she did wish to read it.

"I dinna know if you will understand the technical bits. . . ."

"I doubt very much I'll understand the technical bits, but I would know more of what is to be done to me, even if the details do not make sense."

"And when ye have read the essay?"

"Then I will decide if we should proceed."

Mac sighed. "And I thought it merely a question of bringing the silly machine here and using it. Will we have an argument, lass?"

"Of course you will have to argue," said Lady Fuster-Smythe tartly, wishing everyone would shut up and eat their food, so the next course could be served. "But *not* at the dinner table, if you please!"

Jaycee, noticing that at least three of her guests were not eating properly, giggled. "Oh, yes, please. Do you have the least notion what Cook will say when so much food is returned to her kitchen? Tibbet, do go immediately and explain that it is *not* the fault of the food? You will know what to say whereas I have never been good at dealing with Cook's tantrums."

Jaycee sent a coaxing look toward her butler. Tibbet nodded and, with stately tread, removed himself from the dining room after only one warning look toward the first footman who was in charge in his absence.

The rest of the meal avoided all talk of medical problems, skirted discussion of Jaycee's ball, and managed to involve no controversy which would again lead one or another around the table to decline the offered edibles!

Later that evening, after she'd more than once been on the receiving end of one of Sir James's very special looks, Anne returned to her room. She reviewed her day as Kitty prepared her for bed and, once she was settled, Anne wrote a long letter to Kitty's reverend which Kitty agreed she'd deliver on her next half day.

Perhaps there was true hope? Perhaps her aunt's way was not the *only* way?

Perhaps?

It took Lady Anne several days to skim Charles Hunnings Wilkinson's *The Elements of Galvanism,* a two-volume work reporting the surgeon's experience in various applications of the differing techniques. She had taken one look at the article which aroused Mr. Macalister's enthusiasm and agreed that not only was the technical discussion beyond her, there was so little general discussion she understood no more than before. The doctor had promptly sent one of Jaycee's grooms into London with a letter to a friend. The servant had returned with Wilkinson's work which included instructive discussion of the various techniques. Only a portion of the work was relevant to Lady Anne's case, but she found the subject so intriguing she'd been unable to put the volumes aside.

Sir James read right along with her and they'd had a grand time arguing the various uses Wilkinson had listed. Anne was convinced that certain types of mental derangement might be helped by the doctor's treatment where Sir James feared *more* damage might be done. Nor did Sir James like the use of Galvanism in the case of headaches. In fact, in any case except the toothache, Sir James had an aversion to placing the wands near the brain!

"But that is not relevant in your case, Anne," he said, as he carried her to the room near the kitchens which had been given over to the young man and his Galvanism equipment. "You'll see. Mr. Ryder has finished testing everything and the machines are not at all frightening. We'll soon have you walking again. I'm convinced of it."

"I hope so."

But Anne frowned slightly, her flying eyebrows giving her a rather devilish look. She said no more, but she herself had not been convinced by what she read. As Mac had once told James the results were uncertain, unreliable, inconsistent, often unrepeatable, and occasionally had actually worsened a condition!

Voices could be heard as they turned into the hall leading to what had been a nearly empty storage room. Very soon they could distinguish Lady Fuster-Smythe's voice asking, "But why does that do that?"

A tired young male voice responded, "My lady, I do not know. No one knows. We call it electricity. It is a name. The fluids moistening the piles cause something to happen, in the same way the old Leyden jars caused something to happen."

"Electricity. But you said it was Galvanism! How can it be both?"

"Galvanism is a term limited to what happens when you apply electricity to a living preparation."

"Preparation?" Lady Fuster-Smythe's voice sharpened. "And just *how* do you prepare the living creature?"

"It depends on the creature and the purpose of the experiment." The voice was becoming choppier, more brittle. "My lady, I have work to do. I cannot answer all your questions."

"One more," insisted Lady Fuster-Smythe in her most autocratic voice. "Will Lady Anne be subjected to any *preparations* which would be counter to her modesty?"

Sir James arrived in the doorway just then. He saw Mr. Ryder straighten from where he'd been leaning over a Voltaic Pile and stare at Lady Fuster-Smythe. "Modesty?"

Her ladyship grimaced. "Surely you know the word? Propriety, if you will. I must be assured the procedure will not offend against propriety."

"Would it not be simpler, Lady Fuster-Smythe," asked James in a silky tone, "for you to sit yourself in the corner during Lady Anne's treatments and supervise that little problem at the time, rather than harass poor Mr. Ryder when he very likely cannot answer, not knowing just when and how you feel propriety might be offended?"

"Modesty seems rather unimportant," added Anne, "when one thinks that without the treatment I may never walk again."

Lady Fuster-Smythe bridled. "Modesty and propriety are never unimportant. And I will certainly chaperone your treatments. Why does that table have glass legs? Surely they are not sturdy enough that one might actually dare to use the table?"

"They are perfectly sturdy," growled Mr. Ryder. "The patient must lie on such a table. A normal table will not work."

"Nonsense. Glass breaks."

Sir James moved to the table in question and sat Lady Anne on the edge. He took one hand, saw she was balanced and backed away. "See, my lady? The table is certainly strong enough to hold a wee wren such as our Lady Anne. She's no weight at all. Now if we were to treat *you,* Lady Fussy-Puss . . . !"

His eyes twinkled and, as he'd hoped, Lady Fuster-Smythe stalked from the room, not even waiting for her footman to help her, the poor man having to hurry to catch her up and offer his arm.

"And now, Mr. Ryder," he said once her ladyship was beyond hearing, "I fear there are still more questions to be asked. Lady Anne wishes to see the equipment about which she has been reading. Is there, for instance a clockwork contact breaker such as Cuthbertson invented, or will the practitioner control the timing?"

"In this procedure, the operator causes a contraction in the particular muscle and waits for it to relax and then touches it again. In muscle contraction you don't need a clockwork breaker because you aren't wishing for repeated contacts. Sprenger of Jena invented a breaker that would cause the circuit to be made and broken every second. That sort of treatment takes maybe four minutes, five at most. Something nearer fifteen minutes, twice a day, is recommended for our work here, but you time it by how fast or slow the muscle works," the young man finished a trifle pedantically.

"Will you use a Voltaic Pile or a Leyden Jar or a Galvanic Trough to supply the energy?" asked Anne.

The young man gave her a look of astonished respect. "We'll use the pile, my lady," he said. "You see I've assembled the column here. This one is constructed from a dozen plates, zinc and silver discs, separated by pasteboard soaked in saltwater, such as Anthony Carlisle used."

"Hmm. And that is the wand with which Mr. Macalister will touch me?"

"Yes, my lady. You'll see here in the middle a handle by which it will be held. That way—" Ryder made a rather heavy-handed joke. "—the operator needn't worry he'll get the treatment instead of the patient, you see?"

"I see. What is in that small box?"

"Ah. Now that's most important," said the man who enjoyed showing off his expertise to pretty Lady Anne as he had *not* enjoyed old Lady Fuster-Smythe's inquisition. He opened the box and brought it nearer. "Here you'll see real gold. It's been pounded thin as thin can be. Each little circle will be moistened and stuck on the skin where you are to be touched. The electricity comes from the battery through the wand and into the muscle through the gold. When we've done the treatment, your maid can rub the affected area with this flesh brush which will restore the blood to the area. You see, my lady, we've thought of everything to make your ordeal as comfortable as it may be."

Anne's lips compressed. She feared it would all be excessively *uncomfortable,* but said nothing. If there was a chance, and her reading suggested there was, that she would walk again, then she must accept whatever discomfort might result in the process. And, if no other good occurred, Wilkinson had been clear in his belief that the treatment counteracted the usual wasting process that happened in cases of paralysis. Anne had no desire to be like her patient who had finally begun to walk again, but had had to gradually build up new muscle because the old had deteriorated! If nothing else, the treatment would insure against that.

"When will we be ready for the first treatment?" she asked.

"I'll have this lot ready in another hour or two. I want to test every thing once more before we try it on *you,* my lady," he said, grinning as if that were a great joke.

"Are you ready to go?" James asked and she nodded. "Perhaps," he suggested, "a game of chess would take your mind from what is to come?"

"I think not. Sir James, would you take me to the music room? I believe I'm finally ready to try that piano. If, that is, you can find some very simple studies with which I may begin again?"

James hid his surprise at the request. "An excellent notion." Why, now of all times, had she decided to return to her music? Had she recalled how much she'd loved it? Would she discover her talent lost after so many years? James decided he'd stay near just in case she found the work too frustrating.

"If you'll have Kitty bring me my bell, I'd prefer to be alone while I try to recall some of what I used to know. I'll ring the bell when I'm finished or when I decide it is hopeless!"

"In that case, I'll await the sound in the room across from the music room."

"That is not necessary, Sir James. A footman will respond."

"It may not be necessary to you, my wee wren. It is, however, very necessary to me."

Anne bit her lip. "Very well," she said in a slightly strangled voice.

"But you wish I would not admit such need?" he asked, keeping his tone light and nonthreatening.

"I cannot think it proper nor can I understand why. . . ."

"Why? But that is obvious, my little bird. You are everything I ever wished in a woman. I don't expect you to feel the same about me, but that won't change what I feel for you." He smiled. "Anne, you mustn't worry your head about it. When you can walk again, then I'll woo you, but I promise I'll not bother you until you are capable of flying away whenever you will!"

"I am not a bird."

He chuckled. "My wee brown wren. When you finally realize you should not wear that ugly cap, but should show that magnificent hair to the world, I'll not be able to call you a wren. Then, perhaps, I'll call you . . . hmm. Now what bird has a wonderfully russet-colored crop of feathers?"

"The pheasant. I do not believe I'd find it the least amusing to be likened to a pheasant!"

James threw back his head and laughed loudly. "A partridge, perhaps?" he asked when he could speak. "But you are not plump enough, Anne. I'll have to think about it. I believe there is a red headed bird in North America. A striking bird it is, too, but not, perhaps, just in your style. Here we are," he added as he approached the music room door.

Some fifteen minutes later Kitty had brought the required bell, Sir James had retrieved the Wilkinson's volume he'd been studying, and Anne was, tentatively, rediscovering her long-lost music.

It would be time enough to think again of her treatment when Dr. Macalister arrived. He wished to oversee their first effort, she knew, but he had gone into London early that morning saying, testily, he didn't have a notion when he'd be free to return. Anne hoped it wouldn't be too long. She feared her concentration on her playing would not be strong enough to prevent her nerves getting out of hand!

Ten

"Lord Runyon," intoned Tibbet. He turned on his heel, leaving Jaycee's guest standing just inside the salon door, hat in hand.

"Oh!" Jaycee stopped in mid-pace, put her foot down and turned. "You're here, Lord Runyon?"

"Only briefly."

Runyon had attempted to hand over his hat, cane, and gloves, but the butler must have had something in his eye. Tibbet had blinked rapidly and said, "I'll announce you," without reaching for the items. Since he was holding them, Runyon was obligated, by polite usage, to stay only minutes.

The worst of it was that Jaycee didn't appear to care. Inwardly, Runyon fumed. Every time he'd concluded he was making headway with the lady, some contrary wind would blow up and turn her in another direction. She was the most vacillating child, her interest caught one moment by this and then, an instant later, by that. He'd never had such a time with a woman.

"I came," he said, once he'd controlled his volatile temper, "to see if we'd be riding this afternoon." As an explanation for his presence, it was a trifle lame, but he could think of nothing else to say. Holding the blasted hat truly limited one and left one very much at a disadvantage. "I am looking forward to it," he added, using the insinuating tone some women reacted to with giggles and the more sophisticated with equally meaningful looks.

Jaycee did neither. She merely looked blank. "Ride?" Her features took on a look of enlightenment. "Ride! Oh, no. The . . . the weather is too blustery for me. I'm sorry." Jaycee turned away.

"Are you?" he asked softly, approaching.

She looked around, obviously startled. "Am I . . . ?"

"Sorry." Runyon still spoke softly allowing none of his growing irritation to show.

"Sorry? Why should I not be sorry? Of course I am. You don't know how awful it is."

"Awful?" To what did she refer? Their ride? The weather? The chit didn't make sense. Or perhaps . . . ! "What is awful? Have you news your erring husband returns?"

"My husband?" Jaycee stared at her guest. "You've had word he's left Vienna?" she asked.

Had there been a touch of eagerness in that question? Runyon eyed his prey. She blew hot and then cold and just now he'd felt a truly frigid breeze down the back of his neck. But at least her distraction wasn't due to word from her husband.

"I can think of nothing more awful," said his lordship, returning to his careful pose of intense interest which he'd perfected long ago.

Jaycee sighed. "I've heard nothing from Martin."

Was there the faintest of wistful notes in her voice? Runyon very nearly gnashed his teeth. His careful plans for seduction were making no headway at all. But why not? Had she a friend in Vienna who wrote to contradict his false news?

"If it is not your husband," he said, "your concerns can be nothing of great consequence. And it is not so very blustery, after all. Exercise will keep us warm."

"Exercise? Oh. The ride. No, I think not. I've much too much on my mind just now. Oh, the worry of it all!"

She still made no sense. . . . Perhaps, she'd overspent her allowance, and become apprehensive at what her husband would say. If so, Runyon desired to know nothing about it. He was never well up in funds but, even so, had, on occasion, found it necessary to dig into his slender resources to aid a woman. Right now that would be impossible so he'd best ignore the chit's turmoil—although his curiosity was making up solutions with every breath!

With effort Lord Runyon controlled himself. "Tomorrow perhaps?"

"Tomorrow?" Jaycee gave him another blank look.

Runyon managed to keep his hands from her neck, but only barely. How did Montmorency put up with her skitter-witted idiocy! Almost, Runyon felt sorry for his enemy.

Embarrassed, Jaycee said, "Our ride! I do not know, do I?"

"I'll come by and see if you would find it amusing," said Runyon through clenched teeth. "I must go now."

"Very well. I do apologize for my abstraction, but it is all very unpleasant and I am a trifle upset."

She held out her hand and Runyon tipped it over, putting a kiss in her palm. Runyon's anger faded into satisfaction when she closed her fingers over the kiss. To hide his triumph, he quickly turned and left the room. As usual, he was seen off the premises by the footman hovering outside the door.

Lord Runyon would have been far less pleased had he turned back for a moment because Jaycee opened her hand, spreading wide the fingers, and rubbed it, hard, against the side of her gown. Opening her reticule, she pulled out a handkerchief and scrubbed her palm, again, with that. For the first time since she'd begun her dangerous game with Runyon, Lady Montmorency felt thoroughly disgusted. *Oh, why,* she thought, *does not Martin come home?*

While Jaycee paced her salon and chewed the end of one dainty finger, worried about what electricity might do to her husband's house—to say nothing of her husband's sister—Lady Fuster-Smythe sat in her special chair in a corner of the converted storeroom and watched, eagle-eyed, as Lady Anne was laid on the table. She stiffened when a sheet was placed over the young woman. And she actually struggled to her feet all by herself when Dr. Macalister lifted the bottom end of the sheet and hooked it to hooks hanging from the ceiling.

"What are you doing? What has that to do with the treatment?"

"I prepare my patient, Lady Fussy-Pussy."

"And what has that sheet to do with it?" she asked, suspicious.

"It is better that Lady Anne not be aware of exactly when the instrument is touched to a muscle. The sheet prevents her watching the procedure. And," he added sternly, "at the slightest interference from you, you'll leave this room. Do ye understand me, my fussy friend?"

"I'll have no lurid goings on!"

Macalister rolled his eyes and grimaced. "Lady Fussy-Pussy, I must be able to reach the appropriate muscles."

"So?"

Sir James stepped forward. "So he must be able to *see* them, Lady Fussy-Puss. Sit down now, do," he coaxed. "I must stay on the other side of the sheet, for modesty's sake, but, if you behave, you can watch and see that nothing beyond what is necessary is done to Lady Anne."

"I'll not have that man touching her!" Lady Fuster-Smythe raised one arm and pointed an arthritic finger at Dr. Macalister.

Macalister heaved a great sigh and rolled his eyes. "Her maid will do the actual touching once I've shown her exactly where to place the bits of gold and taught her how to do it correctly. Once I have trained the girl, she will do the work and I will merely observe."

"But you'll be looking at the chit's legs," said the horrified Lady Fuster-Smythe. "It ain't right."

"Nae, then," soothed Mac. "It is perfectly all right for a

octor. It would nae be proper for Jimmy-lad here which s why he'll stay on that side of the sheet." Macalister eered around the edge and saw that James, hidden from ady Fuster-Smythe's view, had collected Anne's hand in oth of his and held it closely. The doctor frowned, caught is friend's eye and shook his head.

James looked down at his hands holding Anne's and back o Mac. His brows arced. "No?" he mouthed very nearly ilently.

Macalister looked around the room and discovered a stool nade like the table. It too was furnished with heavy glass egs. He hooked it toward James. "You too, might as well et your feet off the floor, Jimmy-lad."

James realized he could not hold Anne's hand and keep ontact with the floor if he were not to endanger her. He arefully contorted himself so that he was seated on the tool with no part of him touching his surrounds. He cocked is head as he reached for Anne's hand. Macalister nodded nd ducked back around the sheet.

"Oh, aye, then," he said, turning to Lady Fuster-Smythe. 'That Jimmy-lad have my view, that *would* be wrong, I loubt it not. But," he repeated sternly, "it is a far different hing when it is a doctor, my lady."

"I do not know what to permit," she said crossly, but she lumped back in her chair, defeated.

"May we simply get on with it?" asked Lady Anne. "I'm a trifle nervous and would prefer to discuss the moral and ethical aspects of my treatment once it is over."

James chuckled softly. "My sensible henny-penny," he whispered. He caught her gaze with his own. "Do you think 'd allow Mac to do anything which would harm you?"

"But . . ." She bit her lip and looked away.

"But you are not so stupid as to accept a story cut from whole cloth as I did that one!" Anne's mouth smiled but ner eyes remained solemn. "You are correct," he said. "I cannot guarantee that absolutely nothing will go wrong. But it is very unlikely, you know."

"Yes. I do know. Which is why I've agreed. But I do not like pain and however careful the doctor is, there is likely to be pain, is there not?"

Macalister, listening from beyond the makeshift screen, answered that. "We cannot predict whether you will feel our work, Lady Anne. It is possible that the paralysis will prevent you from feeling any of it."

Anne smiled and seemed to relax. "I had not thought of that. I never feel it when you pinch my poor toe, do I? So it is unlikely I'll feel this. Lady Fuster-Smythe, I know the procedure appears scandalous, but with you here to chaperone my treatment, I've no fear that anyone who hears of it will think it the least odd. They will trust that you have seen to that."

"Very true." Her ladyship returned to her usual rigid posture. "Why didn't I think of that? My credit with the ton is such that they cannot possibly think nasty thoughts when it is known *I* remain at your side."

"The only thing wrong with that," said Sir James softly to Anne, "is that while she is *here,* my sister is *not* and heaven only knows what mischief she'll get up to!"

Anne tugged at the hand he held. "I, too, fear dear Jaycee may succumb to boredom and do some rash thing which she'll regret."

Jame's hand firmed around Anne's. "If she does, then so be it. I'll not leave you to face this alone."

"There, now." Macalister's voice interrupted their soft-voiced conversation, his words directed toward Kitty: "If you move that bit of foil just a fraction higher, yes, like that," he said to Kitty. "And the next one . . . yes, you have the idea, do you not?"

The maid, red-faced that a man was observing her mistress's limbs well up above her knees, had caught her tongue between her teeth and concentrated on doing exactly as she was told.

"Now then," Mac said a bit later, "we mark those spots with this ink so you can put the bits of gold back in the exact same place each time. Yes. Like that . . . Lady Fuster-Smythe? Did you note how the maid moistened each circle before placing it just so? I expect *you*," he said sternly, "to see she does it exactly the same way later today and then twice each day until the treatment is ended."

Lady Fuster-Smythe sat up still straighter, a relieved expression relaxing her rigid disapproving features. "You mean to say you'll not be here beyond this morning?"

"I'll return to check on our Annie's progress whenever I can, but I need not observe each and every occasion."

"Well. You might have told me that. I feel much better about the whole thing."

"I wish I did. Please get on with it," said Anne, raising a despairing gaze to James who tightened his grip on her hand.

"Now . . . Kitty, you are to take this wand. Yes. Like that. When Mr. Ryder nods from over there at his table in the corner, you touch the end to the first circle. Yes. That one. Only briefly. The more quickly the better, lass. Yes. Just like that. A moment now. . . . Go on to the next . . . and the next . . . and the next. Hmm. Very good, lass. You have the makings of an excellent researcher, does she not, Mr. Ryder? Verra delicate you are with the wand, my child. Verra delicate indeed." The doctor peeked around the sheet. "And, you, Lady Anne? How do you do?"

"Is it working?"

"It is working just fine, lass."

"But I don't feel it. A faint jerk, now and again, but that is all."

"The muscles contract, ye see. And that pulls the rest of your body a wee bit. It is good that they are forced to work themselves. Yes, Kitty," he interrupted himself to say, "you begin with the other limb now. Slowly! Give the muscle time to relax before you go on to the next spot."

When Kitty finished with the second leg she was told to go back to the first. And so it went for what seemed like an hour to Lady Anne, but could have been no more than twenty minutes from the time Kitty placed the first circle until she carefully removed the last and put it in the small box in which they were kept. Anne's skirts were pulled down and propriety satisfied. The sheet was unhooked and removed. It was over.

With the sheet down Lady Fuster-Smythe could see the whole room. She frown. "Sir James, what are you doing with Lady Anne's hand?"

"I've been holding it, my lady Fussy Puss. Do you object?"

"I *object*," said her ladyship, "to the fact that you hold it *still*."

James looked down to where Anne's hand was clasped between his own. His gaze moved to meet Anne's. Her lips compressed slightly, but couldn't hold back a smile. He grinned, his eyebrows arching. "So I am. Now why, I wonder, did I not notice?"

"Hurumph!"

"Now Lady Fussy-Puss, that isn't a nice noise at all!"

"Have you," said her ladyship, her voice sarcastic in tone, "now noticed you still hold Lady Anne's hand?"

"I believe I do."

"You will release it at once," ordered Lady Fuster-Smythe.

"I will?"

"James Collingwood, don't you try that sham innocence on *me*. Let go of Lady Anne's hand. Now."

"But of course." James did so but only to move to the side of the table and scoop Anne up into his arms. "Come along Kitty. After her ordeal, I think Lady Anne should rest. You will come and prepare her for a nap."

"And if I do not wish to nap?" asked Anne, crossly.

"Then you will read or write letters or something of that sort. Something quiet."

"I would prefer to go to the Green Salon and work on my book."

"I will come for you when the lady's luncheon is served and, once you've eaten, you may work on your book."

"Sir James, you are a tyrant."

"Lady Anne, you are more tired than you think. Is she not, Mac?"

"If the lass is not, then it's a remarkable constitution she has," said Mac, looking up from the notebook in which he recorded the day's session. He hoped to coax Lady Fuster-Smythe into keeping his journal. Whatever else might said about the old woman, she was observant, and her handwriting was impeccable—far better than his own, actually. And, besides, if she could be cajoled into taking a part, then she'd be less likely, in future, to argue against the procedure. "Did you say something, Lady Anne?" asked the doctor, coming out of his fog.

"Lady Anne wishes to know if she can expect any immediate improvement."

"Immediate improvement? Unlikely, lass," said Macalister getting up and coming over to where James stood with Anne in his arms. "It takes time, ye ken?"

Anne sighed. "I know. I only hoped there might be an instant change. And now that I've relaxed some, I freely admit I am more tired than I thought. Please take me to my room, Sir James."

Followed by Kitty, he did just that and then returned to the hall. He stopped on the bottom step when Tibbet approached him. "Yes, Tibbet?"

"That Lord Runyon were here again."

"While we were well occupied? He times his visits well, does he not?" James's gaze jumped to the butler's startled expression. "Tibbet?"

"I just wondered if perhaps his lordship has suborned a servant to take him news of such opportunities?"

"I'll leave it to you to check. Now, tell me what the cur talked my idiot sister into."

"Oh, no, Sir James. Lady Montmorency was rather preoccupied and not at all welcoming. His lordship did not stay long at all."

"Perhaps he invited her to ride with him or something of that nature."

"He did so, indeed. . . . I believe, however, that Lady Montmorency feels it too blustery. They, er, will not ride."

"Tomorrow?"

"I cannot say."

Sir James eyed the butler for a moment as that starched-up figure stared into the middle distance, his face expressionless. "I see. You overheard the first but no more. Thank you, Tibbet. I would appreciate any other news you might happen to hear—just in passing, of course."

He slipped the butler a coin which, much to Tibbet's surprise, was a guinea rather than the shilling he'd expected.

Macalister strolled into the hall just then. "Ah, Jimmy-lad. It went well, did it not?"

"Well? I had hoped Anne would be able to walk after her treatment, but that did not happen."

"Verra doubtful that it would. Do not despair, my friend."

"No. And even if she never walks again, she will still be the woman with whom I fell in love."

"Oh, aye. It *is* love, then?"

His face red, James looked quickly around the hall. Luckily Tibbet had gone off and no one else was there. "Did I say I loved her?"

"Well, Jimmy-lad, the last I checked my ears they were working fine and I verra much fear you *did*."

"Don't tease, Mac. *My* fear is that she'll not have me. I'm too frivolous. A mere fribble."

"Fribble."

"I jest at all the wrong things and when I should not."

"Ah."

"And she doesn't like it that I make decisions for her, that I tell her what to do, but . . ."

"But ye have been telling your womenfolk what to do for many a long year now," said Mac solemnly, "and ye canna change your ways all in an instant."

"But she doesn't see that I will try to change!"

"Ah."

"Mac, I wish you'd just laugh your head off and get it over with."

The doctor chuckled. He put his arm around his friend's shoulders. "What you need, Jimmy-lad, is a long ride and a day following me around the hospital which experience will bring you down from the clouds and make you much more sober and, or so you believe, more to Lady Anne's taste."

James held back. "You don't know how that offer tempts me, Mac, but I've said I'll carry Anne to her luncheon and from there to the salon and later, of course, back to that room we just left."

Mac grinned. "And yon footman could never do it so well." He nodded toward the baize door at the back of the hall.

James glanced to where one of Jaycee's overly tall and exceedingly well-built footmen appeared. The young man wore a silly-looking and totally inadequate apron over his livery, and carried a pot of wax in one hand and a rag in the other. He looked to neither left nor right as he stalked across the hall and through the entrance to the east wing. Very likely he was to work on the paneling. James had noticed the smell of lemon oil here and there around the house. It was a pleasant scent, but he suspected the work of applying the wax to the woodwork was not half so agreeable as the result!

Mac chuckled. "A busy man that. Too busy to bother

with your Anne, hmm? So. Another time, Jimmy-lad. I'll
not renege on the offer."

"Thank you, Mac, I appreciate it. Will you return this
evening?"

"Nae, then. A few days, unless you send word there has
been a change in Lady Anne's condition, of course. . . ."

The two looked at each other.

"An outcome, devoutly to be desired."

"Oh, aye. Nae doubt of *that.*"

With that Macalister took himself off and James was
again left at loose ends. He recalled that Runyon had been
to visit his sister. Would Jaycee tell him of the visit if he
confronted her? Should he challenge her with fact of the
rake's presence and demand that she order Tibbet to refuse
the man entrance?

Debating the effect of such a demand, James looked into
several salons before he found his sister in the large, rarely
used formal salon. He watched as she paced to the far end
and turned. Her usually immaculate coiffure was coming
down and her lips looked as if she'd bitten them repeatedly.
In fact, she looked anything but the immaculate creature
she affected to be!

"Jaycee?" demanded James, on observing her agitation.
"Did that scoundrel *offend* you in some way?"

"Scoundrel?" Jaycee blinked. "Oh. Runyon. No. Of
course not. I'd forgot he was here. James," she went on
before he could comment on such an odd and unexpected
revelation, "is everything quite all right?"

"You mean with Anne? She is back in her room and
resting. The procedure went off very well, according to
Mac."

"Anne. Yes, of course, it is important that Anne is all
right, but . . ." Jaycee wrung her hands. "No, I do not mean
that. Of course I was worried about Anne, but . . ." She
cast a despairing glance at her brother. "James, that machine. That electricity. Would . . . would Martin approve

that it is being done in his house? Will there be damage? Is it not dangerous?"

"Where did you get such silly notions?"

"They are not silly! I remember someone boring on about that man in the colonies. I mean in what were once our colonies. Anyway, it was something about proving that lightning is the same thing as electricity and I know lightning can start a house on fire. I remember when we were children and that lovely old farmhouse burned. You know. Farmer Lister's and . . ."

"Jaycee. Hush!" James put his fingers over her mouth and she glared at him over his hand. "Stop it. Right now! You refer to Dr. Franklin's work in America. And, yes, you are correct that lightning can cause a fire. But, Jaycee, lightning is like hundreds and hundreds of machines such as Mr. Ryder brought here. This one cannot possibly do the sort of damage a bolt of lightning might do." He studied his sister. "Do you not believe me?"

All the muscles which had become tense with Jaycee's fretting relaxed. Not that the state into which she'd worked herself was surprising. Jaycee rarely did anything that wasn't done to excess! So now, at the relief, she burst into tears. Since this also was a normal reaction, James did not panic. He merely drew his sister into his arms and allowed her to cry herself out. When she hiccuped, he held her away.

"Better now?" he asked.

She smiled, radiant. "You can't imagine how worried I've been. Why," she said, startled, "I believe I actually may have been rude to Lord Runyon! I must apologize when next I see him. Do you think you and I might go riding?" she added, before James could object to the notion she would offer up an apology to Runyon even if she had been *exceedingly* rude to him—which he wished she had been, but doubted it very much!

"Riding," he said, diverted. "I thought you told his lordship you thought it too blustery."

"How did you know that? Has Tibbet been listening at doors? Never mind," she added, "I don't care if he does. As to the wind, why the exercise will keep us warm."

There was a faint snort of muffled laughter from just outside the door where a footman stood. Lord Runyon had said the exact same thing! Quite a sense of humor her ladyship showed, thought the servant, using the good-for-naught's words that way.

Jaycee was a trifle put out that James insisted their ride wait until after the luncheon which would be served in midday.

"But I do not wish to wait," she said, stamping her foot.

"And I do not wish to break a promise."

Diverted, Jaycee tipped her head and stared at him. "A promise? You mean to eat lunch, perhaps?"

"No, of course not. But Lady Anne is resting until it is served and I promised I'd carry her down to it and then to her place in the Green Salon so that she may work on her book. I do not wish to renege on that, Jaycee."

"The footman . . ." She broke off as James shook his head, his look solemn. "Well. It is too bad of you. Perhaps I'll go anyway. With a groom," she added when James opened his mouth to object.

"Jaycee, I would like very much to ride with you. Can you not wait?" he coaxed.

Jaycee tipped her head. "That is the first time I can remember when you have *asked* me to do something."

James stared at her. "How can you say that? I am always asking you to do something!"

"Oh, no, James. You are always *telling* or *demanding* or *ordering* me to do something. You do not *ask.*"

"Will you wait?"

She tipped her head. "Will I wait, *please.*"

"Please?"

"That's better. Yes, James, since you ask so nicely, I will

wait." With that Jaycee flounced out of the salon and disappeared.

For a long moment James stared after his volatile sister. Then, his review of their conversation complete, he threw back his head and laughed so loudly the footman, daringly, peeked in the door. "My lord?" he asked.

James stifled the last of his chuckles. "That woman will be the death of me," he said and chuckled again. "She truly will!"

And that, wondered the bemused footman, *is something about which one would laugh? I will never understand the quality if I live to ninety!*

Later that afternoon two men pushed away from among the bushes growing at the verge of an ancient grove. One chewed a twig. The other scowled at his scuffed boots.

"Think it'll do," said the rougher-looking man.

"Yes. A perfect hiding place. You will take the stage and bring back the special carriage, drawing it in there. I don't want anyone catching a glimpse of it. You must choose your time exceedingly well."

"You know I'll do it right."

"I know no such thing. You become slothful the moment I'm not there to see to things."

"I'll do this right. Don't want the Red Breasts finding it."

"The Patrol is composed of far too many busybodies! But remember, it would be your neck if they did."

"Yours too, guv."

"Oh, no. I'd be furious to say nothing of astounded to discover my groom was involved in smuggling. I'd denounce you. And I'd be believed."

"Too likely," muttered the groom, scowling.

The man was wrong. Too many tonnish men had wondered where Lord Runyon found the funds to live as he did. It was quite likely the groom *would* be believed if he accused his master of masterminding their business dealings with some enterprising fishermen who sailed from the Sussex coast west of Bognor Regis. It had been a profitable trade until the war ended. Now, with France open to anyone with the price of the packet, smuggled goods were still lucrative, but far less so and Runyon, more often than he wished to admit, was thinking of alternative ways of raising the ready.

"Stage goes soon," muttered the groom. "Better see if there's room."

"Certainly. You do that. I'll ride a bit before returning to the inn. Despite Lady Montmorency's belief the weather is too cold for such exercise, it is my belief anything would be better than my room there!"

"And speakin' of her irritating ladyship, ain't that the wench riding beside that swell on the black?"

"Nonsense. She said she'd not ride." Runyon was angered by the thought Lady Jaycee would deny him and then go off with someone else. "Where?" He scanned the region beyond the hill on which they stood and saw what his groom had already seen. "By God, it is! Blast the woman. Too cold and blustery, is it? I'll . . ."

"No ye won't, guv."

Runyon relaxed. "You are correct. I'll *not*. Let us go," he said and stalked around the brush to where they'd left their horses. They mounted, but neither rode off until they were certain the pair they'd seen cantering toward Chelsea where quite out of sight. Then, after one more look to see that no one observed them, they moved to the road.

"She's just a mort, guv," said the groom in a pacifying tone. A quick glance had warned him his lordship's temper was on the boil. It would do their business no good if the hothead went off on one of his starts. He'd ruin all. Since a night with the wench had been promised to the groom once Runyon finished with her, the servant wanted nothing to go wrong. He'd never had a night with a well-born woman. The thought of such fragile flesh had him licking his lips in anticipation. "Just a silly flighty senseless mort."

"So she is," said Runyon, smiling tightly. "And easy prey, if we do our planning well."

"Right you are," said the groom, encouragingly, seeing his master unwind. "You just put your mind to what we do once we have the wench cold."

"Yes. I'll plan our route to the coast. Do you think we might destroy the scent for anyone following, if we were to head for our friends in Sussex?"

The groom thought of the smelly fishing boat. He'd been forced to go with those men once. And been sicker than a coal-heaver was the morning after receiving pay. But the thought of a noose around his neck, which would be his fate if he were caught abetting a kidnapping, had the groom nodding. "A real good notion, that. When I get the carriage out of sight, I'll just take a day or two and have me a ramble down to talk to 'em?"

The more he thought of the notion, the better Lord Runyon liked it. "You come back to the inn once the carriage is well hidden. I'll have a better notion of what you should say to our friends. Remember. Every detail must be seen to."

"We'll do it. We done it before, ain't we?"

"Nothing quite like this," said Runyon.

For the first time he wondered if he'd finally bitten off just a trifle more than he could chew. But he put the thought aside as he again pictured both Sir James and Lord Montmorency's state of mind once he'd been the ruination of Jaycee.

Eleven

Lady Anne, unhappy her treatments seemed to do no good, lay quietly on her chaise. Her books were to hand, her lap desk properly placed and her pen . . . well, the ink was drying on the nib.

Instead of working, Anne stared out toward the ancient yews which today, under a lowering sky, stretched in a dark rank. The double row began not far from the old wing of the house and marched up and over a slight rise. On the other side and, where it could not be seen, it curved back toward the house. The trees had been originally planted for the comfort of the ladies of the house. The double row sheltered a path which allowed a stroller gentle exercise while free from chilling winds. The trees were so old they had nearly grown together, making the path quite narrow.

Even so, Anne wished she could be out there. Wished she might enter that long walk, could stride along freely, or amble slowly, or march like a soldier, or . . . or anything but lie on her couch totally dependent on those around her for her every need.

Anne sighed softly and forced her mind from such useless thoughts. If she were to be a burden on others for the rest of her life, then it behooved her to learn ways of easing that burden. It was also true, she had decided, that she must insist that Sir James's increasingly particular attentions cease. At once. Could she, she wondered, order him to leave Montmorency Park? If she did, would he go?

The answer to that was a resounding "no." Sir James believed himself responsible for her fall, responsible for her present inability to move . . . and one sure thing Anne had learned about the man, was that he never shirked his responsibilities. Even when they irked him no end, as Jaycee was known to do. Even now when it might be said his responsibility to his sister was ended, that it was her husband's duty to see she didn't fall into the briars, he had rallied round the instant he realized she needed him. Not that Jaycee would ever admit that need, of course.

So, wondered Lady Anne, how was she to make him understand that she, herself, did *not* need him? She knew, from what her brother, Lord Montmorency, had been kind enough to tell her, that she had money inherited from her mother. It gave her a very good income. There was no reason why she could not use it to hire those servants which would be necessary if her situation did not change. She laughed softly at the notion she'd have to model herself on Lady Fuster-Smythe and have special footmen who would move her and whatever special chair she might have, from place to place!

But however much she might appear to others to be a second Fussy-Puss, she could and would care for herself. Or, at least, she'd make it possible to be as independent as someone might be when they could not walk. If her paralysis continued she'd order a bath chair! In it she could move around more on her own. And, once she convinced her brother she should have her own home she'd plan a special herb garden which she could supervise. She'd have a room in which herbs were cured, mixed, and made into health-giving tonics, salves, balms, and syrups. And she'd find other doctors who felt as Dr. Macalister did and supply them with herbal remedies for their patients. She would have a useful life, despite her inability to move freely.

So why did she not feel more satisfied? worried Lady Anne. It was exactly what she'd already planned for her life—except that, thanks to the revelations about Lady Prem's true motivations, she'd concluded that it would not be necessary for her to settle in an isolated area far from the temptations she'd been taught were her bane.

Instead, Anne thought she might like a place here, near Jaycee and her brother, where she might have them to a meal occasionally or actually join them here at the Park on informal occasions. But even that, although so much more than she'd ever thought to have, was not totally satisfying. . . .

Anne's blank stare was drawn from the line of yews to the nearer prospect, the arrival of a bent gardener catching her eye. He set down a wicker basket and choose from it a small saw and a pair of clippers. Then he turned to the nearest rose bush. She watched him work, carefully pruning away a limb here, a twig there and wished she could join him in the fresh air, perhaps use her own small secateurs to clip the smaller twigs.

But that was to feel sorry for herself and, although it seemed her guardian had been far too harsh in her methods, many of the principles instilled had a great deal of value. Self-pity was to be avoided!

Anne looked at the blank sheet of paper laying before her. She glanced at the careful drawing set where she could easily see it. After a moment, she set her pen to paper and only then realized the ink had dried. She dipped the pen in the ink and carefully printed the words *White Hyssop* at the top of the page.

White hyssop, she mused. Again the pen dried as she let her mind wander, this time into the past. She'd learned of this particular herb's use from a farmer who cut himself when trimming the hoof of one of his young horses. He'd looked around, found the hyssop for which he'd searched, and stripped off the striped leaves. He bruised them thoroughly and placed the resulting mess over the cut which he bound with a none too clean handkerchief.

Anne had questioned him concerning his use of the herb. He'd looked surprised and said it was what his father had done and *his* father afore him. Years later Anne had read a reference to the herb which suggested mixing a little sugar with the bruised leaves. The writer had attributed his knowledge of this recipe to John Parkinson on whom the title *Botanicus Regius Primarius* was bestowed by King Charles I. At that memory Anne frowned. She was not convinced the sugar added one iota to the cure.

Over an hour—and several versions—later, Anne gave her essay a final reading. She nodded, set it aside, and put the cover on her ink. She wiped her pen on a pen-wiper and set it into the case in which she kept a selection of pens with different width nibs. Then she stacked the books laying open around her into a neat pile—except for one which had fallen from the edge of the chaise and was out of reach. She stretched, couldn't quite reach it, but before she could decide what to do, it was lifted and handed to her.

Anne, accepting the volume, glanced up. "Sir James!"

"When you work, you are lost to all around you, are you not?"

"I suppose I must be. I've never before had reason to notice."

"Did you finish?" asked Jaycee's voice from where her embroidery frame stood.

Anne turned her head and Jaycee grinned at her, her needle held poised above her work. "That herb is finished, but it begins with an H. Can you imagine how many more I must do? How was your ride? And have you solved your problem with your embroidery pattern?"

Anne shut her mouth. She was babbling. She never babbled. But the way in which Sir James had looked at her . . . the warmth in his smile . . . the kindness and the . . . the affection? All of that brought back to mind her decision that she tell James it was time he return to his own home.

He must not waste his time pandering to her wishes—especially when those wishes included the hope he might actually fall in love with her.

With her! Anne almost laughed aloud at the thought. Her insignificant self with her head of ugly hair. . . . Suddenly all hint of laughter fled. Once again she turned blind eyes on the row of yews striding along their path up the rising ground. . . .

"Anne? What is it?" When she didn't respond, James moved between Anne and the window. "Anne, why do you look as if you'd been struck!"

"Struck?" *Struck,* she thought, *by a notion so strange I cannot credit it!* "Oh, merely a thought . . ."

"Perhaps if we discussed it . . . ?" When she shook her head, he went on, "Is it then, something you cannot discuss with a man? Are you in pain?"

For half an instant Anne again got that blank thinking look. Then she raised her eyes to meet James. "Pain? You fear that what I will not discuss is something embarrassing?" She chuckled softly. "Well, perhaps it is at that, but not in the way you imply!" She raised a hand when James opened his mouth. "It is merely something about which I must think before I air the idea!" She glanced at the clock set into the side of a tiger which rested on the nearby mantle. "Is it not," she asked with a faint sigh, "time I was taken to our torture chamber for my afternoon session with Mr. Ryder?"

"You are very brave," said Jaycee before James could speak. "If it were me I'd do everything I could so that everyone would forget it. I'd certainly not mention it that way!"

"Anne is brave, Jaycee. And she knows the sessions are designed to help her. So she will suffer the embarrassment and, perhaps later, pain so that soon she'll walk again. Is that not true, Anne?"

"I will do what must be done," said Anne, firming her mouth into a stern line.

She wished Sir James hadn't such a high opinion of her bravery. It wasn't so much courage as that she'd learned, living with Lady Preminger, that to face a punishment and get it over was far better than thinking about it and fretting and worrying and *anticipating*. Anticipation, she'd discovered, could be very nearly as bad as the punishment itself! Lady Prem had been a great one for making the anticipation as bad as it could be.

Sir James picked her up and, more comfortable with his touch, she put her arm around his neck. But she still couldn't look at him even though she knew he'd bent his head to her. Instead she told Jaycee she'd have a tray in her room because of her need to recover from the ordeal of her treatment.

"Fiddle!"

"Fiddle?" repeated Anne.

"Jaycee, do you think it is not an ordeal?" asked Sir James sternly, when he'd turned them to face his sister.

"Oh!" Lady Jaycee instantly colored. "I didn't mean to imply. . . . Oh, no, not that poor Anne wouldn't. . . . Truly I didn't think. . . ."

It appeared Jaycee would continue lost in half sentences forever. "Is there a problem, Jaycee?" asked Anne, interrupting.

Jaycee heaved a great sigh. "It is nothing so very important. Merely that the cards for my Valentine's Day ball have arrived from the printers and I'd hoped that after dinner you and Lady Fuster-Smythe might help me address them. And that perhaps we could discuss decorations while we did so."

Anne smiled. "I would be happy to help, but I've never been to a ball, so I doubt I'd have much of a notion concerning decorations! The invitations, though? Perhaps part of the list and some cards could be brought to my room?"

"But it is more fun to do such things together. . . ." Jaycee eyed Anne. "Perhaps you'd be rested by then and able to return downstairs?"

"I don't know. . . ."

Jaycee pouted.

James shifted Anne's weight a trifle. "Nana would tell you your face will freeze like that. It is not the most attractive of expressions, you know."

"What . . . ?" Startled, Jaycee glanced at her brother.

"Your face." He emulated her expression.

Much to Anne's surprise Jaycee did not become angry. Instead she laughed. "I don't look at all like *that.*"

James raised his brows. "Are you certain?" he asked.

"Yes, of course I am. I know *exactly* how I look."

"How can you possibly know?"

"Because, silly, I have practiced my expressions in my mirror, as does any sensible woman!"

"I guess that tells you," said Anne to James. "Jaycee, I'll have Kitty come down later to tell you whether I can join you and Lady Fuster-Smythe. I'll have several hours in which to recuperate. Very likely I'll feel able."

"Good. And James can play for us."

"Play?" For once Anne looked into Jame's face which was so close to her when she was in his arms—and discovered he was quite red. "The pianoforte?"

"I play a little," he said, an off-handed answer that told Anne he played a lot! "I can't believe anyone would wish to listen. . . ."

"He is very very good and he *will* play for us, will you not, James?"

What Jaycee began in a demanding tone ended as a wheedling request and once again Anne felt like smiling. It amazed her how often she found reason to smile or laugh now she lived in her brother's house. For an instant, Anne felt resentment toward Lady Preminger who had insisted laughter was bad. It wasn't. It couldn't be. Surely nothing which caused such lightness of spirits could be bad! It was, Anne decided, just one more way her ladyship had attempted to ruin Anne's life. And, until now, had succeeded.

As James carried her through the long halls to the treatment room, Anne made a decision: The cross bitter old woman would *not* be allowed to win. Life *was* better. It would become better and better. She would analyze all Aunt Prem's teachings, each and every one, and decide for herself which were based in truth and which were not!

James entered the storeroom just then and lay Anne on the table. As he removed his arm from under her shoulders her cap caught on his sleeve. Since it was a day cap and tied under her chin, it did not pull clear away, but only shifted back from her forehead, revealing a narrow stripe of hair.

Anne, preoccupied with what was to happen, didn't notice. James opened his mouth to warn her but then, loving the color, the white of the material intensifying and deepening the wonderful deep burnished chestnut red, he closed his mouth and, instead, feasted his eyes whenever he dared.

Kitty arrived, breathing heavily, obviously having rushed from somewhere to join them. Lady Fuster-Smythe shuffled through the door, her hand clutching the arm of her footman. Another footman carried her chair and set it down where the doctor had stood that first morning watching the proceedings. Looking a trifle self-conscious as she always did, Lady Fuster-Smythe settled herself and opened a large notebook. The footman set an ink well on a nearby table and laid pens beside it. She waved her servants away and they took themselves off.

"I am so afraid I won't do a proper job of taking notes for the doctor. It is such a terrible responsibility he has given me," said the old woman solemnly, her eyes wide.

"It certainly is," said James, winking at Anne who smiled. "But I know of no one who would do so well. Kitty? Will you begin?" James settled himself on his special stool and reached for Anne's hand. After a time Anne's body jerked slightly and she bit her lip.

"Pain, Anne," he asked softly.

"Not . . . really. More a certain discomfort. . . ."

It happened again. James turned to where Ryder sat with his battery. "You have not increased the powers of that thing, have you, Mr. Ryder?"

"I've done exactly what the doctor asked me to do."

It was hours later when James realized Mr. Ryder had not, exactly, answered the question asked him! And it was days later before Dr. Macalister, who would have answered it, once again arrived at the Park. By then James had adjusted to seeing Anne bite her lip as a stronger current jerked her slightly with each application of the wand. He had, actually, when Lady Fuster-Smythe was bent over her tablet recording one of the muscular responses, peeked around the edge and watched the next contraction. At first he'd been bemused by the sight of all that smooth skin. But then he'd felt something approaching horror at the strength of the movement the wand's touch caused and wondered that Anne felt nothing . . . or at least admitted to feeling no more than the twitch the movement caused to the upper portions of her body.

The horrid thing about it all was that they had nothing of a positive nature to report to Mac. Even after several days Anne could not make her muscles respond to her will and she still spent her time on her couch or her bed or in the specially padded chairs James had designed for her comfort.

Each day Lady Anne worked on her book, enjoying the fact Jaycee sat nearby setting careful stitches in her needlework and James in another chair with a book or writing letters or doing some other quiet thing . . . such as simply watching the expressions flit across her narrow face as she worked to find just the proper words for her writing. The best occasions of all were when everything was moved into the music room and James played quietly in the background as she and Jaycee worked.

It was all very pleasant—except for the twice daily visits

to the store room—and only occasionally, now, did Anne wonder if it were *too* pleasant, if it was wrong of her to feel so much quiet happiness. Each time the worry crossed her mind she would remind herself of the letter she'd received from Kitty's minister. She had read and reread the message, gaining peace and self confidence from each reading. And then there was the analysis she was making of Lady Prem's teachings, deciding what she should adopt and what she should discard. And finally, to her great joy, she'd accepted that happiness was *not* wrong or evil or something to avoid.

The icing on the cake was that Lord Runyon had ceased his visits. Nor did Jaycee appear to miss him. James hoped the man was gone for good, but, although he voiced the thought on one occasion, he did not truly believe it possible. Lord Runyon was both too stupid and too cunning to have taken any hints handed him that he was unwanted. James just wished he knew what his lordship was up to while he was not harassing their peaceful household.

He also wondered how soon he could expect a response to his letter to Martin. He'd not asked it of his friend, but what he really hoped was that the information would bring Martin hot-footing it back to England. If Anne were correct and Jaycee's games since her wedding were merely a misguided attempt to make a splash, then Martin need not feel concern that she'd either stopped loving him or had never truly loved him at all . . . which, James thought, was his bitter friend's deepest concern.

And if Martin were to arrive in time for Jaycee's Valentine Ball? Well, that would be an excellent occasion for a reconciliation, would it not? That special day when, according to the country people, all the little birds were billing and cooing and pairing off?

And his own hopes for the ball? Very nearly silently, far too quietly to be noticed by either Anne or Jaycee, James sighed. He was beginning to fear his particular little wren, his Anne, would *not* recover by then. And if she did not, did he dare proceed with his own plans?

If he dared all and asked for her hand in marriage, would she not say him nay simply because she'd feel it too much a burden to wed when she could not care for herself? James knew Anne well enough he was almost certain that would be her response. And how, he wondered, did one go about convincing her that nothing would please him more than to spend the rest of his life caring for her?

If he were to simply tell her that, Anne would scold him, saying it was not necessary for him to feel such guilt.

But it wasn't guilt. It was love. Love for a strong uncomplaining woman who, for far too long, had not been allowed to enjoy life. He wanted to supply that entertainment, wanted to watch her experience new and wonderful things, wished to discover new ways of teaching her to let free that rare but delightful laugh that bathed him in warmth and made him feel as if he were smiling all over his body. . . .

It was the oddest sensation. As if somehow her laughter painted him with a glow, a gentle warmth. It was wonderful. He only wished it happened more often!

Jaycee had nearly finished the pillow top and was pleased with the way the clusters of violets had turned out. She wondered what she should begin next. Several flowers were possible. There was the common wall flower which she'd always admired in cottage gardens. Or possibly the marigold? Although it was a stiff little flower, it had wonderful color. . . .

Lady Fuster-Smythe sat in her chair and poured over the notebook she was keeping for the doctor. She was so proud of her work. She wondered if he'd find interesting the little comments she occasionally made if some reaction was not quite what was expected.

Today, for instance, she'd added a rather long note. Even she could see that during the second sweep down the left leg the muscles had been slow to recover. They had taken far longer than usual to relax so that Kitty could go on to the next gold circle. What, she brooded, did it mean . . . ?

For the first time in years, Lady Fuster-Smythe had found something other than gossip and disaster to entertain her. It didn't occur to her to ask for books which she might read and learn from. But she was occupied for long periods of time thinking about what she saw and wondering why it happened. . . .

Their peace was abruptly disrupted. Tibbet stood in the door and cleared his throat, catching everyone's attention except Lady Anne's: Anne was thinking deeply about a sentence which simply would not come out right.

"Lord Runyon," intoned Tibbet.

Jaycee smiled a welcome. "A new face! We've had no company for days now. Have you been to London? Tell us the news. Any new engagements? Are any entertainments scheduled? Have you heard," she asked, casting a mischievous eye toward her brother, "the latest crim cons?"

"Oh, it's you," said Lady Fuster-Smythe and laid aside her notebook, mentally girding herself for battle with the rake.

"Runyon," said James, a scowl replacing the dreamy look which had been on his face up to that moment. He stood up.

"How, hmmm, pleasant," sneered Lord Runyon. "A family party." He turned to his hostess. "The weather has improved, Lady Jaycee," he said smoothly. "I hoped you'd come riding with me."

Jaycee looked at her brother and bit her lip. She would truly love to go for a ride. It had been several days since the weather had permitted much exercise. "James? What do you think?" Before he could answer, she added, rushing her words, "I'd very much like to go, but we had plans for the two of us to go later, did we not? I don't wish to disappoint you. Perhaps you'd come with us now?"

There had been no such plan, so James, correctly, interpreted his sister's words as a request for his chaperonage. "Of course I'll come now. It is, as you say, only a bit sooner than we thought to go. Will you change?" He looked at his feet. "I must get into my boots. Come along, Jaycee. I'll walk you upstairs."

As they strolled out the door, he heard Lady Fuster-Smythe hurumph in that way she had. "Didn't know the chit had so much good sense. Now Lord Runyon, tell me, why did . . . ?" The door closed, shutting off her words.

"I wonder what she is asking him," said Jaycee, stifling a giggle. "I would have thought she's already quizzed him about every peccadillo he's ever committed!"

"If you have such a good understanding of the man, why do you encourage him?"

Jaycee pouted. "He is amusing." When James didn't respond, she added, "But I do not wish to be abducted, so I asked you to come with us."

"You believe he might actually abduct you and you still have anything at all to do with him?"

"It was Lady Fuster-Smythe's notion. I'm not at all certain he'd go so far. But I'll not leave the house with him. I assure you of that. Just in case?"

"As Lady Fussy-Puss said, I hadn't a notion you had so much good sense!" James chucked his sister under the chin. "Don't be long, my dear."

Jaycee grimaced. "Why did you have to spoil it?"

"Spoil what?"

"You gave me a compliment which was very nice, but then you had to spoil it by adding on an order."

"Order?" He stared, then blinked. "That you not take long changing?" She nodded. "Jaycee, that wasn't an order, but merely a request. I don't like having that man in the house. I don't want him spending time with Lady Anne. All I did was request that you not dawdle!"

"It sounded like an order to me. But I'll hurry. I haven't been out for days, it seems, and a good ride will do us both a world of good. *You* have become a bear, James, and I truly wish to go."

"And if you did *not* care whether you went or not?"

Jaycee got that mischievous look James liked so much. "Why then, I would tarry just as long as I might so as to teach you a lesson!" She flicked her skirts at him as she swung around on her heel and sped down the hall to her room.

James shook his head. What in the world could one do with a sister like Jaycee!

Twelve

Lord Runyon's groom returned to the inn nearly an hour after Runyon himself did. "What happened?" snarled the exceedingly cold man, his hands held to the meager fire which was all the landlord allowed in the room's tiny grate. He eyed the punch bowl sitting in the ashes which Runyon had nearly finished and growled, "Well? Why'd you leave me hanging like that?"

"Silly wench insisted we take her brother," said Runyon, scowling. "Then they wished to ride west along the river. There was no doing a thing about it if I didn't wish to give away the plot."

"You coulda returned by way of my post," said the groom. He no longer awaited Runyon's offer of a cup of the hot punch, but served himself, using Runyon's abandoned mug. He tossed it back and ladled up the dregs which he drank more slowly. "Can't take forever collecting the wench," he warned.

"I know we can't. The men will wait in port for only a few days. I'm well aware fishermen are unhappy when their nets are empty—whether empty of fish or kegs! But I'll not complicate matters if I can avoid it. Knocking Sir James over the head is a last resort, one I'll come to if I must, but we've a day or two, maybe a week, before taking desperate measures."

The groom cast a sneering look at Runyon's back at what he considered a weakness. "Don't see, myself, why you hesitate," he said in a laconic voice. "We'll have her away and no one the wiser where we go. What matters it if you cosh the brother?"

"Unlike you, I may wish to return to England someday," said Runyon. "Not immediately, of course. I owe too much money to return any time soon, but I won't, if I can avoid it, make it *impossible* to return."

Silence followed for a long moment. "You promised me a certain sum when this was over so I could set myself up, proper, in the Canadas. I tell you to your head, you'd better not be so far into the basket you can't come across with the ready or I'll make you sorry you were ever born."

Runyon winced. "I'll have what I promised you. Don't concern yourself about that. Although, why you need to feather your nest further, I cannot say." Runyon stared into the smoldering fire. "It's my belief you've saved up a pretty penny from your share of our smuggling venture. . . ."

It was, perhaps, a good thing Runyon's groom stood behind him. He'd have questioned the black look turned on him and he'd have been suspicious of the strange flexing of his groom's fingers which were a dead giveaway the man was restraining himself from engaging in violence.

At Montmorency Park, Anne glared into her mirror. "Such ugly hair."

"Pardon?" said Kitty, pausing her gentle brushing. The maid wasn't certain she'd heard what she thought she'd heard.

"Hmm? Oh. Just my hair. It's such an ugly color. Why could it not have been golden like Jaycee's or black or even a plain brown. I hate it."

"Is that why you keep it covered?"

"A Jezebel's hair," said Anne.

"Jezebel? Ahab's shameless wife? What does she have to do with you?"

"My hair. It reveals my nature. A nature like Jezebel's."

"Nonsense."

"Lady Prem . . ." Anne sighed, met her maid's eyes in the mirror. "Is that another thing she lied about? Was Jezebel's hair not red?"

"It doesn't make a bit of difference what color that bible woman's hair was. What has she to do with you? What I think is that that woman made you cover it and told you it was ugly because she was jealous of it."

"You didn't know her, Kitty."

"No, I didn't. I don't have to. I never heard the like, telling a young girl she was destined to be like some other woman just because of the color of her hair! That's nonsense. Our hair doesn't make us good or bad. It's what we believe and how we act and you are the nicest, the most wonderful woman I've ever known. You'd never behave like a Jezebel!"

Anne blushed at the fervent praise. "You don't think I need hide my hair? You don't think it ugly?"

"I've itched to put it up proper-like ever since I first saw it, to show the world how lovely it is! I thought it was a religious reason you kept it covered, like the Friends who live near my home. Quakers, you know? But I don't think even they are so strict as you about not showing a single strand!"

"I'll admit I'd begun to wonder," admitted Anne, ". . . but *beautiful?* No one has hair this color. It must be a sign of *something!*"

"I've seen hair *almost* that color."

"You have? You mean there *are* others . . ."

"You ask that doctor fellow. He's from the north. He'll tell you it isn't at all odd."

Anne frowned. "The north? Scotland? I believe one of my grandmothers was Scottish. . . ."

"I'll bet my garters she had lovely deep auburn hair just like yours."

Anne muffled a chuckle. "Kitty, not only is it wrong to make wagers, but, if you *did,* you'd never bet such a thing as *that!"*

"If your granny didn't have red hair I'll take them off and give them to you!"

"And if she did?" Anne smiled. "What then should I give you?"

"You've already given me so much," said Kitty, sobering.

"I've given you nothing at all!"

"Yes, you have. You did my picture which made my mother very happy and you've let me be your abigail even though I wasn't never trained to be a lady's maid and you don't yell at me when I do something wrong and you are kind and thoughtful and . . ." Kitty burst into tears and, dropping the brush, threw her apron over her head. "It ain't right, you not walking," came her muffled voice. "You should dance and sing and fall in love and everything good," she added, pulling the apron back down.

"Kitty . . . Kitty . . ." Anne didn't know what to say.

Kitty stooped and retrieved the brush. She held it poised over Anne's head. "You let me do your hair proper. If you insist on a cap, then let me ask Lady Montmorency's maid to find me one. Her ladyship would loan us a proper cap with lace and everything."

"You consider one of those dainty bits Jaycee wears a proper cap?" Anne chuckled. "Oh, dear, you cannot mean it!"

"I do mean it."

"But . . ." Anne stared at her own face. Finally she shook her head. "Kitty, let me think about it. Maybe one evening, soon. But not tonight. I haven't the courage. You see, I've never let anyone see my hair. I can't just all of a sudden change my ways. But . . ." Anne stared at herself a bit longer, her eyes huge in her narrow face. In a very soft voice she asked, "You truly think it beautiful?"

"I do. Sir James does too," said Kitty, teasing. "I've seen

him stare wistfully at that ugly cap of yours. He saw your hair when you fell, you know, and I think he wishes very much to see it again."

Anne's skin paled. "Then Aunt Prem was right. She said my hair would give men bad thoughts, bad desires. . . ."

"Nonsense. There's absolutely nothing wrong with a man wishing to feast his eyes on beauty. It's natural, like. The only bad thing would be if he let his desires make him *do* something bad."

"Isn't it wrong to tempt him?"

Kitty chuckled. "I see you think Lady Montmorency a very bad woman? All the time?"

"Jaycee? Why would I think her bad?"

"Doesn't she wear such dresses and do up her hair and practice her attitudes just to tempt the menfolk?"

"Practice her . . . what is that, please?"

"Her maid calls them attitudes. Poses. They are supposed to mean something."

Kitty moved away, tipped her head, put one finger to her forehead and stood with her other arm extended, the wrist limp. Kitty's version was a caricature of something Anne had once seen Jaycee do. Seeing Kitty do so badly what Jaycee had done so gracefully was exceedingly funny. Anne covered her mouth and giggled.

Kitty straightened, smiling. "Guess I need more practice, don't I? That's supposed to mean Serious Thought or some such thing. There's lots of them. Lady Montmorency practices before the big mirror in her room." Kitty returned to brushing her mistress's hair. "So, is she bad?"

"I never thought of it that way. Jaycee flirts, does she not? But she does it in such a light-hearted way, it very obviously means nothing at all. Perhaps what Lady Prem did not tell me was that society has rules about such things," mused Anne, her hands tightly folded in her lap.

"Then I can fix your hair proper like?"

Anne smiled at her maid's hopeful tone. "Not tonight. It

may take awhile to actually accept that it is all right for me to show my hair."

"Maybe I could braid it like usual, but get a pretty cap?"

"Maybe—" Anne bit her lip and shook her head. She could not do it! "—tomorrow night?"

Kitty smiled.

"Or the next perhaps," added Anne, doubtful that she'd have discovered the courage so quickly to depart so far from her usual practice.

Kitty sighed. If Lady Anne would not allow a pretty cap which showed off the hair rather than hid it, perhaps she'd allow her own caps to be prettified a little. Kitty decided to make her mistress a new cap of a pretty white material she'd been saving for a fine new chemise. She'd redesign the cap so it was not quite so off-putting and add a bit of trim. If Lady Anne would not wear one like Lady Montmorency's, then maybe she *would* wear one which had a bit of lace and could be set back a trifle so a narrow band of front hair showed? Kitty decided it wouldn't hurt to try.

And if Lady Anne refused to accept it Kitty would have her mother put it away in the chest with her other things for the future: the linens she'd been embroidering since she was a mere child, the lovely nightgown her mother had made and embroidered, the thin cotton chemise she'd spent her off time embroidering only last winter . . . and the dwindling hope she would ever need any of it. If only the second footman weren't so enamored of Cook's assistant!

The invitations for the ball went out and returns began arriving almost instantly. Jaycee was pleased and read off the note on one at breakfast one morning. "She says, 'What a very pleasant notion during this very dull time of year. I accept with pleasure.' It's signed Mary, Dowager Duchess of Bayswater. I always send her an invitation, because she was my mother's godmother, but rarely does she accept. Oh dear. Now it is more important than ever that the decorations be something special!"

"Why does her grace's attendance make it more important?" asked Anne, toying with a slice of toast.

"She . . . she . . . I don't *know* why I cannot simply ignore her, but she always looks at me as if I were a clod of dirt and I hate it."

"Who?" asked James, entering the conversation just then. "The duchess, did you say?"

"The *dowager* duchess. She uses dowager to underline the fact her son has *finally* married. One did wonder if he ever would. Hmm. I wonder if *they* will come. . . ." Jaycee frowned slightly as she slit the next envelope and the next. The little pile threatened to fall over.

"If you like," said Anne, "I'll keep the list of people who have promised to come. . . ."

"I've a copy of the list already. I merely put a check by their names when they say they'll come and cross the name out when they deny me," said Jaycee, reading still another acceptance. "Oh, listen! 'A very pleasant notion,' she says and then accepts for her daughters, her son and herself. That's Lady Barryworth. Her son never goes to parties. I wonder why he's agreed to come to this one?"

"Maybe to see his family has proper escort," suggested James. He stood at the sideboard and couldn't make up his mind between very nice-looking kippers and deviled kidneys.

"That reminds me. I must notify the Horse Patrol so they'll put a heavy guard on the route out from town that night. Martin did so when we held the garden party last year. I thought it an excellent notion."

"Since I'll be in town today, I'll stop by the Home Office and ask that the Red Breasts be notified," said James, deciding on the kidneys.

"Thank you. I really must do some serious thinking about

decorations. Hasn't anyone a notion?" No one said a word. Jaycee sighed. "I see you'll be no help at all."

She immediately settled into a glum-looking posture which was emphasized as she left the breakfast room with dragging footsteps. She dawdled around the house, looking into a room here and backing out, moving somewhere else, returning to where she'd been and, wherever she might be, very likely getting in the way of some maid's work.

Much later that afternoon a shriek was heard throughout the house: "Eureka!" Jaycee came running in a very unladylike way indeed into the Green Salon.

"Good great heavens!" scolded Lady Fuster-Smythe, who had been so startled she'd actually dropped the ginger biscuit she'd just taken in hand for a sustaining nibble. It was, after all, well over an hour since she'd called for a tray of a little something which, she hoped, would hold her until dinner time. Luckily, since it had not, she'd squirreled away the biscuits! "Really, Jaycee. How very unnerving of you. I thought that, at the least, there were housebreakers and you were being slain!"

"Nonsense. Tibbet would never allow housebreakers. It wouldn't be good ton, would it?"

"If you are not being killed, then why that awful noise?"

"Because I've thought of the decorations. Birds!"

"Birds? You mean those dirty little creatures that live in cages and always leave a mess around them no matter how often a maid is set to brushing it up? Those silly little yellow things? And parrots! No, Jaycee, I cannot abide parrots. You'll not bring a parrot anywhere near!" When Jaycee merely grinned, she added in less a blustering fashion, "You won't, will you?"

"Not *real* birds, my lady, but ones which have been stuffed for display of their feathers, and I'll have drawings of pairs of birds and toy birds and . . . and well, just every kind of bird possible!" She glanced at her elderly guest and added, "Except *live* birds, of course. It is a very good notion. . . . But, don't you see?" she asked when no one looked the least bit excited.

"Perhaps I do," said Anne thoughtfully. "You are using as a theme the belief it is on Saint Valentine's Day that birds choose their mates?"

"Yes! Is it not perfect?"

"Then you are choosing love to be your theme?" asked her brother. "You might add an Eros here and there with arrows well aimed."

"Eros? Oh. Cupids . . . well, perhaps. Chubby little boys with wings and mischievous looks? Hmm . . ."

Unconsciously she adopted very much the pose that Kitty had shown Anne as an example of an Attitude and Anne had very great difficulty stifling giggles which she knew would not be appreciated. To distract herself from the memory of Kitty in the same pose, she said, "The more I think of it, the more I like it, Jaycee. The pairs of birds are a very nice idea."

"Unusual too," said Lady Fuster-Smythe, searching her pockets for another hidden biscuit and, much to her surprise, received a grateful look from Jaycee. "Don't think I've ever seen it used, so you'll likely be remembered for it," she added.

Anne quirked a brow that Jaycee actually blushed at the added praise. She had noticed before that praise was much appreciated by her sister-in-law but now she began to wonder if it weren't more. Did Jaycee actually *need* to be praised? Was she insecure in some way so that it was necessary to her to hear that she'd done as she should or done something well or thought up something special? Anne decided she'd discuss it with James when they were next alone. . . .

And then she wondered at herself, that her immediate thought was of James, of talking it over with him, of hearing his views . . . and that if he agreed with her theory, discussing what might be done about the problem. Surely she wasn't becoming dependent on having the man around! Or finding his company necessary? She mustn't.

Or then again . . . might she? Dared she? Surreptitiously she glanced at James and discovered he was looking at her with that pensive look she'd occasionally surprised on his face.

What did it mean? What was he thinking when that meditative, almost wistful, look was turned her way? Was he worried about her? Or was he wondering how soon he might get back to his usual life which he must miss very much? Did he hope he'd soon be free of the duty he'd imposed on himself to see that she recovered movement, assuming that were at all possible?

Or could it possibly mean what she'd finally admitted, if only to herself, she hoped it meant: that he felt affection for her and liked her and was thinking of her in good ways, wishing she returned his . . . affection?

Anne stared at the household book which lay in her lap, a collection of handwritten recipes going back for more years than she wished to count, and written in more hands than one might have expected. It had been James and Jaycee's mother's book last and would be put in the hands of James's wife once he married. He'd brought it to her, telling her it might have something of interest to her since he remembered his mother going to it when she needed something for the headaches his father had suffered toward the end of his life.

Anne had found that particular recipe. It was, as she'd expected, an infusion of willow bark, although this recipe had had added to it, in a different hand, that a small amount of laudanum was of help when the case persisted beyond the usual. Anne knew there were cases where laudanum was invaluable for a sufferer of persistent pain, but she had strong reservations about its use for everyday ailments and she was especially rabid about the all too common practice among nannies of giving repeated doses to young children merely to make them quiet and passive and no bother to their caretakers! No, she'd not recommend the pernicious stuff in her book. Not at all.

There was, however, another recipe in the journal which intrigued her. For coughs, the writer recommended adding a teaspoon of wild cherry bark extract to an herbal drink such as chamomile or horehounds. It was claimed the bark extract would relieve an irritable cough and was one she'd not heard before. It was certainly worth a try. She'd first have to make an extract of the cherry bark, of course. . . .

"Anne?"

Vaguely hearing her name, Anne looked up, glanced around. "Yes? Someone said my name?"

Everyone laughed. "You are amazing," said James.

He spoke in that warm tone Anne wanted to hear but, alternately, felt it was not, somehow, quite proper. "Amazing?" she asked after a moment which she used to regain control over her emotions.

"You concentrate so deeply you have no idea what goes on around you. I find that amazing," he explained. "Jaycee asked a favor of you."

"A favor?"

"I asked if you would draw some large pictures of pairs of birds. I thought I'd have transparencies made and set along the drive up to the house with lanterns behind them. You know the sort of thing I mean. They had magnificent ones last summer during the celebrations in London after Boney was sent off to Elba. I can contact the same people and have them do up mine. . . ." She went off into her mind, another notion obviously brewing. Her face lit up. "Do you think that sort of thing would shed enough light that I could have them inside the ballroom and use them to light the dance floor?"

"No."

Jaycee glared at her brother. "You never like my ideas!"

"Jaycee, I think having them along the drive a wonderful

notion and one that no one has used before, so, as Lady Fussy-Puss told you, this will be a ball to be remembered. But you cannot have them in the ballroom. There is too much danger of fire. Remember the Chinese structure which burst into flames in the park? It is only the merest chance no one was killed."

"But that was fireworks!"

"So it was, but illuminations are as dangerous. Do you have any notion just how strong a lantern is needed? It would not be safe. I cannot believe Martin would like it if he returned to find the Park burned to the ground!"

"I could have a footman stationed at each one with a fire bucket. . . ." When James shook his head she sighed. "I hate it when I cannot use an idea I really like. It was such a good notion, too."

"You couldn't illuminate them, of course, but could you not have medallions with your love birds on them placed around the room and perhaps decorate around them some way?" suggested Anne.

"Decorate them—" Jaycee got that pensive, thinking look again. "—with ribbon gathered into ruffles perhaps. And lace. Red ribbon, I think. And perhaps make the medallions heart shaped? The heart is the seat of love, is it not? So that makes the shape suitable for lovebirds."

She went deeper into that dreamy, thinking state of mind which always worried James no end because all too often it ended with Jaycee doing something which caused everyone a heap of trouble.

This time when she came out of it, she giggled. "I know what I'll do. I'll have cupids sitting on the edge of the medallions and I'll have them point their arrows at the birds which will look at each other in a besotted way."

"Can birds look at each other besottedly?" asked Lady Fuster-Smythe.

"Birds, I think, are very practical creatures," said Anne

thoughtfully. "Perhaps you should have famous lovers decorating your medallions," she suggested.

"The birds," interrupted Lady Fuster-Smythe, "will do very well for your illuminations, Jaycee, but in the ballroom I would prefer to see people. I cannot like birds, somehow. Dirty silly things . . ."

"Famous lovers . . . ?"

"Antony and Cleopatra," said Lady Fuster-Smythe.

"Romeo and Juliet," suggested James.

"Prinny and Lady Hertford!" added Jaycee, and she glanced from one to another, her mischief-look back.

"Jaycee! Don't you dare," scolded her brother.

"No, of course I would not dare. Why do you always think the worst of me?" she asked, again pouting.

"I suppose," he said and sighed, "it is because, in the past, you have proved you are capable of anything!"

"But I am grown up now."

"Anyone who had grown up," he said, sternly, "would not allow Lord Runyon anywhere near herself."

Jaycee burst into tears. "You do not understand. You never understand!" She ran from the room.

"Oh blast and bedamned!" James exclaimed.

Lady Fuster-Smythe tut-tutted.

"What? Oh. I apologize. I should not have used such language. But my sister drives me to the verge of insanity."

When he began pacing the room, Anne asked, "What exactly has she done to upset you this time?"

"Why the devil—sorry—why," he said more calmly. "Did she burst into tears just now?"

"Because you do not understand," said Anne, a small smile playing around her lips. "She made that perfectly clear, did she not?"

"No, she did not," said James, slightly exasperated with Anne's teasing when he was so upset by his sister's emotional outburst. "What is it that I do not understand?"

Anne sighed softly. "James, it is only speculation on my

part, because I am not certain I understand her myself, but I think that she wishes to make her husband so jealous he'll come flying home. *Ventre a terra,* of course."

"If that's what she hopes, she's a fool."

"Very likely," agreed Anne. "But I believe it is only that she's a Romantic and she would drop the stupid Runyon if only her husband returned."

"It is true I thought she forgot about him those days when he did not make a nuisance of himself. . . ."

"She doesn't like him above half," said Lady Fuster-Smythe. "Anyone with eyes can see that. She is merely using him. She has no more notion than a baby how dangerous it is to use a man of Lord Runyon's stamp! She'll come to grief if she isn't very careful indeed," said her ladyship in the sepulcher tones of a Cassandra. "Or, for that matter," added her ladyship, finding still another gingersnap which she'd secreted in her reticule, "even if she is."

"Is what?" asked James who had lost track.

"Is *careful,* of course."

"You don't trust him."

"You don't either," said Lady Fuster-Smythe in a tone of voice which did not require an answer.

James responded anyway. "You are correct. I do not. But I haven't a notion what to do about it."

"No more do I," said her ladyship mendaciously. As far as she was concerned, she'd already done the necessary. She'd written an old friend in the government and demanded that Lord Montmorency be returned home at once. She patted her pockets, peered into her reticule and, when she found no more biscuits, called for her footman. "I'll just go up now for a little nap before dinner. You, Sir James, had best take yourself off so that Lady Anne is not compromised."

"Set the door ajar, Lady Fussy-Puss and I'll close it when I leave."

Her ladyship glared at James. "Do you swear it will be no more than a few minutes?"

"Fifteen at most," he said, stretching the time as long as he dared.

She stared at him for a long moment, impressing on him how very angry she'd be if she discovered it was more. When certain she'd cowed her godson thoroughly, she said, "Very well."

Once Lady Fuster-Smythe was beyond hearing, James turned to Anne. "You have done it again, have you not?" he said admiringly.

"Done what?" asked Anne a trifle warily.

"Why, explained the complexities of my sister's mind. I have never been able to understand her. Yet you, who have known her so briefly, do."

"I don't claim to have a true notion of her character, but I have noted several things in her behavior. Have you ever observed, for instance, how important it is to her to be told she's done well, that someone is pleased with her. She is hungry for approval, Sir James."

He was silent for a moment, his head bowed. "Hungry for approval and most of my dealings with her since she was quite young have been to complain or lecture her." He sighed. "I tried my best after our mother died, but I didn't do a very good job of raising her, did I?"

"I suspect you cannot have been so very old yourself and you also had responsibility for your estate and all those dependent on a land owner."

"You do not add that I am not terribly observant and prone to think everyone reacts to situations and other people as I do myself!"

That little smile she so rarely got played again about Anne's mouth and her eyes twinkled. "I should, perhaps add," she said in an exceedingly prim voice, "that you are not terribly observant and prone. . . ." She laughed as he approached, flexing his fingers and pretending to growl.

He straightened. "How wonderful to hear you laugh, Lady Anne. It is a lovely laugh."

She sobered instantly, her gaze turning to the long row of yew beyond the window. "I have been taught to think laughter wrong. It is only since I've come among you all that I see how terrible it is that I'd forgotten how to laugh."

"But you have remembered," said James quickly.

She turned to look up at him, a smile in her eyes. "Yes. I have and I'm glad. As you leave, Sir James, would you ring for Kitty? I would like to spend the time between now and my next treatment working on my book."

It was dismissal and James wondered if he'd offended. He hesitated, wanting to ask, but Anne had turned back to stare out the window. With a sigh only barely repressed, James turned and left the room, telling the footman to find Kitty and send the girl to Lady Anne who needed her.

For himself, he went off to find his sister and, after a thorough search, discovered her in the last place he'd have expected. She was in the dim library, seated in the chair Martin most often sat in of an evening on those few occasions James had visited while Martin was at the Park. She was almost lost in the oversized, well-padded chair. And she looked very young.

"Jaycee?" he said softly.

She hadn't noticed his entrance and visibly started. She looked up and, by the watery winter light which managed to find its way that far into the room, James could see her face was wet.

"Do you miss him so very much?"

"You cannot know."

"Then why do you not write and tell him so?"

"He . . . should . . . not . . ." Jaycee burst into noisy tears.

James closed the distance between them and lifted her from the chair. He seated himself with his sister on his lap and cuddled her much as he'd done when she was very little, long before their mother died. He wondered why he'd not done so more often in those early years of his guardianship. Love for his sister welled up in his breast. That was something he'd not felt so strongly for a very long time either. The exasperation at her thoughtlessness, as he'd seen it, and the relief at getting her married off and off his hands had somehow smothered it.

"I love you, Jaycee," he said softly.

"Do you?"

She pushed away and looked at him. He nodded.

"I thought you'd stopped loving me. The only time you ever paid attention to me was to scold me." She tipped her head and blinked. "James, do you think perhaps I behaved so very badly just so you'd at least scold me?" When he looked shocked, she added, "That way I knew you'd not gone off and forgotten me, you see."

"Jaycee," he asked, with sudden insight, "did you feel as if our mother deserted you, perhaps?"

Jaycee bit her lip. Gradually she relaxed so that her head lay back against his chest. "I wonder. Do you suppose I was afraid you'd go away, too? Everyone went away, it seemed. My father when I was almost too young to remember I had one, and then my mother just when I was beginning to need her very much indeed . . . and then it seemed as if you would look right through me—except you weren't around much even for that, were you?"

"I apologize if it seemed to you that I'd pushed you away from me, but I wasn't all that old myself when Mother died. I suspect the responsibility weighed on me so heavily I lost all sense of perspective!"

"I wish Martin would come home."

"Would you behave differently this time?"

She giggled. "You mean would I stop flirting with all the most rakish men in the ton?"

So, James thought, she's already forgotten the emotional state she was in. His sister's volatility was another thing he'd never understood. "I hope so," he said finally. "That was, however, only part of why Martin decided you did not love him and, perhaps had *never* been in love with him."

"How could he think such a thing as that? I doted on him. I still dote on him. But," she added severely, "you *know* it is not the thing to wear your heart upon your sleeve."

"Perhaps not at the most formal of entertainments, but *never,* Jaycee?"

She bit her lip. "He didn't seem to care. He was so busy. He was always off somewhere. And—" Jaycee covered her cheeks to hide a deep blush "—I thought he had a mistress, because I could not believe he was always with the government. James, what is it that men do that takes up so much of their time?" she asked, bewildered. "Why must they leave their womenfolk alone day after day after day? I *needed* him, James."

"Needed him? Or needed to be the center of his attention?"

"Is that not the same thing?"

"Anyone would do as an audience, Jaycee," he said, as kindly as he could. "One doesn't need a *husband* for that."

"But it is Martin's attention I crave. If he loved me . . ."

"No, Jaycee. It is not proof of one's love that one cater entirely to that person's needs. What of his needs? Do you cater to them?"

Jaycee was silent for a moment, her fingers toying with one of Jame's buttons. "Did he have needs, James? I mean, beyond . . . well, *you know.*"

"We all have needs beyond 'you-know' sort of needs. For instance, I think Martin hoped you'd discover an interest in what he did in the government so he'd have someone at home with whom to discuss his day's work and, perhaps, let off steam where it would do no damage."

"His work!" She straightened away from him again and stared. "But, James, it was so *boring.*"

"Not to him."

Jaycee sighed. "I am very stupid, I think. I do not understand him when he talks about taxes and the high cost of wheat and imports and things like that. I do not like it that I don't understand. . . ."

"So, did you explain that to him and ask him to teach you so you would understand?"

"I didn't want him to know I was stupid, so I just told him not to bore on about it all."

"Which was, I think, one of the reasons he decided you'd married him merely for the status of being Lady Montmorency and not because you wished to be his wife."

She thought about that. Finally she scrambled off his lap, sighing deeply. "I've been very foolish. I thought I could make him proud of me if I became one of the leaders of the ton, but he didn't like that, I think. But I only did it because I wanted him to believe me someone special and not just a silly little girl."

"You were very young. Perhaps too young. You should have known he loved you and thought you special or he'd not have asked you to wed him."

"It wasn't just because I was your sister and you and he are such great friends?" she asked wistfully. "I thought it merely that I was *there*. . . ."

James looked up at her. "You really don't think very highly of yourself, do you Jaycee?"

Jaycee pouted. "You have told me so often how terrible I am, I am forced to believe it."

"Then it is my fault. Again I apologize. My scolding of you was not because you were terrible, Jaycee, but because you were always into mischief and I didn't know how other to deal with it."

"But you thought it terrible I was into mischief. So I was bad, wasn't I?"

James ran his fingers through his hair, mussing his valet's careful arrangement. It was something he only ever did when agitated beyond bearing. "Jaycee, how can I make you understand that punishing you for doing something you shouldn't is not the same as disapproving everything you do. Where I failed was in telling you when you did well. You should *know* that, for the most part, you have grown to be a very lovely woman who is lovable and nice to be around. But then you do something silly like encourage Lord Runyon and we have an argument and you think I don't love you."

Jaycee put her finger to her lips as she thought about his words. "I will tell Lord Runyon he is no longer welcome here."

"Merely tell Tibbet to deny your presence."

Jaycee adopted a pensive look. "You don't think it would be more polite to tell him myself?"

"Jaycee!"

She grinned, giving him a saucy look. "Very well, James. I will inform Tibbet that I am no longer at home to Lord Runyon."

Just as she whisked herself from the room James realized she'd been teasing him and chuckled. Was his sister finally growing up a little? Would things be better between them? And between herself and Martin when her husband finally returned home?

James hoped so. Despite loving his sister and, perhaps, understanding her a bit better, he still wished to hand over the responsibility for controlling her starts to another! *Just how much longer would it be,* James wondered, *before Martin returned!*

Thirteen

His heart a little lighter now the worry about his sister had been removed, Sir James took a delayed ride into London. He saw his agent about a few items pertaining to his estate and then went, first to his own home to collect any mail which might have arrived and not been sent on and then, having dealt with that, moved on to the Montmorency townhouse. He'd just lifted his hand to knock on the knockerless door when it opened.

"Martin!"

"James?"

For a moment the old friends looked at each other, nonplussed.

Martin recovered first. "Good. You've returned from wherever you've been off too. Excellent. I've a few things to discuss with you before I return to the continent," he said in a cold tone totally unlike his usual warm-hearted and contented self.

When Martin turned back into the house, James hesitated, then followed. "You're up on your high horse," he said. "Does that mean you did or did not get my letter? I suspect not. It hasn't had time to reach you and you still have time to get home."

"Ah. A letter? Then you did think to warn me my wife was planting antlers on my head?"

"She is not!"

"According to an impertinent letter your Fuss-cat sent

my superior at the Foreign Office, she either is or is about to do so. And according to half the gossips in London, it is the former."

James sighed. "Martin, do you remember leaving London in something of a snit?"

"I had reason."

"Well, you thought you had reason. But, because you were thinking with something other than your mind, you forgot just how silly my ridiculous sister can be. *Her* belief is that she was merely becoming, in the only way she knew how, *all the crack.* She also resents it a great deal that you flirted with Lady Commerce and don't tell me it's tit for tat, because I have it on the best of authorities that it isn't the same thing at all!"

"The best of . . . Jaycee?"

Martin relaxed his stiff shoulders a trifle, but James thought he was not yet ready for a reconciliation. "I suppose you've heard about the debacle at the Cyprian's ball?"

Martin's lips compressed and he nodded.

"That's the gossip to which you refer?"

"Runyon of all people! How *could* she?"

"Oh well, if she wished to make you jealous, I can't think of a soul who fits the bill better." James stared up at the ceiling and whistled softly. When Martin didn't comment, he added, "Of course, it is also true that she had no idea the man she was using might be using her for his own purposes, and, in fact, has not yet accepted that it was through his machinations her presence at the ball was revealed." Still Martin didn't say anything. "Think, Martin. If Jaycee decided to attend such an unacceptable function as that ball, would she allow herself to be unmasked? She is far too canny for that, as you well know. She had *help* making herself a byword."

"Runyon," agreed Martin, disgusted. "He'll ruin her just to make me a fool."

"Me as well, remember. Jaycee is his ideal revenge. We

were both involved in that rescue. But he'll have far more difficulty now you've come home. And, besides that, Jaycee has admitted, finally, that Runyon was not a good notion on her part and has informed Tibbet she is no longer at home to the man."

Martin relaxed another notch. "You believe she took up with that cur simply to make me jealous?"

"Yes. It's all very simple once you understand your situation. You, you see, are supposed to read her mind. You are supposed to *know* what she is thinking and why she does things." James sighed. "I've only just discovered that myself. She has some crackbrained notion our mother, if she'd lived, would have done so, and the fact we do not is merely because we don't try. Or worse, don't truly love her. Or something of that sort. I didn't understand *all* the nonsense she spouted before she began to see sense."

"*Your* sense, correct?"

"Don't laugh. I mean any sense at all. I never knew such a child . . . except there have been one or two indications recently she may be growing up. I have difficulty crediting it, but although *once* might be an accident, she has shown surprisingly good judgment more than once. I discovered, for instance, she never allowed Runyon into a closed room and ordered Tibbet to station a footman outside the door . . . in case she wished to order refreshments or something of that sort, you understand . . . ?"

Martin chuckled. "That last sounds like Jaycee all right. My only difficulty is in thinking it one of those indicators to which you refer. Knowing Jaycee, it may be the literal truth! She may have had him there merely in case she wished to . . ." He broke off, laughing. "You still rise to the bait very nicely when Jaycee is under discussion. She is mine now, James. You needn't concern yourself."

"When you go off to Vienna and leave her here alone? You truly think that was nothing about which I must concern myself! Nonsense. You knew very well I'd see to her . . . except of course, I failed. Somehow I should have prevented that ill-fated night at that ball!"

"Read her mind, maybe?"

The men laughed in the easy fashion they'd been used to do before Martin's marriage to Jaycee had added stresses to their relationship, changing it somewhat.

"You couldn't have known she'd do something so silly," said Martin. "In fact, that bit was very likely my fault. I might have warned you, if it had occurred to me to do so. She'd expressed a wish to attend an earlier one and I'd put my foot down, telling her it was not at all the thing and that she could not under any circumstances do any such thing."

"Which immediately set my perverse sister to planning just how she would manage it! I wish you had thought to mention it. . . ."

"The damage is done, James. Perhaps if we're seen together and amiable, the rumors will be scotched. I was about to go to our club. Not that I want to *see* anyone. I get very tired of the snickers ill-hidden behind hands, but Cook is having an off day and I want something edible. Shall we go together?"

"If you are willing to eat so early I'll dine with you, but I must be on my way back to the Park at a reasonable hour. I promised Anne . . . Lady Anne, I mean . . . I'd carry her—" James slapped his forehead. "—You don't know, do you!"

"Don't know what?"

"You didn't get my letter and Lady Fussy-Puss obviously didn't mention Anne's situation. She fell down the front stairs, Martin, and is paralyzed," James explained in a contrite tone. "It is my fault and I feel terrible about the whole thing. She is undergoing Galvanism, a special treatment to stimulate the muscles which will not function, and I sit with her through it twice each day. My poor wee wren . . ."

"Do I hear something a trifle warmer in your voice than mere guilt would impart?"

Although his ears warmed, James gave a quick grin in response to Martin's teasing. "You do. Come to that, it is a *very* good thing you've come back. Anne is of age, of course, and, technically, she doesn't need your permission, but I suppose I ought to ask it before I approach her." Humor fled and James sobered. "Assuming, of course, I ever do."

Martin eyed James. "Why would you not?"

"You don't seem to have understood. She is *paralyzed*. She can't walk. She may never walk. It is a tremendous adjustment to make. I fear to add another complication, so I do no more than ease her way, occupy her mind as much as possible. . . . It is a very good mind, by the way. She plays an excellent game of chess, and she is an author—" James grinned at Martin's quick look of surprise. "—Ah ha! You didn't know that either, did you? My lady knows far more than Macalister about herbs and herbal cures and you are aware he's something of an expert in that humble field. And she draws. Her art work is fantastic, Martin. Have you seen it? She's illustrating. . . ." James paused and stared at his friend's raised hand. Finally he said, "I'm babbling, right?"

"Very like I did when I realized I was in love with Jaycee." Martin nodded solemnly. "Yes, you babble and I feel pangs of something I think must be hunger. Shall we go?"

Later, once they'd eaten, James asked Martin if he were riding out to the Park now or later.

"Neither. James, will you do me a favor and not mention I've arrived? I'm briefing Lord Liverpool on what is, or should one say, what is *not*, happening at the conference. The government wants a detailed account of all those things one dare not put on paper. It's complicated by daily shifts in coalitions, innumerable conflicts, interminable maneuvering. . . . I'd already been called back so they didn't send

Lady Fussy-cat's letter, although yours must have gone on. Reading it was a shock. Overhearing gossip made it worse and ignoring off-color jokes—*not* about my wife, *of course*—had me about ready to divorce her! I've thought seriously of merely leaving, once done here, and returning to Vienna without seeing her."

"And thereby solving all the problems? I didn't think you a coward, Martin."

"I'm not." James gave him a speaking look and Martin colored. "Except where Jaycee is concerned!" he admitted. "It is the very devil when one's emotions are wrapped up in a problem. They interfere with rational thought!"

"But you will not simply run away?"

"Oh, no. Not now you've explained, but until I've finished with the prime minister it would be far better if I not have to deal with my wife as well."

"I suppose that will be all right so long as you've finished before St. Valentine's Name Day. Assuming you do, all should be well."

"What the devil has a saint named Valentine to do with anything?"

"Only that your beloved wife is holding a ball that evening and if you are known to be in London and do not attend, I think you might as well run away. All the way to India, perhaps? Or even so far as the antipodes?"

"If I remember my globes, that is a rather watery spot."

"Australia, then. That would be nearly the antipodes. . . ."

Martin chuckled. "I think I can promise to finish here and come to the Park long before the 14th of February."

"But in the meantime . . . ?"

"In the meantime," said Martin pensively, "you will oblige me by making no mention of the fact you've seen me."

"I hope this doesn't land us in more briars."

"Why should it?"

"Someone will write Jaycee and she'll rescind her order to Tibbet and I'll have to cope with that blasted Runyon again!"

"If someone writes her, tell her you've seen me, but that until I can give her my full attention, I'd rather pretend she is nowhere near. Because, once I can come to her, I don't intend to part from her again."

"May I add that last?" asked James politely.

"No. Because she, poor love, would take it as absolutely literal truth and I mean it a trifle more symbolically." Martin frowned. "She will return with me to Vienna, of course, and she'll enjoy it no end, but somehow I have to make her understand I'm a secretary in the mission and that my time is not altogether my own! I don't know. . . . We're talking about Jaycee. . . . Do you think she *can* assimilate that?"

"We've commented on the fact our Jaycee is not a stupid woman, but, up until a few days ago, I'd not have given much for your chances. Now . . . ?" James actually considered the point. "If you put it the right way, you may have less difficulty than you think."

"And the right way?"

James grinned. "I have yet to figure that one out, but you might ask Anne. She seems to have a surprising capacity to see into Jaycee's mind and heart and perhaps she'll have advice which will help!"

"You said something about Anne being unable to walk. . . ."

"Have you just remembered that?" asked James sternly, perhaps a trifle dangerously.

"You must remember that Anne does not loom large in my thinking. I settled her at the Park only days before I left for Vienna and have had no opportunity to get to know her again. Time to do so is complicated by my work to say nothing of my darling wife who is taking up far too much of my mental processes. I assume you've had a good doctor?"

"Mac, of course."

As they strolled away from White's, James explained, again, what had happened and what had been done and what was hoped. If he occasionally drifted into encomiums about Anne's character or looks or intelligence, Martin listened with understanding and tolerance. After all, James had had to listen to him, when he'd first fallen in love. Reciprocation seemed called for, but Martin did wonder, once or twice, if he'd sounded quite so silly or so totally besotted. Surely not . . . !

Runyon stormed into the inn and stomped up the narrow stairs to his room under the eaves. As he'd gone through the public room, he'd jerked his head and moments later his groom ducked his head and followed him into the small dark room. Runyon, yanking his coat from his shoulders, threw it on the bed. He scowled at the lanky man leaning against his door with arms crossed.

"Blasted trull has denied me!"

The groom's small eyes narrowed until they were nearly lost in their deep-set sockets. "Ye say her ladyship has forbidden you entry?"

"That's what I said, didn't I?" Runyon swore fluently, his admiring groom adding a couple of new curses to his already extensive vocabulary. When he'd run down, his lordship went to the dresser and lifted the bottle sitting there only to begin cursing all over again. "Get me more brandy."

The groom didn't move. "Landlord says no more on tick. He wants to see the ready before he hands over the doings."

The swearing began still again while Runyon searched his pockets, including those of clothing hanging in his clothes press. He came up with the required coins and the groom lounged off for the brandy.

The man had watched that procedure with lips compressed. If Lord Runyon had that much difficulty coming up with a handful of coin, where was he to get the reward promised for the work they were to do? Maybe it was time to ask for something up front . . . ?

"Took you long enough," muttered Runyon when the bottle appeared. The groom carried two glasses and Runyon glared at the second, met his groom's eyes, and, seeming to diminish slightly, poured out a second portion. "All right," he said once he'd settled himself before the ill-made fire. "We have to plan."

"You ain't giving up?"

"I'm more determined than ever. The vixen will be brought to my den!"

"And how you going to talk her into it if you can't get to her?"

"I won't. It's too late for that. Look here, you'll have to watch and discover her habits. She must stroll out for exercise, since she doesn't ride daily. You find out when and where."

"It's cold out there."

Runyon stared at him.

The groom explained. "Didn't plan on standing around in the cold when we started this gig."

"Money," said Runyon bitterly.

"Money," agreed the laconic groom.

"I don't have it with me."

"So when will you have it?"

"I will get what I have before leaving for the continent."

"Bah."

"Don't play me the fool!"

"If the dibs ain't in tune by tomorrow, maybe I'll jest walk."

"Tomorrow! Can't do a thing by tomorrow." Runyon pursed his lips, a black scowl, turning his usually pleasant features into something closely resembling a Gothic gargoyle. "Look here, as soon as we know when we can snatch her, I'll get it all together. We'll make the snatch, drive hell for leather for the coast and get into France as soon as maybe. I'll pay you once I have the wench properly cowed and in my hand."

"No."

"No!"

"Happen I don't trust you to come down with the ready."

"We've a problem, then. I don't trust you to stick with me once you have it!"

"I'll stick 'til I have the other thing you promised."

Runyon stared, comprehension finally dawning. "Ah. A chance at the mort, you mean. I see. Don't drool," ordered Runyon coldly, noting the lascivious look on his servant's face at the thought of bedding a lady.

Runyon wondered if he really would give Jaycee into the man's hands. He'd long ago discovered his groom had some decidedly nasty habits where women were concerned and, perhaps, Jaycee didn't deserve *that*. Especially if she behaved as he wished and accepted she had no choice but to play his whore before all of Paris! But then perhaps he could frighten her into behaving by explaining exactly what would happen to her if he allowed his servant to have her.

Runyon nodded. "I'll have part of what's owing you tomorrow night, but you get yourself stationed somewhere you can't be seen and observe the comings and goings. I want to know as soon as possible when we can take her. With no admittance to the Park, I've no excuse to remain here and if her bloody-minded brother catches on to the fact I've stayed on, he'll also twig there's a plot. Get on with it."

The groom pulled a battered flask from his pocket and filled it from the brandy bottle. He screwed on the top and slid it into his pocket.

"What the devil do you mean by that!"

"Told you." When all he got was a glare from Runyon, the groom explained further. "Gonna be cold as a witch's ti—"

"I get the picture."

"—ts out there tomorrow. Need the brandy to keep me warm." He didn't wait for a further response, but walked out of the room, remembering just in time to bend his neck so he'd not run into the exceedingly low lintel.

Runyon's soft curses followed him down the stairs.

"Your cheeks have a delightful color," said Lady Anne to Jaycee who had just strolled into the Green Salon, Tibbet hovering at her heels. "I saw you out near the yew walk."

"Hmm. I don't like walking in the alley between the trees. It's too narrow," said Jaycee. She noticed her butler and, shrugging out of the warm coat designed to emulate a man's driving coat complete with a couple of capes, she handed it over along with a scarf from around her neck. "It was very nice out. You should have come," she said a bit mischievously to Lady Fuster-Smythe who, it was well known, did as little as possible.

"Much too chilly for an old woman like me," said her ladyship in an absent tone. "Lady Anne," she added, "are you quite certain you cannot walk?"

"Quite certain."

"I don't understand it."

"What is it you don't understand, Lady Fuster-Smythe?" asked Jaycee looking up from her embroidery by which she'd seated herself. She was trying to decide whether one more violet in the current cluster would add or detract from the design.

"Hmmm? Oh, I saw a twitch this morning."

"I thought that the whole purpose of the treatment, that I twitch," said Anne.

"Yes, but this was *before* your maid applied the wand. I wonder . . ."

"Before . . . ?" asked Anne, a trifle of sharpness in her tone.

"What? Oh, yes. The girl paused in her movement to adjust her hold on the wand. I am convinced the muscle twitched *before* she finally touched it. I do believe I should write Dr. Macalister. He did say to report anything unusual . . ."

"I moved . . . ?" said Anne very softly. Hope revived. Just perhaps she *might* someday walk again. Her heart lightened a bit. Perhaps, she thought, it is not totally self indulgent to dream of Sir James. Just maybe if I can walk again and if, unlikely as it seems, he *does* fall in love with me, as I've fallen in love with him. . . .

"Perhaps before you write you should see if it happens again," suggested Jaycee, drawing Anne's attention away from thoughts which were agitating in the extreme.

"But it won't happen again, will it?" asked her ladyship. "The maid has never paused that way before and is very unlikely to do so again, don't you see?"

"Hmm . . ."

"No, Jaycee," said Anne, smiling.

"No?"

"You are not to suggest to Kitty that she deliberately become erratic in her touches!"

"I am not?"

"Jaycee, she was trained to do her task in a certain way. You must not change that. Not without the doctor's agreement, at least."

"So! I *shall* write him," said Lady Fuster-Smythe, who, as she explained to Jaycee why it *would* not happen had had the same thought that perhaps *she* could talk to the maid and make it happen, but dear Lady Anne was correct in that nothing should be done that the doctor had not approved.

"Well, I think it silly to waste so much time . . . what's that noise?" she interrupted herself to ask, her face turned toward the door beyond which the bumps and grunts of laboring men could be heard.

"Sounds like someone has arrived with all their bags and baggage," suggested Lady Fuster-Smythe, perhaps thinking of her own heavily laden arrival everywhere she went.

"Guests? No! Martin!"

"I hope she isn't disappointed," said Lady Anne who thought the sounds were not quite what one would expect of mere band boxes and a trunk of two.

"Very likely she will be. He hasn't had time to get here, has he?"

Anne blinked. "Lord Montmorency is coming home?"

"He will if he has an ounce of sense and I always thought him the best of all James's wide acquaintance so I expect he'll arrive in another week or two."

"You wrote him?"

"He is needed here," said her ladyship, scowling. "Can't have that Runyon running tame in his home, can he?"

"But Lord Runyon no longer comes here, does he?"

"Couldn't know Jaycee would have so much good sense, could I? She's never shown a sign of it before! I sent off my missive some time ago, you see."

Jaycee dragged back into the room. "It is merely the decorations for the ball. Crates and crates of birds." She sighed. "I haven't a notion what I'll do with them all and it was very likely a silly notion and I'll just have to think up something else. The illuminations have arrived as well. The one I looked at was very nice, I think. . . ."

Gradually, describing what she'd found in the opened crates, Jaycee talked herself into a better mood, but she was still a trifle subdued when James arrived. When he discovered she'd thought Martin had come and that her disappointment had been so great it still affected his volatile sister who never seemed to feel anything for very long, he compressed his lips and fought an inner battle. Jaycee won.

"I promised," he said in a stern firm voice, "that I'd not tell you and if you set up a screech or if you go off in a snit I'll never tell you anything ever again. Will you listen to me and hear me out to the very end before you jump to conclusions or otherwise do something foolish?"

"You have news of Martin?" Jaycee asked eagerly.

"He's in London, but deeply involved in his work. He wants desperately to see you, but you'd only be a distraction. He wishes to wait until he can come and not have to run off to daily meetings with other important people."

"Other important people?" Jaycee's eyes widened. "Do you mean to say my Martin is *important?*"

"Good heavens, Jaycee, of course he is! I should have thought you'd have known that. He is considered one of the government's rising stars and he's being groomed for very important work. The hope is that perhaps one day he'll be foreign secretary or perhaps even prime minister!"

"My Martin . . . ?"

"Jaycee, he has always played a role in government circles. You know that."

"Yes, but it always seemed such nonsense, spending all that time talking about dry stupid things which no one is ever interested in."

"A very great number of people are interested!"

"Yes, but no one important."

"Important?"

"Lady Jersey or Brummel or Lord Byron or . . . but no, perhaps Byron *is* interested. He's such an oddity. . . ."

"And what of Wellington and Castlereigh and Liverpool?"

"Oh, those people. Well, but they are so much above anything the common everyday sort of person. . . ." A startled expression crossed Jaycee's features. It transformed into a bemused look which, if the situation weren't so important, would have had James chuckling. "You mean," she asked, on a rising squeak, *"Martin* might someday be important like they are?"

"You begin to understand. The work people of that sort do, Jaycee, affects thousands and thousands of the common everyday sort you just mentioned. And at the moment, their work affects the whole of the continent and beyond."

"My goodness."

James chuckled. "So, until he can put that aside for a bit and concentrate on you alone, he can't be distracted, do you see?"

Jaycee was silent for a long moment. "He is in London and he does not come to me."

"Have you heard one word of what I've said?"

"He does not come because he'd be too distracted to pay attention to either me or his work."

"Very good!"

"But I *want* him to pay attention to me, James. Only to me."

"That is rather selfish of you, is it not?"

"Selfish?"

"When Martin is a man who is capable of great things, you would have him wait upon you as a servant or a dog?"

"But . . ."

"But nothing is of more interest than your common everyday self?"

Jaycee giggled at that, but her eyes glistened. "Is it so very selfish to wish to be loved beyond everything else?"

"Do you love Martin that way?"

"Yes."

For an instant the simple response disarmed James, but he immediately recovered. "I see. Then it is not important that you ever again visit your modiste or organize a ball or attend another's party?"

Jaycee dropped her gaze to the hands she had tightly clasped in her lap. "I see. You believe those things are for me like Martin's work for the government?"

"Are they not?"

"They *aren't* important, James. Not to me. I dress well because I wish to be a credit to Martin and I give and go to parties because that is what one does. What I would like

bove everything is for the two of us to retire to his estate
p north and never see anyone else ever again."

"Nonsense, Jaycee. You'd be bored within a week!"

"Would I?" she asked, a wistful note in her voice. "Well,
erhaps you are correct and I would." In a firmer tone she
dded, "But if Martin is in London and will soon be coming
ome, then it is important I talk with Mrs. Tibbet. His
ooms will have to be turned out and all his favorite foods
ot in stock and . . ."

Jaycee was still planning out loud when she disappeared
ut the door and shut it. James looked at the blank panels
nd shook his head. He would never understand his sister!
He fished his watch from its pocket and opened it. He
napped it shut, but he was halfway to the door and on his
vay to carry Lady Anne to her next treatment before the
vatch was safely tucked away.

Fourteen

Only a week remained before Jaycee's ball. Just the preceding evening Lady Anne had realized, that without thinking about it, she'd set that date as the dividing line between believing she'd walk again and accepting that she would not. Now she lay on the glass-legged table, every sense alert, waited for the first touch of the wand, the first jerk to her body. The process had become somewhat painful in the last few days. She'd been unable to decide if it was the Galvanism causing the change or if it was merely that she was excessively tense, hoping that each touch would be the one to cure her.

When the process was finished for that session and nothing new resulted from it, she found it necessary to fight back tears.

"It *will* help. You *will* recover," said James softly when he noticed. He held her gently, but a trifle more closely than was proper. "Cry if you wish, Anne. It helps."

"That would be to admit to a weakness," she muttered, turning her head so he could not see her face.

"Ah! Another of Lady P.'s canards! Even the Prince Regent weeps." Anne looked back, found him looking down at her. "Can royalty be wrong?"

"You should not have added that bit," said Anne, the beginning of a smile tugging at her lips. She actually felt herself relaxing and, for the moment, allowed both her fears and hopes to slide away.

"What should I not have said?" he asked.

"I was *almost* convinced," she explained, "when you suggested Lady Prem might have lied, but when you added that bit about Prince George, well, he is not known for his strengths, is he? I am forced to think my aunt correct in his respect!"

James chuckled. "You have caught me out, have you not?" He adopted a pensive look. "On the other hand, *I'm* not particularly weak and *I* have been known to shed tears." His voice roughened with remembered emotion. "I cried for my mother, Anne, when she was so ill and in such terrible pain just before she died . . . I have cried for you, my little bird."

"But those tears were for others, were they not? Mine would be for me alone."

"Then weep them for me, my wee brown wren," he said, his voice still rougher. "You cannot know how I ache for you."

James realized what he'd just said and felt his ears warming. He hoped Anne was unaware of all the many ways he ached! The pain of guilt and the pain of wishing her well again were the ones he'd meant. But there was also the ache to hold her, to keep her for himself alone, to have her at his side for the rest of his life . . . and in his bed.

Setting aside such unworthy thoughts for less selfish ones, he asked, "Will you go to your room, my little bird, or the Green Salon . . . or perhaps the music room?"

"My room, I think. I'll come down for luncheon and then I'll practice and then I'll move to the salon to work on my book."

James was startled into a sound of faint distress.

"What is it?"

"Nothing of importance," he said. "Merely that I'd thought to ride into Town today once you were settled, but it can wait." Had that fleeting expression touching her face

been one of disappointment? Or only wishful thinking tha
he saw it?

Anne's tone was firm when she spoke. "Nonsense. Jay
cee has several footmen who are strong enough they giv
me the same feeling of security you do. You must no
change your plans just to carry me from place to place."

So. Merely wishful thinking. "Ah, but you don't under
stand," said James, making a joke of his emotions. "It i
pure self-indulgence on my part." Her flaring brows lifte
questioning him. He explained. "When I carry you I hav
you close. I like having you close to me."

Anne flushed a rosy red and James chuckled softly.

"Do I embarrass you?" he asked. "I don't mean to," h
added, somewhat tongue in cheek, because, although he ha
not meant to embarrass her, he was not unhappy his word
affected her. "You do not like lies so I only tell you th
truth, you see."

"Nevertheless," she said, sternly repressing the bubbl
feeling his comment roused, "you will oblige me by no
changing your plans. You will leave for London on the in
stant."

He pretended to drop her and, alarmed, she gripped mor
tightly around his neck. "You did say on the instant," h
teased.

"I guess I didn't mean it quite literally. Perhaps yo
should not leave *quite* that quickly!" She gave him a ruefu
look. "But, James, you must go if you have a duty to se
to. Or even if you go for amusement," she added in wha
was obviously an afterthought.

"It is true I made an appointment I do not care to break
and, since you insist, I'll go but will return as quickly as
can. And here we are. Kitty, I see, has popped up the back
stairs and has already prepared your bed for you. I'll jus
sit you here on the side so that she can prepare *you.*" James
hesitated, glanced at the maid and then, greatly daring, ben

and dropped a warm kiss on Anne's forehead. "Kitty, take good care of your mistress." Very quickly he left the room.

Anne stared after him. She lifted trembling fingers to her brow but didn't quite touch the spot where his lips had burned against her skin. She turned her gaze to Kitty, a question in them. Kitty merely smiled and nodded. Anne looked back toward the door through which James had disappeared.

What, she wondered, *did he mean by it!*

She remembered that he'd once promised he'd prove to her she was not unattractive. Had he decided she was well enough to begin—or that she'd never be better than she was now? Had he begun his teasing campaign? Or had he only meant a bit of comfort because she'd felt so very low when they'd left the Galvanism session? He surely did not mean that he loved her . . .

"He couldn't possibly . . . ," she muttered, the words trailing off to nothing.

"What, my lady? I didn't quite hear. . . ."

"Hmm?" Anne felt heat rise up her throat as she realized she'd spoken out loud. "Nothing, Kitty. Nothing at all."

Later that afternoon, Jaycee ducked her head into the Green Salon. "Is there anything I can do for either of you before I take my walk?"

Anne held up her pen and looked around. "Nothing, thank you."

"You may tell me if your cook is busy at this hour," said Lady Fuster-Smythe, quickly swallowing the last crumbs of a ginger biscuit.

"My cook . . ." Jaycee blinked. "I haven't the least notion what she does at this hour!"

"Hmm. Do you not? *Usually* at this hour, in *most* households, servants have a rest period. That would be the best time to talk to her, I think. . . ." Her ladyship beckoned to her footman, one of whom was *always* on duty, and, with his help, rose to her feet. "Since you do not know, I'll just go see."

"See?"

"Hmm. I'm still hopeful, you understand, that I'll manage to coax from her the secret of her ginger biscuits! Now, not so fast," she added as her footman started toward the door. "Just you let me get my breath, first," she scolded.

"Should I go with you?" asked Jaycee on a doubtful note.

"I think not. If I decide to bribe the woman, she might say 'not' simply because you are there."

"Bribe . . ."

"Of course I'll not try that—" Her voice dropped to a conspiratorial tone for the next few words. "—except, of course, as a last resort. One should not coddle servants, but if there is no other recourse. . . ." She glanced at her footman. "You did not hear that!" He grinned and scolding, her words trailing behind her, Lady Fuster-Smythe disappeared out the door.

Anne chuckled and Jaycee giggled. When the laughter subsided, Jaycee asked again, "There truly is nothing I can do for you?"

"Nothing. I hope to finish two of my essays today. This one, Lavender, has been going very well, but it is a fairly simple herb, used occasionally for relief from aches and pains. . . ."

"Like when I have my maid bathe my forehead when it aches with a handkerchief dipped in lavender?"

"Just like that, but it is more useful to the household as an insect repellent or merely for its lovely scent. The Licorice root, which is next, is more complicated and may take several revisions."

"That awful stuff! I cannot abide the flavor."

Anne chuckled. "I have discovered it is one which a person either likes very much indeed, or, conversely, is intensely averse to. There seems to be no middle ground!"

"I am definitely among the latter," said Jaycee. "If there is truly nothing you wish just now, I'll take my walk."

"Will you go along the yew walk as you sometimes do? I mean along this side of it?"

"I think I will. Just to the top of the hill and back. It is just the right distance to warm one's body and make one feel energetic. When you are walking again we must go together." Jaycee noted that Anne immediately seemed to shrink. "Of *course* you will walk again," she chided. "It is impossible that you will not!"

"Why do you think it impossible?" asked a bemused Anne.

"You will walk again before my ball. You see, I have decided. . . ." Jaycee, her eyes wide and twinkling, quickly put her hands up over her mouth, stopping the flow of words. *"There!"* she said after a moment. "I almost gave away the secret! That would never do, would it now?"

"One should not tell secrets," said Anne solemnly.

"I have always been very very good at keeping secrets, but you, Anne . . . For some reason it is so easy to talk to you that I very nearly told that one! Now, no teasing to find out!" she warned. "I won't tell!"

Since Anne had made no effort to discover Jaycee's secret she was initially confused by the warning tone, but then she wondered if Jaycee meant exactly the opposite, that she *was* to tease and cajole and attempt to discover it.

Sounding a trifle disappointed, Jaycee added, "I'll see you later."

Jaycee's tone indicated she had wished to be urged and, as one so often did with Jaycee, Anne gave into the temptation to give the young woman exactly what she wanted. "I *did* hope to discover your secret!" she said. "Now I'll not be able to work for wondering," she added when Jaycee looked doubtful.

Jaycee grinned. "It is very strong willed of you that you did not *immediately* ask me. I am never able to control *my* curiosity, even for an instant! But I'll *not* tell you, so I'll leave you to what work you can manage . . . !"

She whisked herself out the door ignoring Anne's chuckle. For a moment Anne looked out the window toward the yews. The day was slightly cloudy, but there appeared to be little wind. Jaycee would enjoy her walk. . . . Anne bent her head to her writing, discovered the ink had dried on her pen and, deciding exactly what she wished to say next, dipped it, and wrote steadily.

When Anne next looked out the window she saw Jaycee, all bundled up in her long blue coat with the mannish capes. She decided her sister-in-law had come from a back or side door, since it wasn't possible she'd walked all the way around the house in such a short time.

Jaycee was speaking with the old gardener and, it appeared, might be forced to postpone her walk, since he was gesturing toward the roses. The young woman and the age-bent gardener strolled nearer, approaching one particular bush. Once there Jaycee, her head tipped, listened as the gardener spoke with more verve than Anne would have thought possible.

What they discussed could not be seen from Anne's position in the Green Salon. She was too far away for such details, of course, and could hear nothing through the windows. After a moment she bent to her work. When she looked up again Jaycee had reached the nearer end of the long line of yews. She had paused and was leaning over, looking at something laying on the ground. She bent and picked it up, shoved it into the oversized pocket which Jaycee had designed as decoration for the coat. It was only after she'd begun wearing it that she'd discovered how useful a pocket was.

Anne smiled as she remembered that particular conversation with her sister-in-law. Jaycee had insisted, that from now on, she'd have pockets of one sort or another fitted into or onto all her clothing! Anne thought it one of those enthusiasms Jaycee would soon forget. A mental vision of a lovely ball gown shaped itself in Anne's mind. She added a pocket. The resulting image had her laughing softly and she hoped Jaycee had more sense than to spoil the lines of important gowns with something so mundane as pockets!

Thinking of Jaycee and how much she'd enjoyed getting to know the young woman, Anne leaned against the back of the chaise. She put her elbows on the lap desk and fingered her pen with both hands as she watched Jaycee stride alongside the row of trees. It was not a particularly ladylike gait, thought Anne, but it looked healthy and purposeful and matched up with the odd coat. Did Jaycee save the coat for when she wished a particularly energetic walk? Anne smiled at the notion of different coats for different sorts of exercise. What nonsense . . .

Jaycee had reached the hill now. Surely she'd slow as she went up the rise, gentle as that was . . . but no. She walked right along, swinging her arms briskly in time with her steps. What a spirited young woman she was. And what a combination of contradictions. Because, spirited as she was, Jaycee was also surprisingly insecure. It had amazed Anne when she'd first realized that. Jaycee, like everyone, wanted and needed to be loved. The only problem was that she never seemed quite sure that she was!

The hill became a trifle steeper just then and Jaycee slowed a bit. A movement at the top of the hill caught Anne's eye but she saw nothing when she looked up. A bird, perhaps, which had flown from the yews . . . ?

But then Jaycee neared the top, hesitated . . . Anne leaned forward. What was the matter? Why did Jaycee stop in that strange way? Why was she turning . . . running. . . .

"Oh dear!"

Her eyes never leaving the horrifying scene at the verge of the hill, Anne rose to her feet. She pressed next to the window and glanced quickly in both directions, but the old gardener was not in sight. She glanced back up the hill and saw Jaycee kick viciously at the man trying to hold her feet, while the other, one hand over her mouth, his second around her waist, did his best to control the squirming woman in his arms.

Anne turned and ran from the room. "Someone! Anyone! Where is everybody! Oh, help!"

"Anne, what is it?" Sir James returned her call and, moments later, hurried down the hall toward her. "Anne! You are walking!"

"Never mind that. Jaycee . . ."

"What about my wife!" asked a voice Anne didn't quite recognize.

She knew her brother, however, when he came up behind James, a frown marring his high brow. Anne clutched at James's arms and he held her by the waist, but she didn't look at him but at her brother. "You must save her!"

"Save my wife?"

"That villain . . . !" Anne sobbed. "He kidnapped her!"

"Runyon!"

"Yes, Sir James," she said, turning her anguished face up to his. "I just saw them."

Martin looked at his fingernails. "You are quite certain," he said in a cold voice, "that she didn't not go with him willingly?"

Anne glared at her brother. In an equally cold tone she said, "Not if the black eye one of the blackguards will sport is an indication!"

Martin relaxed. "That sounds like Jaycee. Tell us."

"Yes, Anne, but come sit down," said James, still concerned that she was on her feet. "You haven't walked anywhere for nearly a month. It cannot be a good notion for you to overdo now." He swung her up into his arms and headed for the Green Salon.

"Walk?" Anne looked to where her legs dangled over his

left arm. For the first time she realized she had actually *walked*. "I *walked*. I did it! I can walk!"

"Yes. And at a goodly clip, too. But no more for now." James seated her on her chaise and Martin, who had impatiently allowed the diversion, asked for an exact description of what Anne had seen.

She obliged, pointing out the window and explaining.

"So." Martin's forehead wrinkled into a mass of lines, as he thought. "I must be off at once. The question is, where would he take her?"

"Martin," said James, "remember what's been said the last few years? That the wretch has been getting income from some unknown source but no one knows where? I've occasionally wondered if he was engaged in some aspect of the smuggling trade. The agent end, perhaps? Selling what was brought over from France?"

"Which would mean he is involved with someone with a boat. Which would mean he'll use that boat to take Jaycee out of the country." Martin groaned. "The whole of the coastline to search!"

"Why would he take her that far?" asked Anne, her heart still pounding with fear for her friend.

"Because he's determined to gouge the last iota of revenge from this escapade," explained Martin. "If it were me, I'd take her to Paris where I'd make everyone believe she's my mistress."

"Really, Martin, you don't think you are carrying this a little too far? If Jaycee won't cooperate, which at this point I'm quite certain she *won't*, it will be *he* who is ruined, not *she*." James started to add to that, glanced at Anne, and then heard her say what he'd thought too rough for her to know.

"But she *will* be ruined . . . just being in the man's company for several days is enough to ruin her. Even if he is charged with kidnapping, she will be shunned." She lay her hand on his arm. "James, you must stop him! He must not be allowed his way in this!"

Martin crossed the room and pulled the bell pull several times. A clatter of feet were heard rushing down the hall from both directions. Tibbet beat the two footmen by no more than the inches necessary for him to enter the room first.

"My Lord Montmorency!" he exclaimed in horror. "You've arrived home and no one to greet you!"

"That makes no odds, Tibbet. Lady Montmorency was just kidnapped by that fiend Runyon. Lady Anne saw the whole through that window. I need every man available. Every horse. We must search the countryside in all directions. I fear he'll try to get her across the Channel as quickly as possible, so we need to discover the existence of every strange carriage or unexplained cart heading toward the coast in whatever direction. You," he added pointing to one footman. "You go to the stables and order every horse tacked up and explain why, can you do that? Tell the grooms I'll be out to talk to them and set them their orders as soon as maybe. You," he added, pointing to the other footman, "take one of those horses, ride into the village, and rouse it for the search. I would like to talk to the innkeeper as soon as possible. He may know something of Runyon's plans since I would suppose that is where the rogue stayed while waiting for my wife to walk out and get herself kidnapped. Damn!"

Lord Montmorency swore long and fluently until James, seeing how it distressed Lady Anne, placed a hand over Martin's mouth and nodded in her direction. "I know how you feel, but that won't help. Come now. We'll have Cook pack up a meal of sorts and get this search organized. Anne, I don't know when we'll return, but we will return. And when we do it will be with Jaycee. You must not feel too concerned."

"I am sure you will do everything possible," she said. "Good luck!"

But she said the last to their backs as they strode out the door. When even the sound of their passing had disappeared, Anne looked around herself and gasped in shock. There her ink had spread in a dark stain into the lovely carpet. Elsewhere her papers were scattered in all directions. One of her precious books lay, its crumpled pages in the edge of the spreading ink. What an awful mess. Had she done that?

Anne attempted to remember exactly what had happened and what she'd done. She had seen Jaycee hesitate near the top of the hill. Her sister-in-law had turned, begun to run back down toward the house. The men had appeared, Runyon grabbing her from behind, one hand over her mouth. He'd tried to pull her back up the hill, over the top and out of sight, but Jaycee had fought, squirming and kicking, and the other man had tried to control her feet. . . .

And while that happened, Anne had stood at the window watching her, watching her kick and kick at the second man, who was attempting to lift her feet so they could carry her away . . . and finally succeeding? They must have, although by then Anne had moved, had run out into the hall, had shouted for help!

Had walked.

Actually, she had *run*.

On her own two feet. Anne looked to where her feet rested on the floor. She had walked. She could walk . . . or could she? Could she *still* walk? Anne's heart beat strongly, painfully, as she tried to bring herself to the point of attempting the formerly impossible. She had moved. She could move.

She tried very hard to convince herself, but could not banish the fear that if she were to try now she'd fail!

At that moment Lady Fuster-Smythe bustled into the room, her footman helping her seat herself. "Now then,

Anne," said her ladyship, "I want a round tale instantly. Those men were exceedingly rude. His lordship did not even bother to say hello! Nor would they stop even for a moment to explain what all the hustle and bustle might be."

Anne stifled a chuckle at her ladyship's look of outrage.

"Sir James," continued Lady Fuster-Smythe, "said I was to ask you."

Once again Anne described what she'd seen. She did not add that she had walked. The whole time she spoke, however, she never took her eyes from her toes. *If I try to wiggle those toes,* she wondered, *will they move?*

"Kidnapped? Nonsense. All a ruse so we will think she did not go willingly."

Since she was preoccupied with the fact she'd walked, might still be able to walk, her ladyship's words sank in slowly. When they did Anne lifted her head and glared at Lady Fuster-Smythe.

"You will never say anything so vicious ever again," she said in exactly the tone her Aunt Prem had once used on an erring servant. It startled Anne to hear those stern tones in her own voice, and for half a moment she thought of apologizing. Then she decided Lady Fuster-Smythe deserved every word. "Well?" she asked. "Did you hear me?"

"How dare you speak so to me? I have watched Lady Jaycee flirt with Lord Runyon with my own eyes!"

"Before we convinced her the man was dangerous. When she decided that *was* the case she forbade the villain entrance, did she not?"

"Well . . ."

"She has not shown the least sign she misses him either, sighing and moody as one becomes when suffering a benighted love affair. You know that is true."

"But . . ."

"But it would make a much better story *your* way, would it not?"

Lady Fuster-Smythe brightened. "Yes, it would!"

"However that may be, you will *not* embroider on the situation," said Anne in a silky, dangerous tone. "You will tell everyone who asks, how hard Jaycee struggled and fought against being carried away. And you will speak only to those who ask, since it is possible no one will ever know what has happened. Assuming *you* do not tell . . ."

"Not tell . . . ?"

"Do not look so aghast. After all, such gossip is beneath you, my lady."

"It is?"

Now her ladyship looked so wistful, Anne had to suppress a strong, nearly hysterical, desire to laugh. "It is," she insisted. Her ladyship must be distracted from Jaycee, but how . . . ? "You will have quite enough to tell when you describe how you have helped with my cure."

"Ah. My note-taking for the good doctor . . . cure?" Her ladyship's head snapped up. "You said *cure?*"

"Yes."

Taking every ounce of willpower in hand, Anne braced and pushed herself to her feet. For another long moment Anne just looked down. Would her limbs work? Then, a trifle more complacent now she'd proved to herself she could stand, she asked, "If you would be kind enough to loan me your footman . . . ?" Anne looked at Lady Fuster-Smythe who was gaping at her. "Your footman, my lady? I think I'd like his very strong arm for a moment. My lady?"

"Arm . . . oh. *You!*" she called and the footman appeared. He looked at his mistress after half a glance toward Anne. "Help her."

"Just your arm, if you will?" asked Anne when he approached.

Facing her, he held his arm so she could grasp it with both hands. Hesitantly she moved one foot. More carefully, feeling like a child learning to walk, she took a second step. How had she managed to run like the wind down the hall? She took another. She had not, of course, been thinking about what she was doing. The footman backed up and she took another careful step. Perhaps that was the secret. One simply walked. One didn't think about lifting a foot, swinging it forward, setting it down and moving one's weight.

"You don't seem to be walking very well," said Lady Fuster-Smythe.

"Likely that is because it's so long since I've done so." Anne took another step, another. She stopped. "I'm tired now. Please return me to my seat."

The footman hesitated. "My lady?"

"Yes, you had best pick me up and carry me back. I know it isn't far, but I seem to be trembling and don't wish to suffer a relapse!" She was soon settled in her usual place. "Well, my lady?" she asked. "Will that news satisfy those with whom you correspond?"

"I should think so! And the first who must have this news is dear Dr. Macalister. But first, I will write up exactly what I've just seen in the notebook. At least . . . I know it is not the machine and the Galvanism, but it is relevant, don't you agree?"

Anne nodded. "Very relevant, Lady Fuster-Smythe. Mac will wish your every observation and thought. I fear," she added with a sober face, hopefully hiding that she very much wished to be alone, "that may take you some time, since it is such a change from not walking at all and you will have much to say . . . ?"

"A very great deal. In fact, I believe I'll just go to my room where I will have no distractions and set down every word." She gestured to her footman who, with his usual care, helped her ladyship to rise. Then, matching her mincing steps, he slowly led her from the room.

As he left he turned back and winked at Anne. She didn't know whether to laugh at his audacity or scowl at his cheek! But her concern for Jaycee soon put either impulse to rout.

Fifteen

The front door slammed so loudly Anne heard it at the back of the house where the Green Salon was situated. She immediately, without thinking, rose to her feet, determined she'd know at once what had been discovered. She was half-way across the room when its door, too, burst open and James strode in, strode directly to her and pulled her against him, burying her head in the cold lapels of his coat.

"Never!" he said. "Never-never-never put me through what Martin is suffering now!"

"Of course not," murmured Anne, wondering if her heart would burst, it pounded so.

He grasped her shoulders and pushed her away, looking earnestly down into her face, "Anne, he's so afraid, so worried. . . . I've never seen him in such a state."

"You, sir, are no less worried." Surely his behavior was only because of that. Anne took a deep breath and demanded, "Tell me what has been done, what is happening."

Anne reached for James's hand and turned, leading him to a divan against the wall. When they'd seated themselves she tried to retrieve her hand, but he would not let it go. Her pounding heart, which had begun to return to normal, once again increased its pace.

"Please," she said, "I need to know what has been done and why you are here. . . ."

"Umm?" He seemed to return from somewhere far away and the burning look with which he'd bathed her features in fire became slightly more tepid. "You wish to hear about Jaycee. We discovered what we believe to be the proper carriage. It has been well hidden for days in the spinney atop Gritter's Hill—or so we were told by a young limb of Satan who accosted us shortly before we entered the village. He also knew it was moved early this morning to a lane beyond the yews. He claims it is headed toward the coast by the Brighton road, so we think it is on its way to a hidden cove somewhere near there. Would you believe the brat demanded a whole shilling for sweets before he'd tell us that last?"

"Surely you didn't give it to him?"

"What else was one to do?"

"But the poor boy will be so sick he'll never eat another!"

James chuckled. "Which will teach him a lesson, will it not?" He sobered, his eyes again studying her face.

"Then my brother," Anne said, "is following the carriage. Why are you not with him, Sir James?"

"He and a pair of grooms have gone on and I wish I *were* with them. . . ." James scowled "The trouble is, we cannot be absolutely certain, can we? What if we are wrong in our theory Runyon will take Jaycee to France? Perhaps the carriage is a red herring, or what if it turns off somewhere and Martin loses it? It is possible this is an old game for Runyon. Perhaps, instead of taking her across the Channel, he'll demand ransom for her return. . . . You see, Anne, no one can explain how it is he has lived so well for so long on nothing a year—although it is my belief he's run a smuggling operation. The thing is, we cannot *know!*"

"Surely word of such a nasty trick as kidnapping tonnish women would have leaked out?"

"Not if he threatened to make a byword of the lady's honor the moment anything was said." The frown which had faded slightly as he explained the situation returned. "You know, Anne, I have always been amazed at how easily he worst is believed—even by people who know the parties involved. It is almost as if they *wish* to believe the worst!"

"Perhaps it makes their own particular lives seem better f it is known there are others in more trouble, in deeper waters, in greater difficulty. . . ."

"Whatever it is, I've always thought such willingness to ccept, unquestioningly, that the nastiest possible interpreation be put on a situation is at best childish and perhaps, t worst, a sin!"

Anne recalled Lady Fuster-Smythe's immediate response o the present situation and nodded. "Perhaps," she offered, "it is also that, for some, life is so boring, such tales give t a bit of spice?"

"It would be better if they lived life for themselves, rather han needing to be entertained by others!"

Anne tried once again to retrieve her hand, but found her effort only led James to clasping it with both his hands. She looked up, wide eyed, into his face which was softening, warming, looking back at her with such a look as she'd never before seen on a man's face.

"James?"

"Ah, Anne. My little bird. My wee wren. Will you do something for me?"

"If I can . . ."

He grinned at her, and his eyes twinkled devilishly. "Take off that blasted cap!"

"Take off . . . !"

"The thing I thought most often as we raced over the countryside chasing after that benighted carriage was that I wanted, desperately, to see again your magnificent hair."

"Magnificent . . ."

"Anne, when you fell and were unconscious for so long?"

"Yes . . ."

"You may not recall, but it was uncovered. An accident," he added quickly. "My sleeve caught at the cap and pulled

it off when I lay you on your bed, but once I saw your hai
I could not imagine its ever being hidden away again. An
yet you became so agitated when you discovered it wa
flowing free and alive and beautiful, and you insisted s
firmly, I found I had to give in and put one of your ugly
caps over it. I've wanted so much to see it again. Waite
so long . . . Anne, will you remove that ugly cap?"

"Aunt Prem . . ."

". . . Told you it was awful! Of course she did. Pleas
Anne?"

"Please Anne what!" came the abrupt tones of Lady Fus
ter-Smythe's deep voice. "What sinful request have yo
made of that maiden in my absence!"

James sighed and rolled his eyes upward which cause
Anne, who never giggled, to do so!

"I will know at once what it is you have requested o
Lady Anne," repeated her ladyship.

"Merely," admitted James, "that she take off that awfu
cap and allow her hair the freedom it needs. It cannot b
healthy for it that she keeps it covered day in and day out,"
he said piously. "I am," he added, a distinctly wicked loo
in his eye, "merely thinking of her health, you see."

"Poppycock!"

"Not at all. Anne? Will you? Please?" He let go he
hands and reached for the bow.

Anne put her fingers on his wrists, stopping him. For a
long moment they stared into each others eyes. Anne's
hands dropped to her lap. She closed her eyes, as if having
them shut somehow denied what was happening. She fel
the tie loosened. She felt his fingers at the hem, easing the
drawstring back into its casing. She scrunched her eyelids
more tightly closed as she felt the heavy cotton slide back
over her head and drop away. And she heard the deep breath
James drew in when her hair braid fell free from its con
finement and down over her shoulder.

"I thought I remembered its color perfectly," breathed James.

"Why, it is lovely!" said Lady Fuster-Smythe, a note of evident surprise in her tone. "I had assumed there was something wrong with it because why else would you hide it?"

"The color . . ." said Anne, embarrassed.

"I've not seen its like in years, of course. Not since your grandmother on your mother's side turned gray," said Lady Fuster-Smythe. "She came from the highlands, you know. She fell in love with your grandfather, a British earl who was visiting Edinburgh, and was disinherited by her father when they eloped. Everyone predicted disaster, she with her wild highland ways and he with his very strict, very proper, very cold-seeming manners. But they delighted in each other. Very odd . . ."

"My grandmother . . . ?"

"I said so, did I not? Doubtless Lady Preminger never mentioned her. She had no liking for the dear lady with her light-hearted insistence people should be happy! If I recall, it was your grandmother who informed your father one was not allowed to marry one's sister and Lady Preminger had become his sister when he married *her* sister, of course. He promptly married your mother, which is what he'd wanted all along. Despite all Lady Preminger's plots to thwart him."

"Anne," asked James, taking her hands again in his, "are you all right? You seem a trifle pale. . . ."

"Aunt Prem . . . she was so certain, so absolutely positive, so convincing, so . . ."

". . . terrible," James finished for her. "Perhaps even evil. You must never again think of those awful years, Anne." His hands tightened. "I will *make* you forget them. I will make you so happy and gay you will never have reason to think of them again!"

"I cannot put it behind me, James," she said quietly. "Recently, I've been thinking carefully about the things she taught me. There is much one can believe, you know. *Should* believe. A very great deal of good sense concerning good behavior and a proper attitude toward others and an insistence on doing one's duty as you know very well we all should do and . . ."

James covered her lips. "Then you will decide what is to be your own personal creed of behavior and will throw out all the rest. *Particularly,*" he said with mock solemnity, "you will forget her strictures about your hair."

James could resist no longer. He lifted the heavy braid. The curly end, with a seeming life of its own, wrapped itself around his wrist. He raised his arm to his cheek and smoothed the hair against his skin. A faint growth of whiskers caught individual hairs, pulled them free. They fell against his skin, held there as if magnetically, making a pattern of lines.

Anne raised her hand and pulled them away. "You must not," she said softly.

"I wish you'd give me the right to do so," he said equally softly. When her flaring brows flew up into a wider vee he chuckled in embarrassment, two revealing spots of color on his cheeks. "Yes. Awkwardly and with no particular courtship, except that you must have noticed how well we match, how much I love you, I ask you to marry me. Will you, my little bird?"

"Here now!" interjected Lady Fuster-Smythe. "What is this? A proposal and her brother nowhere near to guide her!"

"I've already asked his permission. Go away, Lady Fussy-Puss. I wish to be private with my Anne, with my little bird, my precious love."

"She is *not* your Anne. Not yet at least. And if she has any sense she'll not say yes unless you promise to stop calling her that silly pet name of yours! Little bird, indeed! Nasty dirty creatures . . ."

"Lady Fussy-Puss?"

"I will not leave you alone. I know my duty and my duty is to chaperone her ladyship."

James ground his teeth. Anne touched his wrist and he glanced at her. "You truly love me?" she asked on a breath of air.

"Yes!"

Anne mouthed the word "yes." And then realizing what she'd done, her mouth opened and she looked utterly stunned. "Did I say yes?" she asked, again on the softest breath of air.

"You did." He touched her cheek. "Did you mean you'll wed me?" he asked. Anne looked up into his eyes. She nodded. "You *will*," he repeated. "Lady Fussy-Puss, we are officially engaged and you may *go away.*"

Lady Fuster-Smythe snorted, but she called for her footman and took her leave, saying, sternly, as she moved across the room, that they could have fifteen minutes only, and that she would then, without fail, return. She even directed her footman to close the door as they left.

"You see?" said James, smiling broadly. "She isn't such a bad sort." Anne looked doubtful and he chuckled. "And now, my love, we will share our first kiss which will bind the agreement!"

Anne put her hand to his chest, holding herself away from him. "Did I truly agree to wed you?" asked Anne again, wide eyed and a little pale.

"You most certainly did and there is no way I'll allow you to renege!" He gathered her close and, staring down into her eyes, drew in a deep breath. "Ah, Anne, my dearest love . . . I don't want to frighten you, but I have waited so long to kiss you, to taste you, to hold you close, to . . ."

Her fingers stopped the flow of words and very shyly moved to his neck. She gave one thought to Lady Prem's description of lovemaking and decided the ugliness of it must have been another thing about which her ladyship had lied. She pulled James's head down.

"You will not frighten me," she said against his lips.

The fifteen minutes stretched to nearly twenty before a loud clattering noise in the hall penetrated their preoccupation with each other. Very quickly James set Anne off his lap. "It can't have been fifteen minutes," he muttered, his voice thick, but he straightened her gown and moved himself somewhat away from her.

Anne blushed, deciding that Lady Prem had indeed lied about the wonders of a lover's way. She reached for his cravat, her busy fingers easing it back into proper creases and finished just as the door opened allowing them to hear a gruff, warning, "harumph."

"It's all right, Lady Fuster-Smythe. We are all proper and prudent and polite. At least, we'll attempt to be polite." His heated gaze drew another blush from his Anne.

"I will just have my chair put down at that end of the salon. You may discuss all those important things lovers discuss," she said portentously, "and I'll not hear a thing. But you will behave yourselves and no more nonsense of the sort. . . ."

"My lady," said Anne, before further words would make it all too explicit what they were not to do, "will you favor us by not announcing the engagement immediately? Until Jaycee is found and my brother's problems settled, it would be less than tactful to make a parade of our happiness!"

Reluctantly Lady Fuster-Smythe agreed it would not be quite proper to announce the engagement. Anne turned to look at the footman who instantly sobered and gave a small nod. He too would hold his tongue. Anne breathed again. Very soon they had as much privacy as was proper. "I don't know how I had the *courage* to say yes," admitted Anne when James told her he'd not expected her to do so.

"Why would it take courage?" he asked. "Am I so frightening? So terrible?"

Anne's lips twisted into that funny half smile she sometimes got. "You are forgetting Lady Prem. She taught me all men are terrible! *Of course* you are frightening," and added after a slight hesitation, *"As is the whole world* for that matter. James, are you certain you wish to wed me? I have so much to learn! So much to forget! I may never feel truly free to take my place in the world you inhabit naturally. I will be forced to think of my every action and reaction!"

"I wish to wed you from the depths of my soul, but if—mind, I only say if—you were not to wed me, what did you plan for your life?"

She blushed, and looked at her clasped hands. "You will think it silly. . . ."

"I doubt that very much, Anne. I've never known you to be silly. Now if I were to ask that question of Jaycee . . . !"

Anne chuckled. "Yes, I can see there is something of a difference between us, although I doubt she is half so silly inside where it counts, as she makes it appear on the surface that she is."

"I'm beginning to believe that myself, but I've no desire to discuss my sister. Anne, tell me what you planned?"

She told him of the small house with a bit of land, the herb gardens, her hopes she could supply salves and infusions and other preparations to doctors. "It was all I could think to do with my life, James. The only thing of interest to me and something which might be a bit useful to others. . . ."

"Anne, would you teach me about your herbs?"

She looked up at him quickly, wonderingly. "Teach you . . . ?"

"I think I told you quite early in our acquaintance, although you might not remember," he said hesitantly, since he never spoke of his early ambitions, "that I once wanted, desperately, to be trained in medicine. My father could not allow it. If I'd had an elder brother, perhaps. . . ." He shook his head. "But it is I who is responsible for the estate. But this. Could we not work together organizing a small farm for growing herbs, and then perhaps we could build a proper facility for curing those herbs, and doing the extractions and mixing and all those things one must do? I'd hire you the help you need and you could train them. And couldn't such remedies also be sold to poor people who will not go to a doctor because of the expense, but only to their local apothecary? You could write up directions for their use. And . . ." He stared. "You are laughing."

"Merely because you have gone so far beyond my plans for a humble little garden and a small but well-equipped still room I cannot think! It would be wonderful, James, and of course I will teach you what I know. Perhaps you cannot be a doctor, but there is no reason you cannot be a supplier to doctors!"

"That is almost as good, is it not?"

"Yes. That is almost as good."

Taking her hands again, he asked, urgently, "Anne, when may we be married?"

"Soon. . . . But not until Jaycee is returned to us. James, will Martin take her back if she is gone—" Anne hesitated. "—too long?"

A muscle jumped in James's jaw. "She will not be gone too long."

"But if . . ."

It was his turn to cover her lips with the tips of his fingers. "Anne, he is following closely behind that odd carriage which we believe to be Runyon's. With any luck, it will not leave his sight. Martin will rescue Jaycee as soon as it reaches its destination. They will be home tonight. Or, at latest, they'll come tomorrow, because, if he finds she is too distressed by her adventure, he will, of course, stop at an inn so she may rest."

"I hope all goes well," said Anne and leaned against his arm.

James rearranged them slightly so he could hold her. He lay his head on top of hers and for a long time they sat that way, staring into the fire and worrying about Jaycee and Martin.

"Stop right there," said Martin.

Runyon and his groom froze, their struggling burden no longer wriggling, but sagging between them.

"Put Jaycee down. Gently," Martin directed next. He motioned with his pistol.

"Don't know what you mean," blustered Runyon, adjusting his grip. "Just a boy who drank too much. Taking him to his father. . . ."

"Put Jaycee down at once or I'll shoot."

The groom set her feet against the ground and backed away across the pebbly beach, his hands in the air. "Don't shoot, guv," he said. "Only following orders. Not my doing!"

"Put Jaycee down, Runyon. Easy!"

Runyon scowled. "Damned if I will, you marplot!" Again he altered his hold, this time bringing Jaycee fully in front of him. He backed toward the rickety wharf and the small boat in which a man sat, the oars shipped. Farther out a fishing boat was anchored, its sails loosened and ready to raise. "You shoot," warned Runyon when Martin raised one pistol and sighted it, "and you'll hit your wife."

"I think you know my reputation. I hit what I will. Jaycee?"

"Shoot, Martin. Shoot him! Oh, please shoot him!"

"Fool," hissed Runyon. "He'll hit you."

"No, he won't," said Jaycee with passion. "He's a truly excellent shot!"

The groom hitched his pack higher onto his shoulder and made for the boat. "Don't shoot *me*. I didn't have nothing to do with it, I tell you!"

"Yes, he did," said Jaycee. "They argued all the way here about how much he'd be paid, and Martin, don't let them

take me. If you cannot stop them, then shoot *me* instead."
Everyone could hear the fear in her voice. "They argued
about . . . other things, too," she finished on a hoarse whis-
per.

Martin again raised one of the pistols he held trained on
Runyon and his wife. "Put her down, Runyon, and I'll allow
you to get away. Take her one step further and I'll kill you."

For a moment Lord Runyon hesitated. Then he looked
over his shoulder to where the oarsman was setting his
blades in the water. He dumped Jaycee onto the strand and
raced the last few yards to reach the boat before it pulled
away from the rough dock. "Move over," he said roughly
to his groom. "And put that blasted sack on the floor with
the rest of the luggage. There isn't room for it on the seat
with us!" The groom obeyed.

By this time Jaycee was in Martin's arms. "I feared I'd
lost you forever," he muttered. "We've been fools, Jaycee."

"Yes. But I've been the bigger fool. James said . . ."

They argued about who had outdone the other in senseless behavior as the dory moved into deeper water, but
looked up at a roar of anger mixed with fear. They were
just in time to see Runyon push his groom into the water,
to see the groom grasp his lordship's wrist, to see the two
of them sink immediately under the choppy wavelets. The
sailor shipped his oars. He looked over each side for his
missing passengers and then bent over the stern and stared
down into the water.

"Why don't they surface?" asked Jaycee after a long moment.

"I don't understand it," said Martin, holding her more
tightly.

"Oh Lord, surely it cannot be!" Her voice was gruff with
horror.

"Jaycee, what are you thinking?"

"Oh, Martin," she wailed, "Lord Runyon speculated
about how much the groom had saved over the years. From

his share of their smuggling?" Martin nodded. "He intended to go to the Canadas, you see, and start over. Runyon guessed all sorts of wild totals. You could hear he was jealous, having spent his own share. And once he said something about gold. . . ."

"And just now he insisted the groom put his pack on the floor of the boat and that *before* he pushed the man overboard. You think he thought the groom's wealth was in the pack which he seemed to have a special care for?"

"Yes, but he must have had it secreted on his body!"

"Which meant that when he went overboard, he immediately sank. The question is, did he manage to hold onto Runyon long enough that *he* drowned as well," finished Martin thoughtfully.

"He isn't surfacing. . . . Oh, Martin, how awful."

"I'd call it poetic justice myself!"

"He could be very entertaining, you know."

"And because he could be entertaining," asked Martin in that cold voice Jaycee hated, "you think he should be saved?"

"Good heavens no! Martin! I didn't say that!" He glared at her. "Martin, I just don't like thinking bad things about the dead. My nanny used to say let the dead deal with their sins while everyone else was to forget them. Don't you see? One must think only of the good things . . . ?"

Martin hugged her tightly. "Jaycee, I always forget what a delight you are." He grinned down at her. "Will you return with me to Vienna?" he asked.

"Of course."

"Hmm. But not, I suppose, until after this ball which James tells me you've arranged?"

"Oh! I'd forgotten the ball! Martin, we must return at once."

"But the ball isn't until the fourteenth!"

"I know that, but you don't understand. I've less than a week in which I must somehow manage to make James and

Anne see sense so that I can announce their engagement at my ball!"

Martin threw back his head and laughed. "Jaycee! Jaycee! I suppose this is the thing which will give your ball special cachet, is that it?"

"Of course," she said, as if that should be obvious. "St. Valentine's Day is the day birds choose their mates, is it not, and James is always calling Anne his little bird, so it is appropriate, you see, that they announce their choice on that particular day?"

Martin grinned at her wide eyes and solemn tone. "But you must make them see sense. . . ."

"But of course," she said on a surprised note, as if that should also be obvious. "Do hurry, Martin. We must go home at once!"

"But I am too tired to go at once," said Martin pensively. "I have ridden far and worried about you and . . . I'm very tired."

"You are? Oh, poor Martin." She reached up and brushed back his hair. "I'm so thoughtless. Do let us find an inn and . . ."

"Yes! *Do* let us find an inn!"

Jaycee gave him a suspicious look. He pretended to yawn. She giggled. He leered. They laughed and, joining hands, strolled up the beach to where a rough-looking inn sat just above the tide line. They could not be certain it had a room for rent, of course, but, assuming it did, Martin had no intention of going one step further. It had been far too long since he'd had Jaycee in his arms, and having her there, once she was rescued, had instantly reminded him of that fact!

In deciding to stay the night at the inn, he gave nary a thought to those at home who were worrying. . . . In fact it was one of the grooms who took it on himself to ride the several hours necessary to reach Montmorency Park

where he informed the household that Lady Montmorency
had indeed been rescued.

The groom was well rewarded for his trouble and felt a
trifle smug when his friend grumbled he could just as well
have ridden home if only he'd thought of it and it wasn't
fair . . . but he wasn't truly unhappy with his share of the
reward Martin gave to all who had had a hand in the rescue—including the village lad, whose mother was astonished at the sum: It was quite enough to apprentice her boy
to most any trade—assuming he survived his mischief years
to reach the proper age for doing so!

Late the following afternoon following Jaycee's rescue,
a postilion brought a post chaise to a halt before the Montmorency Park front door and Martin stepped down. He
handed down his wife and, arm in arm, they entered their
home.

All the servants had assembled in the grand hall the moment the knife boy, set to watching for their arrival, announced their approach. Tibbet made a moving speech in
which, eventually, his words became so tangled Mrs. Tibbet
stepped forward and finished for him. "Lady Montmorency? My lord? We are very pleased your adventure
ended so well. We would all like to say welcome home."
She curtsied, the other female servants following her example in a ragged line behind her. The men bowed low. "Now,"
said Mrs. Tibbet, a great scowl marring her features, "every
last one of you, *back to work!* You've no more excuse for
slacking off and we've a deal to do before the ball next
Tuesday." She made shooing motions with her hands, following the last of the maids beyond the baize door at the
back of the hall.

Tibbet bowed again. "The household has assembled in
the Green Salon, my lady, my lord." He turned in his most
stately fashion and led the way. Throwing open the door,

he announced loudly, "Lady Montmorency. Lord Montmorency."

The two entered with far less dignity than their butler espoused, Jaycee rushing to embrace Anne who stood to greet her. Martin met James halfway and the two shook hands. There was a great babble of conversation, no one truly listening to another until Lady Fuster-Smythe, forgotten by the others, banged the arm of her chair with her notebook, collecting everyone's attention.

"You will stop this gibbering, sit down, and Lord Montmorency will tell the story so we can understand it."

"Perhaps," suggested Anne, hesitantly, "Jaycee might begin, and tell us what happened to her after those awful men dragged her over the hill?"

"Very well," agreed Lady Fuster-Smythe. "Jaycee will begin."

Jaycee blinked. "But there is nothing in particular to say. They forced me into that awful carriage which, although it is very well sprung, has no padding. It was very hard sitting and I was very angry and they rode in front and wouldn't talk to me—only to each other and then only to argue about money. It was a most boring journey."

"But you must have been exceedingly frightened," said Anne.

"Yeeessss. When I'd allow myself to think about it, but I was mostly sad, because I was afraid Martin would think I'd gone willingly and would never forgive me and my whole life was ruined, and only because I was such a fool as to flirt and make a byword of myself. . . ." A tear traced a ragged path down her cheek. She turned to Martin and he hugged her. "I still don't quite understand why you did not leave me to suffer for my mistakes . . . ?"

"You can thank Lady Anne for that," Martin said, smiling at his sister over Jaycee's tousled head. "She saw those villains take you. She said you fought like a demon, but, of course, a little thing like you would be no match for two great big men, so of course they managed to drag you away."

"Anne saw them take me? How wonderful." Her smile faded and a frown creased her brow. "But then I wasted all that worry!"

"Not at all," said Martin, smoothly, winking at Anne. "If it kept you from fearing Runyon's plans for your future, then it cannot be said to have been wasted!"

"That is true," agreed Jaycee. She looked up. "Now you tell your tale. How did you find me?"

"I suspect James has already told that part, but *you* do not know, do you? There is a very bright little boy in the village who spends most of his time prowling the countryside. He discovered where those rogues hid the carriage while they waited a chance to take you and he knew when it left and the direction it went. A very bright lad indeed."

"So *he* told you. . . ."

"Yes. And James and I and a couple of grooms set off after it. We weren't so very far behind and traced it with fair ease. Once we had it in sight, I sent your brother home."

"And he went?" asked Jaycee, wide eyed.

"He went. You see, although we believed you were in the carriage, we could not be absolutely certain. If a ransom note, for instance, arrived here, one of us would be required to deal with it."

"You thought Runyon might ask a ransom?"

James shrugged. "It was a possibility, Jaycee. Runyon has no obvious income, yet he lives very well. He must get his funds somewhere."

"Lived," said Martin, a dry note to his voice.

"You think he'll not manage much income where he's going?"

"He'll not need any income where he's gone."

"Good! You had him arrested. I didn't think you would, because you'd not wish Jaycee made a focus for gossip."

"No, James, you don't understand," said Jaycee, turning

in Martin's arms and speaking earnestly. "Runyon won't need funds because, you see, Runyon is dead."

"Better and better! Martin was forced to shoot him!"

Anne blanched. "Surely not. That would be murder. . . ."

"I let him go," said Martin quickly. "His greed did him in. He believed his groom had his savings in a certain pack the man guarded carefully. He forced the groom to set the bag in the bottom of the boat and then, when they reached deep water, Runyon pushed the man out of the dory."

"So?"

"So," explained Martin, "the groom grabbed Runyon's arm and pulled him out, too."

"And?"

"They sank instantly. Jaycee and I think the man had converted his wealth to gold and had it about his person. The weight . . ." Martin shrugged.

"So the villain did himself in?"

"That is our belief. We watched for some little time and neither man surfaced."

"Which means neither will tell the tale. Now," said Lady Fuster-Smythe complacently, "you need only shut the mouths of all the countryside and no one will ever know Jaycee was kidnapped and carried away!"

"I'll not try. It would be impossible. Jaycee *was* carried away, but we rescued her and she's safe. If anyone wishes to make anything of that, I'll simply be obliged to prove to them it is otherwise!"

"Oh no!" said Jaycee, once again turning in his arms, this time to clasp him about the waist and burying her head in his chest.

"No?" He pushed her away. "You would rather imaginative tales of your ravishment and who knows what else, went the rounds?"

"I will not have you fighting duels over me! I will not have you hurt, maybe killed, just because I was fool enough to become angry when you flirted with Lady Commerce. I

vill not have it!" Jaycee grasped his forearms and tried to
hake him, but he was too big and strong and, instead, she
ather shook herself! "Do you hear me? You *must* not!"

Martin grinned. "Jaycee, love, with my reputation as a
lead shot, do you really think it would go so far?"

"I don't know, do I? Men do stupid things all the time
ind how can I tell what some idiot would do?"

"Women, of course, never do anything stupid at all?"

Jaycee hung her head. "I have admitted it, have I not?"

"And it was unkind in me to remind you. Come, love.
We will go up to our rooms and change from these very
grubby and exceedingly wrinkled clothes. And you will be-
ate me all you wish for being merely a stupid man,
ummm?"

He tipped up her chin which she raised only reluctantly.
But when she saw his expression, Jaycee relaxed. "Oh very
vell, but you truly must *not."*

When they were gone James and Anne discussed the situation. They were both worried that Jaycee would suffer from
this latest escapade.

"You, Lady Fussy-Puss!" said James, inspired.

"Me? What has it to do with me?"

"If," suggested James, "we carefully craft a letter which
you then send to your most gossipy cronies, do you think
t might scotch at least some of the rumors which are sure
:o run their course? People would listen to you, my lady.
You have a reputation and are, after all, a witness, are you
not? You would be believed, I think."

"Of course I would be believed," huffed her ladyship.
"But I will not lie and I would have to say Jaycee encouraged the man, would I not?"

"You *might* say so!" said James. "But you would also
have to mention she later informed her butler she was not
at home to his lordship."

Lady Fuster-Smythe pouted. "But she *did* encourage

him." She blushed at Anne's steady look. "Well, at first she did."

"Even then," said Anne, carefully, "Jaycee was very careful to never be behind a closed door when Lord Runyon was present. She always had a footman stationed directly outside the open door." Anne's expression was definitely pensive. "I cannot think one could call that *encouragement* exactly."

"There is that," said her disgruntled ladyship who saw a juicy bit of scandal slipping away. "But she went to that ball where she should *not* have been discovered! What of that?"

"She went, but she'd not have done so if his lordship hadn't encouraged it and, having gone, she'd not have been discovered if he'd not organized her downfall. My silly sister went, I think, not because she wished to have an evening with Runyon, but because she wished to teach Martin a lesson."

The argument continued, James or Anne countering every objection Lady Fuster-Smythe raised. Finally the three put their heads together to produce the carefully worded missive which Lady Fuster-Smythe copied and addressed to three ladies of her acquaintance who could be counted on to spread the word far and wide. She finished her task, which James kept her to, just in time to go up to her room and change for dinner.

It wasn't until later that evening that Jaycee realized Anne could walk again. When she signaled the women, after dinner, to leave the men to their port, Anne simply rose to her feet and began to follow Lady Fuster-Smythe toward the door.

Jaycee turned from having a last word with Tibbet concerning coffee in the Green Salon, and screeched, loudly bringing everyone to a halt. Startled, Lady Fuster-Smythe squawked; Lord Montmorency held his glass half way to his mouth and blinked rapidly, glancing around to see what danger now menaced his wife; James half rose from his chair. One footman dropped a handful of silver which clattered across the polished floor and the other jerked the bottle he held and sloshed a great spreading red pool of port across the highly polished table. Tibbet merely stiffened to immobility.

"You are walking!" said Jaycee, pointing to Anne.

"Of course. Oh! You did not know. And it is all your doing, too. I should have remembered to thank you, Jaycee," said Anne, smiling.

"How can it possibly be my doing that you walk again?"

"But it is simple. There was no one nearby when you were abducted by those villains. I had to get help. At once. I didn't think about it: I merely stalked off to find someone. Luckily, Sir James and my brother had arrived at just that moment."

"Perhaps, because you were not thinking about it, you could walk?"

"I presume it must have been something of that sort. Also, the great need I felt to get help for you must have played a part. So you see, your abduction was not altogether a bad thing!"

"It cured you!"

"I think you might say that my fear for you cured me, yes."

"Then," began Jaycee on a teasing note, "I must remember to thank Lord Run—" Jaycee, remembering Runyon was dead, glanced wildly toward Martin and rushed from the room.

"Oh dear. I think she recalled she *cannot* thank him," said Anne.

Martin sighed. "She will very likely have nightmares, vividly recalling that moment when he fell in and didn't come up. I'd better see how she is."

Before he could leave, the door opened and Dr. Macalister strolled in. "What is this? Dinner finished? Hello,

Martin, you home? Am I too late to be fed, Tibbet?" He
glanced on around, his eyes suddenly turning back and fix-
ing on Anne. "You are on your feet! Can you walk?"

"Yes. It happened late yesterday." Anne turned to Tibbet
and suggested he have a plate of food brought to the dining
room for the doctor. "I think I'll leave you here, Dr. Macalister. James and Lord Mont—" Anne noted her brother's
pained expression and forced herself to use his name. "—
Martin will tell you all our news.

"Except that *I* am on my way to my wife's side. *James*
will tell you while you eat." Martin moved through the door.

"How rude," said Lady Fuster-Smythe.

"No," said James. "He has his values in the right order.
Mac will be here once Martin's seen that Jaycee is all right.
You and Anne go on to the Green Salon where Tibbet has
ordered the coffee set out. I know how you like your coffee,
Lady Fussy-Puss."

Her ladyship glowered at James, but didn't contradict
him. Instead, she headed out the door. Anne told the doctor
who wished to test her reflexes at once that they would wait
until he'd eaten. "You may come to the Green Salon when
you've finished and, hopefully, James will have told you
the whole story so I'll not have to do so!" Anne reached
the salon to find Lady Fuster-Smythe was fuming that her
footman was taking far too long to retrieve her precious
notebook.

"The doctor will wish to discuss every word," said her
ladyship and, once the notebook arrived, she clutched it to
her bosom with one hand, keeping the other free for her
coffee. She'd finished her third cup when her white-faced
maid appeared in the doorway. "Perfect? What is it?" Lady
Fuster-Smythe set down her notebook and rose to her feet.
"Tell me! At once."

"Lady Comfrey!" said the maid in a fading tone. "I cannot quite see . . ." Perfect suddenly seemed to become
boneless and slipped to the floor.

"Bah! She is always doing that!" Lady Fuster-Smythe stalked across the room and, groaning, knelt. "Come now, Perfect. This will not do. Comfrey, you say? But did she not go to France? Or do you not refer to the dowager? Perhaps her son's wife? *Perfect!* This will not do! Come now. . . . Explain!"

The maid groaned. "I see a horse. Lying on its side . . ."

"Lord Comfrey? . . . Come now! You must speak to me!"

"Dead . . . ? Maybe? . . . Maybe . . . not?"

"Oh dear!" Huffing and puffing, Lady Fuster-Smythe rose to her feet. "Come now, Perfect. You must get up. It is not suitable that you lie around this way. Someone might stumble over you and, besides, you must pack us up on the instant. At *once,* Perfect. Anne, dear," said her ladyship, her hand to her breast, "would you be so kind as to ring and have my courier sent to my room." At a gesture, a footman came to help her ladyship from the room.

Once no one paid her the least attention, the maid lifted her head, sighed, and, with some effort, it seemed to Anne, climbed to her feet.

"Do you need help, Perfect?"

"What, my lady? Oh, no. I've work to do. Sorry to make a spectacle of myself, but—" A faint smile hovered around the maid's lips. "—her ladyship is better pleased by dramatics, you see, and when I'm right, which most always I am, she gives me a guinea. One day soon I'll retire in comfort!"

Anne gave the maid a speculative look. "It was your doing, then, that she arrived here at the Park when she did?"

Perfect blushed, nodded, and then her eyes widened and she paled. "Oh dear. You won't tell anyone, will you? Her ladyship would be very angry. . . ."

"I'll not tell. I don't think anyone would believe me if I did!"

"That's all right then," said Perfect earnestly and added,

"From now on you'll have a happy life, my lady. A long life with three lovely children, two girls and finally a boy, and Sir James will be faithful and you will be loved by many." Perfect beamed.

Anne blinked. "Er, thank you, Perfect."

The maid chuckled. "You don't believe me, but it's all true. I only tell people's fortunes when they are good. No one wants to hear *bad* fortune." The maid turned and, dropping a curtsy to Sir James and Mac who approached just then, she left the salon so they could enter.

"What was that about good fortune?" asked James.

"Perfect told my fortune. She says I'll have a long life, lovely children and a faithful husband." Anne chuckled at Macalister's distaste for the notion. "Nonsense, of course, but it was nice of her to wish me well, which I believe is what she meant by it, do not you?" she asked, looking from one man to the other.

"But true," said James softly, "to the degree I can make it true!"

"What is this, then? Not only can the lassie walk again, but she has already agreed to wed you? But this is piracy, Jimmy-lad! I intended, myself, to offer for the lady!"

For half a moment Anne thought Macalister serious, but then she decided he was teasing. James, who knew him far better, gave him a quick look, was reassured by his beaming friend's expression. It was very likely true that Mac, having discovered a woman who had an interest in the work he did, had toyed with the notion of asking for Anne's hand, but his emotions had not been engaged, and he was not hurt by her betrothing herself elsewhere.

"Will you congratulate me, Mac?"

"I congratulate you on winning a great little lady and wish Lady Anne a long and happy life. If he ever does ought to cause you grief, you tell me, Lady Anne, and I'll set him straight!"

"I don't believe that will be necessary. My James is a surprisingly thoughtful and sensitive man."

"Except where Jaycee is concerned," said James, mournfully. "I could never seem to do the right thing with her."

"But that is all better too, is it not? Perhaps you were just too young when first required to deal with her and you got into some bad habits, but that is changed now, and you and she will get along much better!"

"I hope it may be so," said James.

"And now, if you have that settled," said Mac, turning from friend to professional, "I wish verra much to test those plaguey reflexes."

With a sigh Anne agreed. James pulled the bell pull, requesting the footman who answered to ask Mrs. Tibbet to come to the salon. Even now that they were engaged he would take no chances with Lady Anne's reputation. They needed a woman standing by when Mac examined Anne's reflexes.

Mac, when finally able to make his tests, was very pleased with his patient and told her so. "And now, lassie, what excuse will I have to spend time in your company, learning from you about your herbs!"

"But why do you need an excuse?"

"You may come when she gives *me* lessons," suggested James. "Then she'll not need to say things twice."

"So long as you continue to invite me into your home, I'll be happy," said the doctor. He saw the coffee pot and went to pour himself a cup, but found it empty. "Ah well, I dinna need it. Coffee is pernicious, I believe. Once one becomes accustomed to it, it is very difficult to do without it."

"Which likely explains why Lady Fuster-Smythe is so fond of it."

"Oh dear! I must go."

"Where? What is it, Anne?"

"Lady Fuster-Smythe! She is packing to leave and she

once expressed a desire that Cook supply her with a nice box of ginger biscuits for her carriage when she did so. I must go at once and ask Cook if any are available and if not would she please bake some before morning!"

Anne whisked herself out of the room and James sighed. "You know, Mac. In some ways it was better when she could *not* walk!"

"Nae then . . . !" Mac took another look at his friend. "And how could it possibly be so?"

"Because when she could not walk, I knew at all times exactly where she was! Now I'll never know!"

The men laughed, and if James's chuckles were a trifle rueful, neither commented on that fact.

Sixteen

The sun rose February 14th on a cold clear day with bright blue skies. One of Jaycee's concerns, the weather, sloughed away from her mind leaving merely a myriad of others with which she could drive everyone quite crazy. She was actually a little disturbed to find herself listening, every so often, for one of Lady Fuster-Smythe's diatribes on skitter-witted ways and was more than a trifle rueful when it occurred to her that such a lecture might actually settle her down a bit.

"Why is it," she asked as, early that evening, she and her husband entered the huge formal salon used only for such company occasions as this ball, 'that when one gets that for which one has devoutly wished, one discovers that perhaps it is not exactly what one wanted after all?"

"Are you regretting your arrangements for the ball?" asked Martin from where he lounged against the mantel.

"Heavens no. If it didn't sound smug, I'd admit I think they've turned out very well." Then, wondering if her husband's question had been something of a hint, she gave her husband a worried look. "Do you not agree, then?"

"Very well, indeed. I was surprised by how effective the illuminations are. While waiting for you to come down, I strolled to the gate house and back, to see that all are properly lit. Very impressive, Jaycee. I believe our guests will be delighted by the effect."

Jaycee breathed out a whoosh of air. "Excellent. I've feared you'd think them silly."

"Not at all. But if it is not that, then the arrangements for the food, perhaps? Did you not have Gunther's cater what could not be produced in our own kitchens?"

"I am not concerned about the *ball,* Martin. Nothing so simple." A dainty frown creased her forehead in a delightful fashion. "It is quite ridiculous, but I believe I miss that terrible old woman! All day long I would hear her voice in my head telling me to calm down or telling me not to harass the staff and let it get on with its work or telling me I would wear myself out with all my hithering and thithering. It was most disconcerting!"

"Ah." Martin, almost successfully, hid a grin. "I'd think that *might* be rather unsettling!"

"But no! Not at all! I'd immediately calm myself and *think,* and then do as I ought. *That's* what I meant. I wished her gone almost from the moment of her arrival, and now she *is* gone, I am rather of the opinion I did not value her as I ought." Jaycee's features fell into pensive lines. "Martin, it rather worries me. I'm afraid I'll never . . . that perhaps I won't . . . Martin, do *you* think I shall ever grow up?"

"My dear, I hope you don't *grow up* too much. You would no longer be the delightful chit who forever keeps me on my toes if you were to mature into a properly staid matron!"

Jaycee, relaxing, grinned a very unmatronly grin. "Even if I manage to become a proper matron, I doubt very much, my lord, that I'd allow you to become complacent!" The impish twinkle in her eyes was very much Jaycee at her best.

"Good. I never want to live through another few months as have just passed, my love, but I don't wish to take you for granted, either. Or you, me."

Jaycee instantly sobered and was all solemnity when she suggested, "Let us promise to talk to each other, Martin, and discuss those things which bother us. Sometimes people think they understand me and they don't at all. Perhaps it is the same for me. I think I understand you and I am bothered, but I don't ask, so I don't really *know,* do I?"

"I so promise," said Martin and caught her face between his hands, kissing her to seal the promise. It was a careful kiss. Martin was a well-trained man of the ton and he didn't muss her gown or ruffle her hair as he might otherwise have done. "I wish," he said, as he released her, "that it were later. *Much* later . . ."

The door opened just then and Sir James bowed Lady Anne into the room. Jaycee, backing away from her husband, her cheeks glowing, turned to greet them. But she gave her husband a wry look just before turning, saying softly, "Now *there* you see one of my problems! I did *not* succeed with them as I wished, did I?"

Martin smiled, but shook his head, indicating now was not the time to discuss James and Anne's relationship. "Ah, James." He shook his friend's hand. "And Anne, my sister. How very lovely you look."

"Jaycee insisted I have a new gown for this evening," said Anne and became delightfully rosy from where the modestly low cut of the neckline began and continued on up to and including her ears. "I don't know. . . ."

"Look at *me,* for heaven's sake," said Jaycee. She pulled back her shoulders to show off her own décolletage. "This gown is not particularly revealing and it is much lower than yours. My dear Anne," she finished, just a touch of horror in her voice, "with your insistence on that silly lace, *you* verge on the *dowdy!*"

"Better the lace than that I die of embarrassment," said Anne, a smile in her eyes. "I've never worn a gown which showed so much of me. Add to that, that for the first time, I will come into company with my hair uncovered. . . . Jaycee, I may become such a wreck I'll be forced to retire early."

"We're all here to support you, my wee bird," said James.

"And besides, you have nothing to be ashamed of," said Martin kindly. "You are very nearly as lovely as your mother, you know, and she was accounted a true beauty."

Anne blushed again. "But that is nothing about which one should feel pride. One has no say in how one looks. It is how one behaves and what one feels, those things are far more important, surely."

"Of course they are," said Jaycee. "But those are there *all* the time. When one dresses for a ball, why then it is only important to put one's best foot forward, as a dear friend once told me! And that bit of lace . . ." Jaycee shook her head and sighed. "I do wish you'd allow my maid to remove it before our guests arrive . . . ," she wheedled.

"We've discussed this, Jaycee. Much as I love you, I'll not allow you to do more than you've already done in your attempts to turn me into a more normal young woman!" Anne pretended some horror of her own. "Jaycee, I will forget who I am!"

"You are my sister."

"You are my little bird."

"You are my friend."

"Yes." Again a touch of red colored Anne's clear skin. "But I am also all the things I've always been, a trifle fearful of offending, more fearful of over-stepping, and far too fearful of . . . of . . ."

"Of going beyond any of Lady P.'s strictures and thereby ruining all chance of salvation." James nodded. "But we've already decided Lady P. had a bee in her bonnet and that you will find your own values amongst those she attempted to impose upon you. Remember?"

"It is only *because* I remember that I am here this evening, James," said Anne, looking him in the eye and holding out her hand to him.

"Only that, my dear? I had hoped it was a wish to be in my company which moved you."

She chuckled. "That too, of course."

Jaycee looked from one to the other and then toward her husband who shook his head once, firmly, and glared at her. She pouted and cast him another look. Martin gave another, still firmer, shake of his head. "What does Fussy-Puss have to say to you?" he asked softly.

Jaycee gurgled with laughter. "Her ladyship says I'm pushy and too set with wanting my own way!"

"Has Lady Fuster-Smythe returned for the ball?" asked Anne, hearing Jaycee's clear-voiced comment. "I thought she'd gone to another disaster somewhere and would not be back."

"She is gone, but her lecturing voice somehow lingers on." When Anne and James looked at her with that blank questioning look one often wore when speaking with Jaycee, she giggled. "Surely you understand." When they indicated they did not, she explained. "In my *head,* you see. I *hear* her telling me this and that and ordering me to behave in such and so a fashion and it is all a great bore!"

They were all laughing, even Jaycee who began by glaring, when the double doors were flung open and guests were announced, the first of those invited for the dinner before the ball. Following after, others arrived and soon the huge salon was comfortably full.

They, one and all, raved about Jaycee's illuminations. Their enthusiasm made her forget, for the moment, her disappointment that she'd not be announcing the engagement of her brother to Martin's sister later that evening.

But only for the moment.

Much later Martin and Jaycee found Anne and James half hidden behind an arrangement of Jaycee's stuffed birds perched on dead branches. The display pretty well surrounded the small dais on which the string quartette sat while playing. At the moment it was empty because the musicians were having a short rest before the final sets of the evening and Anne had taken advantage of their absence to snatch a bit of peace and quiet.

The evening had been a strain for Anne despite James's support and the aid Martin or Jaycee had given when they could. She had never in her life spoken to so many strangers, had never had so many kindly people tell her they remembered her mama with fondness, or that they were glad she was finally able to take her proper place in society.

Except she was more certain than ever she did not *wish* a "proper" place in society! And so she'd been telling James when her brother and Jaycee found them.

"Why are you frowning so, James?" asked Jaycee in her forthright way. "Tell me at once what has happened. Did the caterers run out of smoked salmon or crab patties? Did one of the musicians break his instrument? Oh!" A shocked expression crossed her face. "Oh, dear, do not tell me Anne has succumbed again to her malady!"

"I certainly won't tell you that last," said James at the same moment Anne said, "No, Jaycee. I am merely tired, but thank you for thinking of me. It means a lot to me that you should worry about me."

"Well, of course I worry about you, but——" Her face glowed with hot blood roiling up under the skin. "——right now I'll admit I feared something had happened to spoil my ball and nothing must spoil it. Nothing!"

"But why is it so important, Jaycee?" asked James. "You sound as if your whole life is balanced on how it goes this evening."

"It *does!* I'll not have the old tabbies saying that Martin has taken me to Vienna with him only because I cannot manage my life, which they *will* do if anything bad happens tonight!" When the others laughed Jaycee stamped her foot. "You do not understand. It is important to me that they know Martin and I have reconciled. That we are very much in love. I'll not have them whispering he has taken me with him merely because he does not trust me or because I am so skitter-witted and scramble-brained I am a menace when he is not there to see to me! Or because . . ."

She stopped speaking in mid-sentence when Martin hugged her, pulling her head to his shoulder.

"Silly wench," he said in fond tones. "If there is anyone here tonight who has missed seeing how much I love you, then they are either blind, too young to understand, or too old to remember! I've made no secret of my feelings for you, madam wife!"

"Nor have I attempted to hide mine for you. It is very unfashionable," she added, pensively, "but I find I do not care at all. I merely want the whole world to be as happy as I am myself. But *you* are not happy," she said, suddenly, turning a frown on Anne and James. "I heard you, and you sounded distinctly *unhappy.*"

"It is only what I predicted, Jaycee," said Anne in as soothing a tone as she could manage. "It is not that I am unhappy, only convinced this is not the life I wish for myself. I do not like such crowds, and even though everyone has been very kind, it is stressful to say, over and over, the same polite nothings to people I'll never remember meeting. And then, when we do meet again, they'll be insulted because I've forgotten! That sort of social nonsense is not the life I want!"

"Have I said I like it?" asked James when she ran down.

"But you have always lived it. You must like it!"

"Anne, I do what is expected of me, but, when I've a choice, I spend little of the season in London. Nor do I attend a dozen functions a day even when there. There are a few friends I have no wish to turn down and a handful of important people whom I feel I cannot offend, but I make no special effort to be in town for any given occasion. Some aspects of the season I *do* enjoy. The opera, a new play, the annual exhibit of our artists at Somerset House or lectures at the Royal Institution. I think you, too, might enjoy those sessions on those occasions at the Academy when women are permitted to attend. The less formal meetings and experiments, I mean. What I want you to understand is that I do *not* plan my whole life around formal entertainments such as this!"

"But I would be expected to organize and give at least one such event each season, would I not?"

James frowned. "Would that be an impossible burden?"

"I . . . I'm not certain."

"The answer is simple. We'll not come to London during the season!"

"But you'd . . ."

"I might go in for a week at some point, but you need not join me."

Jaycee, who had been looking from one to the other, burst out with, "But you . . . you . . . you . . . you . . ."

"After 'U' comes 'V' and then 'W,' my dear," said Martin as if hinting to a child to finish the alphabet.

Jaycee looked at him blankly, then, as understanding came, she blushed and hit her husband's shoulder with her fan. "You!"

"No, Jaycee, after 'U,' comes . . ." James cowered away from her attack. "Martin! Save me!"

"You have lied to me!"

All three looked at Jaycee, horrified to see tears run down her cheeks.

"But *no!* Jaycee, in what way has anyone lied to you?"

"But you *knew* how important it was to me!"

James looked at Anne who shook her head. "Er . . . Martin? Do you know what she means?"

Martin turned Jaycee gently into his embrace. "I think I do. Jaycee, love, I'm quite as surprised as you, you know. But you have jumped, once again, to conclusions and made a wrong-headed assumption, I fear. And," he said, sternly, "you have insulted our relatives."

"Insulted . . ." She raised her head.

"Have you *told* either of them that you wished to announce their engagement this evening?"

"Have I not? Surely I did. . . ."

Anne shook her head, but James frowned, trying to remember. . . .

"But they *must* have known. . . ."

"How?" asked Martin.

"But it is obvious! All these lovebirds strewn around, the illuminations, the table decorations! Surely the very thing would be to announce someone's engagement and who better than that my brother and your sister have agreed to wed?"

James frowned. "Such a denouement may have been obvious to you, Jaycee, but to no one else. Besides, what has given you the notion Anne has agreed to wed me?"

"Has she not?" Before either could answer, Jaycee added, "Because if she *has* not, I do not think you should be discussing where you will live and whether Anne will be responsible for grand entertainments! And, by the way, Anne, I'll be happy to help you when Martin and I return from Vienna. Or better, why do you and James not come with us?"

"Jaycee," scolded James, "will you be still? You embarrass Anne. Just look at her!"

"Think what Lady Fussy-Puss would say," whispered Martin in her ear.

Jaycee glowered at him and turned back to the others. "You have not answered me," she said.

"About what?" asked James innocently.

"About whether we may announce your engagement, of course!"

"Did she ask that?" he asked no one in particular.

"You have known your sister long enough to add in those bits of conversation she doesn't manage to speak out loud before going on to the next notion in her head! She *would* have asked," explained Martin with the air of a lecturer, "if you'd been near when she'd thought of it and you must just *assume* she did so, even if the words were not spoken."

"You are teasing me," said Jaycee and tapped her husband's shoulder once again. "But if I did not ask, although I am quite certain I must have done, *may* we make the announcement?"

"I think," said James, "perhaps you did mention such a thing, once. But you also told me it would be Cupid's greatest challenge to make a woman fall in love with me, so I forgot about it. Well, Anne? Do we let Jaycee have her way?"

"There are still things we've not discussed . . . ," said Anne, tentatively.

"Anne, can you bear to say me nay?" asked James softly. "All those problems you foresee can be managed, can be discussed later and decisions made . . . because we've made the really important one, did we not? About our life effort?"

Anne nodded slowly and, straightening, bravely turned to Jaycee. "James is correct. You may make the announcement if you wish, Jaycee, but do so just as late as you dare, because I do *not* like the sort of attention we'll receive once it is thought by everyone that they'd be going against propriety if they do not instantly give us their best wishes. I truly do *not* like crowds!"

Jaycee immediately glowed with pleasure and clapped her hands. "You have made my ball perfect! Martin, will you please talk to Tibbet and tell him we'll need all that extra champagne after all and that he and the footmen are to circulate immediately with glasses and tell everyone an announcement will be made after the first dance which will begin in just a few moments here in the ball room?"

"And who will make that announcement, Jaycee? You?"

She looked shocked. "Oh dear me no. That wouldn't be at all proper. *You,* my dear husband! *You* will do it, which *is* proper, is it not?"

"You are worried about propriety?" asked her surprised husband.

Anne, James's arm around her waist and her head on his shoulder, chuckled softly. "Of course she is. It is obvious that Lady Fuster-Smythe is 'talking' to her again, is she not, Jaycee?"

Jaycee blushed, refusing to respond, and, quickly, moved away to organize the grand conclusion to her ball. As she disappeared the musicians came back onto the dais, picking up their discarded instruments, began to tune them. Martin followed his wife and James urged Anne back out onto the ballroom floor. In a daring innovation, the musicians struck up a waltz. James didn't ask, simply turned Anne into his arms, and moved onto the floor where a few brave souls were exhibiting a surprising expertise in a dance which had not yet gained approval among much of the ton.

"Do you mind terribly? I mean, that Jaycee wishes to make the announcement?" James asked Anne softly as they moved gracefully around the ballroom. "If you do, I can still tell Jaycee she may not do it."

Anne smiled. "And spoil her excitement? I would not dare! She would be so unhappy." She smiled up into James's face, her eyes bright with the delight of dancing and never once thinking of what Lady Preminger would have said about the depravity of the waltz!

"Nothing could spoil *my* happiness," he said fervently.

James looked deeply into Anne's eyes and, holding her gaze, hoping she'd not notice what he did, he touched one of the shining curls into which her hair had been coaxed that evening. She reached up and gently pushed his hand away, a gentle rebuke in her look. Unrepentant, James twirled them into one more incredible spin, stopping, along with the music, just before the dais where Jaycee and Martin awaited them.

"Or perhaps one thing might spoil it, my wee sma' bird."

Anne tipped her head in that questioning manner she had, her eyes expressing her curiosity.

With a rueful look, James explained, "If you ever again insist you must hide that magnificent hair I'll be a very unhappy man indeed!"

Dear Reader,

Lady Anne's life with Lady Preminger was harsh, but, given the beliefs of strict "nonconformist" families of the era, her guardian's behavior was neither unusual nor overly punitive. It's unlikely Anne will become as light-hearted as Jaycee, but, with Sir James, she'll enjoy a good life.

My next release, *Lady Stephanie,* is a historical. Since it's set during the Regency, it has the traditional Regency "flavor," but there is more danger and my characters go beyond the usual Regency in the depth of their desires and their behavior.

Lady Stephanie's father, Lord Lemiston, blamed his off-spring for his first wife's death in child bed. Mired in his grief he disappeared, leaving his best friend to rear the twins. Nearly a quarter century has passed when he returns to sell his estate before leaving England forever.

Lemiston's protégé, Anthony Ryder, arrives first. When Lemiston's daughter, Lady Stephanie, first sets eyes on the man, he's seducing a farmer's daughter. Stephanie is not amused. Nor is Stephanie amused to discover someone is attempting to kill Theo, her twin brother.

Lady Stephanie believes her father the villain. Or it might be a trusted henchman . . . and who more trusted than Anthony Ryder, a man Stephanie finds too intriguing for her peace of mind?

When Stephanie discovers Anthony has bought her beloved estate, her growing trust and their passionate relationship crash.

I hope you enjoy *Lady Stephanie*. Look for it in June 1996.

Cheerfully,

Jeanne Savery

Letters sent to *Jeanne Savery, P.O. Box 1771, Rochester, MI 48308* will reach me. I enjoy hearing from my readers. A stamped, self-addressed envelope for my response would be appreciated.

ZEBRA REGENCIES
ARE
THE TALK OF THE TON!

A REFORMED RAKE (4499, $3.99)
by Jeanne Savery

After governess Harriet Cole helped her young charge flee to France—and the designs of a despicable suitor, more trouble soon arrived in the person of a London rake. Sir Frederick Carrington insisted on providing safe escort back to England. Harriet deemed Carrington more dangerous than any band of brigands, but secretly relished matching wits with him. But after being taken in his arms for a tender kiss, she found herself wondering—*could* a lady find love with an irresistible rogue?

A SCANDALOUS PROPOSAL (4504, $4.99)
by Teresa DesJardien

After only two weeks into the London season, Lady Pamela Premington has already received her first offer of marriage. If only it hadn't come from the *ton's* most notorious rake, Lord Marchmont. Pamela had already set her sights on the distinguished Lieutenant Penford, who had the heroism and honor that made him the ideal match. Now she had to keep from falling under the spell of the seductive Lord so she could pursue the man more worthy of her love. Or was he?

A LADY'S CHAMPION (4535, $3.99)
by Janice Bennett

Miss Daphne, art mistress of the Selwood Academy for Young Ladies, greeted the notion of ghosts haunting the academy with skepticism. However, to avoid rumors frightening off students, she found herself turning to Mr. Adrian Carstairs, sent by her uncle to be her "protector" against the "ghosts." Although, Daphne would accept no interference in her life, she *would* accept aid in exposing any spectral spirits. What she never expected was for Adrian to expose the secret wishes of her hidden heart . . .

CHARITY'S GAMBIT (4537, $3.99)
by Marcy Stewart

Charity Abercrombie reluctantly embarks on a London season in hopes of making a suitable match. However she cannot forget the mysterious Dominic Castille—and the kiss they shared—when he fell from a tree as she strolled through the woods. Charity does not know that the dark and dashing captain harbors a dangerous secret that will ensnare them both in its web—leaving Charity to risk certain ruin and losing the man she so passionately loves . . .

Available wherever paperbacks are sold, or order direct from the Publisher. Send cover price plus 50¢ per copy for mailing and handling to Penguin USA, P.O. Box 999, c/o Dept. 17109, Bergenfield, NJ 07621. Residents of New York and Tennessee must include sales tax. DO NOT SEND CASH.

ZEBRA'S REGENCY ROMANCES
DAZZLE AND DELIGHT

A BEGUILING INTRIGUE   (4441, $3.99)
by Olivia Sumner
Pretty as a picture Justine Riggs cared nothing for propriety. She dressed as a boy, sat on her horse like a jockey, and pondered the stars like a scientist. But when she tried to best the handsome Quenton Fletcher, Marquess of Devon, by proving that she was the better equestrian, he would try to prove Justine's antics were pure folly. The game he had in mind was seduction — never imagining that he might lose his heart in the process!

AN INCONVENIENT ENGAGEMENT   (4442, $3.99)
by Joy Reed
Rebecca Wentworth was furious when she saw her betrothed waltzing with another. So she decides to make him jealous by flirting with the handsomest man at the ball, John Collinwood, Earl of Stanford. The "wicked" nobleman knew exactly what the enticing miss was up to — and he was only too happy to play along. But as Rebecca gazed into his magnificent eyes, her errant fiancé was soon utterly forgotten!

SCANDAL'S LADY   (4472, $3.99)
by Mary Kingsley
Cassandra was shocked to learn that the new Earl of Lynton was her childhood friend, Nicholas St. John. After years at sea and mixed feelings Nicholas had come home to take the family title. And although Cassandra knew her place as a governess, she could not help the thrill that went through her each time he was near. Nicholas was pleased to find that his old friend Cassandra was his new next door neighbor, but after being near her, he wondered if mere friendship would be enough . . .

HIS LORDSHIP'S REWARD   (4473, $3.99)
by Carola Dunn
As the daughter of a seasoned soldier, Fanny Ingram was accustomed to the vagaries of military life and cared not a whit about matters of rank and social standing. So she certainly never foresaw her *tendre* for handsome Viscount Roworth of Kent with whom she was forced to share lodgings, while he carried out his clandestine activities on behalf of the British Army. And though good sense told Roworth to keep his distance, he couldn't stop from taking Fanny in his arms for a kiss that made all hearts equal!

Available wherever paperbacks are sold, or order direct from the Publisher. Send cover price plus 50¢ per copy for mailing and handling to Penguin USA, P.O. Box 999, c/o Dept. 17109, Bergenfield, NJ 07621. Residents of New York and Tennessee must include sales tax. DO NOT SEND CASH.

ELEGANT LOVE STILL FLOURISHES —
Wrap yourself in a Zebra Regency Romance.

A MATCHMAKER'S MATCH   (3783, $3.50/$4.50)
by Nina Porter
To save herself from a loveless marriage, Lady Psyche Veringham pretends to be a bluestocking. Resigned to spinsterhood at twenty-three, Psyche sets her keen mind to snaring a husband for her young charge, Amanda. She sets her cap for long-time bachelor, Justin St. James. This man of the world has had his fill of frothy-headed debutantes and turns the tables on Psyche. Can a bluestocking and a man about town find true love?

FIRES IN THE SNOW   (3809, $3.99/$4.99)
by Janis Laden
Because of an unhappy occurrence, Diana Ruskin knew that a secure marriage was not in her future. She was content to assist her physician father and follow in his footsteps . . . until now. After meeting Adam, Duke of Marchmaine, Diana's precise world is shattered. She would simply have to avoid the temptation of his gentle touch and stunning physique — and by doing so break her own heart!

FIRST SEASON   (3810, $3.50/$4.50)
by Anne Baldwin
When country heiress Laetitia Biddle arrives in London for the Season, she harbors dreams of triumph and applause. Instead, she becomes the laughingstock of drawing rooms and ballrooms, alike. This headstrong miss blames the rakish Lord Wakeford for her miserable debut, and she vows to rise above her many faux pas. Vowing to become an Original, Letty proves that she's more than a match for this eligible, seasoned Lord.

AN UNCOMMON INTRIGUE   (3701, $3.99/$4.99)
by Georgina Devon
Miss Mary Elizabeth Sinclair was rather startled when the British Home Office employed her as a spy. Posing as "Tasha," an exotic fortune-teller, she expected to encounter unforeseen dangers. However, nothing could have prepared her for Lord Eric Stewart, her dashing and infuriating partner. Giving her heart to this haughty rogue would be the most reckless hazard of all.

A MADDENING MINX   (3702, $3.50/$4.50)
by Mary Kingsley
After a curricle accident, Miss Sarah Chadwick is literally thrust into the arms of Philip Thornton. While other women shy away from Thornton's eyepatch and aloof exterior, Sarah finds herself drawn to discover why this man is physically and emotionally scarred.

Available wherever paperbacks are sold, or order direct from the Publisher. Send cover price plus 50¢ per copy for mailing and handling to Penguin USA, P.O. Box 999, c/o Dept. 17109, Bergenfield, NJ 07621. Residents of New York and Tennessee must include sales tax. DO NOT SEND CASH.

Taylor-made Romance from Zebra Books

WHISPERED KISSES   (0-8217-3830-5, $4.99/$5.99)
Beautiful Texas heiress Laura Leigh Webster never imagined
that her biggest worry on her African safari would be the handsome Jace Elliot, her tour guide. Laura's guardian, Lord Chadwick Hamilton, warns her of Jace's dangerous past; she simply
cannot resist the lure of his strong arms and the passion of his
Whispered Kisses.

KISS OF THE NIGHT WIND   (0-8217-5279-0, $5.99/$6.99)
Carrie Sue Strover thought she was leaving trouble behind her
when she deserted her brother's outlaw gang to live her life as
schoolmarm Carolyn Starns. On her journey, her stagecoach
was attacked and she was rescued by handsome T.J. Rogue. T.J.
plots to have Carrie lead him to her brother's cohorts who mur-
dered his family. T.J., however, soon succumbs to the beautiful
runaway's charms and loving caresses.

FORTUNE'S FLAMES   (0-8217-3825-9, $4.99/$5.99)
Impatient to begin her journey back home to New Orleans,
beautiful Maren James was furious when Captain Hawk delayed
the voyage by searching for stowaways. Impatience gave way
to uncontrollable desire once the handsome captain searched
her cabin. He was looking for illegal passengers; what he found
was wild passion with a woman he knew was unlike all those
he had known before!

PASSIONS WILD AND FREE   (0-8217-5275-8, $5.99/$6.99)
After seeing her family and home destroyed by the cruel and
hateful Epson gang, Randee Hollis swore revenge. She knew
she found the perfect man to help her—gunslinger Marsh
Logan. Not only strong and brave, Marsh had the ebony hair
and light blue eyes to make Randee forget her hate and seek
the love and passion that only he could give her.

*Available wherever paperbacks are sold, or order direct from the
Publisher. Send cover price plus 50¢ per copy for mailing and
handling to Penguin USA, P.O. Box 999, c/o Dept. 17109,
Bergenfield, NJ 07621. Residents of New York and Tennessee
must include sales tax. DO NOT SEND CASH.*